Blind Pursuit

BY

Joe Richard

1stBooks - rev. 05/10/02

For Sonya
This book is a reality because of her support,
encouragement, and love. May every man
find such a gift.

Also

For Brandon and Jake.
Their wonderful individuality became the added inspiration
needed for my feeble attempt.

And

For my mother.
Who, until this day, still wonders how
I met Ranger Zach Randal.

AUTHOR'S NOTE

While this book is a work of fiction, actual locations have been used in the setting of the story. I've tried to be as factual as possible with state borders, mountain ranges, and the distance between different areas of the country.

With law enforcement agencies, such as the Texas Rangers, different state police agencies, and various county sheriff departments, I have taken great liberties. While much of the investigative techniques used by the characters might actually be utilized in the real world, some facets used by organizations in the story are solely a product of my imagination.

All psychological content within the story has been conjured up from within the dark recesses of the author's mind, and therefore must have some validity. For any content that is judged sound and sensible, I can take no credit. It is nothing short of a miracle that the plot and story design end with any clarity. For any grammatical and punctuation errors, I assume full responsibility.

It has been my intention to complete this entire project without the assistance of editors, researchers, and the usual staffs of assistants that I have only recently discovered are needed to accomplish such an undertaking. I regret any complicatedness that the reader might encounter as a result of my stubborn determination to do it alone.

CHAPTER

1

DEKE SAT ALONE at the stainless-steel counter in the small cafe. Stools with round, spinning seats at the long and curving counter reminded him of the old boxcar restaurants he'd seen along the Canadian border. He was tired, hungry, and lonely. The little cafe had looked so inviting when he'd first spotted it that he circled back pulling right up to the front entrance. After all, daylight was approaching, and a good breakfast might help to improve the frustrating mood that had descended upon him.

Entering the cafe was like walking into his grandmother's kitchen. A powerful and overwhelming memory suddenly made him feel homesick. On Sunday afternoons when he was a child, the entire family would gather after church services for the weekly feast at his grandparent's home. Granny was always up long before daybreak busy cooking. An irresistible aroma coming from the combination of homemade bread, pork roast, fresh snap beans, bacon, fried chicken, rice dressing, smothered cabbage, and apple pie filled the kitchen. This little cafe had that same homemade kind of aroma to it.

Deke Stone was thirty-two years old, and five years divorced. He had had no children while married; a fact that he regretted during the marriage, but eventually became thankful about. She had been a witch, plain and simple. She was a certain breed of woman that the Cajun men called a '*geppe*.' The French word meant wasp, and that was putting it mildly. Luckily, it had only taken six years for him to discover her true colors. Deke had no ax to grind, and even denied the bitterness; after all, what was six wasted years when it could easily have been twenty.

Graduating from a major university, Deke had managed to obtain a Bachelor's Degree in Biochemistry. Originally planning to attend medical school, he one day realized that he had somehow fallen out of love with the *American Dream*. Puzzled by this sudden change in his attitude, Deke began his pursuit of psychology. After acceptance at Texas A&M, Deke began his graduate studies thinking that he would learn enough to figure out what life was all about.

After years of studying every possible variation associated with each of the many symptoms in the hundreds of potential psychotic conditions, from developmental, to adolescent, to geriatric, and even to the criminally insane, he quit. Failing to find any reason behind his lack of interest in the coveted dream, or to the meaning of his life, Deke decided to wander around the country. Packing all of his belongings into his used and battered Jeep, he had headed north.

Two years later, there wasn't a state that he'd not visited. Living out of his vehicle, and sometimes even camping under the stars whenever weather permitted. Deke hustled odd jobs in different towns he visited. He managed very well within the smaller communities. However, in the larger cities people seemed confused, acting nearly alien. Areas such as New York, Chicago, and even Denver, crowded and moving at such fast paces, that nobody looked like they would ever be able to stop.

Deke found the smaller towns dotting the valleys in the Rocky Mountains to be the most pleasant areas, and he had decided to settle down in one of them. Folks spoke to each other like human beings, and even cared about one another. It was something forgotten about along the coastal and plain states.

So, what did that have to do with him sitting in a country cafe this early in the morning in Sweetwater, Texas?

Looking around casually, Deke felt rather uncomfortable being the only customer. It was even more unsettling since he had seen no waitress when entering, and it was a good fifteen minutes that he had been waiting. Deke could hear music coming from behind the double swinging doors that led into the kitchen, a low volume, from what sounded to be a small radio.

The aroma coming from the kitchen was making him feel hungrier by the minute. The slowness of the waitress certainly was not due to how busy she was. Not even a little bell had been left on the counter for him to ding impatiently, demanding service.

A cup of black coffee was all Deke wanted when he first walked in, but after smelling the kitchen's aroma he'd changed his mind. At least he'd found a menu to look at while waiting, and it was a catchy one to say the least, one, as he had never seen before. The backside of the menu had the historical account of the little cafe's ownership written on it.

For over one hundred years, the cafe sat in the same spot. Except for the occasional repainting or replacing of red vinyl seat covers on the stools as cotton fell from beneath them, it had remained unchanged. After spot reading bits and pieces, Deke found himself reading the brief history from the beginning.

SAUL Dodson established the cafe back in the late 1800's, after returning from California where he and his brother, Ben, had been lucky. They managed to mine enough gold to pay all their expenses, and still have a small fortune left over. Splitting the money before leaving California, Ben hugged his brother, Saul, before heading north for Alaska. He had heard gold was as easy to mine as picking pecans. Saul wished his brother luck, and then headed for Central Texas. No woman was waiting for him, and certainly no gold. For three long years, they had panned and mined the dry, hot Sierra Nevada Mountains. At times, wondering if they would ever make it out alive. An old man had staked a claim not far from the Dodson brothers. He said his name was Jackrabbit Slim. Even though he was nearly eighty years old, he showed no signs of his age. As time passed, the men began to socialize. Jackrabbit Slim talked about his life travels with special emphasis on Texas. He spoke of it as if it was a paradise on Earth. Boise was the place where the Dodson brothers called home. Saul had never been anywhere outside fifty miles of Boise, Idaho.

While they sifted through mud and rock, Jackrabbit Slim continued to speak of Texas, until finally one day Saul decided that it was where he would start his new business and raise a family. He had calculated how much money he needed to start a hotel and restaurant, then with high hopes he had set off.

When Saul finally reached Sweetwater he was very discouraged, discovering that the extra money he had to use for travel expenses had run out. In fact, he had used some of the money set aside for his new hotel and restaurant just getting to Sweetwater. Saul had never been in such a desolate and barren place.

Coming from California, he first entered Texas at the panhandle, stopping in Amarillo for one night. Continuing with his journey, he noticed that the landscape failed to improve, but he was sure paradise was just a little farther.

By the time Saul hit the town of Sweetwater he had used up nearly half of the restaurant money, and several days before, his horse had become overheated and died. This forced him to spend more money on a young mare in Lubbock.

Disgusted, but still determined, he was able to build a small establishment. To this day, it is the same Dodson's Breakfast and Bar-B-Que Cafe. The cafe is located at the outskirts of town, since at that time it was the only land Saul could afford.

Saul had struggled for the first year, nearly losing everything because of the distance folks had to walk just to reach the small cafe. Finally, one day, after a rowdy crew of Mexican bandits raided his cafe, taking all of the Bar-B-Que beef, Saul's luck changed.

He had lost a whole side of beef in the raid, and his money was being stretched to the limit. When the Mexican bandits arrived at noon the following day, Saul Dodson's heart nearly failed him. Curiously, they were not yelling and screaming like wild natives as they entered the cafe. To his dismay, the leader of the feared bandits had accompanied the thieving bunch. Smiling wickedly, he approached Saul.

"We have come for the Bar-B-Que Gringo, is that all right?" However, before Saul could answer, the greasy bandit continued, "Today we will pay, we will even pay double, because I think these idiots forgot to pay you yesterday. The food is good Gringo, and I never steal good food." The bandit produced a fistful of cash, which he stuffed into the front pocket of Saul's apron. Saul stood shocked and stammering. The Mexican bandit only smiled widely, exposing a row of gold teeth.

In minutes, they had packed up his Bar-B-Que and carried it off. Word about the incident had spread like a prairie fire through Sweetwater. Thinking Saul must be a close friend of the thieving murderers, people from town began walking the extra distance to Dodson's Breakfast and Bar-B-Que Cafe on a regular basis.

After a while, he was able to save a little money, putting some of it in the bank. Saul began courting a young girl from town. He dreamed of many sons that they planned to have together. Soon the two married and had twelve children, all girls. Struggling for years, Saul's wife got fat, the girls ended up costing him a fortune, and still they had no sons.

Some say Saul Dodson was just tired of trying to get things right. Others disagree, saying it was because of a drinking problem. Whatever the reason, while laying across the bar in the cafe one morning Saul put a pistol to his head, and ended the struggle.

The girls began running the cafe after his death, and by some miracle they had managed to keep it open.

Now, over one hundred years later, Saul Dodson's great great granddaughter, Amy Dodson, is owner and manager of Dodson's Breakfast and Bar-B-Que Cafe. Well-known by the residents in the area, she's been chosen Sweetwater Rodeo and Cattle Drive Queen for six years running. Although considered a pleasant sight, it's rumored that her services greatly outmatch her beauty.

Dodson's Breakfast and Bar-B-Que Cafe promises nothing, but the best tasting, juiciest, most tender, man-sized portions of Bar-B-Que this side of Texas. It has been, and still is, what keeps the local men eating Bar-B-Que by the ton, and business is booming.

In addition to the tasty food, another factor added to the cafe's captivating power. Amy Dodson exhibits a unique status. By having resisted all temptations, escaping the bonds of matrimony, she is still available, and worth every effort for a chance to walk her down the aisle.

Miss Amy Dodson loves the attention and the popularity, so don't be offended, she's never been.

Enjoy your stay, and thanks for coming. Amy Dodson—Owner

RETURNING to the present, Deke could not believe how original the back cover of the cafe's menu was. In front of God and everybody, Amy Dodson was advertising her social activities. However, as Deke thought about it for a minute he realized how ingenious the advertisement was.

What more effective way to create curiosity than by having a seductive sounding owner right in the center of a steamy scandal. Amy Dodson was either a fool, or a very smart businessperson.

As many times as he'd passed through Texas he'd sworn never to return to this barren, abandoned landscape that reminded him of the hot surface of Venus. Even in winter, it was dry, and hot, with mile after mile of flat boring terrain. The wind forever was blowing strong enough to sandblast two layers of skin away.

Deke had been sitting and waiting for nearly half an hour, and still he saw no sign of a waitress. Looking around the cafe, he suddenly felt things were not right. His stomach tightened, and the air became thin. He had not heard a single voice, or any sound of employees beyond the swinging double doors, other than what sounded like soft radio music.

Then, with perfect timing, creating a mausoleum type silence, the radio went silent. Deke slowly stood, taking a step backward toward the exit. Something was very wrong here, and he may have walked right in on whatever that was.

Deke managed to move silently toward the front door, and was only a couple of steps away when something scared him so badly he nearly ran through the wall. Loud, clanging noises sounding like pots or pans dropping onto the floor came from behind the swinging doors. Without warning, the radio began blaring, and Deke knew it was not the same music as earlier.

He could not decide whether to yell and see if anyone would answer, or take off never to return, putting it out of his mind forever. The choice was tougher than he thought. He liked to think of himself as a good person, helping someone if in need. Deke was not fearful of what the consequences were. A quality that Deke wanted to maintain in life. This situation was different from anything he had ever imagined or experienced before. An odor of danger seemed to emanate from within the little cafe now.

Deke reached the door, pushing it slowly open, still torn with indecision of what to do. Music from the radio suddenly increased in volume, so loud he could not hear his heart beat in his ears anymore, and he felt his appetite take a leave of absence, which he feared, may be permanent.

Deke was not afraid of a physical confrontation. He was capable of defending himself. It was fear of the unknown that bothered him. His imagination was displaying assorted gruesome images in his mind, causing his already heightened awareness to climb a few notches higher, where paranoia and panic normally take control.

Still standing in the half-open doorway, Deke's mind switched into a denial mode. Deke's thoughts began rationalizing that nothing dangerous was here, and he was drastically over-reacting. When Deke's imagination ran wild, some kind of check and balance system kicked in, countering his too quick responses to whatever situation it was. The system would begin providing opposite views to the event he was encountering.

You will look like a complete idiot if the waitress walks out unharmed.
Don't just stand in the doorway with guilt written all over you.

Deke hated it whenever that happened. Without any way of preventing a battle in his head, the two opposing sub-conscious levels engaged each other in a deadly grip of conflicting views. Resulting outcomes were for Deke to face the consequences alone. Just when he was about to shut down all his reason, and make a fast get-away, he heard gravel in the parking lot crackling as a state police cruiser drove up. It stopped, parking next to his truck. Trying to slow his heart rate, and appear normal, Deke exited the cafe fighting for a decision on whether to tell the officer about his suspicions. Immediately the two opposing forces began a fresh duel within his head.

You'll look like an idiot.
No, you will not, something is wrong.
That cop will think you are on drugs, wanting to search you and the truck.
He will hunt you down for sure if he discovers anything wrong.

The state patrol officer stepped from his cruiser placing his trooper hat on, as Deke approached him. Watching Deke closely in the predawn light, the officer remained near his car, eyes narrowed as they focused on Deke, who walked hesitantly toward him.

"Excuse me officer, may I speak with you sir?" His voice was not quite right with the shakiness still evident from his scare.

The patrol officer only nodded his head without responding.

"My name is Deke Stone. I arrived here approximately thirty minutes ago for breakfast...and have been sitting..." Deke was rudely cut off by the officer.

"May I see some identification please?" the uniformed man asked firmly.

Deke saw the cop's error, assuming that all he had was a complaint about the cafe's service.

"Yes sir," answered Deke, while digging in his wallet for his driver's license. He was beginning to feel like he was guilty of something. Why did this cop ask for his ID? Reporting the strange incident was not as easy as he thought, and he became even more anxious. His hands were visibly shaking, he only hoped the cop didn't notice. Realizing they were trained to look for and notice such things made him double his efforts trying to breath normally and calm down. The level of nervousness he felt surprised Deke. He was normally a very cool and levelheaded individual, only becoming rattled when something major unfolded before him. Even then, he usually chilled quick enough to respond if the situation warranted. Finding his license, he presented it to the officer with a shaky hand.

Still mute as a stump, the patrolman began studying his ID comparing the four-year-old picture to his appearance today with a full beard and longer hair. Slowly raising his eyes, the trooper made sure to get a good look at Deke.

From the moment Deke saw the trooper the man looked at him suspiciously. The look was still on his face.

Deke wondered how long it took to read a drivers license, assuming this cop could read. Finally, it was handed back to him. "All right Mr. Stone, what is it you wanted to tell me?" Spreading his feet apart, the cop rested his hands on the thick black holster belted around his waist. "Thank you officer. I am not sure if anything is wrong, and I might just be over-reacting about this, but I have been sitting at the counter inside for the last thirty minutes, and have not heard any voices or sounds from the employees. I have a very strange, very bad feeling, and I'm worried about it." He stuttered and stammered trying to describe what could not be described.

"It appeared as I drove up that you were leaving Mr. Stone. I assume you were on your way to tell someone."

"Well, I wasn't sure of what to do, but was very thankful when I did see you drive up," he confessed to the suspicious eyes, closely looking him over. "Did you make any effort to call the waitress while you sat at the counter? They may not have heard you enter."

This cop must think this is a courtroom, and I'm on the witness stand Deke thought. It was just what the country needed: cops pretending to be lawyers. It must be Congress's way of solving the budget crisis. Save money on public defenders and policemen by having them do both jobs.

This guy had his sights set on the legislature, and already Deke didn't like him. "No sir I did not yell out. Something was not right inside, and I'd rather let the people who are trained for that type of situation, like yourself, handle it." His response had a small touché added, emphasizing his admiration, but with a touch of sarcasm. Deke was having trouble figuring this guy's angle. Nevertheless, it was obvious he wanted everyone to think someone like Marshall Dillon had come to town. The state trooper said nothing for several minutes then started for the door. Spinning around before reaching the door, he looked back at Deke pointing a finger.

"Mr. Stone, remain in that spot. Do not leave unless I release you." Then, he spun back toward the entrance while drawing his weapon at the same time. Deke watched him as slowly and quietly the officer entered the cafe. He wanted to yell out and remind him to make his presence known because service was slow, but thought better of it. He stood between his truck and the state police cruiser watching as the trooper slipped into the cafe.

No other customers or employees for that matter were inside the place. The trooper disappeared. The last Deke saw of the man he was in a crouched position with his weapon held high before him. He was either very scared or very excited. These people loved it when something real happened. He wished he could see him through the front windows, but either he was crouching too low or had already entered the back. Deke certainly did not need trouble with the police.

All he wanted was get to Green Mountain Falls, Colorado. He had found and bought a small cabin that was halfway up the side of a mountain, he called it home.

Only one thing was responsible for him being stuck in the middle of this situation. Deke had a controlling passion; strong enough to control even his decisions when common sense was opposed to whatever it was that this passion was attracted. His passion was for the incredibly, magnificent power displayed, when awesome and dangerous weather conditions developed.

Already it was late October, and the hurricane season was quickly winding down for the year. Only one of the gigantic, swirling, powerhouse wonders of nature managed to make it to the American coastline, and it was only a category three storm. Deke had found his way to the center of turbulent weather anyway, enjoying every gale-forced hurricane wind he could find. That was way back in August, and he was like an alcoholic, becoming restless, irritable, and discontent. Then a new storm developed in the Caribbean. Strengthening quickly, the monster, category-five hurricane headed straight for Brownsville, Texas. Within twelve hours of hearing the storms projected path he was on his way. However, like anything in life there are no guarantees. Only one hundred miles from the coast, the storm took a hard right heading back into the Gulf of Mexico where it collided with a cold front sweeping down from Canada. It was literally knocked off course from the mainland, and driven into the Atlantic where it died a slow death harmlessly at sea. Returning from the disappointing dry run, he spotted the enticing little cafe.

Now he found himself standing in a near empty parking lot other than a state police cruiser, and ordered not to move until released. This was more of a whirlwind than he was treated to in Brownsville.

He stayed where he was ordered to, trying to hear or see anything that may be happening, being poised, and ready not to miss anything when it started happening. It remained deadly silent as the sun peaked over the eastern horizon; pre-dawn light vanished as the sun's rays flooded the land. With the same stealth used entering the cafe, the state patrolman exited the door. Stopping at the entrance, he replaced his weapon on his hip. Deke could see something was wrong by his movements. With mechanical stiffness and hesitating behavior, he looked around the cafe entrance. Looking at the ground around the front widows, stopping to wipe perspiration from his forehead with a

9

swipe of his shirtsleeve, and replacing his hat, he turned his attention toward Deke. As the trooper approached him the change in his facial features became obvious. Something was missing in him. He was not the same proud little rooster who'd walked into that cafe. With his head hanging down, his stride was slower and not as deliberate, as he walked back through the parking lot.

"Mr. Stone I'm going to have to ask that you remain here with me until the detectives have the opportunity to get your statement," he stated, matter of fact, looking at Deke. The suspicion was now missing from his eyes, and his countenance had smoothed over. He looked almost friendly. "Sure!" Deke responded, taken a little by surprise. "What did you find? Is someone in trouble?" Curiosity had the power to boldly enter the most uncomfortable of situations.

The officer looked at Deke. A nametag above his pocket read Sgt. J. Hadley in bold letters. Opening the door to his cruiser to call for homicide, and an investigative team, the sergeant looked back toward Deke. While standing with one foot on the cruiser's rocker panel, he reached in grabbing the radio handset, bringing it toward him at the open car door. The coiled wire stretched tight with the radio's mike in the man's grip. Bringing the mike up, he clicked the transmit button, and then released it. He had never taken his eyes off Deke. The intense look of concentration that had been on his face relaxed, as he appeared to reach a decision of some kind.

"Three women are in the kitchen in the back of the cafe, but they're all dead. Someone left them hanging from the ceiling, like meat in a walk-in freezer."

CHAPTER

2

STATE POLICE INVESTIGATORS arrived within minutes after Sergeant Hadley radioed his headquarters, requesting homicide detectives. Deke spent the time waiting and even helped Sergeant John Hadley rope off the crime scene and surrounding area. Hadley was quiet while waiting for the homicide detectives, and stayed busy securing the area.

Trying to handle radio traffic and take care of the crime scene appeared frustrating to Deke. Minutes after calling for homicide investigators, a pair of cruisers and two state police officers arrived offering their assistance. Help from the two additional troopers with radio traffic, and assisting Hadley to clear the line of vehicles backed up by rubbernecking citizens, finally allowed him to properly secure the area. The task had involved more than Deke was aware of, and he was actually impressed.

Sergeant Hadley had begun to soften up, and before long, he and Deke were talking freely about the bizarre situation. Hadley advised Deke not to discuss any of his movements, before or after arriving at the cafe, with anyone. Deke's statement, and any other questions, was going to be handled by the investigators. He also confessed that he would have to advise Deke of his legal rights, but only as a formality, assuring him that he was not under arrest. A little nervous about being advised of his Miranda rights Deke asked, "Well, I'm not a suspect. Am I?" he added a little surprise and sarcasm into the question, but he made sure not to sound disrespectful.

Sergeant Hadley was wrapping part of the yellow police tape around a tree when he turned to face Deke. Taking a deep breath Hadley paused, "Mr. Stone, until we can find out exactly what actually happened, everybody is a suspect. You're a smart fellow, you know that." He said it with the emotion and patience of a father teaching a son. Turning around, he resumed with the task of securing the police line tape.

Deke stood alone, feeling as if a mule had just kicked him in his gut. An overwhelming dizzy, sick feeling swept through his body as he stared in the direction of Sergeant Hadley. He waited until the wave of nausea began to pass before he spoke.

"Well, if I'm a suspect could you at least tell me what it is I'm guilty of?"

Since walking out of the cafe Hadley had said little about the three women he stated were hanging in the kitchen, and Deke was bursting with curiosity to find out every detail.

Deke continued to help Sergeant Hadley as he unrolled the bright yellow **DO NOT CROSS—POLICE LINE—DO NOT CROSS—** tape. Hadley stopped, walking over to Deke.

"Look, I shouldn't even be talking to you like this, but to be perfectly honest, I'm dying to tell someone."

Finally, Deke was able to see through the professional tough guy act. He was just a normal, everyday fellow doing his job.

Hadley began describing the gruesome scene. "The waitress and both cooks are hanging from the ceiling. A thin, nylon, ski rope is tied around each of their necks. Nevertheless, I'm sure that's not what killed them. In fact, I'm positive." Sergeant Hadley spoke in a hushed, respectful tone.

Deke stood facing Sergeant Hadley as he began revealing the details. Hadley kept looking over Deke's right shoulder, nervously describing a ghastly scene inside the cafe, all the while watching the two troopers handle traffic.

"What do you mean? What did you see?" Deke found himself struggling to catch his breath in anticipation.

"It was just as you said. The front of the cafe seemed like a mausoleum. I heard music coming from the kitchen area, but the volume was very low. I didn't see anything as I walked through the swinging doors leading to the back, but the smell of blood was so thick I found myself fighting to keep my breakfast down." He abruptly stopped.

Looking over Deke's shoulder toward the parking lot, satisfied with what he saw, he continued, "The room is **L** shaped, and as soon as I turned the corner I saw where the smell of blood was coming from. Side by side, their feet no more than a foot off the floor, they hung from an exposed metal beam. The ceiling is just an open area filled with ductwork, some wiring, and **A** shaped metal beams. The three women that I saw hanged were not what repulsed me. I've seen my share, but not worse than what had been done to those three women." Again, he stopped abruptly, lifting his head to look behind Deke. A voice boomed across the parking lot addressing Sergeant Hadley.

"Yeah, I'll be right there!" he shouted to the voice behind Deke, and began walking off in the direction of the parking lot. Deke turned around to see the homicide van approaching on the highway.

Suddenly Sergeant Hadley spun around as he had earlier when entering the cafe.

"Mr. Stone, between you and me, everyone's a suspect. But not everyone's under suspicion. If it means anything, I'm betting you're an innocent bystander." Spinning back around, Sergeant Hadley headed toward the other two troopers, waiting on homicide.

Deke found himself experiencing two powerful emotions at nearly the same time. Relief and elation that this cop was not as suspicious of him as he feared he was, and utter disappointment at being so close to discovering what grisly scene the trooper had discovered before being called away. He was so damn close. He had to find out what Sergeant Hadley saw. He was ordered to stay where he was anyway, so maybe he'd get another chance.

He watched as the assortment of law officials went in and out of the cafe like mud dobbers building a nest. He found a spot away from the parking lot where one of the only three trees growing in the county stood, sitting in the shade maybe he'd have a chance to catch up on some rest. He needed to get some serious sleep soon. It was not long before he heard his name being called.

"Mr. Stone?" He heard the Texas Ranger call his name. Deke was facing away from the busy scene. They knew damn well who he was. Deke made a quick bet with himself that the Texas Ranger would try again.

"Mr. Deke Stone?" He heard the Ranger ask.

"Yes sir, I'm Deke Stone," he replied while turning around. Deke was shocked to see a mountain dressed up like a Texas Ranger, wearing a white Stetson and walking his way. Without having to think much about it, Deke decided to cooperate completely with this man.

"My name is Zachary Randal. I'm with the Texas Rangers," the big man said, extending a hand the size of a catcher's mitt down to him. Deke watched his hand disappear from sight as the man wearing the battered Stetson shook it forcefully. Withdrawing his appendage, Deke was relieved to see that he had no broken bones, and he only hoped the temporary loss of blood didn't have any lasting effects.

13

Texas Ranger Zachary Wyatt Randal was a giant of a man, standing at least six-and-a-half feet, weighing all of three hundred pounds. Deke was impressed mostly with the big man's chest, it actually stuck out farther than his gut. It also explained the battered Stetson. It was no doubt a difficult task finding Stetsons in that size. Ranger Randal could probably wear a nurse's cap without anyone objecting. Deke estimated him to be about fifty years old. From the old school, his manners were impeccable. He carried himself like a giant, careful not to step on the little people around him, promising never to hurt them as long as he got whatever information he needed. Deke was sure that anyone this man ever ran into went out of his or her way to oblige.

"Mr. Stone, I'm sure you're aware that a terrible crime was committed in the cafe. We don't know exactly when, but probably within the last two hours. Our boys are estimating somewhere around five this morning. Trooper Hadley tells me that you were inside the cafe at about that same time. Now to save time with this, because I do want to get busy trying to apprehend the person or persons responsible, I am hoping you and I can speak plainly with each other. What I mean specifically is that we cut straight through the bullshit, and get busy milking this cow. Do you feel the possibility of that exists sir?" Despite the intimidation Deke felt resulting from the size of this man, the Texas Ranger remained polite.

He had a direct way of making his wishes known, without really insulting anyone, a charismatic personality that swept a person away. No matter what happened, Deke was going to do anything this fellow asked.

The Texas Ranger smiled politely, waiting for Deke to digest everything.

"Yes sir Officer Randal. All I want to do is cooperate fully. I only want to be on my way back home," he responded with all the enthusiasm he could muster, but doubted that he had impressed the big man very much.

Randal asked him a few questions that were wide in assortment. Nothing Deke thought he needed a lawyer for; besides, he was innocent. The big Texas Ranger was thorough. Just when Deke was sure he could think of nothing else to ask, he'd come up with a rather good question. These people impressed him increasingly as he watched them work. "You're telling me the radio changed in volume, and the setting also changed," Randal repeated with a little skepticism, goading Deke to see how much he'd defend his account. These people were good. If Deke remained strong in his defense, knowing what he saw and heard, they would believe him. If he caved in too easily when pressured, then they would know he was lying.

"I will admit that for reasons which I cannot explain, a horrible fear developed within me. I became very scared, wanting only to get out of that place, but what I heard was not my imagination, nor am I fabricating anything. The radio changed in volume twice, and one of those times the frequency was changed to a different station. The loud noise that sounded like a pot hitting the floor also occurred. Someone was in the back as I made my exit, that's the only explanation that I can see for it." He wasn't giving an inch, and saw as the big man slowly started to smile.

"Mr. Stone, I believe you, but that creates a problem all in itself. I will have to ask that you remain in town for today and probably even overnight. We have other things to discuss. I thank you for your cooperation sir." A big hand plopped down on Deke's left shoulder, the weight and size reminded him of a forty-pound sack of cornmeal. The other oversized paw reached out swallowing his hand, shaking it vigorously. The weight on his shoulder was lifted, and just like that, he was gone. Deke was confined to the city of Sweetwater for at least another twenty-four hours.

WITH State Troopers, Texas Rangers, and homicide detectives converging on the scene, it did not take long before the parking lot was nearly filled. Deke's old Jeep was lost in a pack of police cruisers, evidence vans, coroner vehicles, and an ambulance that would carry away the bodies.

So much activity was going on at the scene that nobody saw her coming, until after the Land Cruiser had maneuvered its way through the parked vehicles, stopping at the front door. When Deke saw the stunt driving techniques on display, along with the increase in activity, he began walking in that direction. He may have missed out on his opportunity to experience a category five hurricane in Brownsville, but he damn sure wasn't going to miss this little storm brewing.

He saw the tiny little brunette get out of her vehicle. Before she could make it through the front door she was surrounded by a group of officers, determined not to let her contaminate the crime scene, or let her see the gruesome bodies, which until early this morning, had been

15

her employees. As Deke neared the little circle of people, he could hear the voice of Ranger Randal.

"Now Miss Amy, you know I can't let you inside even if it is your place of business. Ain't nothing you can do right now, but get in our way."

Every so often, he would stop talking, and then a few moments later start up again. Deke was having a hard time understanding the Ranger. Whenever he resumed speaking, the content did not connect with what he had been saying the moment before. "Miss Amy you know me, and you know everything that can be done at this time is being done. I want these sum-bitches just as bad as you do. And ma'am, you know that I generally get what I want." He again stopped, but for no particular reason. A crowd of officers surrounded Amy Dodson, and Deke could not even see daylight through them.

"Yes ma'am. You know I will. I understand perfectly." When he heard the Texas Ranger say those final words Deke finally realized what had been going on. That big giant of a man was yes ma'aming that little brunette as if she was the governor. Apparently, he would stop only long enough to start listening whenever she would cut him off with questions. She sure did not have much of a voice to match the reputation.

"If that's what you want Miss Amy. I will get right on it ma'am. Yes ma'am, I will be available. Okay. Whatever you say Miss Amy. And ma'am, everyone here sure is sorry about all this, it's a real tragedy, but we will get them." Ranger Randal did everything but salute her as she broke from the circle of officers. Climbing back into her vehicle she left in a cloud of dust.

Deke wished he could have heard what was said. Nearly every cop around had run to stop her from seeing what had happened inside. By stopping her from entering the cafe, they probably spared her many a nightmare. It was an extreme show of compassion on their part especially while in the middle of a triple homicide investigation. Yet, virtually every one of the officers stopped whatever they were doing to pamper the little woman that Deke guessed was not much taller than five feet, and could not weigh much more than a hundred pounds.

Because of all this special treatment, Deke became suspicious, very quick. Something was up, and if his guess was right, Miss Amy was the smartest living woman on the face of this earth. It looked like they were getting her approval on aspects of the investigation. That's one reason he'd wished that whatever they were saying could have been heard.

If he was right about what he thought he saw, those fellows were following orders. For having the kind of reputation the cafe menu claimed she had, lawmen sure were displaying a heap of respect for the little woman. It just did not add up, no matter how he turned it. While everyone was busy with the little interruption Amy Dodson had created, he had managed to wander under and inside the area surrounded by police tape. More than ever, he was determined to find out what had happened to those women. Looking around, he was unable to locate Sergeant Hadley. Deke wasn't about to walk right up to anyone casually asking what happened. Not a chance in hell would he walk up to that Godzilla-sized Texas Ranger for anything.

"Mr. Stone, something that I can help you with sir?" It was none other than that Texas Ranger. Deke nearly wet his pants when he heard the voice behind him, and that gave him a quick excuse. "Yes sir, sure is. I don't want to get in the way, but I've been sitting for quite some time, and well, I just have to locate a bathroom," he answered without having to lie. Randal laughed at his situation. Though Deke was somewhat uncomfortable, it was a little humorous.

"Come on over here, and I'll show you where you can go."

They walked through the front door of the cafe, and headed straight for the double doors entering the kitchen. Deke could not believe his luck, until they turned the corner in the L shaped room. He stopped dead in his tracks wishing that his luck had not been so good. He could have done without ever seeing the display before him.

Three walls were exposed in this extension to the kitchen. Each wall was approximately fourteen feet long by ten feet high. The room ended at a large walk-through freezer looking door, approximately five feet wide.

It was open, and a few of the investigators were inside. It looked like it was for dry goods storage. Forensics lab specialists were taking samples from the wall, the floor, everything and anything that they thought might hide clues.

From the serious attitudes displayed, it was clear they had not run across anything like this before. Sergeant Hadley was correct when he'd said the smell of blood was thick. Deke saw why. Such a strong, nasty smell still permeated the back kitchen, even after having all the doors opened all morning, attempting to remove the smell. Homicide detectives were still taking pictures, no clean up had begun yet. Occasionally one of the officers covered his mouth with his hand, running out the back door for air. It was probably just as much to escape the macabre and hideous sight they were trying to accept as a reality. Each of the women had gray, electrical tape wrapped around her head. The tape completely covered their mouth and eyes. Starting at the collarbone, and extending the entire length of the body, except for the hands and feet, not a square inch of skin remained. Bleeding flesh that had since caked hard and dry had a painful, leathery look to it. The fact that they bled so much was proof that they were alive while being skinned. The nylon rope was tied tightly around each neck, only the odd looking knot visible, extending to the steel beam above them, where the killer had left them dangling.

Before Deke could ask what had happened to the skin removed from them he saw the answer to his question. Colorful, pushpins secured strips of flesh hanging on three of the four walls within the small room. It was a ghastly scene. It was now obvious why the officers had rushed to surround Amy Dodson before she had had a chance to enter the cafe.

Two black women had worked for Amy for nearly thirteen years, cooking breakfast and starting lunch. They also prepared side orders until noon, that was when the afternoon cooks arrived, replacing them. They were good cooks, and had families who did not deserve such evil to be afflicted upon a loved one. Both of the women were old enough for retirement.

The young, white waitress had started working at the cafe only two months earlier. She was single, twenty-four, and running from something or someone. Amy never pried into her personal life, but knew a battered woman when she saw one.

Race had nothing to do with the disgusting nature of the crime, and yet it did. The letters **A** and **Y** were fitted together using skin from the older women. While the letter, **M** had been pinned up on the wall using the young, white skin of the waitress. Even without the bizarre touch, a name tacked neatly against a wall spelled by using human skin, created a deep sense of dread for whomever the message was meant.

"The young girl had been trying to start a new life from what I remember," Ranger Randal stated, realizing what Deke must be thinking. "The older lady on the right was Miss Amy's breakfast and short order cook. The other woman made the best tasting Bar-B-Que in the county. I can see by your response Mr. Stone that you have probably never seen anything as hideous as this. Come on this way, we will use the back door. I can't let anyone use the bathroom facilities until the boys from lab have been through it." He backtracked to a doorway leading out where a large brick Bar-B-Que pit sat. Large, iron grills covered simmering coals, piled high in the brick pits. Stacks of mesquite wood sat next to each of the pits. A shelter made with corrugated tin covered the entire area.

"A good spot is just around the corner where the men have been relieving themselves, I'll wait here." Randal pointed to the right, pulling out a small cigar from his shirt pocket, lighting it. Deke walked around to the side where he found a corner of the building hidden from view. Ranger Randal was very smart. Deke used the excuse of having to find a bathroom to get a look at what was happening inside. Ranger Zach Randal used the same excuse to get a look at what kind of response Deke would have to the horrible scene. As he rejoined the Texas Ranger standing underneath the Bar-B-Que pit shelter, he saw the big man leaning back against one of the large wooden, corner posts. He had the look of someone who was in deep thought, as he stared off across the Texas Plains. Nursing the little cigar, blowing out thick clouds of smoke, he did not acknowledge Deke as he walked up and stood beside him. They remained silent for at least five minutes, staring at nothing in particular. Finally, the silence was broken.

"What kind of person could do such a thing to innocent folks, you reckon, or to anyone for that matter?" Texas Ranger Zach Randal asked. Deke knew that the man did not expect him to answer, and shrugged without replying. He did not know of anything to say. "This is just the sort of thing that makes my job disgusting Mr. Stone, but at the same time makes it the best damned job in the world. I get to hunt down the bastard, and make sure he's caught, and know he can never do anything like this again." He turned looking down at Deke. At that moment, Deke saw something reflecting from the Texas Ranger's eyes, and it sent chills running down his spine. It was obvious from the look in those eyes that this was not just a job to him. It was more a mission, and he took it very seriously. Ranger Randal was at one moment the most pleasant of people with perfect manners, but Deke had discovered, like a chameleon, he had an ability to transform himself. As big as he was, to become so non-intimidating, appearing harmless, was a trick of the trade.

Becoming personable, nearly to a fault, Randal gave a false impression to the guilty, appearing to lose his advantage. Then, with stunning quickness, he transformed his appearance into the most threatening Deke had ever seen. This was not the kind of man anybody wanted tracking them. It was obvious that when Texas Ranger Zach Randal had a case, he took it personal. In Randal's opinion the perpetrator had sinned, and worse, had sinned against him.

Feeling rather uncomfortable, Deke was anxious to change the tone. "What did you mean earlier by saying that you believed me, but that it also created a problem within itself?" he asked.

Turning his gaze away from Deke, looking back out over the Texas Prairie, Randal continued nursing the little cigar that by this time was only a stub. "What did I mean about which part? That I believed you, or believing you created a problem in itself?" he asked Deke, looking at the smoldering stub between his fingers.

"Both I suppose." Deke knew he was being toyed with, but decided to play along, especially after what he saw in those eyes a minute ago.

"The part about believing you means exactly that. I don't think you have that sort of killer instinct in you, at least not the kind that could butcher a woman alive." He paused, allowing the comment to sink in. "That leaves us with the other half of the equation. If you had nothing to do with this, and I know you didn't, then who's responsible was more than likely still inside when you walked in this morning. Believing they were undiscovered, they decided to have a little fun with you, and I do think that is what happened. They toyed with the radio and made the other noises. Which is no big deal, killers with the kind of sickness this one exhibits often do things that way, assuming you'd go on home and never be seen again. But that's where we'll have to take the advantage." Randal was leading in a direction that made Deke nervous. He hoped this wasn't what he thought it was. "I'm not sure I follow you. It is a fact that I did not discover anyone while inside," Deke replied.

"Sure you did Deke. May I call you Deke?" he asked with that charismatic tone and personality that left no other option, but to allow him to do whatever he wanted.

Deke again shrugged his shoulders while shaking his head affirmatively. "From everything we've seen, and have been able to piece together, this is not your run of the mill everyday homicide. Apparently, a whole lot of planning and strategy has been put into this by the killer or killers. It is not easy to solve this kind of crime because of the very nature of it. We sometimes look at the viciousness of such a butchering with comments off the cuff, labeling the responsible party as crazy. Nevertheless, make no mistake about it Deke, this person is not crazy, no sir, quite the opposite. The individual responsible for this is far from crazy, sick maybe, but he is not crazy. In fact, may I venture to say that a very intelligent mind is behind what you witnessed a few minutes ago. Do you agree?" Randal asked. He was building up to something that required a complete and full understanding from Deke.

"I see what you're getting at, but what could that possibly have to do with me? I'm just a regular person, not even involved in crime fighting," Deke answered, trying to hint at his desire to go home.

"It may be true that you have no experience with criminal matters, but you're not just a regular person, and it could have everything to do with you. You cannot tell me that you have no sympathy for the families of those three women. And I know through just the short time that I spent questioning you earlier, you're the kind of person who reaches out and helps when he's needed, because it's the right thing to do." Texas Ranger Zach Randal piled it high. Everything that he said was exactly what anyone would want to hear about him or herself. However, he was so casual when saying it that it didn't feel like any pressure was added. He just leaned up against that post looking out over the horizon. "Ranger Randal, I don't want to sound disrespectful, and I do feel for the families of those women; so, if you don't mind, to borrow a phrase of yours, can we just cut straight through the bullshit, and get to milking this cow?" Deke was tired, and didn't feel like playing games.

Randal only leaned against the post, flicking the stub of cigar away. With a slight chuckle, he finally turned to look at Deke. "Mr. Stone, I like you. You're a smart guy, and I know I can trust you to do the right thing. But all that mush won't do a damn bit of good unless I do things by the book."

"Ethically, and legally I have to inform you of the amount of danger involved. Then after I'm certain that you understand the risks involved, I've got to get a signed consent to utilize you in the investigation." The big man's tone had changed from a Southern drawl to sounding like a corporate lawyer.

"Hell, there's a better way of handling this. Where do you live Mr. Stone?"

"I live just northwest of Colorado Springs, a town called Green Mountain Falls," Deke replied, a little suspicious of the question. "Is

that in El Paso County, or Teller County?" he asked. Deke didn't want
to show his surprise, but was impressed that the Texas Ranger knew
each county.

"It's right on the border, but classified as being in El Paso County,"
Deke stated, having no idea where this was going. "El Paso County, let
me see if I remember. Isn't that where Bill Wright is the sheriff?" Randal
asked after about fifteen seconds of thought.

"Yep, been sheriff for the last twelve years. I don't know the man
personally, but I've met him a few times on cross-country trail rides. A
couple of times we started at the base of Pikes Peak, taking a three day
ride around the mountain, ending up right back where we started," Deke
commented, realizing that he was probably saying too much.

"I've heard of those trail rides. In fact, I was invited on a couple of
them, but I'm always too busy with some investigation. Look, I don't
know what you might think about this, but it may be possible to have
you deputized, avoiding any legal battles with defense attorneys when we
do apprehend the perpetrator of this crime." The suggestion seemed
offered even while he was thinking of it.

"Of course I can't guarantee anything until I speak with Sheriff
Wright. If you were a resident in this county we'd do it here, but we've
got to do things by the book," Randal concluded.

"I don't understand. Why do I have to be deputized?" Deke saw
what was coming, and suddenly resorted to a position of playing dumb.
This Ranger Randal actually wanted him to take an active role in the
investigation. Deke didn't have any desire to play cops and robbers, and
had no secret fantasy of becoming a lawman. His self-esteem was just
fine without having to carry a gun.

"Deke, I know all of this seems to be happening very quickly, and
you seem to be having mixed feelings about everything. You probably
even think the best thing for you and everyone involved is just to take
your time making a decision, not knowing whether to help us out or
not," Randal stated in a compassionate tone of voice. Deke had begun
nodding his head affirmatively.

"The fact of the matter is that while it may seem the best thing for
everyone, it only benefits one person; the sick sorry son-of-a-bitch that
committed this butchering. I have a job to do Mr. Stone, and I plan on
doing it with or without your help." The big man's voice gradually took
on a tone that was far from compassionate, and he had reverted to the
formality of calling him Mr. Stone.

Before Deke could respond, or even bat an eye, Randal had spun to face him. Looking up into the Texas Ranger's face Deke was almost certain he could see fire behind those cold, steel blue eyes.

"A cold blooded killer is running loose somewhere Mr. Stone, and even if it wasn't my job I'm sure I'd do everything within my power to see that he's caught. Especially if I had nothing better to do, with no steady job, no wife, no real home to return to, and the knowledge to help put this psychotic maniac away for good. Now if you will excuse me I really don't have time to be coddling someone who can't decide if he wants to do his civic duty or not." With that said, Ranger Randal turned away from him, heading back toward the rear of the cafe.

"Wait just one minute Ranger Randal. How is it that you know about my job and my marital status?" Deke questioned, sounding a little pissed off at what he considered private, and none of the Texas Ranger's business. It was one thing to try and manipulate him into a triple murder investigation, but another altogether to try and make him feel guilty, nearly referring to him as if he were nothing, but some two bit spoiled brat with no spine.

Slowly Randal came to a halt. Even though he remained facing away, Deke could almost see a smile forming on the Texas Ranger's face.

"Does that piss you off Mr. Stone? Doesn't it rattle you just a bit that I'm able to find out that kind of information about you? Regardless of what you might be thinking, it is my business to know these things, but I didn't try to use it when I was asking for your help. Be thankful Mr. Stone that you have no real job, and no wife. It's more than we can say for the three ladies hanging from the ceiling, isn't it?" Slowly he turned back to face Deke. If a smile was on his face earlier, it had now disappeared.

"Don't mistake my intentions Mr. Stone. I may not get any help from you, making my job less difficult, but neither will I give you the same courtesy. I can live with no cooperation as long as you realize that it works both ways," he stated in a voice that made the hair stand up on the back of Deke's neck.

Turning again to face the rear entrance to the cafe, Zachary Randal's booming voice penetrated the scene.

"Sergeant Hadley! I will need you to escort Mr. Stone to headquarters for a full statement. Do not release him until he has been fully questioned." Turning back to Deke, Randal almost looked apologetic when he stated, "You can call your lawyer from headquarters if you like."

Deke was uncertain if he should be angry or scared. At the onset, he was careful not to underestimate this man's abilities or intentions, but he was now certain that he had. It was apparent, Zachary Randal would go to any extreme seeking assistance with the investigation of this triple homicide. Obviously, something about this man was beyond what he had anticipated, or maybe it was something about this situation than Deke was not privy to.

Sergeant Hadley exited the rear door of the cafe approaching Deke, shaking his head slowly from side to side while the Ranger Randal entered beside him. Deke was stunned at how quick the entire scenario had switched. A part of him admired the big Texas Ranger's resolve.

"What in the hell did I do wrong?" he asked Sergeant Hadley in a low voice as the man reached his location.

"It may not be that you did anything wrong Deke, it was probably that you didn't do what was right, and didn't do it quick enough for Randal. He is a very determined man. Anytime he feels pressured or at a disadvantage, he gets a little impatient, and just doesn't feel like he has time to fool around. Let's just say that some of the facts surrounding this case are more sensitive than you could possible know. In his mind, if someone that he thinks could help with the investigation dawdles a little too long, that person becomes someone that's just in the way. Sort of the attitude that if you're not for him, then you're against him," Sergeant Hadley stated in a matter of fact way.

"But that's not at all how I feel about it. It all just kind of buried me, I guess I became a little confused and...well, scared," Deke confessed. He realized he might have been a little wishy-washy when Randal asked for his assistance, but before he knew it, and without warning, it seemed as if Randal had turned against him.

"I was seriously thinking of offering my assistance, but if the man dislikes me that much I don't know if it would be in my best interest," Deke commented frustratingly to Hadley.

"Oh I think you've got it all wrong Deke. Ranger Randal must think highly of you for him to go through the trouble of courting you as he did. He doesn't do that with many folks. Most of the time he considers it a loss of precious time, and those who don't strike him just right are left behind like fence posts scattered after a tornado. No, I'd say he likes you, and a hell of a lot, to go to that extreme. This particular perpetrator has gotten under his skin, and that's a feeling he just doesn't like," Hadley explained.

Deke liked Hadley; he had a way of explaining things.

"What did you mean when you said that some things about this case are sensitive and how I just can't imagine what they are, and how this murderer is getting under Randal's skin? Does he know who this guy is?" Deke asked Hadley, beginning to realize that just because this was his first exposure to such a crime didn't mean Ranger Randal hadn't run across something similar recently, and maybe was even working on an ongoing investigation linked to these murders.

"I'm not the one to ask those questions to Deke. If you're really interested I suggest you make an effort to get the answers from him," Hadley confessed, nodding his head toward Randal.

With that, Sergeant Hadley put his hand on Deke's shoulder, leading him around the outside of the cafe, back to the front parking lot where his cruiser was parked. Opening the rear door, Hadley motioned Deke to get in the back.

"I'll have to ask you to wait here until some of these boys from the lab move these vans. No way for me to get out of this jam until then," Hadley stated.

"It shouldn't be too long a wait Deke. Someone will drive your truck to headquarters at that time." He shut the door to the cruiser walking back in the direction where all of the action was.

"Well, that does it," thought Deke. *"Now I'm under arrest. What a turn of events."*

25

CHAPTER

3

AMY DODSON WAS already at the sheriff's station when Sergeant Hadley brought in Deke. Deke could hear her voice from behind a half-opened door as they made their way down the wide corridor toward the Division Office of the Texas Rangers. While being escorted down the hall, he could not tell whom it was that Amy Dodson was speaking.

Deke had not been handcuffed, nor did it appear as if he were a criminal, but he still held his head down, avoiding eye contact with anyone that might be looking through open doorways. He would soon discover that Miss Amy had been speaking to Texas Ranger Zach Randal.

Deke wouldn't need to see him to recognize the voice, making him all the more ashamed, feeling sick to his stomach to know that the big man was already inside the building. He couldn't help not feeling rotten about the fact that they'd had some sort of miscommunication. He was completely innocent of everything, and Texas Ranger Zach Randal knew it. Still, Deke felt sorry that the Texas Ranger had been disappointed in him. The man just had that sort of effect on people. Deke didn't want to let him down, even if all of this business was none of his affair.

"I don't think anyone is here at this time to get a formal statement from you Deke, but I'll have to put you in one of the interrogation rooms anyway. I know I don't have to remind you not to think of trying to leave. That door can only be opened from the outside," Sergeant Hadley stated. It was obvious the sergeant didn't like having to do this, and Deke knew it was just part of his job, making a comment to Hadley assuring him that he understood. Hadley kindly nodded his head in response.

"Excuse me Sergeant Hadley." Deke stopped him just as he was about to close the door, stepping out into the corridor by saying, "Would you do me a big favor and tell Ranger Randal that I would like to speak to him, that is, if he has time?" Deke had the biggest hangdog look on his face, making Sergeant Hadley smile slightly, understanding the request.

"Sure Deke. I'll see what I can do," he responded. Closing the door, he left Deke in the small room alone. Sitting at a simple wooden table bolted to the floor, Deke knew he'd regret the request as soon as he'd made it, but for some reason he just had to clear his conscience.

This was one of the most horrible feelings that he could ever remember experiencing. It was already well after lunch, he'd been up all night driving, disappointed from his failed storm chasing escapade, plus he'd had the tar scared out of him in Dodson's Breakfast and Bar-B-Que Cafe. Topping things off by falling in the middle of a full-blown, triple-homicide investigation, and seeing what was probably the most macabre sight on the planet. Moreover, a brilliant, King Kong-sized Texas Ranger making him feel that he was personally responsible for the hole in the Ozone layer. It was the understatement of the century to say that he was having a bad day.

Deke felt that he'd been sitting in that cramped interrogation room for a lifetime. He'd read every scribbled, carved name, noun, and descriptive adjective on the small wooden table in front of him before he noticed the wall-size mirror next to the door that led to the hallway.

Just when he thought it couldn't get any worse, he realized any number of officers had probably been watching him the entire time. Thinking back, trying to remember if he'd done anything bizarre while waiting, like crying or praying, he felt himself nearly jump out of his shoes as Texas Ranger Zach Randal exploded through the door, stooping down low as he entered to keep his Stetson from being knocked off.

"Sorry I kept you waiting so long Deke. Real busy right now, which I'm sure you can understand." The Texas Ranger was as cordial and friendly as if they'd been friends for years. Deke was extremely relieved to see the big man smiling as he extended his paddle-sized hand for Deke to gamble his extremity with.

Before Deke could open his mouth Randal took charge of the conversation. "Deke, I feel like I owe you an apology. I sometimes get just a little…well, somewhat impatient with folks during high intensity investigations. It's just something I've had to deal with over the years. If I've insulted you I apologize," he stated. Deke was dumbstruck. This guy was either the most humble man on the face of the Earth, or the best manipulator in the universe.

"Well, now that we've cleared that out of the way, what can I do for you?" he asked.

Deke's head was spinning from the sudden turnaround. He sat stammering, having his entire statement smeared away. He was actually going to apologize to Randal for being so uncommitted, wishy-washy, hoping to be forgiven. He was actually fearful that his salvation would be influenced by Randal's opinion of him. Instead, Randal was sitting across the table from him, completely immersed in one of the most gruesome criminal investigations in Texas history, asking what he could do for him.

It was at that very second that Deke recognized the brilliance of this man, and decided nothing anyone could do was going to keep him out of this investigation. He'd studied the criminal mind, discovering variables that created psychopathic personalities within individuals possessing near genius levels of intelligence. If nothing else, Deke wanted to watch this man work. A voice was singing inside his head telling him this was going to be worth ten hurricanes, and he'd be a fool to pass up such an opportunity.

"Ranger Randal, I've been thinking." Deke addressed Randal sitting across the wooden table that had suddenly disintegrated down to the size of a TV tray before the huge man. Randal never moved, keeping a look of concern on his face, giving the impression that whatever Deke had been thinking about was of his utmost concern.

"If you still think I can be useful in this investigation I want to offer myself totally to whatever service you think best," Deke confessed, magically feeling like a ton of weight had been lifted off his shoulders. Randal continued looking at him for several seconds without commenting. The silence that ensued had dropped that ton of weight right back down on Deke. For a second he thought that he'd said something wrong, but Randal finally smiled.

"I admire you for the offer son, but the truth is I don't want you to get involved in something that, for one reason or another, you may regret. Don't get me wrong, I am convinced that I could make good use of your skills and their addition to this investigation, but remember we're dealing with one bad son-of-a-bitch, ain't no telling where this may lead. For that matter, even how long of an investigation this could end up to be. Look, I'm not trying to dampen your offer, but rather to look out for your well being also." His response was the last thing Deke had expected, but probably it should have been exactly what to expect. Deke was a little disappointed in himself, but not having known Randal for very long, he was surprised at how quick the Texas Ranger operated intellectually.

"Before we make any final decisions I think one other person needs to be included in planning our strategy." Here was something that Deke understood for a change. Everyone has superiors, and Randal was smart to seek approval from whoever that person was, probably the county sheriff. Standing up from the table, Ranger Randal turned, rapping loudly against the closed door behind him. A second later Sergeant Hadley opened it from the outer hallway.

"Excuse me for just a minute Deke, I'll be right back. You can leave this door open John," he told Hadley and headed down the hall. Within only a couple of minutes, he could hear Randal's footsteps as they headed back toward the interrogation room. True to his word, he re-entered the small room turning toward the door behind him.

"Deke I'd like you to meet Miss Amy Dodson." He introduced the petite brunette just as she entered. Deke was so shocked, struck by her beauty that he knocked over the chair he was sitting in while attempting to stand. He didn't know whether to shake her hand or kiss it, and had to make a conscious effort to keep his mouth closed.

"I am pleased to make your acquaintance Mr. Stone. I just wish it could have been under more pleasant circumstances," she offered. A voice that sounded like it belonged on a 1-900 recording, but with the authority of a businesswoman.

"As you are aware, a most horrible event occurred at my place of business this morning. While it may appear that I am relatively calm at this time let me take this opportunity to let you know that constant screaming can be heard inside my head from what has occurred. Not only were those women my employees, but they were dear friends also. My greatest fear is that they may have been disgustingly tortured and murdered for something that has nothing at all to do with them. As you may know by now, an ongoing investigation is being conducted with multiple law enforcement agencies regarding threats against my life. Ranger Zach Randal has been in charge of that investigation." Before she could continue, Randal interrupted. She appeared flustered at the interruption of what was apparently a well rehearsed and thought out narrative describing what she'd been living through.

"Excuse me Miss Amy but I have yet to inform Mr. Stone of any details regarding previous incidents thought to be related to the current situation." Randal informed her. At this she calmed slightly, relaxing from the stiff, straight-back position she'd taken from the time she'd sat across from Deke.

"Oh, I see. It appears as though I have jumped the gun. I was under the impression that Deke, may I call you Deke?" she cooed from across the table. "I was under the impression that Deke had offered his services to help authorities in catching this sick and perverted criminal. I apologize Mr. Stone for taking up so much of your time, but I was informed that you may have actually been inside my cafe this morning when the...when the girls were...excuse me, I'm sorry. I am still having difficulty accepting the entire thing." Lowering her head slightly Deke could see that her chin was quivering wildly, and tears began to stream down her cheeks.

Texas Ranger Zach Randal was quick as a rattler, pulling out an oversized handkerchief. "Miss Amy, why don't you let us handle this. You're stretching yourself thinner than a Democrats viewpoint. We can take it from here. I didn't say Deke wasn't going to help us, I was just letting you know that everything has happened so fast we haven't had time to fill him in on all of it, that's all." The Texas Ranger was as brutal as he was big, but what he said flowed like honey across the table. By this time, Deke was adjusting to the bizarre scene and spoke for the first time.

"Yes Ma'am. Ranger Randal is absolutely right. I have offered my help, and while I have only limited abilities, I am committed to see that this criminal is brought to justice, regardless of what has happened in the past. What I've witnessed today has both infuriated and motivated me to do whatever I can."

He had to make himself shut up before digging a hole deeper than he was capable of climbing. The sight of that petite woman breaking down from what he'd assumed was fear, was too much for him to handle. It may have all been for show, but Deke was too tender hearted to take it; besides, he decided that he liked this show. In addition, what he'd witnessed earlier that day inside the cafe was too brutal to ignore. With that said, Amy Dodson looked up at him with tear-filled, green eyes. Slowly composing herself, wiping her cheeks gently, she gave him the most seductively beautiful smile this side of the Rio Grande.

"Now, you see that Miss Amy, what did I tell you. We have everything under control, and we will catch this perpetrator. Everyone is committed, and with our heads put together, ain't no way he'll get away.

Now go on home, and get some rest before you make yourself ill. We'll keep you informed. Won't we Deke?"

The sudden inclusion of Deke as one of the guys was yet another surprise he was not prepared for. He was beginning to worry that he might get used to this twisted world of Ranger Randal's. He had to be absolutely, completely, and without question, the most unpredictable man he'd ever met. It occurred to Deke that maybe that's why he was so good at what he did. No criminal would ever be capable of guessing his next move. "Absolutely!" Deke replied, proud of himself that he was able to hold to one word. The truth was that he was lucky to get that much out on such short notice, under the circumstances.

Amy Dodson got up out of her chair. Standing erect, and straightening her spine, she lifted her head. "I am, and will forever be indebted to you for this brave and selfless act of courage Mr. Stone." Hesitating, she corrected herself, "I mean, Deke, and please keep in touch, and don't hesitate to call me for anything." Reaching out, Amy took his hand in hers shaking it firmly. Then in a flash, she turned and was gone. Deke sat mesmerized, stuck somewhere inside those eyes, in a trance for several seconds.

Deke noticed Randal staring at him from across the table. Poker-faced, he was impossible to read. Finally, Randal broke the silence, leaving no doubt about what he was thinking. Sitting back in a chair, he reached into his shirt pocket, pulling out one of the small cigars, lighting it.

"Before we go any farther with this conversation Deke, I need to ask you a couple questions. Nothing very heavy, or too important, but it will assist me in answering your next question," he stated, raising a cloud of smoke around his head with a smile on his face. It was clear that he was anticipating a little enjoyment.

"What question? I haven't even asked the first one yet," Deke said in defense of himself.

"I know it, but you will, and if you don't I'll be real worried about you."

The Texas Ranger started with simple questions, "While sitting inside the cafe this morning, you stated that approximately forty minutes had passed. Did you happen to read the menu?" "Well, yeah! I sure did," Deke confessed. "The entire menu, front to back?" Randal was heading somewhere, and Deke was too curious not to play along.

31

"I sure did, and I found the cafe's history most interesting, especially the comments about Miss Amy Dodson. Now I understand to what the menu was referring. Beauty Queen, and apparently well seasoned," Deke admitted. The tone that he used was clearly indicating he thought he knew about what he was talking. As soon as he said it, he realized that it sounded a tad bit disrespectful.

Ranger Randal chuckled with what appeared to be some agreement, drawing heavily on the little cigar. Leaning forward in his chair, nearly eyeball to eyeball with Deke, he blew out the smoke.

"That's what I figured, and before this goes too far to be straightened out, let me show you that you don't know half of what you think you do. What you read on that menu is exactly what any dumb ass would do, coming up with the exact dumb-ass conclusion that you have. And don't get all bent out of shape, I'm not insulting you. What I'm doing is educating you." The smile never left his face, he didn't appear angry, only amused.

"What you city boys are accustomed to are women who put on the sex appeal Friday and Saturday night, getting what they need from you, not what you want from them. I understand, because city women are ruthless bitches. No disrespect intended Deke, but what we have here are refined ladies. That's how they behave everyday, no show, and the real thing. But it doesn't mean they're trying to give away what you fellows are just dying to get. To the contrary, it means they own what you'd sell your soul for, and fellers like you have to sit tight until they decide you've earned the right to taste, not the other way around. I know it may be a little confusing, but you'll catch on. Just don't cross the line without permission. Got it?" Randal concluded his little lesson by crushing out the cigar stub in the palm of his hand, never shedding the smile. His point was made, and Deke silently prayed he didn't break any rules, especially if Randal was the referee.

"Sure, I got it Ranger. I was just a little shocked to see what appeared as a come-on, or something that seemed very seductive flowing out so easily from her. It was so…well, so erotic," Deke confessed, nearly in a state of panic. "I didn't mean anything by what I said."

"I understand Deke. Let me be the first to congratulate you son. That was obviously your first encounter with what we refer to as a real lady. Hopefully you'll have many more such encounters in your life. As long as you know right from the get-go that in my part of the country, the women run the show, making up all the rules." As soon as Randal had completed his commentary on the differences between female personalities and classifications, Sergeant Hadley entered the room with a thick file in his hand. Randal turned to him taking the file, and placing it between himself and Deke on the table.

"Thank you John. I was about to ask for this," Ranger Randal said as he sat back relaxing, opening the file.

"Deke, as you know from my own admission, I'm an impatient man. What we got here is a file documenting a number of criminal violations, consisting of harassment through different methods against one Amy Dodson, Caucasian-female, citizen of Sweetwater, Texas." Ranger Zach Randal busied himself with the thick file, selecting several documents to examine, all the while speaking to Deke.

"I feel like we're dealing with something very similar to what I explained briefly to you this morning as a very cold blooded, meticulous, and brilliant mind. This damaged, but exceptional mind just happens to be inside a body that I have yet to identify, and is our perpetrator. Now, because I feel that we may be on as hot a trail as we have ever been on before, I've already taken the liberty of contacting Sheriff Wright up in El Paso County." This sudden statement startled Deke. Totally unexpected, the revelation came out of nowhere, and Deke found himself at a distinct disadvantage, feeling almost violated by the contact that was made behind his back. Yet, Randal did it without his permission.

"He tells me that you have been a member of his Sheriff's Posse for the last two years, and that he thinks you're a stable man. He confessed you had sort of a hippie attitude occasionally, but for the most part, you're stable. I was glad to hear it, especially since he went ahead and extended the authority of his office directly to this office for the express purpose of having you deputized." Ranger Randal began the conversation by asserting his authority with a tone suggesting that none of what he had done should be questioned.

"Before we get too deep into this file let me clarify a couple of things. Amy Dodson, as you know, is the great great granddaughter of Saul Dodson. Of the twelve daughters that Saul and his wife raised, Amy's mother was the only one never to leave Sweetwater. The other eleven gals either left town or died before they ever had a chance to vamoose. Been too damn many of them for anyone to keep track of; so, just take my word that Amy's mother took it upon herself to keep that greasy spoon of a cafe open for many years. She never got rich. In fact, she nearly starved. Amy's father never hung around long enough to see what a beauty his daughter would become. In other words, Amy never really had a father. You listening to me Deke?"

Deke was definitely listening, and he signaled Randal by vigorously shaking his head. "Well anyway, Amy was just seventeen, and getting ready to graduate from high school when her poor mother accidentally overdosed on some kind of antibiotic medication. It was verified as an accident, and even if it wasn't, it killed her just the same. As if that weren't bad enough, that young, seventeen-year-old, high school senior, dropped out of school three months before graduation to try and run the cafe." It was obvious that Zach Randal was impressed with Amy, and was doing his best to see that Deke was also.

"She not only ran that place, but made a damn good business out of it. It may be true that some of her methods were a little questionable, but by God, she did what she had to do to survive. You getting my drift here Deke?" Each time Randal asked, Deke would resume with the vigorous nodding of his head.

"It so happens, Amy Dodson ain't all that's been printed on that menu. It all started as sort of a joke you know. Fellows always poking good clean fun in her direction, being she's so pretty, whistling at her and such. It worked so damn well with out-of-towners that she just never did worry about getting the story straight. All the folks from around here knew better anyway. It may be true that she's single, and has been courted by a couple of dozen fellows, but Amy always figured marrying one of them would just hurt the feelings of thirty or forty other guys. She seems to be perfectly content to be everyone's girl. Do you see where I'm coming from Deke?"

Deke saw exactly where he was coming from. Amy Dodson was the town sweetheart, and there was not a soul around that would accuse her of being anything more, or anything less than that. Deke silently wondered about the one opinion in town that had suddenly shifted to quite a different extreme; after all, Amy was suddenly chosen as somebody's target.

"All Right, I'm glad we got that out of the way. As long as you're aware ain't no need for me to explain any further, but since I'm going to be relying on a certain amount of brain work from you, I didn't want you starting off on the wrong wavelength, thinking that little lady is anything less than the courageous person she's been all this time.

"Remember Deke, she's the victim here, and it's our job to protect her. Lord knows we did a piss-poor job protecting those poor ladies at the cafe. Just between you and me, that's where this bastard may have just slipped up. I still haven't made up my mind whether to believe it's the work of one or two men. God help us if it's just one madman doing all this."

For the first time Deke saw a glimpse of fear come from the Texas Ranger, and seeing it sent shivers through him.

"What is it that troubles you about it being one man Mr. Randal?" Deke asked his first good question. Zach Randal had been staring off at nothing in particular, but immediately turned toward Deke with a look of encouragement, and launched into an answer.

"First of all Deke, just call me Randal, or Zach. Everybody else does and that's okay, I expect. Whatever you call me behind my back I could not care less about." He was one tough old cob. Not a bone in his body was worried about what kind of impression he gave to folks.

"Now. Getting back to your question Deke, I know what you're thinking. One man must be easier to catch than two must, and in most situations that may be true, but not in this type of a depraved and isolated mind. I'd prefer two or even three of them. The criminal mind Deke is grounded in a thing that we rarely experience under any normal conditions, and that's a constant state of paranoia. You see, to a man like that, everyone is out to get him. Ain't a soul on this Earth that he can trust. Along with that elevated state of paranoia comes a constant and dynamic force of inner competition. Now, this maniac is not against you or against me personally, but against the damn world. Do you understand where I'm coming from son?" Deke wasn't sure, but he was so captivated by what this man knew that he was not about to interrupt.

"If this killer is a loner, then we lose probably our most valuable advantage. Only he knows what he's up to, and he'll never share it with even the devil himself. Now, if it happens to be two people, then half of my work is usually accomplished by one or the other. That inner competition that I was telling you about gets extremely fierce and aggressive, yet it usually remains well hidden. That paranoia dominates any relationship if it's more than one perpetrator and before long the struggle for power will secretly pit one against the other in an attempt to eliminate what they perceive as a major threat, and visa-versa. Do you see where I'm coming from Deke?"

35

Deke suddenly became filled with enthusiasm and excitement. He was definitely getting it. His brain had not been this stimulated since dealing with his ex-wife's lawyers. The difference was that he loved this. Deke found himself so anxious to learn all that this man was thinking that the questions just seemed to pop out of his mouth.

"What is it that makes you think it might be more than one person involved?" Deke asked, fully aware that he knew nothing about what was in the file, but the question had already been asked.

Without any conscious effort from either man, this investigation had just received what it had been lacking most; a fresh dose of hungry enthusiasm. Texas Ranger Zach Randal scooted to the edge of his chair, leaning in Deke's direction, becoming magically energized with the dialogue.

"I'm glad you asked me that son. Actually, it was not until today that I seriously entertained the thought. Let me explain. You told me this morning that when you arrived at the cafe it was somewhere close to 5 a.m. Right?" he began. Deke confirmed that it was indeed very close, if not 5 a.m. on the button.

"Well, you see, that's what has me suddenly looking at this thing from another and totally different angle. Those three ladies arrive for work every morning at 4:15 sharp. Been doing it ever since they started working for Amy, and I confirmed it with her. In fact, a time clock was just installed three weeks ago where they punch a card just to keep track of their hours. It just so happens that on this particular morning they all remembered to do just what they were supposed to and punch that card. When I checked each of their time cards for the time they clocked in, it was exactly 4:16 a.m. That leaves exactly forty-four minutes from the time when they arrived at work until the time when you say you walked in." Ranger Zach Randal paused for a minute. Pulling out another one of the small cigars from his front shirt pocket, he lit it before continuing.

"But I got a little suspicious Deke when I noticed four trays of home-made, buttermilk biscuits inside one of the ovens in the kitchen. In addition, a gallon-sized bowl of pancake batter that had already been stirred up, and two dozen eggs inside a mixing bowl ready to be scrambled." Zach Randal slowly sat back in his chair, looking at Deke. He was waiting to see what, if any, conclusion would be made by Deke from this observation.

Deke was a little puzzled, but knew Randal was waiting for questions; so, he went ahead and asked, wishing he could have given his opinion instead.

"That must have been their normal routine every morning, right?" He attempted at giving an intelligent statement, while at the same time asking a question.

"Exactly right Deke, and that's where the troubling part comes in. How did one man manage to subdue and completely skin three grown women, hang them from the ceiling, pin up that grotesque message made from the skin, and do it all in the amount of time available before you walked into Dodson's Breakfast and Bar-B-Que Cafe at five am?" The question was in fact a statement, declaring the high degree of improbability.

"The women had obviously been busy with their morning duties for what had to be at least twenty minutes, which, at the most, leaves another twenty-four minutes before time is up." Even as Zach was making the declaration, he seemed to ponder over the mystery. Leaning farther back, looking up, his eyes followed the drifting smoke from his cigar. It was such an obvious deduction that Deke was a little taken aback by the conclusion, and found that he had to agree. It did present a new twist to the entire scenario.

After Randal commented on the mystery, admitting that he was not completely sure of anything at this time, he sat with a look of intense thought across his face. Ranger Randal seemed to completely forget about Deke, or that he was even in the room. Saying nothing, continuing to gaze up at the ceiling, he nursed the cigar stub.

Deke followed along with the extended silence existing between them, beginning to activate his own brain cells by trying to figure out what part of the crime scene Randal had now decided was worth expending so much brain activity on.

As Deke sat in silence, he discovered that he too began thinking about the bizarre circumstances, theorizing to himself about the different aspects. Then, from somewhere inside his brain, the realization hit him. Randal never intended to have him interrogated today. To the contrary, Deke had been put in Sergeant Hadley's care with clear instructions given by Zach Randal.

No one was to be allowed in the interrogation room without him. Most importantly, to make certain that not a soul was around with whom Deke could get friendly. The damn news media was going be all over the story, and if they found out about Deke, they'd be all over him too. He had to be protected by someone. The last thing they needed was to have Deke Stone reduced to nothing more than potted meat by a pod of media leaches pouncing on him.

The entire interrogation thing was nothing, but an informal meeting set up by Ranger Zach Randal, having Sergeant Hadley escort him from the scene to headquarters.

All that time Deke had fallen for the act put on by Randal. The stage was being set with a stacking of the deck, so to speak, making Deke think that Zach was angry and disappointed. Before Randal was able to play his hand by asking Deke to reconsider and help them, Deke had volunteered.

Hell, if the big man had decided to push a little harder Deke might have offered his services for life. Just as they reached an agreement, it was secretly realized by both men that the experience was going to be beneficial for everyone involved. Neither man could have been any happier, thinking they were getting the best part of the deal. However, to admit that would in effect be giving up what they found most enjoyable.

Leaning back in his chair, Ranger Zach Randal lifted one tree trunk-sized leg at a time, propping his boots up on the small table. For the first time, Deke wasn't surprised. Randal was still in his dream-state.

What Deke didn't know and really had no way of knowing, was what Ranger Zach Randal seemed so caught up with, had been happening for quite some time. It constituted everything that had occurred from the very beginning up until that point.

One thing about Randal, he was unpredictable.

"No way of telling what he'll do next." Deke thought.

The Texas Ranger spoke, "Deke, sit down and get comfortable. It ain't very often that I stretch myself into telling someone about past events, we may be here for a spell."

CHAPTER

4

IT WAS SEVERAL YEARS EARLIER...

ZACH RANDAL had not yet experienced the pleasure of meeting Amy Dodson, whom he'd heard was a shrewd business woman, in addition to her other attributes. By this time, Zach Randal had developed quite a reputation himself. Miss Amy Dodson was familiar with the rather impressive record that Zach Randal had developed, long before ever meeting up with him.

Several years after she'd decided to run the cafe alone, things started to look up; she actually began thinking she was going to make it. Customers were returning on a weekly basis after discovering the delicious food at Dodson's Breakfast and Bar-B-Que Cafe. That was just one of the attractions. They were also pleasantly surprised at how reasonable Amy's prices were. She didn't believe in the highway robbery prices most restaurants imposed on their customers.

Soon, she discovered that by setting her prices at exactly one half of the amount that the other restaurants were charging, she significantly increased the number of patrons visiting the small cafe, as well as the frequency of their visits. Nevertheless, Amy had made enemies by doing this, specifically, one of the fancier restaurant owners, one who had suddenly discovered that his restaurant was half empty, and on a regular basis.

Without any warning that Sunday morning, the owner of the fancy restaurant barged recklessly into Dodson's Breakfast and Bar-B-Que Cafe. Immediately Amy recognized him, and knew from experiences that he was half crazy and even worse, he was completely drunk. The crazed restaurant owner raged, while slobbering over the cafe's counter, claiming that Amy had crossed the line of decency by reducing her prices, stealing the patrons that he'd been serving meals to for years. He began his protesting with what she'd considered as a degree of reasonableness, near acceptable measures, but after realizing Amy wasn't going to listen to his demands, he made a fatal error.

In deciding that he would force Amy to respond, and compelled with making ridiculous insults, he'd committed his first mistake.

Any experienced fighting man knew to always watch his back. With Amy behind the wide counter, he found himself standing on the tip of his toes, reaching across wildly with his hands. Grabbing Amy around her neck, his intentions were clear. Behind the drunken man were the front doors that he'd used entering the cafe.

As this bizarre scene was unfolding, Texas Ranger Zach Randal had parked out in front of the cafe with thoughts of having a big breakfast, maybe even getting a chance to meet the much talked about Amy Dodson. While sitting in his car, deciding what he would say and how to introduce himself, he happened to look through the large picture window in the front of the cafe. What Zach saw made him jump so quickly that he nearly crushed his Stetson flat on the top of his head, clambering to get out of his vehicle.

Ranger Randal wasn't sure how long this man had been squeezing the life out of the innocent and frail, little bomb-shell, but as the restaurant owner began dragging her limp body up and over the counter, the biggest, meanest son-of-a-bitch in the state of Texas came flying through the front door.

Zach's appearance was not his usual good-old-boy, Texas Ranger look, but one of a raging and rabid beast about to relish the next moment. Jumping immediately against the restaurant owner's back, Zach Randal wrapped one huge, left arm around the man's neck, pulling him backward, and simultaneously shoving his catcher's mitt-sized right hand between the restaurant owner's legs from behind. Reaching up from behind, he latched onto the man's genitals, squeezing the handful of flesh like an over-ripe tomato.

Turning in a state of shock, the man displayed a look of horror, immediately releasing Amy. Zach Randal slowly clenched his hand with the effect of a tightened vice. Without a word, Zach lifted the man two feet off the floor, tossing him several feet through the air and out the front doors. Landing in a disfigured heap, the inebriated man began making strange noises, sounding like a cow's feet when pulled out from two feet of sludge at the bottom of a drainage canal.

Zach Randal, wanting to make a good impression, had found himself deep within a struggle between two powerful forces. The sight of a man attacking a woman was one of the most despicable acts on the planet, and he was known to exact his own measure of punishment when handling men who degraded themselves with such animalistic behavior. The battle raging within him had one side wanting nothing more than to take this guy in the woods, slowly beating him into a broken state of helplessness. The other side of him knew well that criminals must be properly arrested, charged, jailed, and judged by a court of law. The only solace in that scenario was the small amount of satisfaction he felt when arresting a criminal.

Grabbing the man by the seat of his pants, with one hand he lifted him. Texas Ranger Zach Randal walked through the parking lot straight in the direction of his parked vehicle. Not many customers were inside at the time of the incident, a few folks who happened to be traveling through while on vacation with their children and several older couples who frequented the cafe for breakfast. It had all happened so fast that some of the folks still held forks in mid-air, halfway to their mouth, frozen in the pose. The waitress was in the back area where the kitchen is located when the entire ruckus broke out. She quickly ran to check on Amy, seeing that she was all right.

Lying across the counter, holding onto her neck in a state of obvious terror, Amy appeared to be more frightened that hurt. As she slowly recovered from the attack, realizing all that had happened, she'd become embarrassed, especially with her position on the long, curving counter. She broke out in a cold sweat, trembling as she remembered that it was in the same position that her great-great-grandfather, Saul Dodson had been discovered, with a bullet through his head.

Holding her throat with one hand, Amy signaled with the other for something to drink. After a glass of water, and half a glass of Jack Daniel's, she began feeling better, talking slowly with a deep raspy edge to her voice. By the time Ranger Randal returned to the cafe, his appearance had completely changed. Looking closely at his face as he entered, Amy was certain that she'd noticed a touch of embarrassment in the big Ranger. She was suddenly very intrigued.

A deputy sheriff arrived a few minutes later, responding to Randal's radio call for headquarters to transport the prisoner. The berserk restaurant owner was arrested and transported to county hospital for treatment of the mysterious injuries that oddly were consistent with a severe beating. Probably had been injuries from the man's failed attempt to escape. After receiving proper medical attention, he was brought to the county jail.

Texas Ranger Randal was determined to get his breakfast, and Amy was pleased to prepare every breakfast item listed on the menu. Placed before Zach Randal on a large platter, was a breakfast fit for a king. Amy insisted that Zach Randal accept an additional gift of appreciation for what she'd considered a courageous act of valor. Without a doubt, she was certain that his quick intervention had saved her life. She gave him a coupon to Dodson's Breakfast and Bar-B-Que Cafe. It was pre-stamped GOOD FOR ONE LIFETIME. The two have been very close friends ever since.

THEN, THIRTEEN MONTHS AGO...

ZACHARY Wyatt Randal had stopped at the cafe one morning for what he'd called, *"A shot of hair from the dog that bit me."* He was extremely tired, having been up all night, chasing an escapee across the desert. The prisoner had run nearly the entire length of Cottonwood Creek, just outside of Sweetwater, trying to get to Rotan, which was a small, secluded town where the prisoner's girlfriend had been waiting for him in a stolen car. The two thought they could make it to the Mexican border. Randal chased him in the dark all night long, and before daylight, he had caught both of them.

It was just after dawn when he'd decided to stop at Dodson's Breakfast and Bar-B-Que Cafe; it was one place he would find the friendliest service south of the Canadian border. Zach was not a drinking man, and had even cleared out the entire inventory of alcoholic beverages from his home. However, that morning, he'd told Amy that he thought he deserved just one glass.

With a smile that could melt an iceberg, Amy poured him a glassful of Jack Daniel's, handing it to him as he sat heavily on the stool at the stainless-steel counter. He really looked tired, and Amy felt a deep sorrow for this good man who she considered one of her dearest friends. She thought of herself as one lucky person to have such a friend, and she'd never forgotten the way they'd first met on that Sunday morning.

As Zach Randal sipped on his second glass of Jack Daniel's, he began feeling the effects, and for the first time in many days, he began to relax. Amy watched with concerned eyes, able to detect as his body began to unwind. She was glad that the big man dropped by; he had a comforting effect on her, making her feel safe regardless of her situation. He was a giant, and well respected within the community. However, his intimidating size was no reflection of the way he treated the women in his life. Amy had even come to feel somewhat like a daughter for the first time, and Randal checked on her nearly every day while enjoying a lifetime free meal at the cafe.

Amy had often sat with Ranger Randal in a booth, just watching him eat. As time passed, their relationship grew, and Amy had learned about the trials and hardships that Zach had endured during his lifetime.

Zach Randal had been married to one of the most respected women in the county, and who was well known in the city of Austin. Her father, at one time or another, was involved with every political leader in the state...

DURING the early 1940's, while the world was at war, Zach's future father-in-law had managed to purchase plots of land throughout West Texas. He was not rich, but as he was able to save a little at a time, he'd purchased cheap, sand and dirt packed land, barren of trees, and with actually very little of anything spread out across it.

He and his wife had always dreamed of having a large family with many children, building a ranch with horses and cattle to enjoy the rest of their life.

It had been a difficult pregnancy, and an equally difficult labor and delivery. After Zach's wife, Katherine Alicia was born to her parents; they were told of the complications. Oh, the baby was fine they said, but Katherine's mother had suffered extensive damage, and would never be able to carry a child to term again. Naturally, they were devastated.

The ranch had never been built, but Katherine Alicia was never deprived of the great love that her parents felt for her. Discouraged, and with their plans unsure, her father thought of selling the property that he owned. Before he could act on a sale, several gentlemen approached him with a proposal to drill exploratory wells on the property. They carefully explained how everything worked concerning the royalties if oil was actually located. The men were courteous and polite. Katherine's father agreed.

When Katherine Alicia's parents, who were by that time Zach's in-laws, died in a private plane crash in Montana five years ago, Katherine received her fathers estate, totaling over twenty-three million dollars.

Everyone was somewhat shocked, but not Kate. She was crushed by the death of her parents, and in an attempt to ease the pain of her loss, began drinking heavily. After only two years of intense grief, her struggle ended.

Zach had considered it a blessing for Mrs. Zachary Wyatt Randal. His Kate was buried next to her parents three years ago, a victim of alcoholism, severe depression, crushing sadness, and a 38-caliber bullet. Zach never talked much about it. He once confessed to Amy, it was the only pain he'd ever experienced that he had been unable to handle.

SITTING, watching Zach Randal sip on his Jack Daniel's, Amy shook the memory from her mind. Each time she thought of Zach's Kate, it produced sadness within her that she knew she couldn't handle. Zach looked intently at Amy, and he knew where she had emotionally allowed herself to wander.

Trying to avoid an uncomfortable situation, Zach asked what was bothering her. It was then that Amy began to reveal what he could never have imagined. Without any encouragement, Amy launched into a bizarre and horrifying story…

EVERYTHING had begun about two years ago. Amy had started receiving letters through the mail, which were very sexual in nature. The suggestion seemed to be that Amy had been living a secret life, one that was immersed in drugs and pornography. The disturbing letters were signed only…FROM A SECRET ADMIRER.

Without fail, every Monday, just as sure as Texas was hot; Amy would get another letter in the mail. At first, Amy thought that they were from someone who had only been playing a sick joke. Whoever the writer of the letters was, they stayed up-to-date on events in and around Sweetwater. The secret admirer would flatter Amy about her beauty, but the things that were written about next, referred to her anatomy, and made Amy realize that this was no practical joker.

Months passed, and before long Amy had acquired an impressive collection of the letter sized envelopes with her address scrawled onto them. They were all written in that same scratched handwriting, on ripped out pages of a composition book. Without a return address, they were always stamped as having been mailed from Dallas.

Amy began to worry about the bizarre letters appearing in her mailbox every Monday. Occasionally she would receive two letters in a single week. She was a single young woman, living alone, on a ranch miles from town, who was receiving letters from an individual who was in no uncertain terms seriously deranged and obsessed. Even though the letters evolved from a harmless flattery, to twisted perversions with disgusting sexual overtones, it was clearly time to think seriously about reporting this harassment, even if by this time Amy rarely opened any of the letters anymore. Months went by while Amy struggled to keep the cafe open. Then, on one of the due Monday's, she opened her mailbox with the small key fitting the lock. Expecting to find another letter, her face suddenly turned ghostly white, and Amy became very weak. No letter had come from the secret admirer, as she had expected. That was when Amy realized how terrified she had truly become of this individual. As long as he was predictable, Amy knew what to expect and escaped the fear of the unknown. Had he found out about her plans to report him, resulting in no letter arriving today? Should she be happy that the letters had stopped? Amy had a bad feeling that something was very wrong. What she now felt was an intense and deep feeling of impending doom.

Because Amy was a survivor, she entered into what she called her state of heightened awareness. A specific title has been given to this particular state of heightened awareness, and it has even been classified as a major psychiatric symptom in Diagnostic and Statistical Manuals used by psychologist and psychiatrist across the country. Considered to be associated with forms of mental diseases, or more accurately, insane afflictions, it is often called by a more recognizable term, paranoia.

Several more months passed, and every Monday at 10:00 a.m. a slight feeling of nausea would sweep through Amy as she routinely checked her mailbox at the small post office. However, her mail remained free of the easily recognized letters, and slowly she began returning to her previous self. The cafe kept her busy enough for her to almost forget about the disturbing events.

WITH more emotion than Deke had yet witnessed welling up within him, Ranger Zach Randal continued...

"Fourteen months ago, as Miss Amy was busy getting on with her life, and becoming involved in Sweetwater community activities, she started to feel like she belonged. The cafe was nearly filled, with every table taken by noon on a daily basis, all for the tasty Bar-B-Que and friendly service. Folks would come in discussing politics and religion. Before long Amy had to increase the size of the dining area, but left the original cafe just as it had been built by Mr. Saul Dodson."

AT her ranch, Amy was like a different person. She'd bought six horses, two young cows that she hoped to get fresh milk from one day, so many guineas and chickens that she'd lost track of the amount running around, and four Chesapeake Bay Retrievers that were constantly by her side whenever she was home.

A large breed of retriever, they were named after the area where they had become famous, having the strength to swim rough, frozen waters, retrieving ducks and geese for their owners. Besides the extra bulk and size that these dogs possessed, they were also known for having a certain amount of stubbornness, and a very headstrong disposition. A quality Amy decided she liked. With the stubbornness came a devotion that was unparalleled. The dogs were excellent guards, and spent their time patrolling the ranch whenever she had to work late.

Amy loved their unique rust-color, and the thick fur coat they had compared to other breeds of retriever. Chessies, as their owners affectionately called them, had hair that was just a little longer than a Labrador's, with curls and waves throughout. After a few weeks, she was nearly able to recognize them individually. Since there were four of them, their names were obvious: John, Paul, George, and Ringo.

The birds were singing and the sun was shining brightly over the Texas plains, but that day was going to be different. It was early fall, and the state had been blessed by a wonderful cold front that swept down across the country, a little earlier than expected. Nobody was complaining, the crisp cool air felt wonderful. It had been a good weekend at the cafe, and Amy felt rejuvenated as she entered the small post office.

Opening her mailbox without a care, Amy saw the letter sitting inside. She stood frozen. The amount of time that she silently stood staring into her mailbox was anybody's guess. It took a significant amount of struggle before she had been able to break away, deciding what to do next.

Time passed and weeks turned to months. The letters resumed arriving every Monday. Amy was not one to seek out assistance for every one of life's small inconveniences, and the thought of asking for help was a little embarrassing. What would happen if it turned out to be a harmless prank? She feared being labeled as someone who cried wolf.

As long as her feelings came at her one at a time, whether it be fear, shock, dismay, or disgust, Amy was capable of holding them at bay, at least until enough time had passed allowing her to overcome them without seeking help. But the day came when she was helplessly overwhelmed, and even breathing seemed too much for her. A combination of every emotion the letters created had surfaced within Amy simultaneously and she relented.

Texas Ranger Zach Randal told Deke how he began profiling the person who may have written the letters, using only the information Amy had provided. He was shocked at the amount of time it had been going on, and even more shocked that Amy had tried to ignore the letter writer. Zach was certain, if Amy would have had any clue as to how dangerous these things were, she would have confided in him at the start. However, even as shocked as he was, it was nothing near the degree of anger that began to boil from deep within him.

Zach Randal had to remind himself that this was a situation that would be better solved without having his emotions involved; however, things were much easier said than done. His good intentions were far from what he seemed to be capable of, while remembering to stay within a hair of reality.

"I'm scared Zach, and I don't know what to do. Please help me!" Amy's plea for help had set off red warning flags with buzzers inside his head, and it had him worried.

"Amy I'll do anything within my power to help you, but first I need to know what is it you're not telling me." The Texas Ranger was tired, and after one drink had more alcohol in him than he usually had in a six-month period. Nevertheless, true to his reputation he was able to spot something that had Amy in the grips of fear, a fear so evil it made even him shiver.

"I'd like to tell you something about what you may be feeling. Will you let me do that?" Randal spoke with the patience of a saint. Amy looked away, beginning to feel foolish as she shook her head yes. "Emotions are something that we experience everyday Amy, and in addition, we experience these emotions in a wide range of intensity.

Multitudes of levels exist to all of the emotions we possess. In my opinion, when experiencing certain emotions which produce feelings of intense fear and pain, actually symptoms, the reason for the pain and fear is to activate an awareness preparing us for impending negative or harmful events related to the emotion that initially triggered these feelings." He then became silent.

Amy finally lifted her head to look at him, and he continued, "In straight talk, Miss Amy, it's a warning." He spoke with such confidence in what he believed that sometimes Amy wondered where all this knowledge had come from.

"Now, what I heard in your voice was a degree of fear that honestly gives me the shivers just hearing it; so, spill it all out. Then I can get this guy, and put you at ease again." His voice was one of compassion, but also one of urgency. He was worried.

Texas Ranger Randal continued, as Deke remained spellbound...He explained to Deke that ten months ago Amy had received a strange package in the mail. A small, light box wrapped in brown paper, similar to what's used by delivery services. Amy should have been a bit suspicious about the package because rarely did she receive any additional mail, and had even discouraged anyone from writing to her after the initial letters started. Amy had gone through a considerable effort to keep her address a secret, which was on the south side of Sweetwater in a mailbox at the local post office.

Looking back on each development, Zach could not help thinking that it seemed to be a lifetime ago.

Deke Stone could not help realizing that Randal was right. Randal's opinion about the fear that Amy had been made to suffer was meant to harm her, but the emotion, or the feelings that she experienced were because of that fear, and it was definitely a warning.

Thank God, the big Texas Ranger had shown up that particular morning at Dodson's Breakfast and Bar-B-Que Cafe, and for the wisdom that he possessed. Enabling him to look into her eyes and immediately recognize a serious issue had her in a state of turmoil.

Ranger Randal stated that an intensive investigation had been started as soon as he learned the details from Amy. Especially after he'd been able to study each of the letters, in addition to the contents mailed to Amy in the small, inconspicuous packages. As bizarre and unusual as it was to believe, the gruesome discovery of a human ear had indeed been mailed to her. Unbelievably it had been sliced away from someone's head, and then placed in a small box for Amy Dodson. Immediately the evidence was sent to Dr. Josh Sinclair at the FBI Crime Lab in Wichita Falls. The facility was about one hundred and fifty miles northeast of Sweetwater, the closest state-of-the-art crime lab at Ranger Zach Randal's disposal.

Texas Ranger Randal remembered hearing about a new forensic pathologist that had recently been appointed director of the lab, earning a reputation of possessing extraordinary skills helping to solve difficult cases. He was the kind of guy that you'd never suspect to be a big shot physician or pathologist. The young new doctor was missing a critical component that most physicians came equipped with: a God complex. It was probably what kept him from being elevated to the status of a deity, and even made him downright friendly. Well-liked by District Attorney's because of the plain English in which he spoke to any jury whenever having to testify in court.

During the previous ten month period, since first confiding in Ranger Randal, and since Amy had received the first package, more surprises had come in the mail, and with even more shocking contents.

To date, Amy had received five of the strange little packages. With each package came a piece of human anatomy. Zach Randal had so far collected two ears, two eyes, and one tongue. Each specimen had been sent directly to the FBI Crime Lab at Wichita Falls, and Dr. Josh Sinclair.

It was a baffling situation, and Zach Randal knew too much to consider the unfolding events to be the work of just some lovesick, mentally deranged, misguided fool. Texas Ranger Randal had seen too many psychotic cases over the years to write this off as misguided. In his opinion, it was very well guided.

Deke Stone listened with a keen ear, realizing that what Zach Randal had just divulged to him was incredible, yet critical pieces of the deadly puzzle. Deke was still unsure of what role he would be playing in the investigation, but was smart enough to realize each piece had a significance that was all its own, and might not get repeated. For this reason Deke was extra careful, categorizing each and every event into areas of increasing importance. Deke was attempting to prioritize the information, judging in reality, whether the information was a result of events, or a catalyst in causing those events.

Intermittently the letters would appear, but always on a Monday. However, when Randal began his full-blown investigation, they stopped.

He confessed that by that time it had become more than an investigation, actually bordering more on being an obsession. Randal questioned Amy for hours, prying into the private and secret areas that women struggle to keep private and secret. Zach's only answer to Amy's persistent objections, crying foul whenever he crossed into sacred territory, was the fact that no other way existed for him to do this. Zach became relentless. His overall concern was for Amy's safety, but by trying to ensure that safety, he was slowly driving her toward a mental breakdown.

Along with the countless hours came fatigue, but a bond was also created between Zach and Amy during the questioning, a powerful bond. It was a rare kind of bond that few people experience. More often than not, people fortunate enough in life to experience such a friendship had no idea what to do with it. Confounded by the ease and comfort, the popular opinion usually ended up being something like...it must be love.

By acting on the error in identification of the friendship, the two people more often than not, jumped into marriage, resulting in tragedy. This type of linkage or bond or soul mate connection was not the marrying type. It was better. It created a friendship for life, unconditional acceptance, nonjudgmental, sticking closer than a brother did.

Contrary to the popular opinion around Sweetwater that surfaced as folks noticed the new friendship between Ranger Randal and Amy Dodson, the closeness of their relationship was as far away from sexual as the Pope was to Jimmy Swaggert. Plus, if the killer was as disturbed as Zach Randal expected, he needed to get him out of circulation. Amy was motivated in new and strange ways for Zach, with a renewed resolve and attitude toward solving the case.

Zach had made a habit of taking Amy home, or having a deputy to escort her every evening. Amy hated all the intrusions into her life, and often times would lash out at Zach. He took every one of the mental beatings in stride, understanding the reasons behind each one and why he had become the target of them. It was not only interference that Amy had to endure, but also suddenly being exposed to ghastly and repulsive objects mailed to her, followed by questions revolving around these body parts.

In the meantime, with no progress made on the case, two additional detectives were assigned to assist Texas Ranger Zach Randal. He could assign them to any part of the case he saw fit.

With Deke up to date on how the investigation had managed to become so confidential, Zach Randal leaned back in his chair, reaching for another one of the small cigars in his front pocket.

"That's the whole nut in a nutshell Deke. I can't see how telling you everything is gonna help, and I really don't know what you can do with the information, but there it is."

An obvious strain had come over the big man's face, and Deke realized that this case was taking more out of him than he would ever admit, but in reality, it was Zach's way of asking for help.

Sounds accompanied by footsteps were coming from down the hallway. Deke Stone and Zach Randal looked at each other quietly as the footsteps stopped just outside the interrogation room door. Several seconds passed as they waited. Randal motioned to Deke that the person on the other side of the door was listening to see if the room was occupied. Suddenly, the door was jerked open and two rookie detectives stood side by side, looking as guilty as Al Gore inside a Buddhist Temple.

Deke stayed uncomfortably silent as introductions were made. The two rookies sat leisurely around the table, discussing one case after another.

It was a favorite past time, and time-killer of detectives. Discussions about different cases afforded detectives who were not very successful and suffering from a lack of motivation an excellent opportunity to boast or spout off theories. If the case that was being discussed happened to be one that was not assigned to them, then theories and suggestions increased in quantity and volume, with an equally impressive increase of criticisms.

It was soon quite evident that Zach Randal was not impressed with their style. He was already suffering enough with his own self-criticism. Zach did not reveal quite everything to Deke. Only a few months earlier…

RANGER Zachary Randal was feeling outsmarted by the sick, bastard genius that had been terrorizing his friend. So far, after receiving the first package in the mail, Amy had been the only person to find four more packages. They weren't in her mailbox, not in her truck, and not at the cafe either.

The second of the small boxes that she'd discovered was left inside the Chessie's food container. Amy usually ordered dog food in bulk quantity one hundred pound containers. While opening one of the containers she suddenly froze, spotting a small package.

The soft, fleshy, human ear wrapped inside had nearly freaked her out on the deep end, as had the previously collected parts. The package had been sent straight to the Wichita Falls lab and Dr. Josh Sinclair.

Randal had been at headquarters sitting in the interrogation room, which was his office when not in use, going over notes to see if he might have missed anything. Something had to be here, hiding in plain sight. Zach was positive that they were passing right over hidden and critical pieces of information. A diamond in the rough was what he was seeking.

The night desk sergeant called out his name from the front of headquarters. He had a call on the hot line. The hot line was a strictly enforced, private line used only for active investigations. The private phone number was given only to those persons involved with departmental investigations, and who had been judged as possibly in danger of their life. Zach Randal knew, even before he answered the phone, that it was Amy calling him on the Hot Line.

"Hello Amy! Are you all right?" Wanting the answer to that question, Zach spoke first and fast.

"Yes. I'm okay, physically, but you had better come on over Zach. I got another one. I found it mixed with the groceries as I began to save them; it was in my bag of groceries Zach! How is that possible? Who is doing this?" Amy's voice was calm and steady when Zach first picked up the phone, but she was entering a self-destruct phase. It was the very thing Zach Randal desperately feared, knowing that it was only him she trusted, and who possibly could prevent her from sliding off the planet.

"Amy calm down. Do you hear me Amy? I need for you to stay calm. Do not touch or move that package in any way. Where are the Beatles?" Zach Randal could not be sure that his attempt to calm her was having any effect. Amy hadn't made a sound after the initial statement. Zach could hear her breathing, and was confident that she was still on the phone. He had to get her back, before she was able to drift too far.

"Amy did you hear me? Where are the Beatles? The Beatles Amy, tell me where is John, Paul, George, and Ringo?" Randal felt sure that if he could only get Amy to answer, then she would be all right, and if anything in existence could stimulate Amy to return to reality, it would be John, Paul, George, or Ringo. Yet, the situation had unrepentantly deteriorated to a critical level, even before Zach had been aware that it existed.

"Too fast, it's happening too fast," he thought. Zach could still hear the sounds of breathing, but Amy refused to answer. Amy knew that if she didn't answer Zach, he'd be coming, and he'd be coming with hell and death not far behind.

When Amy did answer, it was in such a low whisper that Zach nearly missed it. It was in the way that Amy chose to answer him that hit with the force of a slamming door. In a split second, Zach changed tactics.

In the lightest whisper that Amy could possibly give, yet still hoping Zach Randal was able to understand, she began desperately repeating the message. Barely loud enough so that she could hear her own voice, she began pleading.

"ZACHARY, HURRY PLEASE! SOMEONE IS IN THE HOUSE!"

Throwing the Hot Line's receiver at the desk sergeant, Randal instructed him to keep the line open, monitoring it with a sharp ear because Amy Dodson was in danger and could only whisper! With that, Zach was out the door.

Driving at dangerously high speeds, Randal knew it was going to take him at least twenty minutes to get to Amy's ranch. He was sick with worry. If someone was in the old ranch house and meant to kill her, Zach could do nothing to prevent it. That was why he'd continued to ask her where the Beatles were. She would be as safe as anyone could keep her if the four Chesapeake Bay Retrievers were by her side. Over the last several months, Zach gained their trust, but was surprised at how much work and time was necessary to invest with them before they would ever give away the proud independence that they were famous for possessing.

Driving south on Highway 70, he thought about the old ranch Amy had managed to buy a few years ago. He knew of only one dirt road that led to the ranch and it was right off of Highway 70, but it cut back at a backwards angle, difficult to locate. The actual spot where the road cut back had to be memorized, and Zach hoped that he hadn't already passed it up. Driving in daylight was a different story when going to Amy's ranch.

53

His concern was legitimate. During daylight hours, he usually drove between sixty and seventy miles an hour, having to slow down to look for the correct turn off. It sounded much easier than it was.

Highway 70 passed straight through Sweetwater. From a northeasterly direction, it entered the city, and then turned at an angle going straight south. What bothered Zach Randal on a fairly regular basis was the Highway number 70. Highways were numbered with either even or odd numerals for a reason. All even numbered highways ran either east or west. In addition, all the odd numbered roads headed either north or south.

Either way, even if Highway 70 did nothing but make complete circles, it was a very difficult highway to remember landmarks, because nothing was alongside the highway to use for landmarks or reference points. He was hauling ass, heading south, hoping that he estimated the location of the road to Amy's ranch correctly.

"Damn!" Zach whispered to himself. He had missed the turn-off.

He hit the brakes hard; traveling at that speed might cause a spin. Sure enough, the vehicle spun twice, then came to a stop in the center of the highway. But he was facing the opposite direction, which was all right since he'd passed the turn-off about a hundred yards back. His estimate was pretty damn close. He smiled to himself, looking at the turn-off to the ranch. The small driveway was very narrow, and Randal was glad about that. At least he knew if someone were at the ranch that person had to cross his path heading for the highway to escape.

"Wait! What was that?" Zach spotted something just ahead.

CHAPTER

5

AMY'S RANCH WAS nearly two miles off the main highway. The narrow, single lane, dirt road that lead to her ranch was unmarked, and if a person didn't know where it met the highway, chances were they'd never be able to locate it. Amy had always said that she had no real use for visitors whenever she was at home. The occasional company of friends was always welcome at the cafe. Her home, however, was her place of refuge.

It had been after dark when Amy approached the ranch road, returning home and hoping that she could find some type of relief from the horrible events of the day. It was all so crazy, and sometimes she felt as if she were caught in a dream unable to awaken, helpless as events that were beyond her imagination played out in the nightmare.

"Something is wrong," she thought as she drove up to the ranch. Because her mind was so preoccupied with the day's developments, she'd assumed that it was just the difficulty of trying to make some sense of the confusion surrounding her.

Amy arrived back at the ranch under a cloudy, moonless sky. It was pitch black as she unloaded the groceries from the back of her Land Cruiser. Leaving her headlights on, she followed the sidewalk through the fence gate and up the wooden porch that surrounded the old, log house. She opened the front door. It had been left unlocked. She never locked her doors. Learning years ago, if a burglar was going to break in, a locked door was not going to stop him, and she'd rather give easy access than pay for damages created by the burglar trying to get inside.

She had two, full, heavy bags of groceries. With all that happening she was neglecting her home, eating all of her meals at the cafe. Turning the lights on inside the kitchen, she began unloading groceries.

Suddenly she realized what the object she was holding on to was. Reaching into the grocery bag, removing her items, it was so unexpected that a wave of fear swept over her with such intensity that she actually became sick. Running into the utility washroom connected to the kitchen, she barely reached the large basin that was used to wash the

Beatles in time, before throwing up. Sitting on the floor for several minutes, Amy calmed herself down.

That was when she figured out what was missing: the Beatles! Where were they? Just as she was about to call out for them, she caught herself. Zach knows more about these kinds of situations than she ever will.

The fears that emotions produce are symptoms, preparing a person's response, sharpening and equipping them for eventual negative events to occur.

Gathering her courage together, standing slowly in the utility room, she looked through the door into the kitchen from where she just came. It was very quiet. She saw nothing. Slowly, she began walking toward the doorway. Stopping suddenly, she thought she heard something. It was above her on the second floor. She listened for a long time. Unable to hear anything else, she continued.

Reaching the island in the center of the kitchen where her groceries and that damn package were, she cocked her head to the side slightly looking at it. Something was familiar about the package, but she couldn't place it. Reaching out, she nearly picked it up, her curiosity temporarily blanking out everything else and then managed to shake herself back to reality. She knew she had to call Zach; he was the only person she could rely on. Whether it was a state of heightened awareness or paranoia she didn't care. That state of mind just might keep her alive.

Amy looked around for her purse. She needed the hot line number to call Zach. According to him, who also suffered from states of heightened awareness, the phone line was specifically for situations such as this. He'd told her it was the only line not monitored or recorded. Either with taps or bugs. He refused to trust the detectives that were assigned to assist him. They were never given any updates from him that could screw up his strategy, even though he had not developed one yet. Zach told her to be patient, he was confidant they'd find someone to assist them that could be trusted.

Quickly she scanned the kitchen for her purse hoping that it was here, but she knew that she'd left it in the Land Cruiser, carrying in the bags of groceries first. The hot line number was in her purse. She tried to remember the number, but her mind was so overloaded that it was useless. She would have to go back outside to the truck. She shivered when she remembered how dark it was as she drove up.

Desperately she searched for a flashlight in the kitchen, refusing to go through any of the other rooms. She was wasting time and she knew it. She'd just go outside, run to the truck, get her purse, and run back inside. That was her plan. So why was she having such a hard time with it?

"Oh, shit on it!" she said. "Where are the Beatles?" She was about to begin crying when she heard the sound again; it definitely was coming from upstairs.

Pulling herself together, Amy took a deep breath. Bolting out the door, she ran along the porch, jumping off onto the sidewalk leading to the fence gate. When she reached the fence gate, she stopped for just a moment, catching her breath. Reaching from deep inside, she grabbed the gate handle. Jerking it open, she bolted toward the Land Cruiser. Jumping in and grabbing her purse, suddenly it occurred to Amy that she had a vehicle. She nearly laughed aloud with a surge of relief, realizing she was going to escape. With such a deep thanks to God for making her stop and think, she reached for the ignition. The keys were gone!

She became frantic, fumbling with the ignition area with her hand. Where were they? This was impossible! She'd left the keys in the ignition, she was sure of it. Being so positive, she tore open her purse searching for her keys, searching, searching wildly. They were not anywhere!

Turning the interior light on inside the truck, she jumped down onto the floor scanning the area, running her hands under the seats searching, feeling. They were nowhere to be found.

Amy sat in the truck, turning the interior light off. She was unable to stop herself this time and began crying.

"Why? What did I ever do to you?" she asked aloud, with nobody to hear her plea. She thought of staying in the truck until daylight. She'd lock the door, and in the morning, she'd call Zach. While still thinking it, she discarded the possibility. Again ripping her purse open, she looked for the number to the hot line. Finding Zach's Texas Ranger Division Business Card, she turned it over. The number had been written by Zach. She exhaled deeply, not realizing she had been holding her breath the entire time.

Once again, Amy Dodson gathered her courage, encouraging herself by thinking that she was getting good at this. Opening the door of the Land Cruiser, she bolted out! Running toward the fence gate, then she allowed something to happen, which she knew instantly was a big mistake. Her imagination began to run wild, but instead of ignoring it, she began feeding it. In a flood of panic, she felt someone was right behind her. Her heart was pounding in her chest with the strength of a sledgehammer. She ran so fast she nearly hit the fence when flinging the gate open, passing through. Amy had been blessed finding the ranch when it was placed on the market. It was not far from Sweetwater Lake and the only area with enough water in the soil to sustain trees. Old oak and massive gum trees surrounded the ranch house.

Her imagination had someone hiding in those trees, waiting for her to run by on her way to the porch. She'd thought of taking the long way around and climbing onto the porch from the other side of the house, then following it back to the kitchen door. Instead, Amy bolted straight ahead braving every one of the murderers behind each tree. As soon as she reached the porch, she pressed herself flat against the outside of the house as she made her way to the door. She was breathing so heavily that once she entered the kitchen it worried her. It took some time before she was able to return to breathing anywhere close to normal. Reaching out she picked up the receiver to the phone. Her imagination popped back into action as it told her the phone lines were cut. Slowly she raised the receiver to her ear. She had no idea how beautiful that familiar buzz of the dial tone could be.

Dialing the number, she felt herself stiffen up in fear, as she looked down at the package still sitting on the kitchen island, along with her other groceries. When she heard Zach, she began pouring out frustrations, with him trying to calm her, asking where the Beatles were. In the middle of their exchange, she stopped listening to Zach, and started to listen to other sounds, upstairs, strange haunting sounds, moaning cries.

Ignoring Zach, she was praying that she was not heard by whomever she was hearing. Whispering ever so low, she began pleading for help, knowing if Zach heard her, then he was on his way. She knew him well enough to know that. If she could just hold on until he arrived.

RANDAL was driving like a wild man. The road seemed longer than usual. He was certain he'd caught a glimpse of something just as he turned onto the narrow lane. Becoming anxious, he began driving faster than he should have, hoping to find out exactly what it was. After driving nearly a mile down the dirt lane and seeing nothing, he gave up looking, and proceeded toward the ranch where his main concern was.

Even if he'd spotted someone he could not have given chase, not sure of Amy's safety.

Finally, the ranch came into sight. Randal was surprised to see how dark the exterior of the ranch looked, this was getting worse by the minute. He saw her Land Cruiser parked near the gate; the driver side door was left opened. Before reaching the house Randal shut his lights out and slowly pulled off and away from the house, letting his vehicle coast to a stop.

Randal began feeling that this was one of those rare occasions. Referring to the Colt Python 357 he carried in his hand, he'd been asked by the County Sheriff and even by a couple of US. Marshals, the reason he had for not wearing an approved personal sidearm. That was at a time when he didn't care to have a human being ever speak to him again in his life. After he buried Kate, he became a horribly mean and hard-hearted man. Bitterness, sorrow, hate, and regret were a perfect recipe for de-humanizing a man. That particular combination had destroyed many lives. He had been lucky.

He wasn't very excited about the darkness that seemed to be smothering the ranch, nor the unbelievable silence, on top of the fact that the Beatles weren't anywhere around that he could see. That was the deciding factor about this situation; convincing him that something was bad wrong. It wasn't very difficult to approach without being detected. As he reached the porch surrounding the home, he began peering into windows, hoping to see someone or something. This was taking too long, and he was not a patient man, but for the sake of Amy's safety, he endured the torture. He wanted to get inside the house where he'd hoped that he could find her quickly. He remembered the door that opened into the kitchen just ahead on the porch.

If he remembered correctly, it even had a rectangular window cut into it. Probably about six inches high by ten inches wide, it was right at eye level. Well, he might have to bend down just a little to look into the window.

AMY stood at the exact spot from where she had called Zach. Horrified at the silence and terrified by the sound she was hearing. They were sounds she could not identify, never having heard such moaning, haunting wails.

Amy grew up street wise and matured at a young age. Missing most of a childhood filled with stories of ghosts and goblins. She never believed in the supernatural or in afterlife entities that were so popular in movies. Having to stand so long, listening to such deeply mournful and melancholic wailing, so humanly sad, she'd seriously begun to question her beliefs.

"ZACHARY should have been here by now," Amy whispered softly. Enough time had passed for her to renew her courage, and to rather get accustomed to the incredibly sad moaning sounds above her. She'd decided that she was going to investigate. This was her home, and the home of John, Paul, George, and Ringo. The thought of possibly losing them had her twisted in knots.

Since returning and realizing they were not around, she'd immediately put it out of her mind, hoping that they were out roaming the ranch property. They should have been back by now. It was time for her to do something.

She moved slowly toward the kitchen door. Maybe she could get out onto the porch. As dark as it was she could follow it around the house. She made it to the door without a problem. Sitting on the floor with her back against the door, she wanted to look out the small window before opening it. She slowly pushed herself up with her legs, sliding up to the level of the glass. With a twist of her neck, she looked out onto the porch just as Randal lowered his head peering through the glass into the kitchen.

Zachary Wyatt Randal was a proud man who'd worked hard at maintaining, and expecting a certain degree of respect. His character was something he'd developed over the years, reaching a point in his life where his integrity was established. Through one simple and innocent act of peering through that glass, coming eyeball to eyeball with Amy Dodson, who at the same moment experienced an exact but opposite view of Zach Randal, years of discipline and sacrifice establishing a good reputation had been destroyed, along with his own self-respect.

After living fifty years, he was stunned and surprised at this new development. The scream itself was at such a high pitch, that initially, just hearing this blood chilling cry left him with no option but to respond in like fashion. To his horror, he realized that he had been the one producing the hair-raising scream, which now increased in volume in response to this new and disturbing discovery. Her response was just as disturbing, but Amy had an advantage in this situation since she had experienced it many times. She recovered quicker than Randal, who was at this time making every effort to cover up his overwhelming state of embarrassment. In an attempt to help, Amy continued reassuring him repeatedly that no one would ever find out that he screamed like a woman.

They entered the kitchen, no longer concerned with trying to stay quiet, in fear that someone may hear them. Fully recovered from his little fright, Ranger Randal was very relieved to find Amy unharmed and safe. Amy was beside herself, speaking so fast, trying to fill him in on everything, that he had to stop her, and make her start from the beginning.

Before Amy could start over, the low haunting and moaning sounds started again. Amy started to say something, but raising his big hand, he silenced her. Randal listened carefully while looking up at the ceiling. His brow creased, looking very puzzled, he turned to face Amy. "That's the Beatles!" he announced, a smile on his face.

Amy looked at Zach Randal sympathetically thinking that maybe the fright had affected him badly. Nevertheless, without delaying, the big man moved with an agility and speed that shocked her. It would seem that Amy had a good reason to think the episode was an embarrassing moment, created some discomfort between them, but judging from how Zach was refusing to waste a moment, he might have put it out of his mind, no longer existing, even as a memory.

Zach exited the kitchen with his Colt still in his hand, searching for the stairway. It was a very odd feeling to be inside Amy's home running about with such an appearance of disregard. He made a point to apologize later for his rude and rambunctious behavior. He was here on several occasions, but never actually toured the home. Spotting the stairway across the room, Zach was at the bottom step with one leap, with Amy right behind him.

Climbing the stairs two at a time, Zach Randal was at the top landing in seconds. Stopping again to listen, he motioned Amy to join him. As she reached the landing, he looked down at her.

"Give me a quick layout of the rooms up here," he said in a low voice.

Detecting his sudden mood of caution, Amy realized the possible danger.

"Two bedrooms. The first door on the right is the master bedroom, which I use. The door just after that on the left is a bedroom very similar, just a little smaller. The master bedroom also has a bathroom, but not the other bedroom. The last door on the left is a full bath." Amy tried to explain the second floor the best way she could, but found herself suddenly very nervous.

"I'm nearly certain that the sound we heard is from one of the Beatles. I don't know if its John, Paul, George, or Ringo, but it sounds like they have their snout tied or taped shut. That's why you haven't heard them barking, if they're mouth is taped shut, they can't. Now Amy, this could be a trap of some kind. I'd feel a whole lot better if you would just stay right here until I make sure everything is safe," Randal whispered to her as he began to make his way down the hallway.

Reaching the first door on the right, he found it locked from the inside. Glancing back at Amy, he mouthed the word locked, to which Amy could only hunch up her shoulders, displaying her confusion. Abandoning the master bedroom, Zach Randal continued down the hallway slowly.

Suddenly a low, moaning wail broke the silence with the sounds of scratching heard coming from the first door on the left: the guest bedroom. Randal was temporarily halted in his approach, but after a few seconds listening to the sound, he continued to the guest bedroom door.

Arriving at the first door on the left side of the hallway the big man stopped, as did the moaning and scratching.

Leaning against the door, Randal tried the handle. It too was locked. Looking back down the hallway to the stairway landing, he seemed to be seeking permission from Amy. Then, in a voice just above a whisper, Zach called, "John? Paul? George?" Giving a whistle, he then added, "Ringo?"

To this, the scratching began again frantically with more than one moan coming from beyond the locked door. Stepping back into the hallway Randal lifted a huge leg, and with little effort kicked the door in.

The Beatles were inside. All four of them, with gray, duct tape keeping their snouts neatly shut. Before Randal could give Amy the okay, she was in the doorway trying to hold all four of them while they attempted to slobber her with attention. She was beside herself with emotion, thankful that they were all right.

Texas Ranger Zach Randal only stood aside and watched. To him this meant much more than just finding them unharmed. It meant he was after a much more clever criminal than he had initially anticipated. How had he managed to tape up their snouts and lock them away without being attacked in the process?

Standing, watching Amy struggle to remove tape from the snouts of each dog, he thought back to when he first turned onto the long drive leading to the ranch from Highway 70. He was so pumped with adrenaline that when he spotted what he thought was a man dodging behind tall sagebrush, he nearly talked himself into thinking it was just a trick of his eyes in the headlights. Now he was having second thoughts.

Was a man running across the ranch property?

Now that they were back in the kitchen, after managing to get all four of the big Chessies free of tape, and quieted down, Zach Randal was on the phone. Finishing with his call, he replaced the receiver, and turned to Amy.

"A slew of lab folks will be showing up within the next hour Amy. I want you to stay down here in the kitchen while I look around. You'll be just fine now that the Beatles are with you. Don't touch that package. The lab will pick it up to send on to Josh Sinclair at Wichita Falls," he instructed.

With that, the Texas Ranger slipped out the door, onto the porch that surrounded the ranch house. He circled the entire structure not knowing what he was looking for, but feeling the need to do anything other than sit and wait on the lab, who would no doubt turn the entire house into what would in effect be a mini-crime scene. Although no crime had been committed that he could put a finger on, other than trespassing and the impossible feat of taping the dogs up, not to mention locking them in an upstairs bedroom, he still wanted every inch of the home checked and double-checked.

WITHIN forty minutes, two crime vans arrived, and were busy checking for prints throughout the entire place. In addition, the two rookie detectives assigned to the case to assist Randal also arrived. He had both of them searching the outside of the structure to see if any footprints were left at the base of the windows, in the flower beds, or if anything else was out of the ordinary. As soon as he got the chance, he was going to replace those guys with a couple of officers from the state. John Hadley would know of a couple of good men.

Zach Randal had returned to the upstairs portion of the home, where after a few minutes he was able to pick the lock to the master bedroom. Entering, he found nothing appearing out of the ordinary. The bed was made. None of the drawers had been left open, and nothing seemed to have been rummaged through. The bathroom also appeared to be untouched. Randal began to think that either she had unintentionally, and without realizing it, locked the door to her bedroom, thereby thwarting the perpetrators attempt to gain access. Whoever it was had locked the door just to throw another mystery into all of the confusion. That was what he was beginning to think until as a last resort he checked her chest of drawers.

Apparently, Amy kept her underwear in the top-drawer of the huge, solid, oak furnishing. That was where Randal realized something was not as it should be. The entire top drawer was empty. Opening the others, he found clothing neatly placed and folded. He began having one of those feelings where more was here than he was able to see. Zach Randal returned to the kitchen and asked Amy to accompany him to the master bedroom. Intentionally, he did not mention any of his findings.

"Now Amy, anything you see out of order you have to tell me about. Try not to touch anything. Just look around and let me know what you see," he stated, watching her closely.

Entering her bedroom slowly, she looked around. Randal could not help noticing the fear in her eyes as she scanned the bedroom.

"Everything seems to be in order," she stated, wringing her hands anxiously.

"I need you to be more thorough than that Amy. Look well!" he commanded.

Looking at him as if frightened of what she may find, she walked over to the chest of drawers. Pulling the top drawer open, she jumped back in fear. That was all the response he needed to confirm what he had thought.

"What is it Amy? What's wrong?" he asked.

"My underwear, it's all gone," she stated in a whisper.

"All Right. We'll have to have the lab go through here also," he concluded, more at a loss of what to tell her than ever before. As he walked into the hallway to instruct the technicians, Amy sat on the edge of her bed. Almost absent-mindedly, she reached over and pulled open the small drawer on her nightstand, letting out a scream. Another of the small packages was sitting inside the drawer.

Amy Dodson refused to sleep anywhere else that night; in fact, it was well after sunup before the lab technicians finished their work. The two packages were sent to the FBI lab at Wichita Falls. With Amy's help, they inspected the dogs closely. Randal had a hunch they might find where the dart from a tranquilizer gun had hit each of them. It was the only way all four could have had their mouths taped shut, locked in the bedroom upstairs. Sure enough, a small spot of blood was located on each of their hind ends. It looked like someone had placed a well-aimed dart. Blood was drawn from each of the Beatles by lab technicians for analysis.

DURING the next few weeks, Ranger Randal received information from the FBI lab in Wichita Falls confirming that a tranquilizer had indeed been darted into each of the Chesapeake Bay Retrievers. Blood levels were consistent with it occurring on the night two additional packages were discovered by Amy at her residence. The tranquilizer used in darting the dogs was a drug commonly used by veterinarians for exactly that reason. However, Ketamine is a control substance, and only individuals having a license to practice veterinary medicine or a valid DEA license can legally possess it.

DEA numbers issued by the Federal Drug Enforcement Agency to licensed individuals are used in keeping track of all control substances being prescribed or ordered by that individual.

In addition, Dr. Josh Sinclair discovered that the packages containing the severed right and left ears were from the same adult male; a Caucasian, in his mid-twenties to early thirties. The first two packages, with the eyes and tongue, were also from an individual matching the same description.

Zach Randal suddenly had a direction to proceed in, one that had not previously been thought of. With each of the human parts showing up in small packages for Amy to find, they had to have been a previously attached to a Caucasian male.

With this bit of information, Zach Randal again sought the help of the FBI, along with the help of State Police files in Austin, Texas. He was looking for any recently unsolved homicides, unidentified bodies, or hospital reported cases where any mutilated middle aged men had been seen in emergency rooms, within about the last six months.

It was while waiting for this information to be of some use that Randal convinced Amy to continue with her daily activities. Running the cafe, and trying in one way or another to get back to some resemblance of a normal lifestyle, he told her, was critical. Taking his advice, Amy returned to the cafe. It was a good move on her part, amongst folks with no idea to what was going on in her life. Treated normally without the knowledge of what she was going through was therapeutic, and almost made her forget the nightmare at times.

It had been therapeutic until the morning she visited the cemetery where her mother was buried, bringing fresh flowers, sitting a while to visit. When Amy arrived that morning, she nearly collapsed in fear, nearly unable to drive herself to the sheriff department, looking for Texas Ranger Zachary Wyatt Randal.

In tears, and nearly hysterical, Amy kept repeating to the deputy who first spotted her weeping in the parking lot, that all she wanted was to speak to Texas Ranger Randal. When Zach Randal finally came rushing out of the building Amy could only manage one sentence.

"Another one was left on top of mother's headstone at the cemetery."

CHAPTER

6

"OF THE MANY things I've found distasteful in my life Deke, admitting the fact that I'm no more ready to solve this case than when it started ten months ago has got to be at the top of my list," Randal stated, after bringing Deke up to date on everything.

Sitting in the small interrogation room, Deke began to put together all the small quirky habits he had been observing lately from Zach Randal. What he initially thought to be just bizarre personality traits possessed by Randal were actually traits designed through years of practice. Planned by design to confuse those he may be pursuing.

"So, from what you've told me, I take it you don't feel that anyone can be trusted enough to assist you with the information or that Amy can trust to confide in?" Deke asked. The big man shook his head affirmatively showing just the hint of a smile that Deke took for satisfaction.

"You got it Deke. That's the reason I need you so much on this case. Do you understand why I have a certain feeling of optimism when I consider your abilities? Of course, that's just an accident of good fortune. Even if you had turned out to be the dumbest bastard on the planet, you were at right place at the right time, and it left me with no other option but to use you. With the pitiful progression of this investigation, a certain amount of desperation influenced my decision," he continued, popping any ego balloons being inflated in Deke.

Attempting to change gears before Randal reduced him to minced meat, Deke decided to immerse into the investigation wholeheartedly. Besides, something about Amy he found was very attractive. He was somehow drawn by Randal into wanting to help her, but he now found himself struggling to reign in his enthusiasm, when it came to her.

"The reason you use this interrogation room as an office, and the reason behind Amy's instructions to use nothing but the Hot Line is because you suspect someone here?" Deke concluded.

"Now you see, that's exactly what I thought when I first met you Deke. You're quick. Not that it's something that takes a brain surgeon to figure out, but you were able to pick it up pretty quickly. In fact, you seem to have a cynical sort of attitude when it comes to law enforcement," he stated with a suspicious glance at Deke.

It created a little concern in him for a moment, then Randal continued, "What I'd like for you to do most in this investigation is point out certain concerns that you may have regarding every aspect of the case, things that you may have questions about. Why I focus on certain aspects? What are the other areas you think are more important? How do we make decisions about what happens around here?"

He began to list areas where his technique was now in question.

"Why some things about this or that are not some other way? I want to use you as a sounding board to offer second opinions, another set of eyes that are fresh and unclouded, without a bias. Do you understand where I'm coming from?" he asked. Deke shook his head, beginning to understand what was going on. Zach Randal had no other person that he could trust to back him up. A person to act as a check and balance mechanism. Zachary Randal had now become so emotionally involved that he was unsure whether all of the decisions he'd been making were sound.

"All right, Ranger. I'll certainly do everything I can to help," Deke answered.

"Good. That's all I can ask from you for the time being. As things evolve I'm certain additional areas will crop up where you'll be useful, but for now let's just take it one step at a time," Zach Randal suggested.

"Now that we have all of the basics out of the way, and you know how we've gotten to this point, we've got to decide where you'll stay for the next few days. Fortunately for you, Miss Amy has already offered the ranch house, which has an extra bedroom. Personally, I think it is a good suggestion, especially since she refuses to stay anywhere else, and I would feel better if someone I can trust is staying with her. I can trust you, right Deke?" he emphasized the statement by making a question of it.

"Certainly. As long as you don't think it might create problems. I do not want to be the reason for any public scandal," Deke stated, trying to sound sincere.

"Oh, you don't have to worry about that. Amy can take care of herself, and if by some chance you decide to sneak into her bedroom at night, you will still have the Beatles to contend with," he said with a chuckle. Deke had forgotten all about the Beatles, and had to admit to himself that he was a bit disappointed.

With their initial discussion of the case, the history behind it, and possible direction to take completed, Randal stood.

"Come on, you can follow me out to the ranch. Your vehicle is parked outside."

Standing up, Deke followed the Ranger out. He was not a complete idiot when it came to manipulation, but what Texas Ranger Randal and Amy Dodson had just managed to pull off was astounding. Without knowing if Deke would eventually go along, they had him already set up at Amy's ranch for the next few days.

Stopping at the dispatcher's station before exiting the building, Randal reached in, slipping Deke's vehicle keys off a pegboard. Turning around he tossed them to Deke before they stepped outside. Once outside Randal stopped just beyond the covered entranceway.

"Before we go any farther Deke, I cannot overemphasize enough that everything we've discussed tonight, and everything we discuss in the future is to be held in the strictest of confidence. I don't care if it happens to be the Chief of Police, the Sheriff, the Pope, or Sesame Street's Cookie Monster; you are not to repeat anything. Lie if you have to, but above all do not give out any information.

"Anyone who attempts to get information from you will become a prime suspect. The folks that work here know only that you are staying at Amy's as a favor to her. They have no idea you are working on the case, and think you're a friend of the family, through friends of her mother. If someone does approach you, inform me as soon as possible." Randal was filling him with so much new information that he hoped he didn't screw up.

"Now, one more thing before we leave here. You may find the items in your vehicle have been rearranged. After taking it to headquarters, I had it impounded, more for appearance than for anything else. It was searched thoroughly by the department, also for the sake of appearance, and I'm happy to announce, found clean. That is, all except for the small amount of cocaine found in the center console."

Deke was stunned. He didn't have any cocaine in his vehicle, nor had he ever had any. Zachary Randal read the look on his face. Before Deke could get a word out in protest, he interrupted, "I know what you're going to say, Deke, and you're right. No cocaine was ever found in your vehicle. And to put you at ease, let me say I haven't allowed the illegal substance to be reported. It's in a safe place, of which only I know the location. You're not in any trouble, and will not get into any unless you screw me around, and decide to do anything that's, how shall I say it, not beneficial to the satisfactory outcome of this investigation. Not that I don't trust you Deke, only that I want to continue trusting you," he concluded. Zachary Randal then turned, and walked out into the parking lot toward his personal vehicle.

The Ford Bronco was modified to run at speeds capable of staying with anything else on the highway. It was solid black, and Deke found that he was admiring it as he opened the door to his ten year old, rather run down, Jeep. In only a few minutes, they were leaving the city of Sweetwater, heading south on Highway 70.

Before long they were turning off the highway, at a location Deke thought was a spot for Randal to relieve himself. As far as he could tell it was only a side road that went nowhere. As he followed Randal, he eventually began making out what appeared to be a ranch in the distance. Zachary Randal had not exaggerated when he'd said that Amy lived out of town in a secluded place.

They followed the dirt drive, which circled behind the ranch before ending near a wooden fence. The gate was open, and as soon as they stopped, Randal was out of his Bronco. Deke started to get out of his vehicle when suddenly he saw something come through the gate in their direction, making sounds that sent him scrawling back into his vehicle, quickly closing the door. Zach Randal stood calmly while the four Beatles jumped around, dancing in circles, competing for attention. He laughed out loud bending down to one knee, wrestling with them. For the first time, Deke saw the human side to the Texas Ranger. It reminded him of a young boy playing with his puppies.

Turning to Deke, who was still hesitant to exit his vehicle, Randal waved with his hand telling him it was safe. With much reluctance, Deke stepped down from the Jeep, closing the door behind him. Amy Dodson came strolling through the gate, and Deke suddenly found a bit more courage while approaching the scene.

"Mr. Stone," Amy began. The hardness in her face magically faded away as she re-addressed him, "Deke. May I call you Deke?" she asked, extending her hand.

"Miss Amy," he answered, shaking his head yes to her question while taking her hand and feeling oddly out of place.

"And this is John, Paul, George, and Ringo. Better known around these parts as the Beatles," she offered. Then, with a word, she captured their attention.

"Boys!" she said. They backed away from Randal, all sitting perfectly side by side next to her, and facing Deke. They were beautiful animals, not monstrous in size, but well built. The Beatles were a very formidable looking group.

Speaking directly to the four, she introduced them, "John, Paul, George, Ringo, this is Mr. Stone. He will be staying with us for a while. I expect you to treat him courteously, and do not become mischievous, chasing him up any trees. Do you hear me?" she asked. Deke was not sure if he was supposed to shake their paws or say hello. Questioning if she was serious, he didn't have to wait long to find out.

Turning to the Beatles, she instructed them, "Okay, get his scent." With that single command, Deke found himself surrounded and frozen in fear. The four moved so quickly that he couldn't have gotten two feet away before they'd begun sniffing wildly at his pants and hands.

After a close inspection of Deke, the Beatles were satisfied that he was no threat. Calling them off, Amy offered Zach Randal a cup of coffee, which he politely declined.

"No thank you Miss Amy. I've got to get back to headquarters and finish up a little paperwork. You two get settled, and I'll speak to you in the morning." Tipping his Stetson, Zach turned to get into his Bronco. In a flash, he was gone.

"Well Mr. Stone, shall we go inside?" Amy suggested, turning toward the house walking ahead of him. Deke followed feeling uncomfortable with the arrangements and very tired after what had to be the longest day of his life.

"I'm sure you must be very tired; so, I'll show you to the guest bedroom. Have you had anything to eat today?" she asked, reading his mind.

"No ma'am, but I don't want to put you through any trouble," he stated quickly.

"It's no trouble. Why not take a shower Deke; I'll whip up a quick meal. I'm a late eater anyway and haven't had supper yet."

Deke answered only with a nod of his head. He felt somehow subservient to the woman who without a touch of make-up looked drop-dead gorgeous. He was shown to the upstairs bedroom, where towels and linens were located, and the bath at the end of the hallway. After showering, he felt much better, refreshed to the point of losing his sleepiness. Walking downstairs, he found Amy in the large kitchen with the Beatles. They took up most of the place, stretched out on the floor watching her as she grilled two thick, delicious looking, rib-eye steaks. Seeing him enter the kitchen, the heads of the four Chesapeake Bay Retrievers turned simultaneously studying him.

"Feeling any better?" Amy asked as she continued with the steaks.

"Much better, thank you," he answered feeling foolish as he answered her. He didn't know how to take this woman's hospitality yet. The aroma from the grilling steaks was overwhelming.

"Rare, medium, or well-done?" she asked. Watching the steaks, Amy was being watched also. "Medium-well," Deke answered as he found a stool at the center island, sitting on it. A green salad in a large bowl was already prepared at the center of the counter-top. Condiments surrounded the salad, and Deke suddenly realized just how hungry he was.

"Drinks are in the fridge. Help yourself. I'm afraid my waitress skills have been all used up over the years," Amy commented looking at him for the first time.

Sitting at the tile-covered island, Amy Dodson and Deke Stone ate in silence. Occasionally one of the Beatles was treated to a piece of steak. More famished than either of them thought, the meal soon disappeared. At her suggestion, they retired to the large den, where Deke was encouraged to start a fire in the large, stone fireplace. Finally, settling down with an after dinner drink, Amy started the conversation.

"Deke, what exactly has Zach Randal told you about the investigation?" she inquired.

Immediately he became paranoid, hesitating on whether to answer her or not, remembering the big man's stern instructions earlier that night before leaving the sheriff department. Deke looked at her with a blank expression. Amy realized then that the intimidating Zach Randal had sworn him to secrecy, and she began to laugh aloud. It was exactly what they needed to break the ice, and soon after determining it safe to talk, they became involved in a lively, interesting conversation.

"What I'm having trouble understanding is why, when it seems it would have been much easier at the time, did the killer go to all of the trouble of darting the dogs, taping them up, then carrying them one at a time upstairs, locking them in the guest bedroom, instead of just killing them?" Deke asked, more from pure observation than from the position of wanting an answer from her.

"That's something that I've never really thought about. Now that you mention it, that does seem to be a very good question. Thinking back to that time, I think I was so distraught about everything happening that I was too busy questioning what had happened, to question the things that could have happened," Amy stated, obviously wondering about his questions herself.

"I'm sorry if the question upsets you, but since Ranger Randal filled me in on what he's looking for, in the way of help initially, I began thinking about the entire investigation, and what I've been told so far," Deke explained, trying to avoid anything that may bring confusion to the case.

"No. Really Deke, I'm not upset by the question, just somewhat unprepared. In fact, this is something I've needed for quite some time. Unable to really sit and talk things out with Zach Randal, I think it would be the best thing for me, therapeutically that is, to have someone to talk with. It is the only way I'm able to categorize all that's occurred," Amy confessed. Her demeanor seemed to improve from the one that was bleak and cloudy to an excited state of anticipation.

"What other things have you noticed or thought about? I'm very interested," Amy asked, pulling her legs up on the couch to sit on them. Then, in a complete turnaround, her facial expression changed. "I'm sorry. You're probably very tired, and I'm being a little selfish wanting to finally talk to someone about this whole thing," she confessed.

"No really, I don't mind at all. In fact, it may help to ask you the questions I have before I run them by Randal. He is sort of an intimidating person, and I don't know how I'm suppose to ask questions about his methods or judgment," Deke confessed, sitting on the hearth of the stone fireplace. By this time one of the Beatles, he'd not yet found anything to distinguished one from the other, walked over, sitting beside him. His big head was at the same level as Deke's, and only inches from his face. The Chessie began watching his every move.

Stiffening his posture, Deke looked at Amy, afraid to move too quickly, but desperately wanting to turn and look at the Chessie. With a chuckle, Amy looked at him, finding an amazing amount of humor in the scene.

"Don't worry, he won't hurt you. That's Ringo. He likes you, and apparently finds you interesting. He does that when he finds something he likes. I've never seen him do it with a person though. I've seen him sit for the longest time, right in front of the television, with that stare, watching a program on Volcanoes. I can call him away, but until he can study you enough to become satisfied, he'll find his way over to you again," she offered, giggling the entire time at Deke's response.

"No, that's all right, as long as he's not about to chomp my ear off or something." He was still feeling uncomfortable regardless of Amy's attempt to put him at ease.

"Getting back to what we were talking about earlier, Texas Ranger Zach Randal did give me a brief history about you, and the death of your mother." He saw a response of sadness creep into her eyes.

"I'm sorry, I didn't mean to bring back memories. My parents are still living; so, I can't imagine what you have been through," he quickly confessed, not wishing to upset her and destroy the mood of their conversation.

"Allow me to change direction on you, and ask if you can tell me about Zachary Randal? Where the man comes from? Who is he? And what can I expect of him?" Something in the back of Deke's mind kept telling him that a great big heart must be somewhere within that chest of his, and he wanted to know how far he'd have to go before discovering it.

"Well, I'm very interested to find out what he told you about me," she said, a little embarrassed. "But I can tell you that Zach Randal has not had an easy time of it in the past."

Amy told Deke about how they'd met that Sunday morning in the cafe when he'd rescued her from the deranged restaurant owner who tried strangling her. She also told Deke about the death of Katherine Alicia Randal.

Deke suddenly began to understand the Texas Ranger and his tough exterior. Amy continued with her rendition of the life and times of Zachary Wyatt Randal by telling him a story, which he recalled hearing something about several years back. He had no idea it was this Texas Ranger involved in one of the most horrible crimes of the century. Amy started at the beginning: "A missing persons report had been filed by a man in Austin. He said that his nineteen-year-old girlfriend had not returned home one night from a trip to the grocery store. They found her car abandoned in the parking lot of a local food mart. At the time, nothing could be found to give them any leads as to where she may have gone. She seemed to have just disappeared off the planet.

"For several days the local police did all they could to try and locate her, but to no avail. After running several pleas, asking for information on the three television stations in the Austin area, they received a phone call from an elderly woman. She said that she recalled seeing the woman in the parking lot that night, talking to a tall, middle aged, white male, but the girl did not appear to be in any distress at the time." Amy stopped to freshen their drinks, and Deke noticed she had become a little tipsy.

Returning from the kitchen, she handed Deke a fresh drink. Sitting on the couch she repositioned herself to get comfortable, and continued, "Anyway, they then assumed she had been kidnapped, and the Texas Rangers became involved in the case. Zach Randal was called in, who at the time was going through a difficult time with Kate, his wife. It turned out to be an exhaustive investigation with a life long rapist and murderer as the main suspect. On several occasions, Zach crossed the murderer's path while pursuing him. On each of those occasions Zach arrived at the scene of a brutal murder, just behind the person he was after. Because of the grisly murders, Zach Randal began to have less and less hope of finding the missing girl alive.

"The victims he found left behind by the murderer, were in cheap hotel rooms, they had been raped, tortured in horrible ways, hog tied, and left lying on their backs in bathtubs. Each of the women was discovered while the water was still running. Unable to get out of the bathtub, the three young women he'd found had drowned. He said they were conscious, but because they were hog-tied could not get out of the tub as the water rose above them." She stopped to compose herself while Deke listened. He'd not known about the details surrounding the murders.

Amy continued, "The media was denied all of the gory details by Zach who refused to have the families go through the horror of having that reported about their daughters for the world to see. He was able, after four months of tracking the person, to find a hotel clerk who said he'd just rented a room to a man that resembled the one in the picture Zach showed him.

"Alone, and afraid to wait for backup, taking the chance that he may somehow escape, he approached the room where the murderer was located. Listening closely at the door to the room, he tried to decide whether to gamble his chance to apprehend the criminal. Going against his better judgment, he radioed the state police, and explained his situation, but also notified them of his intentions of going in. The Investigator that he spoke with told him to wait until he had arrived at the scene, threatening Zach with some ridiculous charge, calling him a lone wolf. The Investigator wanted in on the media attention when they captured the guy. The media frenzy by this time was like a pride of lions feeding on bush bucks as they followed the trail of murders." Amy again hesitated, adding to the dramatics of the story.

"Well, Zach waited in the parking lot outside the hotel room for thirty minutes, until the State Police Investigator arrived. He had leaked the potential capture to the local media before leaving his headquarters to assist Zach. They busted in the door, and found the person packing his overnight bag to leave the room. A brief struggle ensued where Zach was wounded in the shoulder by a bullet fired from the gun of the Investigator. Zach tackled the person, and had the upper hand, when the Investigator suddenly fired. He said his intention was to wound the suspect. That wasn't the real tragedy behind the entire episode. "In the bathtub they found the girl reported missing from Austin, the one originally kidnapped. The water was still running. The coroner said that she had drowned only minutes before their arrival." Amy was obviously disgusted with the sad ending.

"That must have been horrible for him, after such a grueling pursuit." Deke was surprised by how compassionate his voice sounded. "It was," Amy agreed, "But another terrible thing had occurred just as the pursuit came to an end. Unknown to anyone at the time, Zach's wife had shot and killed herself that very same morning. She was alone at their home." Amy added the last bit to the horrible event with anger in her voice.

"I don't think he's ever been able to forgive himself for that, and he definitely has never gotten over the anger toward the State Police Investigator. To this day Zach will not call for assistance, earning himself a reputation of being a lone wolf. Secretly, and I'm not sure if even he knows this, but a lot of law enforcement officials have started calling him *'Hunter.'* I guess because he's so effective with any investigation that he's in charge of, and few people question him about his techniques anymore.

"With my case things have gone so slowly he was forced to accept the help of two rookie investigators. I think he really resents their presence, and I know he won't share any information with them," she confessed, explaining more to the methods employed by Zach Randal than Deke could have figured out alone.

The account was such a tragedy in so many ways that Deke was sorry he ever questioned any tactics by the law official. Without the knowledge of what eventually brings a man to employ the style they choose to use, questions are foolish. He was also able to understand why Randal had become so protective of Amy. Apparently, in his mind, Randal was trying to rescue that poor young girl kidnapped each time he began a new investigation. No doubt, he thought of Amy as the victim he'd never allow anyone or anything to jeopardize. It also explained why Amy was so trusting of him when it came to her safety.

"Who would want to do the things that have been happening to you in the past Amy?" he asked in an attempt to return to their previous area of conversation, getting away from what he had found to be an extremely emotional area.

"I have gone over it many times in my head, but I can't think of anyone. It's true, several young men were disappointed when I decided that I could see no future in our relationship, but they were not that unstable or I'd never have become involved with them to begin with," she explained.

Her explanation did make sense as she was giving it, but, then again, most folks had no way of knowing just how rejection could affect some people. Deke saw guys that he thought were very stable, completely lose their perception of reality after rejection by a woman.

It was not, in his opinion, any fault of the woman. In most cases, he discovered it was because of the disgusting ways that men treated some women that drove them to make those types of decisions to begin with. In any case, he saw how utterly foolish and destructive some men became, men who for some reason actually believed they had every right to terrorize and harass the woman who rejected them. Instead of trying to correct the problem leading to reconciliation, they revealed the reasons they were rejected in the first place.

"How long has it been since you have had any type of a relationship with anyone? In other words, when did the last relationship that you were involved with end?" he asked. Maybe he had an ulterior motive for asking the question, but he was so sincere she didn't suspect him to be prying for information on her current love life.

"Hasn't been a man in my life, not even for a single date, in the last two years. I have not had the time it takes to invest in a serious relationship for at least that long. Maybe I never have had the time, and that's why none of the men I became involved with ever had a chance. Not a result of their fault, or because of their shortcomings, but more because of my neglect," Amy confessed, with no hint of regret.

"To be honest with you Deke, I have only been involved with three guys that I would consider as relationships. Of the three, one is happily married, one has moved out of the country, and the third guy was killed in a boating accident, his body was never found," she confessed.

"Zach Randal was told about all three of these people?" Asking with a puzzled look, Deke continued, "I assume they were individually checked out?"

"Absolutely! The married person is still married. The guy who moved out of the country, converted to some Eastern Religion, living somewhere in India. The third guy was declared dead after the Coast Guard called off the search."

"Wow, from what I read on the back of the menu at the cafe, reality seems much more boring," he teased her, chuckling at his gullibility to have put any stock in believing what he had read in the first place. "Randal told me the truth about what was written on the back of that menu, and that I was a fool if I chose to think such things."

"Well, I would not go so far as to say that no truth exist in what was written, most of what you've read is true. Saul Dodson did move to Sweetwater after mining for gold. He was deluded into thinking this was paradise by Jackrabbit Slim. The cafe was almost shut down until the Mexican bandits showed up, and he did eventually marry before committing suicide. My mother was the youngest of twelve girls and kept the cafe open until her death years ago. And I must admit to actually having been chosen as the official Sweetwater Rodeo and Cattle Drive Queen for the last six years," Amy clarified.

Without warning, the happy carefree persona which had begun to take shape in Amy vanished. She dropped her head slowly, and began nervously wiping the condensation from around the glass in her hand. Deke was puzzled as to what could have come over her so suddenly, but soon the answer was provided.

"Did you see them Deke? Did you see what was done to my workers, my friends?" Her voice was breaking as she shook with grief. "Why wouldn't they let me go in Deke? What happened back in the cafe this morning?" she asked him slowly, emotions shattered from fear.

Deke looked at her silently for a moment, realizing not only did they prevent her from entering the cafe, but also she was not told of the gruesome scene. Ranger Randal had not said anything about this, probably because of everything else on his mind. It was one area Zach had failed to give Deke some type of instructions.

Knowing that too much was at risk by being the one to tell her exactly what happened, Deke was not going to go any farther with the situation than he had to. Shaking his head, he averted his eyes from her.

"Yes, I did see what was done to them. Ranger Randal escorted me through the back area of the cafe, but so many officers and people from the lab were crowded inside the room that I really could not tell you exactly how they were killed," he lied, finally looking back at her. He had no idea why, but he found it very difficult to lie to her while looking into her eyes. Amy was sharp, and with a little effort managed a smile, looking straight through him.

"All right, I understand. I won't put you in a position to have to lie to me. It must have been a horrible scene. I suppose Randal has his reasons for keeping it from me, but I'm not a child, and it offends me sometimes that he has taken it upon himself to treat me as one," she admitted.

"But that may not be at all why he has chosen not to tell you. It may be for reasons we cannot figure. You have to admit he does have a different method to nearly everything he does. I know that initially I judged everything he did, but have since discovered that I was wrong to do that," Deke confessed, trying to switch areas of conversation, and surprisingly found that he was defending Zach Randal.

"You are absolutely right Deke. I'm sorry if I put you in an uncomfortable position. It's late, I must be getting tired," Amy stated, starting to stand. As soon as she did, the Beatles instantly responded. John, Paul, and George, who were dozing on the rug in front of the big couch, with Ringo who'd continued to study Deke, shifted their attention to her. Their box shaped heads turning to look at her in unison. So many questions were floating between them that they were both anxious to discuss, but before realizing it, time had slipped away. It was Approaching 3 a.m., and only one more question remained that Deke thought he needed answered. It had been bugging him since earlier that day when Zach Randal gave Deke his speech on Texas women.

"So many things have happened in the last twenty-four hours, I only hope I'm able to remember most of the information that has passed between us tonight," Deke said. Amy immediately realized that he was leading up to something. She narrowed her eyes, looking at him inquisitively.

"Just where are you heading Deke Stone?" she asked.

"Oh, not anywhere considered taboo. It's just that Ranger Randal strikes me as quite a Southern Gentleman. Relatively young, intelligent, good-looking, he's a man with such power, physically, in addition to whatever political status he holds. After the tragedy of his wife's death, women must have been just waiting for whenever he'd recover. Not that he could ever forget about her, but realizing that life goes on, maybe he saw someone socially?"

Deke was trying to ask the question with as much innocence as possible, without exposing more than mere curiosity. Maybe he had an ulterior motive for asking, but he was hoping Amy didn't pick up anything unusual, destroying any trust he'd managed to gain.

Looking at him mildly suspicious, she hesitated for a moment. Deciding that the question was innocent she answered, "You're right, several women. Before I continue, I hope you're not suggesting anything is going on between Zachary Randal and myself. Because rumors that were about exactly that surfaced a couple of years ago. Deke; let me tell you, so many rumors have been spread around in the past that it no longer fazes me when new ones begin, as I know they will. In fact, because I have you as a guest here at my home, the talk will start. But as I said, I don't care, and I hope it doesn't in any way bother you either." She was very sincere in telling him this, and Deke secretly wondered if, as she predicted, any rumors concerning the two of them would take root. Not that he wished it to happen, but the thought rather had an exciting ring to it.

"Zach Randal was a crushed man following the death of Kate. For several months, he refused to be consoled, and rarely spoke to anyone about it. He was told therapeutically it would benefit him to go out socially, speak to people, realize that everyone was aware of the pain he was going through, and that it was all right to show that to folks.

"One day, nearly a year after Kate's death, he offered to help me with the Beatles. They needed to be taken to the veterinarian for their annual checkup, booster shots. As you might imagine they can be quite a handful. That was two years ago.

"When I got my boys they were only a few months old, and I decided to take them to a veterinarian who'd just started practicing in town. I can't say exactly why, but it was like I had known her for years, and immediately I trusted her completely with their care.

"Dr. Vanessa Jansen started her practice about two years ago in Sweetwater. She's about my age, maybe a couple of years older, very attractive, and single. She has no family, an only child, and her parents died years ago. The moment Zach Randal and Dr. Vanessa met I saw a spark of attraction. They dated off and on for nearly a year, and then mysteriously it ended. Their relationship just ceased to exist.

"Nothing specific that I could think of had caused them to abruptly end it, and I was puzzled for quite some time. Thinking that maybe I'd had something to do with it, I questioned Zach. He assured me nothing that anyone had done was responsible, and I was reading more into the relationship to begin with. They were just not compatible. I took his word for it, but felt so uncomfortable that I never could talk to Dr. Vanessa about it. They were cordial when meeting each other in public, but it was obvious that whatever they had in the beginning was dead. Since that little romance, Zach Randal hasn't dated anyone.

"I hear Dr. Vanessa has a pretty active social life. She is said to go out pretty often in the Dallas-Fort Worth area." She finished the account with a hint of sadness in her voice.

It was apparent that Amy had deep feelings about Randal because of the tragedy he'd suffered through in his life, along with his commitment to help her.

That was, more or less, the information Deke was looking for. He was somewhat bothered about how Amy chose not to speak very much about the three guys she confessed to dating, especially the one guy that was killed in the boating accident. He was convinced that it was more than she'd admitted, or that she knew. Almost no compassion was noted in her voice, and that could be her way of hiding some deep-seated pain associated with this guy's death. He decided to change the subject unable to stand the sadness washing over her when she spoke about certain things.

"As far as my presence here is concerned, Randal said he had arranged for it to look like I was a friend, only concerned about your safety. You invited me to stay here at the ranch because you did not want to be alone. Someone who knows you from a friend of your mother's, I think was the way he explained it to me. That should be enough to prevent rumors from running too wild," he offered.

"Deke, you have a lot to learn my friend, not only about being naive, but about Sweetwater," she declared.

Deciding they had stayed up longer than they planned, and realizing questions would still need asking in the morning, Deke and Amy retired for the night. Deke, alone to the guest bedroom, and Amy, in the company of the Beatles to her bedroom.

CHAPTER

7

THE MORNING AIR was chilly as Ranger Zachary Randal drove across town. He was going to Amy's ranch. Several things were on his mind and he wanted to talk to Deke, now that he'd decided to trust someone, he might as well use him as a sounding board. Randal had never set eyes on Deke Stone in his life, but for some reason as soon as he met the young man, he was impressed. He only hoped that he was not making a mistake. When he was given Deke's name and social security number by Sergeant Hadley, the first thing he did was have him quick-checked through the FBI computer banks in Wichita Falls.

The report he'd received, via fax machine from one of the Trooper's vehicles while at the cafe that morning, was impressive. Deke's accomplishments in the field of psychology forced him into the position of having to try to get his assistance. He was surprised at the humble attitude the young man had. Zach thought that by now, he'd have boasted about turning down position offers to assist with experimental psychiatric studies at four of the most prestigious psychiatric institutions in the country. If it turned out he were someone who had a habit of screwing things up, he'd have to kill him.

As soon as he turned onto the dirt lane leading to the ranch, he remembered the strange feeling he'd had on the night the Beatles were drugged. He'd been so sure that he saw someone running across the property, but whoever it was had managed to hide behind a clump of sage. Apparently, the person had remained hidden until after he'd passed. The next day he'd searched and searched for some kind of sign, footprints, maybe a piece of fabric torn from clothing, anything. However, nothing was ever found. It was another dead-end. Nevertheless, ever since that day, he'd remained positive that his lights had briefly caught someone leaving the ranch. On the other hand, with each day that passed, he talked himself into becoming less and less positive. That bothered him more than anything. He was at a point in his career when evidence that seemed promising suddenly had become questionable. With such long and dry periods passing without any piece of evidence to gather, it was a bad sign when you started questioning the

83

only possible evidence you might have stumbled on, crucial to the own investigation.

That was one reason Deke was so hurriedly put on the case, and the reason he was on his way to the ranch this very moment. It was past the time when he should doubt himself, and Deke was going to confirm the fact that he was still in control, doing the best job possible.

Just after five in the morning, it was dark as he drove up behind the ranch, seeing the vehicles belonging to Amy and Deke parked as he had left them the night before. As he looked closer, he noticed something was different. He had to study them for a moment before realizing the difference, but saw it, and began to worry. No lights were on that he could see, and the Beatles did not come running through the fence gate. It was not unusual; they usually slept with Amy anyway. Turning his lights out, flipping off the ignition key, he cruised to a stop. Not sure of what to do just yet, he sat in the Bronco, in the darkness, waiting, watching, and thinking.

Randal could not be certain from this distance, especially in the darkness, but he thought he saw something scrawled on the windshield of Deke's Jeep. It looked like something was smeared or splattered on the glass. As the morning dragged by, and daylight began to filter across the horizon, he saw clearly enough to confirm it. Something was written on Deke's windshield, and it was written in red.

Randal debated whether to scrub it off, sparing both Amy and Deke from the message, but he knew the lab would have to come out and take samples. Getting out of the Bronco, he was sure whoever had left the message was long gone. He walked toward the Jeep. His approach was slow and cautious, wondering who in the community was so damn sick. He read what was scrawled on the windshield.

"THE PUNISHMENT FOR SHEDDING INNOCENT BLOOD IS DEATH!"

By now he'd become used to killers taunting, and felt sure Amy and Deke were safe inside having no idea of what had happened during the night. It was not this person's MO to leave such a message, ending his fun and challenge by killing them so soon. He decided he would wait until daylight arrived before walking over to the ranch house, waking them.

Studying the message, he realized it was written in blood. He also thought it looked like the same handwriting used to write the harassing letters.

Digging in his front shirt pocket, he pulled out one of the little cigars. Lighting it, he wondered if he would be able to get the jump on this killer by using Deke. Had this cruel message been left out of fear, thinking that Deke may come in handy? On the other hand, was this was a sign of total fearlessness? The killer might be under the impression that he'll never be caught. If he has that much confidence in his ability, then it was definitely something Randal could use to his advantage. He liked it when they became cocky and self-assured, that was usually when he dropped the net catching them. What was different with this case was his failure to discover where to place the net. This person was good, making no mistakes thus far.

DEKE'S mind seemed to be returning from out of a thick fog. It was warm and damp, a smell that reminded him of playing with puppies as a child. With a jerk, Deke awoke, opening his eyes. Ringo was standing straddled over him in bed, his nose nearly touching Deke's as he stared down at him. He had no way of knowing how long Ringo had been standing over him, but it was starting to worry him a bit. Ringo was a huge dog with strange behavior. Deke thought it would be much easier if he understood, but speech was the one thing they had not yet mastered. He wondered if that was an intentional disability, realizing the ability to speak with humans would only be confusing, for the humans.

Sitting up slowly in the bed, he did not have the advantage of Amy Dodson's protection should Ringo decide to be mischievous. Without warning, Ringo jumped down from the bed, running out the door. As Deke sat confused, he heard the rest of the Beatles running down the hallway stairs also. Thinking something must be wrong; Deke quickly got out of bed, slipped on his jeans, and ran down the hallway and stairs behind them.

He ran through the living room, passed by the den, and into the kitchen, but they were gone. Looking around, he was certain they had not gone through any of the other rooms. Walking over to the door leading out onto the porch that surrounded the ranch house, Deke opened it. He saw Randal coming through the gate with the Beatles around him.

"Good morning Deke. I hope you're not already running around the place half naked. I just dropped you off a few hours ago," Randal stated as he approached Deke. Reaching him, the big man extended his hand. Deke looked at the huge dip net-sized paw with hesitation, remembering the last time he shook hands, but he had no permanent damage. Deke extended his hand in response, watching as it disappeared.

"You got the coffee made yet son?" Randal asked, releasing Deke's hand and continuing through the door into the kitchen. "Hell boy ain't a drop of coffee made! Well, I guess I'll have to show you how to do that too," Randal stated. Deke was still examining his hand out on the porch. Deciding he had escaped serious harm, he followed Randal and the Beatles into the kitchen. Seeing Deke had entered, the Texas Ranger called him over.

"All right, now this here is what they call an automatic drip coffee machine. I'm going to show you just one time; so, pay close attention." Randal began to set up what was apparently going to be a demonstration.

"This is where the coffee is kept, right here in this canister. Now pay attention Deke cause I'll expect you to have mastered this by this evening. Every time I come over for a visit, I want a fresh pot of coffee ready for me. These here white, paper things, that look sort of like a nurse's hat, are coffee filters." He was not letting up, and Deke was at a disadvantage, half dressed, and unsure if Randal was serious or not about this.

"I can see it in your eyes Deke, you're wondering…is this guy serious? Damn right, I'm serious! One thing I never joke around about is my coffee. Okay, now you put this in here like so, then fill this like such." As he was going through the mechanics of brewing a fresh pot of coffee Amy walked in, covered from chin to ankles in a terry cloth robe.

"Good morning guys. How are we this morning? Oh Zach, I can't believe you're showing Mr. Stone how to brew coffee," she blurted out realizing what was going on. "Give me that, I'll do it," she said laughingly, grabbing the filters and coffee from him.

"Amy, you just can't let folks get by without pulling their own weight. I was just showing Deke here the correct technique, making sure that he'd at least learn a trade as he loafed around on the ranch."

That was when Deke realized he was joking. They all had a good laugh. It was kind of scary Deke thought. "This guy was as straight faced as they come, causing me to question him seriously."

He marveled at how simple it must be for Randal to intimidate people, especially if he had a good reason to.

After the coffee was ready, and everyone had a mug full before them, Amy asked the two men if they wanted anything special for breakfast. Ranger Randal forbade her to cook anything, stating he was going to whip up a batch of scrambled eggs with fresh green onions sprinkled in. Before Amy could stop him, he was standing nearly inside the refrigerator grabbing items and handing them to Deke.

Amy immediately discerned Randal was hiding something, and refused to wait any longer before popping his bubble. "Okay, Zach Randal, I admire the effort, but it won't work. Whatever it is you're trying to keep from me, I'll eventually discover. Stop torturing yourself, and get it out of the way. Then we can decide just how to handle it." Amy pegged him. Zach actually flinched as she made it clear that she was on to him. Turning slowly away from the mess he was managing to whip up on the counter, he faced them with regret in his eyes.

"I was hoping to think of a way to not tell the both of you, before you could figure out what you just figured out. It just ain't fair Miss Amy, you never let me get away with anything long enough to enjoy it." Randal fussed about her lack of fairness like a younger brother complaining about the loss of bathroom privileges, his sister occupying it most of the morning.

"Let's have it. Not much surprises me anymore," Amy declared.

Deke was also very curious about what could have possibly happened that was so drastic in the last several hours.

"I'll make a deal with the two of you. First we have a good breakfast, then I'll show you what's happened, and we'll decide what, if anything, to do about it." He was slinging egg yolk and green onions with a whisk all over the kitchen, bargaining with them.

"Deal!" Amy stated. She looked at Deke looking for his answer. "Deal!" he repeated. They sat down to one of Zach Randal's famous egg smorgasbords. As they sat eating at the counter, Randal began asking Deke questions about where he lived in Colorado. His inquisitiveness became a little too extreme after several of the questions. Deke and Amy looked at each other, getting suspicious at the exact same time. Randal also realized that he'd become a little too obvious with his questions.

"All right, I guess enough is enough damn it! I'm about tired of having to baby-sit grown up people anyway. Get yourself something to wear on your feet if you don't want to lose your toes from frostbite,"

Randal instructed them. He stood to show them what he'd found written on the windshield of Deke's Jeep.

Amy slipped on a pair of rubber boots that she kept in the utility room. Deke ran upstairs grabbing his sneakers, putting them on without the benefit of socks. Zach Randal waited for them on the porch, watching the Beatles as they sniffed around the big oak trees along the wooden fence. They were probably picking up that bastards scent as he'd walked around looking into the windows of the ranch. The pervert probably thought he could catch some hot action. He wished that he knew of some way to get a scent picked up by a dog into a pair of handcuffs.

Amy and Deke soon met Zach Randal on the porch. Randal could not help but notice Amy's wide-eyed nervous look. Deke also seemed to be quite anxious due to the mysterious development. While the three of them approached the fence gate, Randal tried to prepare them.

"When we go through this gate you'll both see that someone was here last night, and they left a message on the windshield of Deke's truck. I truly didn't want to have both of you see this, but I really don't know what else to do. This might be the incident to create a change in the way we've been doing things. I'll need both of you to help me with this." Randal stopped at the gate, not letting them through until he had said his peace.

"Desperate times call for desperate measures, and desperation makes men do desperate things. Remember that, when I tell you my new plan," Randal stated, sounding like a politician.

The message had two entirely different effects. Amy gasped as she read it, her knees started to buckle. Randal quickly jumped to hold her up while the Beatles stood anxiously by her side, watching him closely. They sensed the distraught feeling that she was experiencing and became very jittery, moaning with an occasional growl toward Randal.

Deke, on the other hand, became very angry. The boldness and cocky arrogance that the message portrayed stirred a righteous anger from deep within him. The very thought that someone had written a threatening message directed toward him was not taken very well. He had decided yesterday to help Amy and Zach in any way they needed him. Seeing someone was in need, he felt obligated, sort of his civic duty. Now things had changed, it had become personal. He was being threatened, and that made it a completely new ball game!

"Why would anyone do this Zach? We haven't done anything to deserve this, have we?" Amy pleaded with Randal for an answer, one that he was not prepared to give.

"Come on you two, let's go inside. We'll need to decide what our response to this kind of sick mentality is going to be," Randal declared, urging them to maintain a calm attitude as he assisted Amy back toward the ranch house.

As the initial shock evaporated somewhat, the three of them sat in the den discussing their options. The harassment did not look as though it was going to decrease. Whoever was behind this enjoyed the fact that Ranger Randal was reaching out to obtain assistance from Deke. They had no way of knowing whether the murderer knew Deke was assisting Randal with the case, or if the murderer had believed the story that Randal had purposely leaked.

According to Texas Ranger Zach Randal, Deke Stone was the son of a woman that Amy's mother had become acquainted with, doing volunteer work at a local retirement village for the elderly. Deke had come to stay at the ranch house, helping Amy so she could spend more time at the cafe. Whether or not anyone knew to what degree Deke had become involved, the murderer was determined to target him for the sheer fun of it; after all, that was basically, what had ended up happening at the cafe. Deke had been inside the cafe alone with whoever was responsible for all of this.

"I have a few things that I'd like to run by you two and see how you feel about them. What I'm going to propose may seem a bit bizarre and even chancy, but for reasons that I hope to be able to explain later, it may be the only option that will bring about the results we're looking for," Randal stated.

Amy made sure everyone had a fresh drink. Randal took a deep breath, and they made themselves comfortable. Options, to what had become a desperate situation, were evaluated, studied, and eventually decided.

Zach Randal turned to Deke. "Well son, let me hear what you've come up with so far." Deke hardly had enough time or information to develop any solid profile that he would consider beyond fifty percent accurate, but diving in, he gave his opinion.

"From everything I've observed since this whole thing started, it appears that a man with considerable intelligence and resolve has targeted Amy. Despite an extensive amount of work on Amy's part, to recall anyone having even the slightest amount of animosity toward her, you are still without a suspect. I think this person has the perception of having suffered some harm, with the source for this harm being Amy. Yet, evidence or something that would point to any individual that you could seriously consider as a suspect, proves to be quite elusive. This is very disturbing, especially with the brutality of such a crime." The vague explanation for past events seemed pathetically weak, but that was all he could safely assume, considering the lack of evidence.

"Deke, more than anything, because I happen to be a man who harbors a certain amount of pride concerning the work I've dedicated my life to, it has been tremendously difficult for me. When recruiting you, as late as yesterday, I felt such frustration by not being able to offer the first piece of substantial evidence aiding with apprehending this individual. I guess that I should also confess, and hope that you understand, about having your whereabouts closely monitored for the last three weeks. You have been under the surveillance of the Kerrville, Texas Rangers. I made a special request personally. It's no secret to some folks in law enforcement that on three different occasions within the past eighteen months you have been the critical factor responsible for capturing serial killers. Moreover, I know this was information held very confidential, with media outlets never finding out about your involvement.

"In short my friend, you have been set up, but the incredible development of your presence at the cafe when these murders occurred was never anticipated. That was what I strongly suspect as being a brilliant move on the part of the killer, one that I still marvel about, and do not ever expect to figure out."

Texas Ranger Zachary Wyatt Randal dropped the information on Deke like a thousand pound bomb from the belly of a B-52. The effect was nearly as shocking as an explosion from such arsenal. Deke sat dumbfounded, completely speechless.

"I do not want you to think this is an accurate reflection of what my capabilities are. Although I've made what I consider to be a monumental choice in recruiting your service as a civilian for help, please do not become suspicious of anything or anyone except the individual committing these horrible crimes. Even though I have had you tailed, and monitored, the decision to help has always been one that I wanted you alone to make. I also realize that the person with the most opportunity to commit such acts and with the best chance at pulling them off would be me. It could also be that the motivation for this individual to commit these murders was to frame me. Nearly every time we've had stuff left behind by the killer, such as messages or clues, I am always nearby, or at the scene. My only concrete alibi is Amy's testimony, categorically refuting any possibility of my involvement. On a couple of occasions, when she was being terrified by someone here at the ranch, I was the one answering the Hot Line as she called to report them." Zach Randal appeared weary, and he despised having to defend himself from something that he was innocent. But to a greater degree, angry, having to defend his actions from the very thing he worked so hard to prevent.

"What it all boils down to is the fact that we're completely on our own. We are without a single person that can be trusted, with the consequences this extreme. In addition, this individual seems to know everything in advance, or at least is making a good impression of having knowledge about plans we've entertained. In short, I can't say for sure that anywhere is safe, nor can I say that this person couldn't reach out and kill if he wanted to." The Texas Ranger was having a difficult time trying to describe the helplessness of the situation. It was not something that he accepted well.

"Therefore, I have come to the only option I think we have left. With your help, having the training and exceptional judgment concerning psychotic criminal behaviors, and your humble attitude to remain incognito, I feel we may be effective. It is also the most daring and dangerous of all the methods I've ever used. However, if we are very careful, observant, and persistent, we will effectively turn the tables on our nemesis. Thinking he is the predator pursuing his prey, it will be too late to do anything when he realizes the situation is reversed." As Randal spoke, a smile crept across his face.

Deke was pretty sure he knew what Ranger Randal was up to, and it was beginning to make him just a bit nervous. He was still astonished by the covert actions and intellectual planning by Ranger Zach Randal, but chose not to comment in any way about what had just been revealed to him.

Amy had no idea where Randal was headed, and Deke was doubtful that she would go along with what Randal was thinking, unless Randal was better at persuading her than he thought. The tension reached a critical level, and they realized if any decision was to be made, they needed to make it now. Any additional stress was most likely to affect their reasoning and logic, in one direction or another. Afraid of the potential to over-react or under-react drove Zach Randal to force them into making a decision.

Turning to Amy, Randal started to unfold his plan, one page at a time, giving both her and Deke adequate time to process the information. He was confident that this was their best chance to draw out the killer, apprehending him while staying alive.

"Earlier when I began asking Deke about his home back in Colorado, and about the surrounding area, I had more than just casual curiosity in getting his answers. We have been operating from a defensive position since the investigation began, waiting on the murderer to make a move, before making our move in response. It's a bad position to be. Anytime you're in that situation, options are limited due to the lack of available room to move around in. The killer keeps the upper hand by planning each of the shots. We have no choice, but to respond. In effect, he can, and probably does, anticipate our every move." Amy listened intensely; both men were encouraged by her looks of enthusiasm.

"Not too many ways exist to suggest what I want to suggest without just coming out and making the suggestion. The both of you know quite well that the best defense is always a good offense. Amy, I think you and Deke should pack up and head toward Colorado. Go to wherever Deke's home is located. I think the two of you should leave within the next couple of hours. Time is critical. We have a chance to catch him off guard by doing this. But it must be done in a double-barrel shotgun approach, firing our guns at the same time." Randal was becoming excited, obvious that he had faith in the move.

"What I hope to be able to do is draw him out. If he thinks his target is getting away, he might just follow you all the way to Colorado. Only, I will be following him while he follows you. We'll be calling the shots, and he'll be responding from a defensive position. The advantage will hopefully shift to our corner, and I'll peg the son-of-a-bitch!"

Amy said nothing for a while, thinking about the plan, judging the enthusiasm she saw in Randal. It was a determining factor she used to calculate possible success, measuring the confidence displayed from Zach while revealing it.

However, Deke's involvement was what she placed her faith in and her hopes on. Amy would not confess to that fact, especially after all the work done by Randal, but it somehow was obvious without being mentioned. Ranger Zach Randal was too big of a man to allow such a thing to deter him from giving every ounce of his effort. Although Deke saw that Randal was aware that he was no longer number one in Amy's eyes, his attitude and behavior was without a hint of change.

"You really think that's what I should do, or that both of us should do?" Amy asked, while switching her gaze from one man to the other, then back again.

"Amy I'm afraid of this person. He's very dangerous and has exceptional skills in covering his tracks, remaining anonymous. Plus, I received information from the FBI lab in Wichita Falls. The forensic pathologist hasn't performed a complete autopsy yet but sent me a fax. From his initial inspection on the ladies at the cafe, he thinks it was someone with extensive medical skills, like a doctor or a medical student. The way they were…well…cut on, suggests that it was someone with some type of surgical training," Randal informed them.

Deke sat listening closely to everything said. As he listened, he began thinking. The more he thought, the more it began to make sense. Silently, he realized that Randal was correct. The best and quickest way to draw out the killer was to eliminate his advantage. This advantage was twofold with his constant knowledge of Amy's location, and still able to keep his location and identity secret. By having Deke escort Amy from the town of Sweetwater, on a journey where their eventual destiny was unknown, they may draw the killer out. Not only did they want to draw him out, but possibly create a sense of panic in him. If this sudden and secret move by Amy, in the company of someone previously unknown by the killer had the effect that they hoped for, the killer would be forced to expose himself.

It was a gamble, but if Deke and Zach had profiled this killer correctly, he was more than likely consumed, even driven, by the power of control. No longer in control, and unable to manipulate factors, he'd no doubt become careless and act impulsively. In a state of panic, trying to regain control, they hoped Randal, secretly following Deke and Amy from Sweetwater, would discover the killer's identity. They'd have to devise a way of staying in touch with one another. Maybe all they needed was a reliable cell phone.

"What do you think about all this Deke? Are you game?" Randal asked him. Deke was deep in thought, planning as the question came. He had to shake himself back to reality just to answer.

"Yes. I was thinking about the advantages as you were speaking, and quite honestly, I believe this just may be the type of thing unexpected by the killer."

Deke's answer was just what the Texas Ranger needed to finish convincing Amy, who by this time was scared enough to agree to anything. She wanted to be free of this dark cloud shadowing her life for so long. She also wanted to live, and for everyone else around her to be free of this horrible curse. As long as this killer was loose, she feared more would die. Her conscience could not handle any more.

"I suggest you start to packing, but don't take more than you really need. Remember, you'll have a good chance by just staying on the move for a while. It's not absolutely certain you'll drive straight to Deke's place, staying until everything is over. This might take longer than anyone anticipated, requiring a change in your destination. You two will have to remain a target until I've had a chance to absolutely identify the killer, and apprehend him," Randal stated. He wanted them to realize that it might be more difficult than just a road trip.

Shaking his head while still deep in thought, Deke nodded his agreement with Zach Randal. Amy looked on, concern written all over her face. Looking at Amy, Deke could see she was worried about more than just the trip.

"What is it Amy, other than the plan itself, that you're so worried about?" Deke asked.

"What about the Beatles? I can't just leave them here. If you think we have to leave that quickly, then I won't have time to bring them to Dr. Vanessa. She'll have to keep them in the kennel," she confided, obviously worried about not having them around. They were, after all, what made her feel safe.

"You two will have to take them along. I don't want anyone to know about this. By calling Dr. Vanessa, you'll expose your intentions, and possibly compromise the entire plan. The Beatles will have to go along," he stated abruptly. Something about his reaction made Deke think he knew more than he was saying, or maybe he was just being forceful in his instructions, making certain the plan was not revealed to anyone unintentionally.

"Oh, and one other thing. The Land Cruiser can't be used. You guys will have to use Deke's Jeep. Should be plenty of room for the Beatles. We need to map out the route that will be taken, at least to Colorado Springs. If for some reason the journey continues farther than Colorado

Springs, it will be because I haven't had a chance to make my move. We'll get together some kind of way at that time, adjusting our plans. Until we can get together, we'll just take things as they come. It's important that we try to stay in touch at least once a day. What do you think Deke?" Randal was seeking confirmation, making sure he agreed to the entire plan.

"I agree with everything you've said so far. What about using cell phones while on the road, just in case of an emergency?" Deke offered.

"That may be a possibility, but we have to consider the fact that this guy is very smart. If he's half as smart as I think he is, then he'll probably have a police scanner, monitoring every frequency," Randal stated.

"But we won't be using any police radio, will we?" Amy asked. Seeming to have emerged from the fog she'd been in since admitting she was worried about the Beatles.

"That's right. We won't be using any of the department radios, but with the right kind of scanner, he'll be able to monitor dozens of frequencies. Law enforcement frequencies are not the only ones he'll be able to monitor. Communication devices such as cell phones operate using frequencies that can also be monitored with a good scanner. I hate to assume he'll have one. Then again, we're getting way ahead of ourselves. We don't even know if he'll come after you. But it's about all we can hope for right now." Randal had been thinking of this very strategy for quite some time. Either that or he was a very fast organizer. Deke was impressed.

"Has this been an option you've been thinking about?" Deke asked, unable to reign in his curiosity.

"To be perfectly honest with you, it had crossed my mind a couple of times. But it was awful chancy back then, being without a backup. That was before you stumbled onto the scene Deke. I'd thought of trying it with just Amy and myself on the road, taking my chances that I'd get him before he was able to get us. Then, I sort of gave up on the idea. I'd forgotten about it until the developments of yesterday morning. You coming aboard did not automatically change my decision. I really had planned to try a few other maneuvers first. However, when I arrived this morning to find the message left on your windshield, I realized it was time to get aggressive with this person. He pisses me off, and right now I want him so bad I can almost taste it!" he commented with enough viciousness in his voice that Deke was glad it was not him the big man was after.

"All Right! Enough chitchat for now. Amy, you get packing, and make it quick. Deke, I suggest you go through that Jeep of yours, eliminating anything you can, and making room for the Beatles. Anything that you will not need can be left here. You can always pick it up later. I've got a few phone calls to make," Randal stated.

He apparently trusted someone enough to make a call. Deke wondered who that could be, then realized it was most likely Sergeant Hadley, who he knew Randal trusted to escort Deke to the sheriff department.

Amy was silent, having drifted back into the fog lost in earlier, but she followed Randal's directions, and went upstairs to pack. Deke was kind of worried about her. Even though she was moving, it was a little slow and woozy, like a drunken man in the dark. Deke went upstairs to finish dressing and gather the little belongings he'd taken from his truck the night before. Though he was alert, he also found himself feeling dazed. By the time Amy was packed, Zach Randal was off the phone, having arranged it with Sergeant Hadley to keep an eye out for any information from the FBI lab in Wichita Falls. Zach planned to check daily for any new developments. Deke managed to re-arrange the interior of the Jeep by removing the rear seat. Now, they had plenty of space for the Beatles. He was fortunate to have a luggage rack on top where the luggage could be placed, leaving more space inside.

"Okay. I think we're as prepared as we possibly can be, with such short notice. Deke, you got money son?" Randal asked, pulling a large wad of bills from his pocket.

"Uh, money. Oh, sure I've got money!" Deke replied, somewhat shocked by the question. He did have some money, but he was far from swimming in it. He was sort of in an uncomfortable position, not wanting to look like he needed it. Honestly, he had not even thought about its significance in their plan.

"Well here. I know you have money, but I do not want you spending any of it. This is an official Texas Law Enforcement Investigation, although they don't realize it yet. I want you to take this, put it in your pocket, and use it as needed. Like I said, we don't know how long you may have to be on the road, and I don't want something like the lack of funds stalling us when we may need it most." He handed Deke a roll of hundred dollar bills. Randal didn't mention the amount, and Deke didn't ask. Anticipating Deke's refusal, Zach stopped him before the objection was attempted.

"Now don't give me any lip. We don't have time to haggle over this." As Deke reluctantly slipped the roll of bills into his pocket, he estimated that it had to be at least ten thousand dollars.

"Let's see, it's nearly noontime, and I want you two to leave here as soon as possible. First, we have to decide on a rendezvous location for tonight. I won't leave town until at least a couple of hours behind you. I want to see if anyone notices the two of you are gone, deciding to make a quick exit from town themselves." Deke now saw Randal was flying by the seat of his pants, planning things as they progressed.

It was decided Deke would drive slow, giving the appearance they were in no hurry. Casually leaving on a trip, without giving an appearance of racing away, would look less as if they were running from someone. It offered several advantages. The obvious one was that their decision to leave town would be considered as a mere vacation. What they planned to gain by taking their time was less obvious and nearly sinister.

Without having a fair chance to catch up with them, would actually reduce their chances of success. They must allow the killer time to react, making certain he doesn't feel that the prey is escaping completely. That might cause him to go for the kill too quickly.

A slow moving target wasn't likely to initiate a hasty response from the killer. After all, they wanted him to take his time also. The plan had many areas where the killer was still calling the shots, but the fact was that he wouldn't know that. If he took pleasure in the chase, dragging it out a little, it was to their advantage, giving Randal time to initiate his move.

They agreed they would stop in Amarillo for the night. As a precaution, they exchanged cell phone numbers. They could use them in the event of an emergency, but decided only as a last resort. Randal's pager number was given to Deke and Amy. As soon as they stopped for the night, renting a room, they were to page him with the number to their location. Whenever he was able, Zach would call them. They'd be able to share any information at that time, and plan their next day's travel. It sounded like a good procedure, relatively safe and simple.

"Not that I expect this to happen, but what if we lose touch with you for some unforeseen reason? Is someone else gonna be aware of what's going on, someone that we can contact?" Deke asked hesitantly. Just the thought of such a situation occurring, sent chills down his back. It was best to be prepared.

"That's a good question," Randal commented. He hesitated when giving the answer, but for a different reason. Trust was such a hard thing to come by as far as he was concerned, but realizing in an emergency they needed backup he answered, "Sergeant Hadley is the only person that will be aware of our little journey. I plan to contact him daily, getting updates, and giving him an update on our situation at the same time. If for some reason you don't hear from me, contact him. I'll advise him to send in the troops and have you two picked up. Use the Hot Line to call Hadley at headquarters. Give me at least until midnight each day, to contact you. I may not be able to get in touch with you guys until then. In fact, I'll call him now, just to be sure that he's aware. I don't want any confusion with this operation," Randal said. Standing, he walked over to the phone.

While Randal was on the phone, Deke took Amy's one suitcase out to the truck. As he lifted it, he realized Amy had been obedient to bring only one suitcase, but it felt heavy enough to contain her entire wardrobe. Laughing silently, Deke strained as he carried the heavy load. Amy saw his response.

"Hey! What are you laughing at? What's so funny Deke?" she asked, offended by his gesture that the suitcase weighed a ton.

"I'm not laughing. This is the expression I display just before my hernia tears open. It's a pretty universal grimace men have when they realize they may be damaging their ability to father children ever again in their lives," he teased, trying to keep a straight face as he said it. When Deke saw the expression on Amy's face responding to what he said he burst into laughter. As she saw him break up, she could no longer hold back, and both of them stood laughing wildly. It was what they needed most. The seriousness of the situation still remained, but they needed to break the mood before it became so intense no one managed to escape.

Returning from outside and securing Amy's luggage, Deke approached Randal just as he was finishing with his call to Sergeant Hadley.

"That's correct John. Regardless of what you hear, if it doesn't come from either one of them or me you are not aware of anything. I feel it's in the best interest for everyone, including you. Yes, they have the Hot Line number. It will only be used in the event that something happens to me. Yes, I will John. You too, thank you." With a look of deep concentration he finished with his conversation, placing the phone back on the end table. The time had come for them to put the plan into action.

UNKNOWN to anyone at the ranch house, the entire conversation that had just taken place over Amy Dodson's phone was recorded. Sergeant Hadley wasn't the only person Ranger Zach Randal relayed information to.

The small button sized monitoring devise was placed in the receiver of the phone on the same night that the Beatles had been drugged. Of all the sheriff department people that were at the ranch that night, not a single person thought to check for bugs or listening devices. It was unfortunate indeed that a search for the possibility of any such device was overlooked.

CHAPTER

8

WITH THE BEATLES riding in the back of the Jeep, Amy and Deke set off just after noon that day. With strict instructions from Randal that they stay in areas well populated, they headed north to Amarillo. The cafe was closed indefinitely, due to the murders, sealed off by law enforcement as the crime scene of an ongoing homicide investigation.

It was a strange feeling for both of them to be leaving on this trip of unknown duration, and without a specific destination. Especially strange because they were taking such a journey accompanied by a person they had never met or knew existed before yesterday. Regardless of the bizarre situation they suddenly found themselves in, it was decided by both that they would make the best of it. While it was true, they knew very little about each other, it was also true they felt some kind of strange familiarity. Secretly, they were also feeling an uncomfortable, but undeniable attraction toward each other, and considering their predicament, they wished it had occurred under better circumstances. At the same time, they realized that the alternative might have proven to be more difficult and stressful.

As they made their way toward an eventual, but unknown future, Amy and Deke began talking. Amy spoke about her mother, how she was shattered by her sudden death, and how she felt so alone when taking over the cafe.

"When growing up I was sort of an outcast because I had no father. All the other kids had dads that were very active in school functions. Sweetwater, at that time, was a very family oriented community. With no father, and a mother who worked sixteen hours a day, I was not included in too many of the outings and parties that my classmates took part in. It was probably just as much my fault as anybody's. I was very withdrawn, and considered a little weird. When anyone tried to invite me somewhere, or even have a conversation with me, I didn't know how to respond, and really blew it. Because we couldn't afford it, I never had any make-up, and boys didn't really notice me. I was what they called a late bloomer. By the time some of the guys did take notice, my mother died. With only a few months left in the school year, I had to quit. I was a minor, with no living relatives in the area. The County Chamber of Commerce, which is in charge of the business ordinance and licensing bureau, declared the cafe to be in violation of the requirements needed to operate legally within the city limits of Sweetwater. They stated that the owner and previously licensed party, who was my mother, were not in possession of an acceptable or valid license since she was no longer alive. Therefore, the building and cafe's business was to be auctioned off by the sheriff department to the highest bidder. I was told that there was no way that I could continue to operate according to the state and county laws, or the city ordinances."

"Wait, I don't understand. Why couldn't you just take over as the rightful owner, being the only heir to your mother's possessions?" Deke asked.

"I was the rightful owner, and heir to the cafe, but one member on the County Chamber of Commerce was running the show, and he wanted the cafe. He thought he could railroad this through without too much trouble. The fact that at the time I was only seventeen years old, and literally broke, was something of which he'd decided to take advantage. He nearly got away with it. Miraculously out of nowhere, an attorney filed a petition with the courts to stop the sale of the cafe until a hearing could be held. A date for the hearing was set by the judge to start six weeks later. Before that six-week period was up, my birthday arrived. I turned eighteen. With the help of the same anonymous lawyer, the court was again petitioned, requesting that it allow legal transfer of the cafe, cafe business, license, and permit to operate within the city limits into my name. As soon as that was granted, the petition by the Chamber of Commerce was denied. The judge's reply was that he considered it a moot issue, and all previous action by them was discontinued." Deke listened, thinking that what she'd endured was incredible.

"So, by trying to save the cafe, you've evolved into a shrewd business woman?" asked Deke. He didn't ask the question sarcastically, but with compassion and understanding, realizing she'd been fighting for her survival.

"I suppose it could be described that way," Amy answered. "So during that time you were too busy to get involved with anyone, I assume?" asked Deke. "Well, it was a combination of factors. Physically, my developmental attributes were actually more of a curse than a blessing. The attention that I started getting was not the kind of attention a girl is looking for. Especially one who is running a business, trying to make ends meet, and exhausted by the time the end of the day rolls around. But being a business woman, and having to deal with everyone in a polite and courteous manner, I probably made mistakes by not being perfectly honest up front and from the start," she confessed. Amy was giving Deke a much more detailed education than he'd received from Zach Randal. He was beginning to understand why such a mystique surrounded her, and why she had allowed the mystique to remain. Unwillingly, she'd inherited a reputation, which was constructed from pure fantasy. Men, who dreamt of possessing her, had conjured up the reputation, written about her, from thin air. She had very little to do with the wild accounts described on the menu, but to her benefit, decided to play along as the colorful character in Dodson's Breakfast and Bar-B-Que Cafe's history. Her reasoning was valid, as she explained it to Deke. Those who wanted to think it true believed her reputation, regardless what was written on the menu. The people she considered her true friends knew it to be only a part of the cafe's way of advertising, and not a part of her real life. Besides, the story helped put the city of Sweetwater on the map, her finances in the positive, and the cafe evolving into one of the most talked about restaurants in central Texas.

Leaving Sweetwater, taking Highway 84 north, Deke planned to catch Interstate 27 in three to four hours, depending on how heavy the traffic was and the speed they drove. Once they were on Interstate 27, they estimated getting into Amarillo in less than two hours. With a little luck, they'd arrive before sundown, locating a hotel to stay in for the night. Then, they could page Randal with the phone number and their room number. Both of them were already curious to find out if anything had occurred after they left town.

Zach Randal seemed to think he might have a chance of that happening, and was the best reason for him to wait around and find out. He was a man who did nearly everything for a reason, but rarely explained any of those reasons to anyone.

"I was kind of wondering when Randal was planning to leave Sweetwater," Deke said in a conversation stimulating voice.

"If you were thinking to find out from him before we left, it's a good thing you weren't holding your breath. Zachary Randal is the most unpredictable man on this planet. I've been dealing with his odd and twisted behavior since the day I met him. Finally, I decided to just sit back and allow him to surprise me. It seems to be what makes him happy. Fear of becoming too predictable, I think, is more of a concern to him than the fires of hell." She sounded very sure of herself.

WITH Deke and Amy gone, Ranger Zach Randal poked around at the ranch house, making sure things were locked up secure. The blood on Deke's windshield was scraped off with a sterile razor, collected, and put in a specimen bag that he kept a supply of in his Bronco. They'd taken a picture of the message before finally washing the rest of it away. That was just going to have to be good enough for the boys in the lab. He decided they didn't have time to call the lab's evidence collection team out, plus he wasn't even sure he could trust them anymore anyway. It certainly was a sad day in law enforcement when corruption, greed, and power ran rampant through the profession, increasing at the speed of a bobcat chasing a prairie dog. Any person with half a brain knew the pay was so pathetic that nearly all those who, for one reason or another, happened to be social outcasts, found law enforcement appealing. He longed for the old days when nobody made much money. It didn't matter back then, because not much was needed to live and everybody did the job for the sheer purpose of catching bad guys.

He'd discovered something about Dr. Vanessa, and had a hard time in trying to handle it. She'd been hiding a secret. After going out with her for ten months, Zach Randal learned she was from back east somewhere. She had no family. Her parents were dead, and she always referred to herself as an only child. Then, one night after having a few too many drinks, she became suddenly depressed. While Zach watched, she seemed to fall over a cliff into a deeply emotional state, weeping for several minutes. When he pressed her, seeking a reason for the depression, she said something very strange.

"Oh, don't worry about me Zach. At times, when I'm least prepared for it, the memory of his death washes over me, and I feel like I'm drowning," she'd told him. When he'd asked who's death, she confessed that she was engaged to a young man who was tragically killed only weeks before they were to be married. After that, she decided to move her practice to Sweetwater. Vanessa told him it was the main reason she moved her practice. Attempting to begin a new life, she thought a new location without the reminders might be the best thing for her. Dr. Vanessa also stated it was a great help, but occasionally, for no reason she was able to figure out, the memory haunted her.

She never did reveal to him how her fiancé was killed, and Zach didn't push. The only information he'd ever managed to learn was quite by accident. One evening while returning from a weekend spent in Dallas, Vanessa dozed off leaning against Zach as he drove. In her sleep, she began whimpering slightly, mentioning the name Jedediah. Zach decided it was best to allow the memory undisturbed. Zach resisted the temptation to research the event, keeping her from having to relive it. He was wise enough to know that if she told him what killed her fiancé she'd think of it each time she saw Zach Randal. Being the husband of someone who had taken their own life, Zach had his suspicions about her fiancé, Jedediah.

He and Vanessa Jansen saw each other only two times after that. On each of the occasions, he felt a certain discomfort had crept between them. He came to the decision that she was in love with a memory, explaining the odd behavior she'd displayed or she was hiding something either embarrassing or illegal. Not sure of what it was exactly, but he did know it was big enough a part of her that he could not compete. Zach Randal even admitted to himself the possibility that he was measuring Dr. Vanessa Jansen against the memory of his wife, Kate.

Feeling it was best, a mutual decision was made to continue with their lives as before, referring to each other as friends. He vowed not to reveal anything to anyone about her painful past; all too familiar with the pain associated from the death of someone who had been a very close friend or lover.

THAT was a whole world away, where a different man had once lived. Zach Randal wondered why he was revisiting the issue at all. He had other things much more important, that needed his attention.

Once he was sure the ranch was secure, he'd left a couple of markers on top of each door to let him know if anyone happened to visit during the time they were away. He located a patch of clover along the porch and picked a few of the small, three-petal clovers to place on top of each door of the ranch house. If any door was opened, the clover was light enough that it would float off its perch. When he returned, he'd check to see if any of the clovers were missing. The trick was relatively foolproof, alerting him if someone had managed to gain access, even if the person used a window to gain access. He'd discovered years ago that in most cases, a perpetrator found guilty for a breaking and entering charge, eventually confessed to the crime in detail. Included with the details was an admission of exiting the home through either the front or the side entrance. It was a fact that was established through interrogation, the perpetrator found leaving through the more convenient doorway was less troublesome and less suspicious than through the window they used entering.

Amy and Deke were gone over an hour by the time Randal decided to make one last walk around the entire ranch house. His walk covered only the property nearest the house. He was unable to shake a feeling that somewhere under his nose, a piece of evidence was waiting to be found. While making the last round, his eyes were trained on the ground in front of him. Passing by one of the ground floor windows, which happened to lead into the laundry area of the house, he spotted something strange. It was a hairpin of some kind, about three inches long. The outline was oddly in the shape of a dog. A type of hairpin used by women, but not something just any woman would wear.

Picking the hairpin up, he wiped the dirt from it before placing it in his pocket. He would have to remember to ask Amy about it. He could not remember ever seeing her wear such a thing, but it was an area that he had to admit, he did not really specialize. Probably were a lot of things women wore that he'd never noticed before, and probably didn't even know what they were called. Completing his walk around the entire house, he continued straight to where his Bronco was parked.

Despite the fact they were never able to find the missing keys, a spare set had been used for Amy's Land Cruiser, and they'd stored it inside the barn several hundred yards from the ranch house. With the doors to the vehicle locked, and the barn doors secure, Zach concluded that it would be safe. Little time was available to store it elsewhere, once they began to carry out the plan that was decided upon that morning.

Starting the engine of the big Bronco, he looked at his watch. More out of a habit than anything else, and he noticed that it was fifteen minutes before 2 p.m. That was as much of a lead that he wanted them to have.

He drove away from the ranch onto Highway 70, heading straight for Highway 84. When he reached the intersection of Interstate 27 and Highway 84, he planned to stop. Parking at the crossroads, he'd easily be able to monitor all traffic heading north along that route. If by some lucky chance, one of the people he was suspicious of drove by in a hurry, he'd be in pursuit of his first suspect. The fact that anyone who

knew him may easily see and recognize him as they drove by did not
concern him much. He hoped the suspect's interest would be on
catching up with Amy, not aware of his presence, hastily trying to gain
on the prey they'd assume was getting away. In no hurry, he'd let them
speed on ahead, knowing that Deke and Amy were going to be stopping
in Amarillo for the night.

If someone he knew did drive pass, he would be very surprised
indeed. It was virtually unknown to anyone in town that they were now
on the run, so to speak. The people he casually referred to as suspects,
were actually folks he'd narrowed down to be smart enough to pull off
such clean homicides. They weren't really suspects, but people who he
used in matching the profile established for the real killer. Zach Randal
had painstakingly devised a profile of the killer, using characteristics that
he was forced to guess about. He knew whoever it was; they had to be
financially stable. The amount of time necessary just learning all that was
known about Amy through surveillance, meant the killer didn't have to
work, or was self employed. No employer would allow any employee
that much time off over the last twenty-four months. Planting the
packages found by Amy meant they knew her habits, and what they
were doing.

Zach Randal was also certain that the killer was in very good
physical health, physically strong, and probably in his early to mid
thirties. No elderly person or any weak, unhealthy person was capable of
doing what was done to the three women at the cafe. Having physical
strength was also something needed to incapacitate, tape up, and carry
four full grown Chesapeakes, weighing more than one hundred pounds
each, up a flight of stairs. In addition, very few people under the age of
thirty fell within the social status that his profile had established. Under
the age of thirty, also didn't fall within the age bracket of folks who were
associated with Amy or her friends, and he was sure the killer was
someone Amy knew.

Finally, and without a doubt, this person had above average
intelligence. His gut feeling told him they were likely near genius level.
Through many years of enforcing the law, tracking criminals, arresting
criminals, and enduring long, drawn-out, court trials, Zachary Randal
had gained special insight regarding the criminal mind.

Some were no-good, trouble-seeking idiots, but these were easily
recognized and apprehended. They left so many clues at the scene that
Randal could nearly track them by following the trail.

Some were individuals who acted out of passion and in the heat of the moment. They usually ended up turning themselves in after a day or two, if they had not been arrested at the crime scene initially. Occasionally however, some were meticulous in every detail, not a thing left unplanned, no evidence left at the crime scene, and not a clue about their identity. The victims, or the victim's relatives, were also clueless. These were the ones Randal dreaded, even feared. They were the ones that were motivated by reasons beyond the average ability to comprehend, but they were relentless and usually unstoppable in their mission. This was the type of person he believed he now had to pursue.

After a careful process of elimination, Randal chose the two people he thought were most similar to the profile he'd developed. He then used those individuals as models. Randal's reasoning was mostly based on the fact that the killer's characteristics, the level of intelligence, the probable social and economical status, along with estimated age, closely matched in theory. To be safe, he chose a male model and a female model, unsure in his profiling of the perpetrator's sex.

It made him chuckle to himself thinking of the two choices that he'd given killer characteristics. He was even more amused when he thought of what response they would have, especially if they knew how he'd used them to model a sadistic, perverted, serial killer. The Mayor of Sweetwater was what Ranger Randal used as his male model, while his old fling, Dr. Vanessa Jansen, was his choice for female. It was a long shot, that the killer would turn out to be anything like these two, but he had constructed the profile with care. Altering methods, being untraditional, and just choosing to do the types of things that are normally called crazy, was what Randal eventually found himself resorting to. Because this case had such personal meaning to it, with Amy a very close and dear friend to Zach, obviously chosen as the target of some demented, dangerous killer, Zach decided that he had no choice but to break his most important rule, and trust someone.

Call it good fortune, good luck, God smiling down on you, or just miraculous, but when Deke Stone entered that cafe, becoming an innocent bystander sitting on a barstool while a serial killer skinned three women alive several feet from him, Zachary Randal's prayers were answered.

Amy's ranch was on the south side of town, and Ranger Randal had to drive by the sheriff department before leaving town, heading toward Amarillo, eventually meeting up with Deke and Amy. He had one last chore to take care of, and the amount of time it normally took him to walk down the long corridors to the interrogation room was about as long as this meeting should last.

On most days, he could detect elevated stress in the department just by what was said or not said, or because of the way that other officers looked at him, or didn't look at him. Over the years, it had become a daily game with Zach. He never let on that he had such discerning abilities, but was nearly always correct with his observations.

Two Texas State Troopers that worked undercover narcotics were in the interrogation room. Both were seasoned men with nearly twenty years between them. Since Zach Randal was making the decision to go out on a limb to catch the butcher who murdered the cafe employees, he asked John Hadley to send him two men who he could trust with his very life. Looking at the two troopers, Randal wondered why Hadley trusted them, but said nothing as he closed the door. Shutting the door was his way of keeping everyone else out, and over the years the other officers realized his intention.

"Okay, I don't have a lot of time, so make it quick. Tell me everything you know, and skip all the bullshit that you use when entertaining your captains back at the State Police!" Randal demanded.

They had to admit, this was a first for both of them, seeing Zach Randal cocked and ready, unafraid to pull the trigger on his emotions, and probably looking forward to it with excitement. They knew Zach Randal. They knew he could smell a lie as sure as if it were bear shit. These two officers had not been born yesterday, despite what their appearance suggested.

"Zach, we'll tell you all we know up front, but it ain't much, so don't think we're holding out on you." The older of the narcotic officers Dan Baker volunteered.

"Fair enough," Randal replied sternly. "So get to telling Dan. You don't have all day," Randal told him. They finally understood that he was in hurry, and whatever they ended up saying needed to be short, precise, and to the point.

Lowering his voice to a whisper, the younger of the two, Officer Bill Frye asked, "You trying to tell us something about what we saw is tied into these women being murdered Zach? Something critical that we should know about?" He held his head low fearful someone may be eavesdropping.

"Nothing that you won't be told about eventually, Bill. Just happens to be something that I'm involved in at the time, requiring my complete attention." Troopers Dan Baker and Bill Frye looked at each other for a split second, confirming the decision they wanted in on the triple homicide their senior officer, Sergeant Hadley, and Texas Ranger Zach Randal were now assigned.

"We want in Zach. All we know is that you're up to your armpits with ideas, no suspects, and not many people that you trust." The statement was about as blunt and accurate as it could be stated. Bill and Dan were both the quiet type, always holding their cards close to their vest. Zach was glad for that, even though he suspected trusting them may be a gamble from the get go. He had to trust John Hadley's opinion, and let them in.

"In my opinion, we are dealing with an individual with above average intelligence and with the lowest of morals. More than capable of unspeakable horrors which I am sure you've heard about." Randal felt obligated in advising them how extremely dangerous he thought this killer really was.

"What exactly is it you're saying Zach? You're not worried about us, I hope. Whatever you're working on has got everything to do with Amy Dodson that's for sure, but why all the secrecy?" Trooper Baker asked. His doubts were not well hidden in the manner of speech he used, or in the tone that he took.

"I'm not afraid for myself or for Miss Amy, and that is being brutally honest with you fellows." Zach Randal made certain not to mention Deke's name in the scenario. "It's my concern for anyone who decides to become involved in the investigation. I know what I'm saying. This killer just might consider a male opponent someone worthy of the challenge." Dropping his attempt to warn the troopers, Randal again brought them back to the matter at hand.

"But forget all of that for now. What I want to know is what exactly the two of you observed after Sergeant Hadley left the building."

"All we know is that the desk sergeant received a phone call right after someone called to speak to the Sergeant, but he'd already exited headquarters. The desk sergeant seemed very attentive to whoever was calling, but said very little. After hanging up, he said he had to check out a certain informant in town about a tip he received." Dan and Bill were telling the story in tandem, one filling in words where the other was too slow and shaking his head affirmatively with each statement.

"What about radio checks? Did he ever call in with his 10.20? Have you two been monitoring scanners?" Randal began grilling them faster than they were able to answer, and it was beginning to piss both of them off.

A loud knock on the door interrupted them, and a large rookie detective stuck his head in. "Sorry to disturb you Ranger Randal, but a guy from Wichita Falls is on the phone, says he needs to talk to you," he announced. Immediately Zach Randal excused the troopers. He more or less forced them out of his office to have privacy with the caller, telling them to get him more details as he shut the door.

"Hello, this is Texas Ranger Randal. With whom am I speaking?" he asked, without the least bit of hesitancy.

"Good afternoon Ranger. This is Josh Sinclair at the FBI lab in Wichita Falls. I'm glad that I was able to catch you this afternoon. I have new information on the victims that were sent to me yesterday. I don't usually make a habit of having something so soon, but when I was able to read over the horrible events that you guys think took place in that small cafe, it just would not leave me alone. For the life of me, I was unable to figure out how someone, even of considerable strength, was able to inflict such a degree of trauma to each of the victims while they were apparently still conscious. I know for certain they were alive, but a possibility remains that they may have been drugged enough that they didn't suffer the agony." The forensic pathologist was bursting to tell someone of his initial discovery.

"Hey Doc, that's just great! What is this discovery of yours? You've got me sitting at the edge of my seat!" Randal replied.

"Well, as you stated in the summary that you sent to me that not much of a window of time could have been available for whoever did this. Either they were extremely powerful, or a master with a scalpel. Yet, neither of those two assumptions seems to hold water. First, while the instrument was more than likely a scalpel or other similarly sharp devise, too many areas have signs that signify the hand doing the cutting had just simply slipped, resulting in uneven incisions, and varied degrees of depth to each wound. This would rule out most surgeons as the likely culprit.

"Secondly, the way the women had their necks tied, reveals to me that contrary to being an individual with amazing strength, it was more likely someone with an average to medium degree of physical prowess. The particular knots used were of a specific design that tightens as the individual struggles, leaving me to think they were disadvantaged, also familiar with usage of the tightening knot. But that was not what prompted me that we might have either a male or a female killer. A much bigger advantage had been used by the killer. I wouldn't rule out the possibly that this was a female serial killer." Doctor Josh Sinclair was a talker, and he was excited. It was a deadly combination if the other person wasn't a very good listener.

"Doc, you got me all wound up like a spring ready to pop. Give me a break will you?" Randal was pleading. "Oh, sorry. Anyway, that was when I thought of the Beatles," Dr. Sinclair declared.

"The Beatles? You talking about the band or the Chessies?" Randal asked, beginning to wonder about his line of reasoning.

"Why, the Chesapeakes, of course! Ranger Randal, do you remember when they were found locked in that second story bedroom with their snouts taped shut? The time when Miss Dodson was home alone and found the package in her grocery bag?" Josh Sinclair was explaining the event with the enthusiasm of a paleontologist finding T-Rex for the first time.

"Yes sir. That I do remember, like it was yesterday," Zach stated proudly, and a little humored by the pathologist's excitement.

"That's your answer, Ranger! It was that simple all along, so simple that we were unable to see the sense of it and the cleverness behind it."

"Doc, I know you must be a real smart fellow, with this revelation just slapping you upside the head, but us fellows in law enforcement sometimes need a little more of a hint to grab hold of such startling information. In other words whatever the hell you're trying to say might be clearer if you went ahead and said it." Randal was able to follow the little tour down memory lane without a problem but it didn't give him an automatic answer.

"Ketamine! Ranger Randal, the drug that was used to render the Beatles harmless was also used on the three women from the cafe. The canine sedative used by veterinarians, the very same sedative that was used on the Beatles, is also present in very high levels within each of the women. They were alive, and possibly conscious, but rendered completely helpless. Drugged and tortured, all without a struggle, and in record time. Oh, and I don't know how important this is, but they were not sexually assaulted. It was simply a matter of time, and he would not have had the time for any of that, it might be the only reason that they weren't sexually accosted. But, I am still puzzled as to why you're suspicious, thinking that the killer may possibly be a woman, and requesting that I assume as much, when examining the bodies for evidence to the fact?" The FBI pathologist was now asking Randal a question, which had but one answer: Guesswork.

"Well, by golly you're right Doc! Ain't that a kick in the head?" Zach Randal stated, ignoring the question from Dr. Sinclair about why he'd suspected a woman. The wheels in his head began turning, and he wasn't sure he liked the message the wheels were grinding out.

Returning to the present, Zach Randal thanked Dr. Josh Sinclair, telling him to keep up the good work, and not to forward any of his reports just yet, since he was going out of town for a few days. Whenever he returned to Sweetwater, he would call and have him send everything over in a single report. Josh Sinclair said he would wait for Zach's call before sending any additional information discovered from the autopsies. With a final good-bye and thank you, Randal hung up.

The information was bad for the investigation, but Zach was glad things were moving along more like a real investigation. The discoveries were disturbing to him, but only because he knew how difficult it was for some investigators to be effective when they were told that a suspect to multiple homicides might be a woman. It just didn't fit in their heads right, and they usually became sloppy and careless as a result. At least Zach no longer felt that he was trying to catch a ghost. The suspect had now entered the realm of the living. That meant only one thing to Zach Randal. This killer would eventually have to make mistakes, and Zach Randal wanted to be the one to catch him or her when they did. Returning the phone to its cradle, he stood from behind the small table in the interrogation room and began pacing. Deep in thought, he fumbled with the different keys to the puzzle knowing one existed somewhere that could answer all his questions. If only he were able to look at the big picture from an observers point of view.

Because of the high degree of emotions involved with such a hideous criminal, different things had to be addressed by Mr. Deke Stone, and he would have to bring each to the surface. He hoped that Deke would also recognize the danger of becoming emotionally involved. Zach just had to resign to the fact that there was nothing he could do to prevent it. Deke had to be his own master, enforcing the discipline necessary to maintain a clear line of reasoning. He'd once again have to allow life to be the best teacher of hard lessons. Snapping back to the present, he stopped pacing, and called the two troopers back into the small room.

"Okay men. I'll have to rely on your good judgment and surveillance skills, trusting that you get the success you need, and quickly. I will be calling daily regarding this case. When I do, I'll be asking Sergeant Hadley to keep me up to date with everything. That is why your job is so important. If he doesn't receive information from you, then I'm also left in the dark. An ability to be in two places at one time has been on my Christmas wish list for many years, but Santa has decided to reserve that ability for himself only. The two of you must help me do what I hope the killer thinks are not possible. Are we straight on this? Do both of you feel comfortable with this?" It was not necessary for Randal to ask questions concerning their comfort or feelings. But asking questions pacified Zach, allowing him some consolation in the fact that his questions gave an appearance of compassion.

"Good luck, and don't screw up!" With a few last minute instructions, Zach gathered folders and stuffed them under his arm. Shaking hands with his new investigators, Bill Frye and Dan Baker, he exited the small office, shoving past the deputies in the crowded hallway.

SUNLIGHT had faded significantly as the fiery star dropped below the western horizon. Zach Randal climbed aboard the Bronco. He was seriously behind schedule, and it was starting to aggravate him. Due to his preoccupation with everything at hand, especially whether the two troopers were capable of what he needed without being killed, Zach never noticed the dark, sports car parked across the street. He also failed to notice as it pulled away from the curb, following him. Zach turned and headed for the expressway, north toward Amarillo.

CHAPTER

9

TRAFFIC WAS HEAVIER than they'd expected as the setting sun left an orange glow over the state of Texas. Watching the sinking sun, Deke was certain about one thing, today would never be repeated or duplicated. He and Amy's conversation had long ago been replaced with a relatively comfortable silence. John, Paul, and George, were stretched out snoozing peacefully while Ringo sat directly behind Deke, studying the back of his head. He appeared to be perfectly content with counting hairs on Deke's head while the other three slept. Amy tried distracting Ringo away from the strange obsession, but it lasted only until she stopped giving him the extra attention, whereupon he returned to his previous position. Deke accepted the dog's critical inspection without any more fear about losing a body part.

"Hey, how about finding a place to pick up some food before we get to the hotel we decide to stay at for the night?" Deke proposed. He was getting pretty hungry, and realized their hasty escape from Sweetwater was accomplished only after the special breakfast Randal prepared for them this morning. Since the early morning breakfast, they'd not eaten. If Deke was hungry it was a pretty sure bet that the others were too, and he had better locate a market where he could pick up a hefty sack of dog food for the Beatles.

"Food sounds great. It's always my favorite part of a vacation. It seems that there's no better tasting food than the stuff you find while traveling," Amy commented. For such a small person she sure had no problem putting away a man's size portion of a meal.

"We took a vacation a couple of years ago. Well, what I mean is that the Beatles and I did. No place in particular, we just took off traveling across the country. First, we drove into Louisiana taking Interstate 10. Places like Lafayette, Baton Rouge, and of course, New Orleans were so much fun that we almost decided not to come home. We especially enjoyed the Cajun cuisine." She was staring off into the night as she spoke, and it sounded as though she were still there.

"You make it sound as if the Beatles were right by your side at those Cajun restaurants you enjoyed so much," Deke said, joining her with memories of his own about New Orleans.

"Of course they were by my side. They seemed to enjoy the food even more than I did, and the people of Louisiana aren't so stuffy and proper that you were not allowed to bring a pet to dine with you in the evening. The Beatles ended up being a big hit with those people. You know, the Cajun people have some kind of special understanding when it comes to dogs, makes you think actual communication is taking place between them when they're together. Having four, rather large Chessies dine with me never even caused anyone to lift an eyebrow in surprise.

"The places we enjoyed eating out the most were the seafood and catfish houses. They serve the catfish any way you like it, and the seafood is Southern fried, in a buffet setting where folks return six and seven times to pile more food on their plate. What I liked best was the way the folks ate peanuts from the shell for little appetizers, throwing the shells on the wooden floors like it was perfectly normal." Amy was reliving the entire dining experience, and Deke saw a light in her eyes that was not obvious before.

"Oh it was such fun just to be somewhere that was different, and not a soul knew you. Pretense seemed not to exist in anyone, believing only certain behavior was acceptable. It was a place that had no boundaries to keep you from being whoever you wanted to be. A place where the only important thing is life, and living it as hard or as easy as you chose that day, being whoever, and whatever you wanted to be, totally free to enjoy life, and living for no other reason except that it's the way life was meant to be lived."

Deke was taken by surprised to hear Amy speak with such rebellion. She was definitely sincere about her sudden confession that life was corrupted by those who had taken it upon themselves to judge what should be done or even could be done in life. The more absurd the leap was that some people felt compelled to take in life, the more taboo it was judged by others to be. According to those who were self-appointed as lifestyle police, anything defined as a gamble was considered the most extreme form of foolishness, and anyone exhibiting such behavior was considered to have suffered a serious and permanent loss of mental function from drugs or injury.

What the ultra careful referred to as a waste of life was what those who enjoyed life most found to be the main ingredient and absolutely imperative to the freedoms they sought so earnestly.

The very fact that failure was always waiting around the corner, and at times left its stinger in you, made life's journey exactly the challenge they desired. What kind of fun or enjoyment could exist in life if all the hazards were removed, where success was ensured before any direction was chosen? Fear driven people are held captive in a prison designed by their own possessions. They soon lose what makes seeking the prize the best part of the adventure, not limiting rewards to only those who find, but to those who dare to seek. Deke's philosophy was rarely understood by those afraid to try.

Deke had three philosophical sayings that he lived by: The first was never to underestimate an over-achiever. Secondly, beware of judging the actions of a man who has been captured by the intoxicating adventure of a dream. Thirdly, that success was only measured by the amount of joy experienced while attempting to achieve it. Without the fun of the hunt, the kill becomes pointless.

Locating an acceptable hotel for the night and the closest restaurant to that location seemed the best thing to do. Driving through the most crowded portions of Amarillo, they were sure the interstate leaving town had a row of well-known establishments with rooms vacant for the night. It was important not to be secluded from activity, but at the same time, they didn't want to be stuck in the middle of it. Before long, they spotted one of the more famous franchise hotels and pulled in. Immediately all four of the Beatles stood, sensing they were about to stop.

"What about these guys? Should we even consider trying to sneak them in or just fess up that we have five hundred pounds of Chesapeake Bay Retrievers in addition to our luggage?" It was a legitimate question since most places frowned on even the smallest of pets in hotel rooms.

"Oh just tell them we'll put a deposit up front to take care of any damages or extra cleaning, even though I'm sure the Beatles are probably more civilized than most of their guests." Amy was right, and Deke wholeheartedly agreed. Besides, they were hungry and tired, all six of them. After checking into a room with only one queen-sized bed, and a two hundred dollar deposit, fifty for each Beatle, Amy decided to take a shower and freshen up. Deke spotted a burger joint a couple of blocks away, and after taking everyone's order left on foot to grab their supper.

As he walked to the burger place he wondered what they'd think when he ordered two regular burgers with everything on them along with the twenty large burgers, with just meat and bread.

OFFICERS Dan Baker and Bill Frye followed the instructions given to them by Zachary Randal. They were not sure how this had been arranged so easily with headquarters, but, then again, several powerful people owed Sergeant Hadley many favors, and he had probably called one of them in. They were to remain together at all times, using an unmarked state cruiser. The two officers were assigned to one specific task. Someone who they had never had the pleasure of meeting, was placed under a twenty-four hour surveillance. However, this surveillance was strictly covert in nature. The individual was not considered a criminal of any kind. To the contrary, she was someone considered in danger of falling victim to criminal activity.

Zach Randal told them where they'd be able to locate Dr. Vanessa Jansen, and set up whatever type of routine they needed, using any equipment they considered necessary. Randal said she drove a black Porsche Carrera 911. Not very many folks in town drove that kind of vehicle. To be exact, there wasn't another Porsche around other than the one Dr. Vanessa drove.

Just as the two undercover officers were cruising past the address given to them by Randal, they spotted the black Porsche returning from the direction of the city. Slowing down as they passed by the Veterinarian's residence, they saw the attractive woman exit her vehicle and enter her home. This, they thought, was going to be a piece of cake. Her automobile was identified, and the good doctor herself had also been identified, on their first drive-by. Deciding the surveillance was going to be easy street, baby-sitting her, the undercover officers looked for a reasonably close spot to park. What they did not know, and had found sort of odd, was what Sergeant Hadley and Ranger Randal thought that she was in danger of?

Dr. Vanessa Jansen's home and Veterinarian office was located on the outskirts of Sweetwater in a rural community which offered open fields, and thinly scattered trees, separating one home from another. The homes in the area were priced well above any blue-collar workers ability to afford. Due to her profession and financial blessings, the Doctor was fortunate to own what seemed to be at least twenty acres of landscaped property, including the kennels and large barn for housing farm animals.

As the two troopers searched along the winding country road to inconspicuously turn their vehicle around, they discussed the strange behavior they'd witnessed in Ranger Randal.

"Dan what do you suppose that big, old, Texas Ranger, Zach Randal and Sergeant Hadley are up to?" Bill Frye asked the older trooper his opinion for the first time since they were recruited for the assignment. While waiting for his answer, which he knew may take several minutes as Dan considered the question, he ripped open a bag of venison jerky packed in the back seat of the unmarked automobile for them to chew on while keeping Dr. Vanessa under protective surveillance.

"Well, that's a pretty broad question considering we're pretty much in the dark concerning this whole mixed up affair." Dan's answer may have been mistaken by anyone else to be incomplete, a way of saying I don't know, but that was Dan's way of winding up before he really started answering the question entirely.

"We know three women were murdered back at Dodson's Breakfast and Bar-B-Que yesterday morning about sunup, and from what we've been able to piece together, it was no picnic. Now they're doing their damned best to keep any of the particulars from getting out to the press, and that means the investigators are pretty clammed up about it, because you know as well as I do Bill, it's always some loose-lipped cop who leaks all the information out to newspapers and television people." Bill was aware of everything Dan revealed to him. They'd been together the entire day, but he knew Dan was still in the warming up phase of answering the original question.

"What occurred back at that cafe was pretty much leaking out all around headquarters, but not because that's what they want. Sergeant Hadley and Zach Randal are like old blood brothers, acting pretty much just alike when it comes to situations like this. Everybody knows Zach Randal will never trust another cop in his life, not completely that is. Especially since that clown from the investigator's office put a bullet in his shoulder several years ago when capturing that murdering rapist who drowned his victims in hotel bathtubs. Even putting all that aside, I got a strong feeling this killer they're so intent on catching, is one of them slashers, skinning his victims. It sounds more or less like one of those perpetrators who makes old, law dogs like Randal real nervous. Hell, worse than that, I think this is the kind of bastard that makes men like Randal plumb scared."

Officer Bill Frye never once looked at Officer Dan Baker, but kept his eyes on the road while chewing a tough piece of jerky. Listening to Dan as he related everything that Bill already knew about the case, he resembled a jackass eating briers, chewing the hard, dry jerky. He didn't look like he was paying any attention, until Dan made that last statement, suggesting Randal was afraid.

"Now hold on just a second Dan. I believe you may be crossing over to that side of the fence where judges and lawyers hide, if you think Zach Randal is afraid of this killer." His defense of Randal was admirable, and completely understood by Dan.

"I didn't say he was afraid of the killer. What I said is that this is the type of killer that makes men like him afraid." The clarification was nearly accepted, but Bill insisted that it meant the same damn thing.

"What in hell's blazes are you trying to say with that kind of double-talk Dan?"

"I know that sounds like a politician speaking at the women's auxiliary, but if you think about what I said you'll realize that there's a big difference between types of fear. The fear that Zach Randal's wrapped up in is not the kind that makes him run and hide, but the kind that, and God help us if it happens, makes him dangerous! A crazy fear, creating unpredictable actions, downright deadly from the start."

With the information that was taking root in Officer Bill's mind, the steady chewing of his cud of jerky stopped. He swallowed the mouthful of venison, nearly choking. Looking straight ahead at the roadway, he asked, "You reckon we done the right thing by jumping into this nest of rattlers as quick as we did?"

Finally, locating a gravel road to turn around at, Officer Dan maneuvered the unmarked vehicle skillfully, utilizing the gravel area to successfully make a U-turn before answering.

"That, I can't tell you. But what we just did in the road is impossible when it comes to this assignment, especially after telling Zach Randal we wanted in. The only two ways you can get out of an assignment with the likes of Zach Randal is when the perpetrator is apprehended, and the investigation is over, or if you happen to be unlucky enough to be attending your own funeral."

Bill Frye turned his head slowly looking at his partner, eyes wide, and face pale, he replied, "Oh shit! Now you tell me."

The two men looked at each other for a second; sharing a pair of grim looks about things they feared might come. It lasted for only a second, and then quickly and automatically shifted back to a mode where nothing was considered beyond their ability to handle, until the moment proved otherwise. It was the well-practiced persona that kept most of these fine men from becoming statistics, while at the same time made sure they remained humble.

Just as they began once again approaching Dr. Vanessa's residence, the two of them had the very same thought. What was that phone call the desk sergeant received all about? Why did he have to leave so suddenly? Where did he go?

They did not have to wait long for the answer. Almost as if conjured up out of thin air just by thinking of him, the desk sergeant appeared. Watching the scene unfold as if in a dream, a patrol car suddenly emerged from the barn that was behind Dr. Vanessa's home and the mysterious acting desk sergeant himself was driving it. His name was Bob Davidson, and he had been with the Sweetwater Police Department for nearly forty years. For the last ten years, he was desk sergeant on the evening shift. Law enforcement was a strange and confusing force within the county, and indeed the entire city of Sweetwater. One reason for the confusion was how each branch of the different institutions was set up.

Sweetwater City Police, the Nolan County Sheriff Department, the Texas Rangers, and Texas State Police all shared the same four story, sixty-five year old building, creating sub-stations as their headquarters. It was an accepted reality in the area as far back as anyone could remember, and each branch of law enforcement pretty much did their thing without getting in the other's jurisdiction, causing competition or hard feelings. As for the individuals, they just figured it was beneficial. Everyone got along, and usually ended up covering for the other. The public at large stayed confused concerning who did what, but that also was considered a benefit. Most folks just tried to stay out of trouble.

As they watched Bob Davidson pull around from inside the barn to the side entrance of Dr. Vanessa's home, they were stunned! Dan Baker edged the unmarked car to the side of the road under a maple tree and parked. They were not noticed, and far away enough not to look suspicious.

Sergeant Bob Davidson parked and exited the patrol car. He entered the side entrance to the home without knocking. He would not be seen again until emerging after dark. When he did emerge, the two officers watching the place would not see Dr. Vanessa Jansen sneak into the back seat of the patrol car with Sergeant Davidson. Both Dan and Bill assumed he was leaving the house alone and remained at their location carrying out the protective surveillance that they were assigned.

Meanwhile, Vanessa Jansen was driven secretly to Amy Dodson's ranch by the desk sergeant, dropped off under the cover of darkness. After he'd driven away from the ranch house leaving the doctor, his next stop was Police Headquarters. Sergeant Bob Davidson would resume his shift as desk sergeant until eleven o'clock that night. He had completed his end of the plan. His small part in what was a much bigger scheme was now finished. He'd resume his job as he had for the past ten years, having no idea what the eventual outcome of his actions would bring.

He didn't want to know, and hoped that whatever happened could never be tied to him. The price that was owed by him had now been paid, and that was all he cared about, praying fervently Texas Ranger Zach Randal never found out about his actions. He respected Zach Randal tremendously, and feared him. However, it was an even greater fear that had caused him to act in such a strange way. He was certain that his actions were not illegal. He broke no laws as he carried out the deed. However, a greater law, unspoken and unwritten had been violated. Zach Randal had been crossed. His investigation may be in jeopardy, and possibly his very life put in danger, with the lives of several other people.

Technically, he was interfering with a felony investigation, but not willingly, or knowingly, and certainly not maliciously. The old desk sergeant was horrified at what may happen if his short errand to drop Dr. Vanessa Jansen at Amy Dodson's ranch was ever discovered. So far, the only thing anyone knew was that he was at her home early that evening, but had left alone.

His main concern at this time was for the safety and health of his wife. She was all he had left in the world, and at the end of the year, he planned to retire. He would get a small pension, but not enough for them to move far from Sweetwater, as they'd dreamed of doing for so many years. They wanted to move to an undisclosed location and never found. Now that he had paid this price, he and his wife could plan that move. It was rotten, but that was sometimes the only way for old cops to survive after too old to perform the job required of them. It was a young man's job, but usually never discovered until that young man had aged past the point of doing anything else. That was when the corruption they fought hard against became a temptation beyond what could be resisted. Sadly, it had become a final means of survival.

While in one location two undercover officers were watching Dr. Vanessa Jansen's home, she was at another location opening the barn door where Amy's Land Cruiser was parked. Desk sergeant, Bob Davidson, gave the set of keys she held in her hand to her. When he gave them to Vanessa Jansen, he reassured her they were certain to fit the vehicle's ignition. After arriving home earlier that day she was informed about the quick exit that Deke and Amy had made from Sweetwater. Anxious to leave as soon as possible, she was determined not to allow the couple too great a head start. Vanessa realized it was much too dangerous for her to use the Porsche. It was much too easily recognized, jeopardizing her attempt, even if she was certain no one was suspicious of her. Thankfully, desk sergeant Bob Davidson was able to eavesdrop on the phone conversation between Texas Ranger Randal and Sergeant Hadley. He told her it was more than likely Amy and Deke were heading for Green Mountain Falls, Colorado, and Deke's home. Amy's vehicle would be much safer. Surely, the Land Cruiser was the last vehicle anyone would think to look for.

TEXAS Ranger Zachary Randal sat in his vehicle at the crossroads watching traffic pass. He was tired, and needed to be on his way toward Amarillo before the night was over. He could not resist watching for a couple of hours to see if any of his theories panned out. So far, there was no word from Sergeant Hadley. According to John Hadley, the two officers were still watching Dr. Vanessa's home, where they saw her return that afternoon.

"Hell John, it don't make a damn bit of sense! I'm telling you either we're pissing up a rope or the woman is involved in some way. Ain't no other variables to plug anything else into." The inside of the truck was dark except for the dim green glow from the cell phone keypad Zach Randal used to speak with Sergeant John Hadley, back at headquarters.

"Zach, I wish that I could do more. I know it's frustrating. It's like that all the way around this investigation. Hold on a second Zach, I got a beep on my phone." Randal sat in the dark holding the small cell phone to his ear knowing soon he would be getting a page from Amy and Deke. He'd have to call them with no progress to report. Still, he was sure things were happening that he just hadn't stumbled across yet.

"Zach you still there? Listen, that was Dan Baker, and he filled me in on a small piece of information that they'd neglected to mention earlier." Zach Randal was all ears, as he suddenly sat up straight in his Bronco. Sergeant Hadley relayed what the two undercover officers at Dr. Vanessa's residence witnessed.

Turning the ignition for the Bronco, Zach fired up the engine and threw it into gear, spraying gravel and squealing tires as he headed north toward Amarillo. "Damn John! Do you realize what may have happened?"

"Not really Zach. Is that your tires or have you witnessed an accident?" John Hadley heard squealing tires as Randal tore out of the crossroads parking spot, heading back onto the interstate.

"Hell yes that's me! I've got to get to Amarillo fast! Tell those surveillance clowns to drive up to Vanessa's front door and ask for directions." He was blurting out orders to John Hadley, realizing what had happened.

"What the heck are you talking about Zach, and what's got you so wound up all of a sudden?"

"Do what I say John! If my guess is right, she's not even home. We've been had, made fools of by one of our own. Leave Sergeant Bob Davidson to me. Do not mention a word to him concerning this. I want him to relax, thinking he got away with it." Suddenly Zach Randal was no longer frustrated. It was happening. He only discovered things after they had begun happening. At that moment, the pager on his belt went off. It was Amy and Deke sending a message advising him of their phone number and hotel room. Now things were suddenly happening too fast, but he liked it better this way. He only hoped that he was ahead of whoever was in pursuit of the bait.

Zach hated to think Vanessa Jansen was involved, but the evidence sure pointed in that direction. Maybe there was an accomplice. Whomever, he was sure they were driving something other than the Porsche 911. It definitely wasn't an encouraging development, but by God, it was a development never the less.

DOCTOR Vanessa Jansen had one distinct advantage over Randal. While she was familiar with the type of vehicle he drove, being a passenger on many occasions, he had no idea what she was driving. It was not that he didn't know Amy Dodson's Land Cruiser by sight, but that he had no idea Vanessa Jansen would be driving it. The same vehicle he personally witnessed being locked up inside the barn at Amy Dodson's ranch. If given time to think about what she may be driving, it still would not have been one of his guesses.

Driving the posted speed limit to avoid any unnecessary complications, Vanessa was not surprised when she spotted the Texas Ranger parked at the crossroads. Having no clue that she was in Amy's vehicle, he hadn't even given the Land Cruiser a second look as it passed him. She was not especially nervous about the trip, but began to get a little paranoid as time passed. She could not bring herself to believe Zach Randal associated her with the trouble Amy was now embroiled in.

He had no way of knowing that her brother, Jedediah, had committed suicide six months after leaving Sweetwater, or about the secret Jedediah and Amy shared. Zach Randal ended up buying the story about her fiancé having a tragic accident. While she was ashamed of her lie, she was sort of proud that the story managed to fool him completely.

The great, Texas Ranger Zach Randal was under her spell and had no idea. Her only concern was not letting Amy get too far away. As long as she was somewhere between Zach Randal and the beat up Jeep that Amy Dodson's friend was driving, she felt certain to eventually locate them. It was vitally important that she reach Amy before anyone else.

She remembered when their poor father had taken his own life. Vanessa and Jedediah were still very young, but she remembered the confusion. She saw how her mother degraded her father constantly in public, creating such despair and despondency that he could no longer face life with hopes for the future.

Because of his suicide, she and her younger brother were deprived of the love and nurturing that was rightly theirs. Her mother managed to steal away the childhood years through her selfish brutality. This was one reason she found it so hard to accept the fact that Jedediah had also committed suicide.

Less than a year after her father was dead and buried, her mother remarried. He was a cruel, evil man who abused Vanessa and her brother Jedediah for years. In her case, the sexual abuse did not stop until she left home for college. What was most disgusting about her suffering was that her mother was aware of the sexual abuse from the beginning, but did nothing to help her.

As she entered the city limits of Amarillo, Dr. Vanessa slowed the big Land Cruiser to below the posted speed limits. Scanning streets as she passed hotel after hotel, Vanessa was becoming frustrated. What made her think this was going to be easy, searching through a large city for this elusive pair, roaming around with four full grown Chesapeake Bay Retrievers?

As she stopped for a red light, next to a line of hotels, she thought about her options. What happened next literally shocked her into near panic, and defied all odds. Emerging from out of nowhere, Deke Stone approached her vehicle, jogging along the sidewalk. Vanessa was in full view, frantic of what to do, and then she saw the armful of hamburgers that he carried.

A lunatic's luck was strange indeed, with powers undiscovered out of that realm. As Vanessa waited on the light, she came closer than she would ever know to that strange force, for she felt certain that she was in a state of lunacy to be in this situation. She watched as Deke entered the parking lot of a hotel only a block away. He looked around to see if he were being watched or followed before turning quickly and entering the room, 116.

Her closeness to their location was going to make things a little hairy, having Amy this near to her while driving the Land Cruiser. Nevertheless, she had them in her sights, and that was what she set out to do. Vanessa Jansen was determined not to allow distance to come between them. She would watch Amy with an allegiance that even the Secret Service would envy.

She found an adrenaline rush starting from being so close to Amy and Deke. It was as euphoric as a thick white line blasting into her sinuses, and she could not keep the silly little grin from appearing on her face. Her perception of reality needed some shifting periodically from the dangerous direction it had been taking, avoiding any stupid mistakes. As the amount of danger increased, there was an equal increase of her appreciation for the situation.

It was almost as nothing could go wrong with her plan, and she took that to be a good omen. Vanessa became so exhilarated that she found herself giggling aloud. Vengeance was such a powerful motivation.

EACH of the Beatles had managed to consume their giant burgers before Amy or Deke had time to finish one. Their bellies filled, the four

Chesapeake's stretched out on the carpet, watching television while Deke and Amy completed their meal. They were so hungry that the conversation consisted of very few words. For the first time all day they finally relaxed, the degree of their fatigue surprising them.

While Deke had been out getting the hamburgers Amy paged Zach Randal with the phone number to their room and a second numerical message giving their room number.

It had been nearly an hour ago since she sent the page, and still he had not called them. They had until midnight to wait before contacting Sergeant Hadley, as decided upon back at Amy's earlier that morning.

"Amy, dozens of questions are flowing through my mind, and I feel if they were answered it may shed some light on some of the mystery surrounding this situation." Deke's voice carried a different tone to it revealing that his frustrations were steadily increasing.

Looking at Deke, sitting across from him on the floor of the hotel room, Amy's expression caught him totally by surprise. She had such an innocent and naive look. Deke was beginning to feel a growing responsibility associated with Amy's confidence that everything would work out fine as long as he was with her. He nearly suggested they talk about it later, but the eagerness that she'd urged him on with was contagious. Before too long, they were spreading theory and conjecture throughout the room like feathers from a shredded pillow.

"For a reason that I might never understand, I have a very negative reaction whenever Vanessa Jansen's name is mentioned. It seems like the entire nightmare surrounds her arrival in Sweetwater, and increases in severity as time passes, as your friendship with her grows." The calm deliverance of his suspicion eased the defensiveness that she would have exhibited before all of this madness developed. Their situation was indeed one that posed grave consequences, the solution to some part of the mystery remaining elusive, just out of their grasp.

"I have never felt any negative feelings from Vanessa when we've been together. Deke, I will not completely dismiss your assumptions, or your suspicion, because of the extreme seriousness that such accusations carry. Therefore, please don't tell me any more about Vanessa being involved unless you feel it necessary and, then only when you can provide the proof to back up an accusation. Necessary by the way in this case means only if there's imminent danger, not just because you or Zachary feel that she is guilty."

While he thought about her emotional response to his observations the phone at the bedside table began ringing. It resulted in both of them having an unexpected scare, along with the four Chessies.

As Deke lifted the receiver, he was cautious not to act too quickly, allowing whoever was calling the advantage of first having to discover their identity. Pressing the receiver lightly to his ear, Deke listened closely without speaking a word.

"Well, you gonna say something Deke, or just stand there shaking in your underwear?" The voice was none other than Ranger Zachary Wyatt Randal's, and he seemed to be in a jolly mood. However, as Deke had discovered, it was an exercise in futility predicting the big man's moods.

"Yes sir. We've been kind of worried, waiting on your call," Deke confessed over the phone to Randal. Amy looked at him genuinely surprised that he'd admit to such feelings of fear, especially in front of a woman. She had apparently lived among the macho, male community for too long, and found it a pleasant experience to be around a man not afraid to voice his true feelings, or his fears.

"Deke, listen to me! I'm not going to pull any punches with you, so get a grip on yourself. And make sure Amy doesn't see your response to what I'm about to tell you."

Deke steeled his backbone and clenched his teeth, not sure of what Randal was about to unload on him. "All right Zach. We were just eating burgers and relaxing. How's traffic? We were caught in what must have been the early Christmas shopping rush." Deke rambled on about nothing in particular, trying to remove the edge that had developed in Amy while they had been waiting for Zach Randal to call. He was creating a decoy conversation, leading her thoughts in a totally different direction as she sat listening to their conversation, but only hearing one side through Deke.

"Good boy Deke, you just keep her occupied with traffic and holiday shopping. I knew I liked you for a reason." Randal picked up on Deke's technique, and was genuinely impressed. "We'll have to devise a little code system from now on because our animal is a very smart one, and probably listening. This lion has already escaped from the cage. I'm afraid that for all I know it might even be a lioness, and one that's heading in your direction, if she ain't already in the area. I have no solid proof of anything, mind you, but it will not surprise me anymore if I'm correct with my suspicions." Deke quickly understood what he was saying.

Whoever the lioness was, Randal was sure that she had a scanner. Randal had expected the killer to utilize one, intercepting their messages by monitoring the frequencies used most often by cell phones.

"Oh I see. Was anyone you know involved in the accident?" With silky smoothness Deke played along, while asking Randal who was the person he suspected.

"Let's just say you don't know her personally, but if this is who I think it is, I've had affairs with her in the past. This specific breed of predator is highly unpredictable, and known to be very vicious when seeking running prey." From the tone of Randal's voice, and the way his sentences were constructed, Deke knew Randal was very concerned, but at the same time having a ball with the chase. This was the type of opportunity Texas Rangers lived for, putting all their skills into action after spending years gaining experience.

"Don't name the establishment you're at, just try giving me a landmark," Randal instructed him. Before Deke was able to answer, Zach changed his mind.

"On second thought, disregard that last request. Probably too risky, but we do need to rendezvous soon." Several moments of silence followed as Randal tried to think up a safe plan. Deke pretended to be listening while Amy eyed him closely from across the room.

"Noon tomorrow, stop somewhere crowded, page me from a pay phone. I'll call you back, and we'll plan our next move." It may be the simplest plan he had ever devised, but sometimes simplicity worked the best.

"Okay, I got it, and don't worry, we'll be fine. The Beatles are fed, loaded, and cocked for action." Hanging up the phone Deke turned to face Amy, pretending what Randal had said was harmless. He soon realized the acting hadn't fool her. She was looking at him with squinting eyes that spoke clearly; she was not falling for the act.

He was unprepared for a confrontation with her, and before he could stop himself he blew it by stating a ridiculous, "What?" Amy had all she needed to confirm what she thought. He was guilty as sin. Randal was playing ball with him and leaving her out.

"Do me a favor Deke, and don't make me pull everything out of you piece by piece. It's just as much my business as anyone's. I demand to be told everything about each development, just as it happens."

RESTING quietly in her motel room across the highway, Vanessa smiled, turning the scanner volume just low enough to monitor any calls. Every word said between Zach Randal and Deke Stone had been monitored, while filing her nails.

Though they managed to communicate fairly well without mentioning names or places, she had no difficulty understanding the exact meaning behind their words. The final phase to her plan may be put into action quicker than she had anticipated. Uneasiness settled about her, the gamble of dragging the game on just for the sport of it was too chancy. She feared for Amy Dodson, yet her safety was also at risk. While applying the polish to her nails, applying the even strokes, she decided to create the first diversion very soon. Vanessa Jansen's previous assumption that Zach Randal would never connect her to Amy's troubles, proved to be recklessly incorrect. She was, to her amazement, the prime suspect being hunted by the notorious Randal. The thought didn't create undue anxiety in her, but rather amused her, even to the point of admiring him and his skill as an investigator. The fact that Texas Ranger Zach Randal had referred to her as a lioness had sexually aroused her.

She still had an ace in the hole; they had no idea what type of vehicle she was driving. While her nails were drying, she removed the black pair of sweatpants and black sweatshirt from her bag. She also carried a black, doctor's bag, similar to those made famous in the days of house calls.

Opening the leather bag on the hotel bed, she inventoried her supplies. Several standard ten milliliter syringes, twenty-one gauge darts, and the incredibly small, newly designed, pistol-type, Veterinarian dart gun she'd recently acquired, were all set aside. A multiple-dose vial of the drug Ketamine was also taken from her bag. The vial contained fifty milliliters of isotonic solution containing ten milligrams of the solute, Ketamine, for each milliliter of the solution. It was enough Ketamine to keep a herd of elephants sleeping for hours.

As soon as her nails were dry, she abandoned the medical bag with its supplies, turning on the shower. The water was hot, effectively reviving her tired body. Dressing in the black sweatpants and sweatshirt after showering, she laced on a pair of black sneakers, then returned to her medical bag.

With a standard ten-milliliter syringe, Vanessa drew up a large dosage of Ketamine. She halved the dosage, transferring it into two twenty-one gauge darts. Loading the state-of-the-art dart gun with one of the filled darts, she neatly stored the second one inside the pistol-grip handle of the small devise, slipping it in a hidden pocket of her sweat pants. Vanessa did not feel comfortable with guns, but realizing she may have to protect herself, had resorted to what she had seen incapacitate large and angry canines. She thought of herself as being very clever, smiling at her ability to avoid handguns. When checking into the hotel where she stayed, Vanessa noticed a diner only a block down the street.

A sign in the window read, *Open All Night.* It was a weeknight, and chances were the diner's business would slow down after midnight. Brushing her hair straight back, rolling it into a bun, she pinned it up, out of her face. With one last look around the hotel room, making sure that nothing was left in sight or out of place; she opened the door and silently slipped out. This was just a dry run, scoping out the location, determining how many employees worked overnight.

Traffic had thinned out considerably. Being nearly midnight she was sure the time contributed to the reduced amount of vehicles on the highway. Without lifting her head, Dr. Vanessa Jansen walked briskly, looking directly at the ground twenty feet ahead of her until reaching the parking lot of the small diner.

Glancing through the large front window, Vanessa noticed only three customers, and two waitresses. The cook must be out of sight inside the small diner's kitchen. Satisfied with the surveillance, she spun quickly around heading back to her hotel room. Managing only a couple of steps in that direction, Dr. Vanessa Jansen felt a crushing blow to the right side of her head, accompanied by a loud noise that created a severe ringing sound in her ear.

Dazed and nearly unconscious, Vanessa slumped to the ground, unable to figure out what had happened. Powerful arms slipped under her falling body, lifting her up before being thrown over broad shoulders. Helplessly stunned from the blow to her head, Vanessa felt herself being carried away into the darkness.

CHAPTER

10

SOME TIME BACK, folks living in a small seaside community along the coast of Maine came to the conclusion that Jedediah Duncan must have been very unhappy. Apparently, after confronting some situation in life, which he'd decided he was incapable of managing, Jedediah placed the barrel of a.357 Magnum revolver in his mouth. With a last gesture of prayer he dropped to his knees, pulling the trigger.

His body had been discovered in a small closet of his bedroom. After his gruesome remains were located, a few people from the area, who knew him best, displayed surprise and shock before quickly accepting what obviously had been beyond anyone's power to change.

Neighbors alerted the local police after noticing a foul odor seeping out from somewhere within the house. His sister, who was away when the tragedy occurred, was not immediately notified after authorities discovered his body. This created an immediate air of doubt and suspicion in her mind. The entire incident became an immediate obsession.

Displaying the highest degree of shock and disbelief, she was the person who knew him best. Authorities probably should have listened to her as she repeatedly insisted Jedediah would never have ended his life intentionally. She'd shared the beachside home with him and had been steadfast in her refusal to accept his death; even after realizing that nothing she or anyone else could do would change what happened. In addition, it appeared as though the authorities were steadfast in their decision that it had been a suicide. She was quick in recognizing that she was alone in her conviction and any new discovery would have to be made on her own.

What Vanessa Jansen did not know and could not have known, was that she would eventually discover the truth about her brother's death. The brilliant accomplishment she would make through old-fashioned detective work was buried deep within a twisted and tragic sequence of events too incredible for anyone else to accept or believe. That extraordinary set of circumstances would be the exact reason that would keep her from sharing the story with authorities. Her findings would remain secret unless she could provide the facts, which were beyond any doubt. Only then would the bizarre account be accepted.

POWERFUL hands, callused and raw, gripped Jedediah with incredible force. In the darkness of his bedroom that fateful day, he couldn't tell who the massive strength belonged to, but he knew one thing for certain; he had been caught totally by surprise and he was terrified.

Jedediah was dragged from his bed in the predawn darkness. With his attacker behind him, jerking his body backward across the bedroom, it took every bit of his effort just to keep the silent marauder from jerking half the hair from his head.

Without warning, the violent attack stopped. Yet the hand that easily covered the top of his skull, was tightly clinched around the fist full of hair, refusing to loosen the grip it had on him. Attempting to regain his bearings, the young man quickly realized they were standing at the door to his closet. With a fearsome jerk, the closet door was flung open, and he and his captor entered the small space. Very few items were stored inside, leaving enough room for the deed to be committed. It was only a few weeks ago that Jedediah had moved into the home. Not enough possessions were brought back with him to fill the walk-in closet.

In a sudden twist of the situation, the powerful perpetrator turned the young man to face him, demanding that he remain on his knees. Without much choice, and unable to maneuver himself into an advantage, he obeyed.

"Well, I doubt that you have any idea why I'm here boy, but that won't make it any less dramatic when they find you." A gravel-like voice belched out in his face. The effect was nearly instant horror, accompanied by a dreaded feeling of impending doom.

Jedediah Duncan had only been living with his sister for six months. He could not imagine why such evil had targeted him, why such venomous hate was suddenly directed toward him. Jedediah had never experienced the feelings that came with having enemies. He was a friend to all, unaware of anyone holding such disregard for him.

Rumors about being associated with a beauty queen in Texas, who'd decided to dump him, preceded his return to Maine. Ever since, it had been a mystery to him where such fabrication could have evolved.

Something in his gut was telling him that this man was not only the source of such falsehoods, but with lightning speed it was also revealed to him that this was the father of the child Amy had been carrying, a child that he'd supported Amy in killing. It was at that moment that Jedediah Duncan knew death was literally breathing down his neck. His last thought was how incredibly loud the shot sounded.

VANESSA Jansen was a Doctor of Veterinary Medicine. She'd been married once, but for only a short two months. One day she awakened to discover her husband had abandoned her, giving no explanation for the departure, or his destination. The doctor's husband had more or less vanished, never to be heard from or seen again. It was the reason her last name was different from that of her brother.

The reason she'd given for abandoning her maiden name, after the failed marriage was that in her opinion Jansen had a more professional ring to it. She liked the sound of Dr. Jansen. It was only one among many reasons she was suspect, but never discovered.

Vanessa Jansen buried her brother, grieved for a reasonable amount of time, and began to ask questions about the life he'd lived before returning to Maine. Despite not finding anything to support her suspicions of foul play and with no firsthand accounts to support the rumors circulating, she determined Jedediah's death must be a direct result of some mystery involving the secret woman back in Texas.

Within only a couple of months, Dr. Vanessa Jansen had re-established her practice, far from Maine and the East Coast. Far away from the haunting memories of death and depression, it was where she claimed her healing awaited her.

When she was asked by the curious New Englander's where she was moving, Vanessa simply replied, "I'm going to find a few answers to life's many questions and maybe discover where true happiness exists." In reality, all that awaited Dr. Vanessa Jansen was a nightmare. Only time prevented the eventual collision of her simple goodness and the rotting evil that Sweetwater, Texas held crouching, waiting for her.

Soon after her arrival in Sweetwater, events began occurring that were of a horrid description and with increasing severity and frequency, until that day when three women were discovered butchered at Dodson's Breakfast and Bar-B-Que Cafe. Fortunately, Vanessa had become a close confidant of Amy Dodson, discovering much of the information that she needed. While managing to stay out of the fray of suspicion, she also managed to become Amy's closest and most trusted friend.

SERGEANT John Hadley was able to contact the two officers who were supposed to be watching Vanessa Jansen's home, instructing them to go ahead and investigate the residence, finding out if Dr. Vanessa was indeed at home. Somewhat taken by surprise by the request, the two veterans obeyed. Within fifteen minutes, they reported back to Sergeant Hadley. They were unable to find any trace of the veterinarian homeowner.

When Zach Randal's phone rang, Sergeant Hadley was ready with the update, confirming that indeed Dr. Jansen was missing from her residence, just as Zach Randal had suspected. Two extremely humiliated undercover officers were at that moment returning to headquarters, yet all the while, volunteering to drive straight to Amarillo to assist Ranger Randal if he still had any faith in them.

"It doesn't seem possible John, but that animal doctor, Vanessa Jansen, just may be the killer we've been searching for." His confession, until now, had been very difficult to admit, and was shocking, almost beyond his belief. But it did add up very nicely in that direction.

Sergeant John Hadley was instructed by Randal to scour State Police computer files, FBI files, even motor vehicle registration files, for anything that had Vanessa Jansen's name attached. He wanted every available bit of information related to her, including drivers license, medical license, marriage license, DEA license, and anything else Hadley could think of, regardless of how remote, or how outdated.

The Ketamine that Dr. Josh Sinclair reportedly discovered in the three bodies from Dodson's Breakfast and Bar-B-Que Cafe, suddenly made perfect sense, especially since it had also been found in blood samples taken from the Beatles several weeks prior. The time span, and the most damnable piece of information of all, Vanessa's confabulated story about her fiancé killed in a tragic accident, seemed to nail her backside to the barn door, being the only plausible suspect for all the killings.

"Well, you want those two fellows to drive up, just in case you need the help? They're at a standstill here in Sweetwater. Ain't nobody left here to investigate anymore, even if we're still not sure where Vanessa Jansen has vanished off to."

"Hell I guess so. No telling what we might run up against the way things are going." Zach Randal's world was the perfect example for inconsistency. One moment he was racing at breakneck speeds, the next he had no idea what direction to go in. His one piece of luck came when he decided to profile the killer, with almost nothing to go on but instinct. After choosing her as one of his model serial killers, he made a request that Dr. Josh Sinclair go with an assumption the killer was female. It was a hunch, a fluke request, and without any solid reason for the request. Dr. Sinclair gave him every reason to believe the killer may indeed be Vanessa. If he had not proceeded with the decision to run her name through state police computer files, he'd never have found a way to forgiven himself.

STRICKEN with a horrifying fear, the physical immobility was what she noticed first. With ankles tightly bound and her hands tied behind her back, she desperately struggled in the storage area of the van.

A combination of darkness, total disorientation, a possible concussion, and an overwhelming fear, effectively rendered Vanessa Jansen incapacitated. She remembered that she was walking when suddenly a loud explosion occurred at her right ear. A sensation of falling, and her vision blurring, felt just before losing consciousness. Moving as if in and out of a thick fog created by semi-consciousness, things remained fuzzy, with lights flashing behind her eyes, and all torturously timed to the painful pounding in her head. He'd tied her ankles together before restraining her wrists behind her back. Vanessa only moaned in despair as her efforts to resist were easily stopped. A voice sounding like rocks in a sack being dragged across a wooden bridge, grunted in anger. Large hands squeezed her with incredible strength in response to her struggling. Heart-stopping fear shocked her like an electrical current. A display of his intention abruptly ended any thought of escape, as Vanessa found herself completely helpless. She recalled a violent, bouncing while on the broad shoulders of a powerful man. Large, strong hands held her lower legs as her head dangled loosely behind, facing the ground in terror. Her captor ran quickly down dark, wet, sewer-smelling alleyways. Finally stopping at a garbage smelling dumpsite, her body was lifted high above the ground.

Her next memory was of waking in the back of a van. Opening her eyes wide, trying to focus on the driver, she could only see the outline of a head with long hair loosely hanging from it. With no regard for anything or anyone on the dark street, they raced recklessly, before finally exiting the city, taking the interstate.

Reaching highway speed, she started taking mental notes of anything recognizable to her. Highway sounds, traffic congestion, train whistles, anything that she recognized was stored within her memory. After considerable effort, she was able to bring the panic levels down, allowing her to think rationally.

It happened so quickly that Vanessa was unable to recall the events previous to the explosive blow. The ear-ringing clap associated with getting hit was the extent of what she was capable of remembering. Battling with the shock of total helplessness, parts of her mind realized how dangerous the situation she had become a victim. With every passing moment, she felt herself slipping away while in the rear of the van. Vanessa was becoming an unknown, falling deeper and deeper into a void, a bottomless hell.

The woman kidnapped along the dark streets of Amarillo was now the number five victim unfortunately captured by the serial rapist, now labeled by officials as a serial killer. The four victims who preceded the current one, never made it back from their ordeal. Their bodies were discovered within several hundred yards of each other in a wooded area north of the city.

A wave of tortured madness was beginning to rise within the woman bouncing around in the dark. Forcing herself to accept the facts, realizing the only way to survive the ordeal was if she didn't panic, remaining calm was still nearly impossible. Fear of not being able to recall anything prevented her from being able to devise a plan. There had to be a way of escape, despite her failure to recall who she was.

THE two men spoke very little as they began the four hour drive to Amarillo. Their embarrassment was painful as they realized how that veterinarian, woman doctor, made them fools. Saving face was their only option, and that was by volunteering to meet Ranger Randal, somewhere north of Amarillo, and committing to catch the murderer. Sergeant Hadley was not a verbally abusive man like most senior officers. His method was just the opposite of those who yelled and screamed, resembling tantrum throwing toddlers. His was the torture inflicted through silence. As long as the effort of the officer under him was reasonable, he saw no justification in chastising a man like a child.

Zach Randal found himself again catapulted from one extreme to another. When he'd last spoke to Hadley, it was clear he wanted no additional radio or cell phone contact until the following day. As he progressed through the city of Amarillo, heading north, the Jeep caught his eye. It was the blue vehicle belonging to Deke Stone, sitting parked under the street lamp at an economy hotel.

Just south of the Colorado state line, in northern New Mexico, sat the town of Raton. Located at the outer edge of the Rocky Mountains, Texas Ranger Zachary Wyatt Randal had forgotten how beautiful and breathtaking this area of the country was. Like switching from day to night, the mountains contrasted to the flat plains running throughout Texas. Raton was a sample of the majesty and power flowing from the Rocky Mountains. Although still early November, snow covered each of the higher peaks, cool breezes sucking the humidity of the lower elevations away from the land. Although Zach Randal stayed ahead of those he was supposed to be following, he had decided to drive straight through to Raton. He'd wait for Dan Baker and Bill Frye once he arrived. A rendezvous with Deke, to plan their strategy and options, had to take place before Vanessa Jansen discovered them, if she ever showed up.

Because he had a head as thick and as stubborn as a mule's, he continued to beat himself ruthlessly for not anticipating the possibility of such developments. If he'd been prepared beforehand, no pursuit would even be necessary like the one they now found themselves involved with. In addition to the tangled web he found himself in, was the nagging question regarding Vanessa. As strong as his gut feeling was on this, he'd hate to blunder it, falsely accusing someone before having the slightest bit of proof.

She was involved, of that he was sure, but to what degree was still impossible to discover. Yet, with such certainty of her involvement, why had she not shown up, or been heard from for over twelve hours? Deciding not to pursue Amy as she fled the area didn't fit the profile that the Texas Ranger had for Dr. Jansen.

North of Amarillo, Zach Randal was in deep thought when his cell phone rang. It surprised him so much he slammed down on his brakes before figuring out what the hell it was.

"Hello! You still awake Zachary?" His old friend John Hadley was checking up on him. When he had no update in an investigation to call him with, John still called his friend on the cell phone, just making sure he hadn't fallen asleep. The friendship had weathered many stormy seasons.

"Why would I be sleeping?" Randal was not going to let his friend think he appreciated the call, even though he did.

"The 'Jedediah' fellow mentioned by Dr. Vanessa while dozing in your truck, was in fact her dead brother. He committed suicide six months after moving away from Sweetwater, which was three years ago." Sergeant John Hadley was able to find out this crucial information quicker than expected; launching right into the juicy development as soon as he was certain Zach was indeed awake.

"Well, I'll be a monkey's," Randal began.

"No, don't say it Zach. That makes your sister an ape. Don't you have more respect for your relatives?" Hadley loved to correct Zach, even though he knew Zach had no sister.

Her past may not match the life of a felon, but more than enough controversy and secrecy was evident to make him skeptical. The horrible suicide of her brother seemed to be the catalyst, which started this cycle of events. Answers had to be hidden somewhere in Jedediah Duncan's past, when he was still a resident of Sweetwater.

As he struggled with the bizarre circumstances, Zach Randal realized how the situation had become confusing, on both sides. Nearly certain that Dr. Vanessa Jansen was involved; he was puzzled about where she could have disappeared to. He found that he was now involved in what was called 'a blind pursuit.'

DEKE and Ringo slept together on the floor, while Amy shared a bed with John, Paul, and George, on a queen-sized mattress. Everyone seemed comfortable and at home with the accommodations.

With the first hint of sunlight filtering through the window, Amy awoke. Remaining in bed, she stared at the ceiling, wondering where they'd be going today and when would this crazy nightmare end. She was not as afraid as when the harassment had first started. She didn't know at what point of time she'd noticed the fear subsiding, but was sure it had to be sometime after Deke had entered the picture. It puzzled her that someone who was a total stranger could have such an effect on her. Here it was only the third day of her life after meeting Deke Stone, and already her courage and determination were renewed. She was as sure now as she had been weeks ago that danger lie ahead, only now she feared that the danger might not be associated with a criminal, but with a friend, a new friend. Stealing her thoughts away from the subject, she realized that a certain amount of infatuation was mixed in with her emotions. In addition, although she knew it was a gamble to pretend she were uninterested, she also knew the atmosphere around them sparked with electricity when together in the same room. She worried that others noticed it too and must do her best not to encourage what in the end might be a mistake.

From on the other side of the bed she heard a slight stirring. Leaning over the side she erupted into laughter as she saw Ringo and Deke sleeping together, embraced like elderly people seeking warmth, not passion.

Opening his eyes slowly, Deke focused on Amy leaning over the side of the bed, smiling down at him. She was a picture of beauty even at this time of the morning. A smile so unpretentious that it lit up the entire room. Marveling at his feelings toward her, he came back to reality. The improbability that anything could last seemed doomed by their bizarre situation. Additional events of any high emotional state were a risk.

"Good morning Miss Amy." His greeting sounded so natural that her automatic response was an even bigger smile. Subconsciously they were becoming friends quicker than planned, but time was one thing they were not guaranteed.

Deke felt a little uncomfortable with the situation, especially when he imagined what he must look like at this time of the day. Her beauty was ever present. All the while, he was sure a nice carpet pattern had formed across one side of his face with his hair matted completely opposite of its natural part.

"We had best be getting on the move. I feel like Ranger Randal is in a mood worse than a mother hen looking for lost chicks, wanting to meet with us to discuss what he was unable to take the chance at saying over the cell phone last night."

Amy was already rolling to the other side of the bed, a sheet wrapped around her. Deke suspected she'd head in a straight line toward the bathroom. This was another first. He did not have to share a bathroom the night he'd slept at Amy's, since an extra bath was available. He wondered how long he might have to wait to pee, having no clue whether she was the kind of woman who rebuilt herself from the ground up every morning or one of the lucky who splashed water on her face, re-hydrating each cell, and in a snap, the re-hydrated cells puffed out to a finished product.

While waiting, Deke began picking up around the room, folding his clothes into a tight ball before neatly shoving them into his duffel bag. Within only ten minutes, Amy emerged, flawless. He suspected she was going to make some lucky guy happy one day.

"Your turn," she announced happily, beginning to pack her bag. He hoped to be back on the road in less than an hour. Sticking to their original plan, they would head north. Deke was familiar with this part of the country and decided the best route was straight through to Raton. Interstate 25 would take them on into Trinidad. Once in Colorado, staying on Interstate 25, Deke planned to head due north, past Pueblo, into Colorado Springs. Green Mountain Falls was only thirteen miles northwest of Colorado Springs, where his humble, log cabin sat nestled in the wild country of the Rocky Mountain Range.

It was a full day of traveling. Amarillo was nearly four hundred miles south of Green Mountain Falls, and their total travel time was going to be at least eight hours. Randal instructed him to stop somewhere crowded around noontime and page him from a pay phone. Deke eventually had to inform Amy of the entire conversation between him and Randal the night before. She would not tolerate being uninformed, or treated like a child. With no idea where Zach Randal planned to be by noontime or even what state he'd be in, it was as good a guess as anything to assume he knew of their plans to be somewhere south of Trinidad, possibly not quite out of New Mexico by noon. It was a guessing game that Deke decided should not affect them either way. Amy was also in agreement with him. It was not worth getting too worked up about.

As they left Amarillo, north on Interstate 27, taking them to Texas Highway 87, he began telling Amy about his home. The surrounding views of the Rocky Mountain peaks were described to her. It brought forth a response from her that he had not witnessed from anyone since childhood. Amy was as anxious as an eight year old, waiting to see the mountains for the first time in her life. It was a sight that he could only describe as magical, and it had a tremendously pleasing effect on him.

The information that was passed on by Randal last night did have somewhat of a negative impact on Amy. She found it a total mystery that Vanessa Jansen may have some hidden evil desire to see her harmed, or dead. It was against the intuition she possessed, as all women do, to think a hidden Vanessa Jansen was beneath the one she had grown to know and love. It was too much of a total departure from what she'd witnessed in Vanessa over the years. Naturally, she pointed out that Zach Randal had no proof to support his theory. Either Zach had nothing to use as proof, or he didn't think it was important enough to mention the fact.

Amy quickly decided that it was such an unpleasant subject for her that they would not discuss it any further, at least until they were given additional information, supportive of the accusation.

WITH his stomach growling, Zach Randal entered Raton. It was still very early in the morning, but he was determined to locate an all night diner where he could at least pick up a sandwich and coffee. Suddenly, deep in thought, a revelation occurred to him. Vanessa might not be in route to Amarillo. Maybe she wasn't even aware of Amy's departure, but in route to another location. The night Amy called him, certain someone was at the ranch, he was sure that he saw someone running across the property. Yet, either whoever it was had been dropped on foot or had a vehicle parked miles away. If Vanessa left secretly with the desk sergeant, where was he taking her? John Hadley reported the desk sergeant was back at headquarters, very soon after leaving Vanessa's home. He needed to call Hadley, finding out exactly where those two undercover officers were. With the way circumstances kept changing, he might have them running back and forth across the state all night.

He did not know about Vanessa Jansen's brother when he spoke to Deke the night before. It wasn't until later that he'd received the call from Sergeant Hadley with the new information. Jedediah Duncan had committed suicide years ago, six months after returning to Maine where his sister lived. He had been living in the town of Sweetwater, before returning to live with Vanessa. Apparently, the suicide of her brother had affected Vanessa in a very powerful way, possibly to the extent that it drove her to the bizarre behaviors surrounding Amy Dodson for the last twenty-four months.

It was just as Zach Randal was turning into the parking lot of a Pitt Grill Restaurant when it occurred to him that Jedediah Duncan might well have been acquainted with Amy Dodson. The possibility of the two having any romantic involvement seemed remote. He had more confidence than that in Amy. Not that she was above the emotional involvement required for a romance, but trusted Amy would have been completely honest about such a thing, especially after Zach had brutally grilled her on every one of her past relationships when the investigation started. The possibility of anything other than a casual friendship occurring was remote. While it was more instinct than actual proof, Zach relied on it, and he believed this might be the missing clue he'd been searching. When he thought about how Vanessa had reacted to the memory of Jedediah, his confidence in the theory only grew stronger.

While sitting in the parking lot, he dialed the Nolan County Sheriff Department. He decided not to use the Hot Line; if a snitch was involved, he wanted to give them a reason to worry. It was better to assume any information he and Hadley shared over the phone would be monitored, and then he'd be able to expect the next move. Zach knew that whoever was listening would eventually slip up, and the fact that they didn't know he was expecting their next move, might be the break he needed.

"John, where are those two fellows that are heading in this direction?" he asked, hearing as Sergeant Hadley picked up. Unprepared to hear Zach Randal calling him on the regular phone line, Hadley hesitated.

"Uh Zach, I think we have a bad connection. Don't you want to call back, maybe we'll get a clear line?" he hinted. He was trying his best to tell him they were not on a safe line.

"No, this connection is fine John. I've got my reasons. Just get in touch with those two, and have them turn back. I don't care where they are. Tell them I need for them to head out to Amy's ranch, give the place a good look-over. I've got a hunch," Zach stated.

"All right big man. I'll get them right on it. Anything in particular that you want them to look for?" Hadley questioned. He was fishing for Zach's sudden decision to turn them around, knowing it was probably hopeless. He'd never get a straight answer to a straight question from Zach.

"Just have them do whatever undercover cops do, look for anything unusual," he replied. Without another word, he hung up.

BACK in Wichita Falls, FBI Forensic Pathologist Dr. Josh Sinclair, was busy performing a myriad of selected laboratory tests, checking out one of his own theories about the investigation. As he began to receive data from the testing, he became somewhat baffled. Through information that Texas Ranger Zach Randal had shared with him, the suspect was thought to be a woman. With an enthusiasm he'd developed concerning the murders, he'd managed to coax a theory out of Zach Randal. That resulted in him making certain assumptions about the evidence, assumptions that he should have been able to prove, if correctly performing the right tests.

He knew that the perpetrator that subdued the Chesapeake Bay Retrievers when they were discovered locked in the upstairs bedroom at the ranch had used Ketamine. Utilizing this canine sedative gave the person guilty of darting the Chessies a powerful advantage, allowing him or her time handling the heavy dogs, not having to worry about being attacked. Conveniently, this created a situation, which a woman would easily be capable of accomplishing. In addition, Dr. Sinclair also discovered high concentrations of Ketamine present in the blood samples taken from all three of the slain women from the cafe, again enabling the deed to easily be managed by a woman. Only one additional test was needed to confirm his theory, leading to the conclusion Ranger Zach Randal was also heading.

His opinion was that it might be possible to ensure all the circumstantial evidence, which was all they had so far, pointing to one and only one perpetrator. Confident that his deductive reasoning was correct, the test was set up and performed. However, the test results were not exactly what he'd expected, and Josh Sinclair was rather surprised, especially when he considered the implications.

Since Dr. Sinclair was a professional and a scientist, results that were contrary to his expectations were not considered disappointing. Having new factors plugged into investigations only increased the intrigue, creating situations that were much more challenging and solving the mystery much more rewarding. If anything, the new test results excited him.

A total of five packages had been mailed to Amy. Ranger Randal had sent all of them directly to the lab. They were all analyzed, according to procedure. Each of the packages contained body parts of a healthy, Caucasian male, probably in his late twenties to early thirties. But that information alone was useless, leading him in no specific direction narrow enough to realistically warrant an investigation. Everything led to a general conclusion about the amount of time needed to process common denominators, if any.

With the new test results in hand; Dr. Josh Sinclair was busy attempting to explain to Sergeant John Hadley how imperative it was that he be connected with Ranger Randal. It was what he considered to be a matter of life and death.

THE cabin was at least fifteen miles from the main highway, leading back to civilization. Constructed from pine logs and mountain stone, it was the perfect hideout, offering the seclusion sought after by so many romantically involved couples.

The situation that it was now being used for was far from romantic, and the couple that occupied it was the least possible to be considered by anyone as seeking romance.

She was still hog-tied in the rear of the parked van. The companions that accompanied her since the initial abduction and through the terrifying two-hour ride remained with her still. Vanessa never invited them, but confusion, pain, paralyzing fear, and amnesia, refused to abandon her. The most recent acquired companion: amnesia, was not appreciated at first, but as time wore on, developed into the most persistent and worst of her fears.

Unable to recall anything, her age, her name, she wondered if the end result would be a total mental collapse, or if she was in that condition previous to being struck on the head.

Vanessa Jansen lay face down, cold and shivering, but aware of the daylight approaching. Her captor made trip after trip from the van to the cabin. She supposed, from the sounds he made, unloading supplies of some kind. Occasionally, she would hear him calling out to her, a voice croaking deeply, dragging words from his throat with such deep resonance that the process sounded painful.

"You still alive bitch? Don't you die on me! We got a whole lot to talk about, bitch!" He was completely void of emotion. But she sensed a deeper reason to fear the voice other than its lack of emotion. Deep grunting sounds came from his direction periodically, completely confusing her, until she identified it as his laughter. She had remained silent throughout the entire trip and continued her refusal to speak. The nightmare she found herself to be stuck in was easier to escape if she continued to pretend it was only a nightmare. By remaining silent long enough, she imagined he wouldn't find her. It was all a part of the overwhelming trauma associated with feelings of impending doom and her injured brain attempting to devise a strategy, leading to escape.

When he came for her, the additional daylight allowed her a sight of who had so easily taken her captive. Feeling as helpless as a bird, trapped by a cat, she recoiled in shock at his appearance.

His size was intimidating. A large man who was well over six feet tall stood before her. She judged him to be in his early thirties. The man had a large square head with fine, blond hair hanging to his shoulders. Deeply tanned, his body also looked square, reminding her of the massively built men roaming Muscle Beach in Southern California. She was relieved somewhat by the fact that he wore dark sunglasses, hiding the piercing eyes she knew must have been looking down at her.

With not so much as a grunt, he lifted her completely out of the vehicle, throwing her once again over his shoulders. He carried her into the dark interior of the cabin; her body was handled with the gentleness of a butcher hanging sides of beef on meat hooks.

A mattress was thrown upon the wooden floor, in a corner of the cabin, next to a fireplace. Using quarter inch ski-rope, with one end tied to an exposed wooden beam overhead, he looped the other end around her neck. She was given enough slack in the rope allowing her to lie on the mattress.

After being secured to the corner, he shoved her down. His strength startled her. Walking off in the direction of the cabin's kitchen, he rumbled forth with a bit of his laughter.

"We hope your stay will be a pleasant one bitch. Nothing has been spared in making certain that you are comfortable, getting your money's worth," he remarked sarcastically. She was beginning to get the feeling that he knew who she was. His calm demeanor was one of total relaxation. It was clear that he feared nothing.

Remaining silent, she began hoping he might call her by name, clearing up some of the fog surrounding her. But instinctively she knew not to reveal anything about her memory loss, believing it might deteriorate the situation. Her fear was of such intensity that she was already resigned to the fact he was planning to kill her. Still, death by his hand didn't create half the dread created by what he was planning to do before killing her.

While he was in the kitchen she frantically tried to get her hands free of the rope tied behind her back. While struggling, she continued to listen for sounds from the kitchen, telling her that he was busy, fearful he may catch her attempting to escape, only to become angry, and kill her all the more quickly.

The knots that he used to tie the rope around her wrists and ankles only tightened with every effort to loosen them. Suddenly, while absorbed in her attempt, she realized it had become very silent. Slowly looking up toward the kitchen, she saw him standing in the doorway. He just stood quietly watching her struggle, a smile of satisfaction smeared across his face. She became deathly still, waiting for his response.

"Pretty good knots aren't they?" he questioned. He was obviously humored by her vain struggling, and proud of his ability to keep her helpless.

"Why don't you save your strength? Look, I'll even make it easy on you. If you're a good girl, just maybe, I'll cut those loose for you. Now, you'll really have to be on your best behavior. I don't want to have to use excessive force on you. It would be a shame to damage such a rare catch. What do you say, is it a deal?" he patronized her.

She supposed that was his game. He would now begin to humiliate her, eventually thinking she'd beg for mercy. Not knowing where the stubbornness was originating from, she found herself glaring in anger. The fear was miraculously evaporating, and a ruthless hate began to surface. It may have been when she realized he planned to degrade her, or some other unknown reason. But a definite change was occurring, a frightening change, a transition from thinking that he may know who she is, to one where she was supposed to know who he was.

Seeing her change of attitude surprised him and he responded by mocking her, "What's this? You're getting mad at me bitch! That's either a joke, or you're trying a bluff." His lips were in a pout as he spoke to her. He began taunting her, treating her like a child. It was his sarcastic way of responding that began to give her hope. He wasn't going to kill her right away; he wanted to play with her. She was here for a reason, a reason that for the time being, only he knew. In time, she determined that she would remember, turning the tables on him. A certain confidence was beginning to grow. It must have had to do with who she had been, because it definitely didn't have to do with the person that she felt she was now.

She wanted badly to know who he was, but couldn't chance asking. If she were supposed to know his identity, asking would tip him off that she had no way of remembering anything.

Squatting on the dirty mattress, bound hand and foot, she silently stared him down while he pulled up a chair. Turning it, the chair's back facing her, he slowly sat down. Biting into a large apple, he watched her with amusement.

CHAPTER

11

THE WEATHER WAS turning from a bright sunny morning with crisp northerly breezes, into one with overcast, gray skies. A threat of rain was in the air, maybe even snowfall once they reached the higher elevations.

Deke had become quiet after telling Amy about a number of the sights they would be seeing reaching the Rocky Mountains. In fact, before he realized it, he noticed that he had been talking for quite a while as she sat listening, rarely responding to what he decided must have been endless chatter. Nearly two hours still remained before it was lunchtime and to carry out Ranger Randal's order, paging him from a pay phone.

As the day deteriorated from bright and sunny, to dreary and cold, Amy sat staring at the vast expanse of tundra and prairie, wondering how it was possible for majestic snow-covered mountains to appear over the horizon. She was very bothered with the implication that had been made by Deke Stone and Zach Randal, suggesting Dr. Vanessa was involved in the horrible things, which had begun two years ago. Although she had not realized the strange coincidence of everything starting about the same time Vanessa Jansen moved to Sweetwater to begin her veterinary practice.

Amy and Vanessa seemed to hit it off right from the start. It was as though they had been friends for years. Amy even shared with Vanessa very private details about her life, details that she would never have told to just anyone.

Some of her past haunted her, and she desperately needed someone to talk with from time to time, especially when the memories hit the hardest. All Amy was capable of doing was to isolate herself, crying for hours. In those desperate moments of her life in the past two years, Vanessa Jansen held her close while she wept. Amy never felt that Vanessa was judging her. She never offered meaningless advice, only held her. More than anything, it was what Amy needed. Of all the people she knew, Vanessa was the first she had trusted with her secret.

THREE years earlier, Amy met a man who seemed to be the answer to all of her prayers. In the beginning, they began seeing each other only casually. Amy would drive to El Paso to see him, where she'd met him at a weekend business conference that he also had attended, roughly twice a month, every other weekend. The fact that this fellow lived somewhere other than Sweetwater was a big plus in her opinion. No one suspected her of having a secret relationship, not to mention an eventual full-blown love affair, and that was just fine with Amy.

The business conference was sort of a workshop and seminar, geared to assist small business owners in handling success. While at the seminar, she met Jack Vermette. He was a professional diver working for several major oil companies. They offered contracts to Jack for underwater equipment salvage.

He was an extremely confident man, one of whom Amy became immediately attracted. Much to her surprise, Jack confessed to having the same strong attraction for her. They saw each other every other weekend. Amy would drive to El Paso, making it clear to him that for specific reasons she preferred to continue their relationship in a quiet manner.

At first, Jack seemed to understand her motives, keeping their relationship a secret. But as time passed, he began pressuring Amy. His calm and mature way of handling the strange arrangement began to undergo a change. It was not a change for the better.

Jack became possessive. Alas, he revealed his true colors to a distraught Amy, who for some unknown reason thought this man was going to be different. From the suspicions that he had developed about her choice to keep their affair a secret, he developed bizarre ideation's, and began accusing Amy of a number of wild behaviors, among which was the standard accusation that she was seeing other men when not with him. He had decided that it was the only reason she'd insisted that they always meet in El Paso, never during the middle of a week, and only on specific weekends. In truth, Amy was still nursing what she considered a fragile state of affairs at the cafe. The weekends that she did not meet him in El Paso, Amy was busy working at the cafe.

After they had been seeing each other for six months, the frequency had increased to every weekend. The kind, understanding, mature man she thought she had discovered, turned into an insanely, jealous individual that had become unpredictable. Amy began to fear him, feeling trapped, and worst of all she was three months pregnant.

She kept the pregnancy a secret from Jack, waiting for a time when she felt he could be approached safely. A time when they could honestly discuss how this unplanned pregnancy may affect their relationship, and eventually their lives. Before that day came, Jack was called upon to dive at a sight in the Gulf of Mexico.

A drilling platform had capsized in rough seas, settling ninety feet down on the sandy bottom. Oil executives were determined to salvage everything they could, and Jack was one of the best. He left after much deliberation, reluctant leaving Amy alone, out of his sight for what could be more than a month. The fact that he needed the work was what eventually made the decision for him. He had been passing up good contract work lately, obsessed with making certain Amy had no secret lover.

Two weeks after he left, Amy decided to write him, mailing the letter to a production platform located south of the Louisiana coast, in block 175 of Southwest Pass. She planned to break the news by mail, telling Jack about her pregnancy. However, at the same time, and in the same letter, she informed him that she had serious doubts about her keeping the child. She was planning to have an abortion. Her biggest reason for this decision was her belief that their relationship could never last. She felt trapped and just wasn't ready to settle down with anyone. She explained how the cafe and the success of her business consumed most of her life. She also made it clear; she had no time for marriage or motherhood in her life.

It was a cruel thing to do to Jack, but the fear she felt whenever thinking about his behavior, left her to think it was the safest way for him to find out. She hoped that before finishing with the salvage contract, and returning, he would have time to think through the situation and agree with her wishes, keeping his temper in check.

Amy never heard from Jack Vermette again. While still on assignment at the submerged portion of the drilling rig an accident had occurred. A seventy-foot crew boat was arriving one night, with supplies for the salvage team. They were only a couple of hundred yards away from the dive sight, when the skipper suffered a heart attack. Slumping over onto the instrument board in the wheelhouse, his hand on the throttle of the twin diesel engines, he accidentally gunned the two engines to maximum r.p.m. A horrendous collision occurred between the dive boat and the crew boat. Jack Vermette was one of the seven men on the salvage crew listed as missing and presumed dead. After search and rescue efforts failed to locate his body, he was declared dead.

Amy never received any response to the letter she wrote Jack, and she was unable to find out for sure if he had even received it. Because of the horrible accident that claimed his life, Amy hoped the letter had never reached him, saving him the anguish and heartache that she knew the decision would bring. Since their relationship had never been discovered, she was spared the discomfort of being consoled and decided not to attend the memorial service held for him in El Paso. In fact, their secret romance had been kept such a good secret that Texas Ranger Zach Randal had just a few weeks earlier become privy to the couple's affair. Soon after finding out about the accident, while grieving in secret, Amy started doubting her ability to go through with an abortion.

From out of nowhere, almost miraculously, a compassionate young man entered into her life. It was while calling a crisis hot line for assistance, feeling she had reached the end of her rope, that Amy became acquainted with Jedediah Duncan.

Jedediah Duncan was a volunteer crisis counselor that occasionally staffed a 1-800 crisis hot line, the night shift. Amy made several calls over a two-week period, speaking to Jedediah, who she'd found to be the only person she could reach out and talk with. He was harmless, just a voice on the other end of a phone line. He was a person that Amy could call without feeling the pressure of any commitment. No strings attached, just a voice in the night, or more accurately, Jedediah had become just a listening ear in the night.

While sharing her fears with Jedediah late one night, he uncharacteristically volunteered something that shook her to the core. What Jedediah said wasn't cruel or rude; in fact, it was more of a question than it was a statement. "Why are you so afraid to commit your love to anyone, including yourself, Amy?" Jedediah inquired. If his question had not been asked with such genuine concern Amy would have hung up immediately. The urge to discontinue the conversation was such a powerful reflex that it startled her. That was when Amy realized the question from Jedediah, although harmless and innocent, had hit her in a very vulnerable area.

She hesitated for a bit, but eventually answered him, surprising her. Even though she denied his observation, Amy found herself inviting him over to the ranch for supper, just for the opportunity to prove him wrong.

That first meeting between the two became a point of revelation for Amy. Jedediah had been right. As their friendship grew, she strengthened, since friendship was all he was offering. Jedediah Duncan was different from any of the other men she had known. He was actually comfortable with the person he was, not trying to become someone he wasn't, never pressuring her in any way for more than the friendship that they had.

It had been Jedediah holding her hand, comforting her, as they entered the abortion clinic. He never gave his opinion unless she asked. He did not judge her decision, nor did he try to persuade her in another direction. Jedediah only supported his friend, Amy. After the abortion, Jedediah told Amy that he was leaving, returning to Maine, where his only remaining family member lived. He never did mention who that family member was, and for a while, Amy wondered if the family member was a parent or sibling. Little did she know the possibility of finding the answer to that mystery would one day present itself to her and nearly at her very doorstep.

Amy found it oddly disturbing when she realized how brokenhearted she was to see Jedediah go. Jedediah did not depart without first teaching Amy many valuable lessons. One of the lessons he reminded her of just before leaving had been about the importance of friends, and how they were everywhere. The only difference between the person who had few friends and someone who had an endless supply had to do with what it was that person sought most in life. Becoming someone's friend and looking for someone to be a friend were very different. It was going to be Amy's choice Jedediah had said. She would have to decide whether or not to take a gamble on life, giving people second chances, and trusting more in herself. The greatest pleasures were directly proportionate to the amount of passion we felt about life.

Amy did not hear from Jedediah again. She assumed that he was somewhere, helping others as he had helped her, giving his friendship freely and seeking nothing in return.

That was a couple of years ago, and in only a few months, the very thing Jedediah taught her, happened. She met a new friend, Vanessa Jansen. Amy had been able to share everything with Vanessa, and their friendship grew. Amy eventually came to love Vanessa Jansen as a sister. Now it was being suggested by the two people risking their lives for her, that Vanessa was involved in her troubles, maybe even the person responsible.

Amy was afraid of what they were suggesting, afraid for Vanessa. But even more afraid that she might have to open up, exposing her deepest wound to save Vanessa, telling Zach Randal and Deke Stone about the secret. It angered her that she may have to sacrifice the most intimate and private part of her life. She would wait; wait until no other options were available, for the sake of her friendship.

Deke slowed the Jeep, pulling off the highway. A row of pay phones was lined against the side of a gas station. Looking at Amy with determination, he displayed an attitude filled with optimism, attempting to break through the walls that she had placed around the tender places of her heart. Reaching out, Deke touched her hand lightly. "We all have moments of despair Amy. But rarely do we have someone so anxious to assist us from that which brings such heartache. Don't let the rare moments pass without taking what is freely offered." Touching the softness of her cheek lightly, Deke turned, heading for the phones. It was time to contact Randal.

"WHERE are you?" Sergeant Hadley asked when Randal answered his phone. "I'm just getting back into my vehicle, still in the parking lot of some greasy spoon just outside Raton. Why? What have you come up with?" he asked.

"Your hunch was right I guess, about Amy's place. Dan Baker and Bill Frye went snooping around. The place was as quiet as a graveyard, except for the barn doors. They were wide open. Ain't no vehicles parked in that barn Zach," Hadley stated.

"Damn! I should have guessed it. That's why she was dropped off I'll bet. Now she's in Amy's vehicle with a head start to who knows where. Damn she's sharp!" Zach Randal responded.

"Put out an APB for that Land Cruiser, John. You might want to call the state boys in New Mexico, having them look for it too, and include Colorado State Patrol. No telling where she is by now," Randal concluded.

"Well, I'll be. She is a slick one. Zach, I don't know where we missed it, but from the get go we had nothing to go on, and all of a sudden we have more than we can handle. You getting the same feeling?" Hadley inquired.

"Yeah John. I know what you mean. Speak for yourself though; being led by the nose is better than having to follow no scent at all. What else you got for me?" Randal asked.

"I got that doctor back at the FBI lab getting the drizzles to be connected to you. Says he has some critical information to give you," Hadley answered him wondering what the FBI doctor and Zach Randal had up their sleeve.

"Well, put him on John! I don't have all night. Hell, we may even have more stuff to help confuse us," Randal stated sarcastically.

"Hello Ranger Randal, this is Dr. Josh Sinclair," the forensic pathologist began.

"Yeah Doc, I know who you are. We can dispense with the introductions from now on. Just get to the juicy stuff, and Doc, talk English for me okay?" Zach Randal requested.

"Absolutely Ranger; however, what I have to relay to you must be preceded with at least a brief explanation to ensure your ability to understand the reasons behind why it is so imperative this not be mishandled. By applying test results in the most effective manner and obtaining the highest possible degree of each potential result of which, very possibly, could be in a wide variety of combinations while avoiding parallel conclusions, it is possible to obtain critical evidence. Please bear with me." The forensic pathologist was persuasive with whatever he was trying to explain to Zach.

"For crying out loud Doc! The only thing I think you guys need more training with is the fundamental aspect on the English language." Zachary Randal rolled his eyes back while wiping his huge bear-sized hand through his hair. Grabbing his Stetson, Zach popped it back down on his head. "Okay Doc. You guys have to get your kicks too I guess," Zach Randal chuckled.

"Thank you sir. In order to obtain specific results and an analysis of toxic substances when testing human tissue, which includes blood, it is often vital that the laboratory have a specific drug, or toxin, suspected in the sample identified, beforehand. In other words, unless the lab knows to look for a certain substance, such as Ketamine, it often will not be identified. This is relatively due to the fact that literally thousands of toxins and drugs exist, and in nearly the same number of combinations. Each can be detected through different testing techniques today," Doctor Josh Sinclair began. He was explaining with such exhilaration that Randal wasn't sure if he had given him the critical information or not.

"Uh Doc, I trust your reasoning. Let's just discuss whatever it is you think is so earth-shattering." Randal was losing his patience and developing a headache to boot.

"Oh yes, forgive me Ranger Randal. What I have discovered may throw a curve in the hypothesis that a female is responsible for all of the recent developments of this case. Specifically, what makes me doubt the certainty that we were so comfortable with earlier has to do with the five individual packages, including human ears, eyes, and one tongue. Having made deductions that Ketamine was used as a tool, creating an advantage in committing the crime for someone not as capable with the power and strength of the average male, the drug created a situation, which could easily fall into that realm where a woman was capable. I theorized the drug must have also been utilized, rendering victims helpless to prevent them from being mutilated," Sinclair detailed, while pausing to catch his breath.

Meanwhile, Zach Randal had become quiet, dreadfully sensing where the pathologist was heading.

"So while confident with this hypothesis, I was willing to test my assumption. I performed toxicological screenings on each of the specimens, specifically listing Ketamine as a target compound for the computer to graph." Texas Ranger Zach Randal now had no problem following the doctor, but didn't relish what he was anticipating the conclusion to be.

"The only problem is the fact that no traces of Ketamine, or any other drug for that matter can be detected anywhere in any of the submitted human tissues. I am afraid the contents of each package were taken without the assistance or use of any drugs, casting a rather large shadow of doubt upon our theory that this was a crime easily carried out by a woman," he concluded.

Zach Randal was silent for several seconds following the conclusion that the pathologist relayed. "Ranger Randal, are you still with me?" Sinclair asked hesitantly.

"Still right here Doc, just allowing the old gray matter to absorb what you just unloaded," he answered.

"Anything else Doc?" Randal inquired.

"No, I'm afraid that's all I have at this time," Doctor Sinclair confessed.

"Thanks a lot Doc. I won't say it's just what I needed to hear, but it's definitely going to shave the way my thinking goes. Put Sergeant Hadley back on the line sir."

Randal was now more frustrated than when he knew nothing. The amount of information had reached a level of sensory overload. His only remedy for situations like this, he'd found, were to catalog every bit into categories on paper. After that was accomplished, then he was able to sort through it, usually coming up with a usable pattern to follow.

"This is John Hadley." Randal heard him answer the phone while still deep in thought.

"John, where the hell are those two Hardy Boy undercover agents? Still at Amy's place?" he asked.

"That's where I last heard from them. They were awaiting instructions. I told them not to move in case you had any more of Sister Zigong's psychic hot-line clues for them to investigate," Hadley stated in a tone confirming that he was now one up on Randal.

"Well, give them a call. Tell them I want them to haul ass to Raton, and I mean run hot. I don't want us to be caught with our pants around our ankles. All this is starting to worry me," Randal said. Instructing the undercover agents to run hot, referring to the use of their flashing emergency lights and siren, he hung up.

Zach Randal remained in the parking lot where he'd managed to grab a sandwich and cup of coffee. He sat behind the wheel deep in thought, watching the mid-day sunshine fade behind thunderclouds rolling south out of the Rocky Mountains.

John Hadley was right. They were suddenly drowning in leads. It was very odd when after nearly two years of nothing, they were now being deluged with information. He knew not to assume anything, and question everything.

Dr. Vanessa Jansen was considered only because of her arrival to the city of Sweetwater coinciding perfectly with the attempts to terrorize Amy Dodson through the letters she'd received, and the packages. The fact that she had easy access to a sedative found in the Beatles, then in the murdered women at the cafe, only resulted in the probability of her involvement increasing.

That information alone was not enough to make Zach Randal rule out anyone else, but she had given those two narcotic agents the slip. Unless some legitimate reason for Vanessa's odd behavior could be established, discovering the barn doors open and Amy's Land Cruiser missing indicated premeditated involvement.

Zach was troubled when he remembered how smoothly she had lied to him, fabricating the story about her fiancé. Then again, finding out it was her brother who she was secretly grieving over was not a clear indication of anything illegal.

She may have made up the fiancé story because of her shame associated with Jedediah Duncan's suicide.

Zach had dated Vanessa Jansen, knew her intimately, but when all the evidence seemed to be pointing in her direction, it troubled him. She was not a killer. The possibility of an accomplice seemed the most logical and probable of scenarios.

This was a most frustrating situation. Devising a plan based on what little evidence they had, he resorted to attempting to draw the killer out. Leaking news of their departure, just enough so that the killer would get wind of, he was sure the case would break open. His refusal to allow Amy to call Vanessa Jansen was based on his anticipation of Vanessa's own informant telling her.

Now the entire strategy hung in the balance because of a flood of newly discovered information. Still he currently had no idea where Vanessa, Amy, or Deke happened to be.

While running everything through his head one more time, his pager went off. He had set the damned thing on vibrate because the high-pitched alarm nearly drove him crazy when it was activated. The sudden buzzing vibrations got him to jumping like a prom queen with a bee down her dress. He hated the contraption. Knowing it was in his pocket, he still came close to hurting himself whenever it went off. It took only a second for him to realize what it was, but the fright was so bad he stayed pissed off for hours afterward.

It was nearly noon. Even without looking at it, he assumed it was Deke and Amy. Digging into his pocket, he read the number. Within thirty seconds, he'd dialed the number and had Deke on the line.

"Well, how far north have you managed to get?" Randal inquired.

"Just driving into the city limits of Raton," Deke replied.

"Good. Keep driving north through town. Before leaving the city and getting on the Interstate, look to your left. I'm in the parking lot. We can talk while parked. That way I can keep an eye peeled," Randal advised him.

Deke hung the phone up and turned to walk back to the Jeep. Meanwhile, Amy was across the highway with all four of the Beatles. It was time for their stretch and bathroom break.

She looked like a young child frolicking with the big dogs. However, Deke was all too aware that appearances and looks could be very deceiving. He wondered what secret she was holding back that could be the key to this entire mystery. It would do no good to press her for it. She'd have to volunteer, thinking it was her decision entirely.

"Hey, let's go! We have a scheduled rendezvous to keep!" Deke yelled. With that, the four Chessies and Amy came jogging back, piling into the truck.

WHILE Deke and Amy were in route to meet up with Zachary Randal, Sergeant John Hadley was posting an all points bulletin for Amy's Land Cruiser. Instead of just placing it on the wire, he made personal phone contacts with every sheriff department along the most likely route heading north. He then called troop headquarters of the state police, alerting them of a possible kidnapping, or at the very least a car theft, in which interstate flight was highly probable.

Undercover agents Dan Baker and Bill Frye were flying through Amarillo, heading north at about the same time. Hoping to rendezvous with Zach Randal before dark, around the Colorado border.

The two men felt about as comfortable as a Barn Owl in a hummingbird's nest. They were nearly in the dark concerning the case, yet were drawing enough attention to be leading a parade.

They could only hope that Zach Randal knew what he was doing.

CHAPTER

12

JACK WATCHED HER for what seemed like hours. While sitting in a wooden chair, he made certain to stay just out of her reach. The filthy mattress that she had been deposited upon lay mildewing in a corner. Although remaining speechless, Vanessa was determined that she would wage silent war with this stranger, who she would eventually discover to be Jack Vermette. Her stare was just as hard and as piercing as his was. She was fairly sure he had not yet realized her true reason for being mute. The courage to utter a single word in defiance against him was not to be found. Time passed. She began to think that what he must be waiting on, while staring at her in such silence, was a verbal outcry of the injustice. For her to question him, plead with him, beg for mercy, would fulfill his expectation of her. Steadfastly, she refused.

Vanessa studied the man's features, desperately making efforts to recognize him. She was certain that she must know him, or at least know of him, but she could not place him anywhere in what had become a dark void for her previous memory.

He was powerfully built and had a deep golden tan covering his body. She made the assumption with his help, him being the typical, macho, male exhibitionist. He'd made a point of leaving the front of his shirt unbuttoned down to his waist. She did her best to send the message that she was not impressed, though secretly she was terrified.

After a long period of silence, and in an environment thick with impending events that Vanessa interpreted as the worst of her nightmares, the man tired of the game, disregarding her challenges.

Standing suddenly and jerking the chair away that was beneath him, he chuckled. His success in startling her amused him. Breaking her composure, he had proven to himself, and to Vanessa, that she was not nearly as tough as she thought, or that she wanted him to believe.

Vanessa could not prevent herself from shrinking back as he stood towering over her. His threatening posture reduced her to less of an opponent than imaginable. Her courage in the presence of this unimaginable threat puzzled her, since it was intertwined with a fear and dread, which had an origin that was lost somewhere within the memory she no longer possessed.

"What's the problem? Having reservations about taking me on?" he needled her while brandishing an amazingly friendly smile. She was frightened, but also very curious. The mystery behind this man and his reason for abducting her was beginning to overpower her determination to remain silent.

However, it was what he next said that shocked her back to the present situation. It was a powerful statement, but filled with a deeper meaning. Due to her disadvantage, she was unable to figure out that meaning. She felt the air leaving her lungs as a shock wave passed through her like a charge of electricity, but the reason for the powerful response remained a mystery to her.

"I don't guess you're any more of a challenge that old Jed." An evil and sadistic smile forming from what had previously been a friendly look. He watched her closely, hoping for a response from her. He seemed pleased with what he saw. Despite her inability to recall anything from memory, she had managed to exhibit a shocking response. Vanessa felt she had been kicked in her belly. Waves of nausea swept through her, and she was having trouble breathing. She feared fainting.

A trace of something that was very powerful, not unlike a memory, was associated with this man. Even with only a subconscious recollection, she knew enough to become ill.

Her abductor found her display entertaining, enjoying the gestures of despair and fear. He remained standing over her, but his posture became less threatening. Instead, he began cocking his head from side to side, giggling almost childlike while watching her.

"Oh I'm sorry. Did that little bit of information upset you?" He was relentlessly cruel.

"Well, if it means anything to you Doc, he begged for his life. You're proving to be a better suited opponent. He just wasn't much of a manly figure before entering that dark closet of his bedroom. He really moaned, like a sick dog dying in the gutter. It was only because of my great compassion, Doc, that I was able to shove that gun barrel between his teeth before pulling the trigger. I refused to allow him to suffer any more than what was absolutely necessary. It offends me that anyone could think that I am anything but humane." His dialogue was like the babbling of a psychotic misfit, a complete psychopath, yet ready to justify his action because of the sacrifice he was convinced that he had made. Vanessa noticed his posture changing as he took a step closer, his hands sliding down to his hips, and a lurid sneer forming on his face.

Vanessa's mind was like a fuse box that suddenly began shorting out connections. Everything she had heard him ranting on about made perfect sense, yet, it made no sense at all. Her ability to filter the information being verbalized was like that of a schizophrenic.

Because the damaged mental capacity of a schizoaffective mind responds to stimuli that are not properly filtered, repeated and vain attempts to react to each and every stimulus occur. Eventually, because of the impossibility of the task, the brain resorts to a complete disassociation from reality. It was that disassociation from the person she was that Vanessa felt she was helplessly entering.

From the stubborn streak that she had acquired as a child, that hard headed refusal to give in, Vanessa was able to successfully escape the emotional turmoil that she had fallen into headlong. Regaining her composure, she emerged from the fetal position where earlier she had attempted an escape. Facing her opponent, she glared into his eyes.

"You try putting anything in my mouth, and I'll bite it clean off, you bastard!" Vanessa made the declaration with such surprising force that even her captor took a step backward.

The moment was totally unexpected, for both of them. A victim of circumstances that she had come to find unacceptable, Vanessa decided to change those circumstances. If he meant to kill her, then he was going to have to work for the pleasure first.

"What's the matter, shit-head? Having reservations about taking me on?" The insult was more than he could stand, and with a wide arching backhand, he struck her across the side of her head. The blow was swift, and effective.

Vanessa heard the explosive sound of the impact as the back of his hand hit solidly. It was nearly an exact duplicate of the first blow he had used to capture her with, the same explosion, and once again, she lost consciousness.

"How's that for a reservation, Doc?" he angrily responded. She was barely conscious while he made his remark, but she heard what was said. As she slipped away into the black void of nothing, she remembered thinking; that's the second time he's called me Doc. Before she could put the clue to any kind of test, Vanessa was out cold.

WHEN Deke and Amy had driven away after meeting briefly with Randal, continuing on their northerly course, Amy discovered a wave of guilt was beginning to swell within her. Was she harboring the secret to all of this mess? Recklessly placing peoples lives in danger, all because of her shame?

She wasn't ready for this. The pain that accompanied only brief moments of any reflection tore at her heart. Amy knew she might not have a better opportunity, but she was frightened. Her heart was not quite prepared. The walls that she had been building were not complete. She needed protection against emotions that would tear at her mercilessly when the time arrived. More than any other time, she knew that it was coming.

When Zach informed Amy about her Land Cruiser's absence from the barn, insinuating that Vanessa Jansen had taken it for what he termed very mysterious reasons, Amy quickly slammed the door on his theory.

"I personally gave Vanessa a set of keys to the Land Cruiser. Sometimes Vanessa needs a vehicle with a hitch for pulling horse trailers. I offered her the use of the Land Cruiser!" Amy declared angrily.

"If that's the only proof that you are using to come to this conclusion, accusing her of murder, I suggest you find an alternate theory to offer prosecutors. You're charge is very weak, and I personally will be the one to eliminate it before any prosecutor or judge!"

Her anger surprised both Zach and Deke. It was venomous, and immediately the assumption of Vanessa's guilt was put on hold. Women can be very naive at times, but both of these men were smart enough to know how incredibly accurate a woman's intuition can be. They would pay closer attention to details, especially after the display that Amy had just given them.

"Well, all right Miss Amy. I just have to cover every angle, that's all. Deke, you two go on ahead and continue to your place. I've got a couple of agents meeting me here pretty soon, then I'll catch up." Amy had shaved Randal down a notch. She was even ignoring his attempt at smoothing things over.

Zach became suddenly uncomfortable around Amy. Before long, he was rushing the pair off for their journey. Amy sat, arms across her chest, staring ahead from the passenger seat while Deke waved to Zach. They drove off without another word.

The weather was definitely changing for the worse. What had been a sunny sky that morning became completely overcast, with a light, but cold drizzle starting. It was going to turn very cold.

Unaware of each other's thoughts, Zach Randal and Deke Stone were both focused on similar fears. Identical twins, some people claim, are so tuned in to each other's feelings that one can feel the pain from an injury inflicted on the other. Zach and Deke had unintentionally become tuned in to each of their thought patterns, and both were hoping it would be only the weather to turn bitter cold, not anything or anyone having anything to do with the investigation.

BACK in Sweetwater, Sergeant Hadley was busy contacting law enforcement agencies across the mountain states, pumping up details, and exaggerating as much as possible in order to motivate some of the troopers to become involved. It was a trick he and Randal employed from time to time. Stretch the truth to an extreme, without breaking it, and it may just be the thing that gets you the needed help in capturing a criminal. So far, no explanation had emerged behind the mysteriously missing Land Cruiser. When, and if it was found, the whole case just might blow wide open.

Agents Baker and Frye were good men, racing across the Texas plains into New Mexico with not so much as a straight answer to inform them of what it was that they were now involved in. Not many officers were left of that caliber in law enforcement. It was the disciplined ability of completely trusting their superior, Sergeant Hadley, that created the rare, but admirable devotion for the work they chose. Too many officers were having to watch each other's back, afraid of getting knives placed in them by supervisors that they supposedly should trust.

The change in weather was something Zach Randal hardly noticed anymore. After Kate was buried, he just seemed to lose a part of him that once enjoyed the grandeur and beauty of mountains. Starting his Bronco, Zach eased over to the farthest corner of the parking lot, waiting for Bill Frye and Dan Baker. This was some embarrassment. He was obviously frustrated. He was a man rarely put into the position of having to admit when he was clueless, but that's exactly what happened when he eventually talked to the two officers who'd finally found him hiding in the restaurant parking lot.

NEVER had Vanessa been so confused. Regaining consciousness for only minutes at a time, she slowly worked backward to the place where her life once existed. Building from time spans of added minutes of awareness, she soon would completely emerge, more or less. Just as Vanessa would begin to break out of the fog, again she would slip away into a blurry sleep.

The fact that she was unable to stay awake for any significant amount of time troubled her tremendously. It meant something had happened to her physically. Maybe she had suffered neurological damage from the blows that she'd received. Waking periodically, Vanessa had estimated the time to be past noon. Aware that daylight was quickly passing into fading shadows; Vanessa would eventually discover that they were hidden under a lurking full moon somewhere in the wilderness. A night of terror awaited her, but the moon would remain mute, a solitary witness, telling not a soul.

Each time she tried harder to shake the drugged feeling off, listening for noises from her captor. She discovered that he was rarely in the room where she was kept, sentenced to a mattress in the darkest corner. She occasionally heard noises coming from the kitchen and even from the outside of the shack on a couple of occasions.

A sharp stinging sensation could be felt on her hip when Vanessa woke later in the night. The cabin was dark except for a dim glow coming from an old coal oil lamp that he had apparently set upon the mantle. He was nowhere in sight, and she stayed very quiet, hoping that he had fallen asleep.

Vanessa became increasingly aware of discomfort and noticed that her hip was very tender. She assumed it must be broken glass somewhere on the mattress, and she'd somehow managed to cut herself. The room had barely enough light for her to make a quick inspection, but it troubled her. She had to inspect the area. The jogging pants that Vanessa wore had an elastic band in the waist. She quickly exposed half of her rear end, hoping no glass was imbedded inside her.

Vanessa didn't find any glass, but to her amazement she found small puncture wounds, at least half a dozen. The reality that finding this new development forced her to accept took time to sink in. But eventually it did, and her fear escalated to new heights. She was being drugged! That was the only reasonable explanation for her sluggishness, with the repeated episodes of falling asleep.

Suddenly, with one half of her backside exposed, still examining the small tender spot, a shadow emerged from out of the corner behind the mattress. The massive, haunting, looming figure moved so quickly that she froze, crying out in panic at the last moment.

"It's so thoughtful for you to drop your pants, but this won't hurt a bit." Thrusting quickly into her, she felt as the needle entered. Terrified that she could do nothing to stop him, the unmistakable burning sensation of medication shocked her, as her captor emptied the contents of a syringe deep into her hip. The air of confidence that he displayed surpassed arrogance, and he knew, that she knew, he owned her.

"If you continue to be such an obedient little girl, I might be tempted to even keep you; after all, the sex is exceptional. I also have needs." He slobbered the words out disgustingly.

At first, Vanessa did not understand to what he could be referring. In reality, she knew but the coping mechanism of denial remained intact. It finally hit her. The last fourteen hours, when she'd been barely reaching the surface of awareness, he had been having nonstop sexual marathons. Like falling through ice in a frozen lake, she became immediately numb, but along with the numbing feeling of cold water came the feeling of being completely alert.

Before she had any time to pull away from him, he had stepped across the mattress. Empty syringe still in hand, and completely naked, she again balled up in the fetal position, at the center of the crude bed. His tall square frame stood above her, gloating with the anticipation of another opportunity. He made no attempt to rape her while she remained alert, revealing the poor self-image and the low self-esteem that he had of himself.

Vanessa's ability to handle the tragic reality, being sexually violated, was going to determine if she had the strength to survive. With another surge of courage, one that seemed to come from her very soul, she turned every emotional response off, with the one exception of anger. All of the energy that had been reserved for other emotional responses, Vanessa now applied to the single remaining emotion left in her. All she could feel was a brutal and determined, wildly unpredictable anger!

"Oh, you know I almost forgot. With all the excitement that's been going on, you must be hungry." The tone of his voice was as deceptive as a minister's, confusing her even more in the drugged state. She was experiencing a near childlike fascination with him. At times, a transformation occurred in his voice that actually took her very breath away.

She refused to respond to offers of food. He had waited a few additional seconds to see if she would verbally request food or water, but realizing she would make no such request, he stood and entered the kitchen. It was just the break for which she'd been hoping. While inspecting her backside, she had noticed an object of some sort inside the hidden pocket of her jogging suit. With the opportunity to inspect her pockets and their contents, she turned her back to the kitchen, pretending to be adjusting her clothing, just in case he walked back suddenly.

What she was to discover was even more puzzling, creating more confusion in her. She knew what a syringe was, and she guessed that she even knew how to use one, but what she found looked like a toy water pistol, only it was loaded with what looked like a small dart.

Like having a word on the tip of your tongue, Vanessa struggled with her identity, swirling below the surface of her ability to remember. The struggle was intense. For a few seconds, she would surface, only to fall back into the darkness, unable to lock her thoughts onto anything for very long.

As despairing as her efforts were, she became encouraged by the progress. She kept repeating to herself the name. He had referred to her as, *"Doc? Why Doc? Who was Doc?"*

As well, she wondered about the discovery of the syringe. *"Why did she have this in her pocket?*

One of the more puzzling pieces of the maze had to do with someone called Jedediah. *"Who was Jedediah?"*

Over and over, she pondered the questions, becoming obsessed with finding answers. Vanessa had crossed her first big hurtle, surviving the emotional trauma that he had inflicted upon her, still intact. Some type of pledge, which she must have sworn to accomplish, had to be responsible for the resolve that was within her. As she thought deeply about what must have occurred for her to have ended up where she was, it added to her determination. If for no other reason, she would succeed. She owed it to the person that she used to be.

With a loud slamming noise, she jumped in fear, letting out a brief scream. He stood three feet from the mattress. At his feet sat a fruit basket that was dropped to the floor, scaring her. It was filled with oranges, apples, grapes, and strawberries. He remained silent as a cat, roaming barefoot and naked through the cabin. He had not seen what she had managed to pull from the inside pocket of her jogging suit.

"Well, you still have your voice. It would be to your advantage to socialize like normal people. It's not healthy to push all the negative feelings down you know. You can talk to me; after all, I am all you have now." What Vanessa heard in Jack's voice within that brief moment of time revealed more to her than the words he spoke. He was obviously mentally deranged, associating himself with the image of being her provider or protector of sorts. The delusion usually had a very negative impact when it came to fruition.

The steel that Vanessa found in her backbone came from tough lessons that she had endured through life. For the time being she could not recall the origin for her determination, after having experienced life following the tragic suicide of her father, a drug addicted mother, and an abusive stepfather. The situation she found herself faced with looked like a Girl Scout Camping trip compared to her previous exposure. It was just good fortune that her current host had no idea, not the first inkling of suspicion about what it was that made up the person who came to be Vanessa Jansen.

"Come on now Doc. You've got to keep your strength up. If you start to peter out on me, things will be a sight more unpleasant," he stated. Initially his attempt to coax her into eating was reasonable, but as quick as lightning, his tone had changed.

"Eat the fruit bitch! I promise it goes down much smoother if you do it yourself."

Even with the fear turned off, and the anger turned on, he scared her. It was time to shift the balance in her favor, even though she knew the result might be disastrous.

"Since you already know my name, and your professional advise is to socialize, what shall I call you, other than shit-head?" she gambled.

She'd try hitting the buttons least expected in him. Throwing his concentration off, even entertaining him was a route she may have to venture and endure.

"Hey Doc, that's pretty good. See, it does help to discuss things. You may call me Sir. To begin with, I think you already know my name. You want to play stupid, trying somehow to trick me, when Amy has probably told you everything."

Quick as a camera flash and just as blinding, a memory shot through her head. The name Amy caused a connection to surge in her brain, but only for a split second. Then, it was gone.

"What if I told you the name Amy means nothing to me, and that I have no recollection of knowing anyone by that name, sir?" Her nerves were as tight as piano wire, but one way or the other she had to start making headway.

"Well, if that were the case I would have to go ahead and kill you. Your value to me is judged by what you know, not how you perform, even if the extra benefit is enjoyable."

With her hypothetical question now asked, and his answer given, she knew more where the boundaries were, and she knew better how to handle any hidden disability, very carefully.

Pretending to be occupied with the fruit that he was forcing her to eat, Vanessa began frantically piecing together some kind of strategy. Making him want to talk, revealing more of the facts was what she must do. She would then know what it was that she was supposed to already know.

If his motive for all this hinged on the information given to her by some Amy, then she damn sure had to play along until it somehow came back to her, or take the first opportunity available, and kill him.

In the meantime, she seemed to satisfy him with her attempt to eat. He was always extra careful to remain just out of Vanessa's reach, appearing to be timid or afraid of her. Vanessa was puzzled by the appearance he gave, as if afraid she may suddenly reach out and touch him. Another strange development that she took note of, feeling it may be worth consideration when the time came for her final plan.

It was not long before Vanessa began to feel the effects of whatever drug he had injected into her. In minutes, she slumped into a supine position upon the filthy mattress, completely zoned out.

Jack smiled at this special prize, which he possessed; it made him feel especially powerful when he thought of the attractive woman completely in his control. To confirm the fact that Vanessa had passed out, he edged closer. He began his violating, taking full advantage of what he had never learned to respect.

CHAPTER

13

THE UNDERCOVER OFFICERS made good time, arriving in the town of Raton late that afternoon. The topic of their discussion in route centered on the fact that neither of them had any clear understanding of what Zach Randal's objectives were. Dan and Bill were not disrespectful men, but persisted in questioning, almost insisting that their effectiveness was only as good as their understanding of each unfolding event.

Ranger Zach Randal quickly understood their confusion, and feelings of discomfort, especially being left in the dark. Zach explained, in very frank terms, everything he knew as fact, which was little help to them. Then he shared with the two men his suspicions regarding Dr. Vanessa Jansen's involvement. They were very surprised at what the information suggested. A woman had managed to commit the most heinous and wicked triple-murder in Texas history! They were astounded, more about how the perpetrator had managed to accomplish such an act, and with relative ease, getting away without leaving a clue. That is, until Dr. Josh Sinclair entered the investigation.

Dan Baker, Bill Frye, and Zachary Randal sat tossing ideas around for a couple of hours. The immediate objective was to kill time, so the idea tossing began as a way to do it without losing their sanity. It was not an exercise in reality, especially knowing that no idea would be considered with any degree of seriousness unless Zachary Randal were the one to come up with it.

Because the atmosphere was so loose surrounding their immediate mission, it became obvious to the undercover officers that Zach Randal had not the first clue of which direction they should go next. Just as their discomfort was beginning to escalate, Zach came close to panicking, yelling aloud, jumping across his truck console, spooked by the vibrating pager sitting in his pocket.

"This is Randal, what have you been able to stir up?" he asked, after dialing the number left on his pager.

"Zach we have what may be a positive on Amy's Land Cruiser, only one drawback, it's back in Amarillo." Sergeant John Hadley had stayed up all night pestering different patrolman in different areas to make extra efforts, and it had just paid off.

"Amarillo!" Zach repeated. Bill looked over at Dan, slapping himself on the forehead in disgust. Immediately, they corrected any display that was less than enthusiastic by encouraging each other, pretending to be ecstatic by the news. They'd be heading south again shortly.

WITH daylight quickly fading, only snow-covered peaks of the surrounding Rocky Mountain Range reflected the remaining sunlight over the horizon. The rest of the country remained shrouded in heavy, dark skies. The odd mixture was in such contrast when looking from west to east horizons, that it created an impression of an early dusk, the descending sun's rays blocked by the western storm clouds, in addition to the majestic mountain range. Accompanying the decreasing sunlight were falling temperatures that plummeted suddenly. In addition, light flurries were promising heavier snowfall later.

Colorado Springs was a much busier city than Amy had ever expected. In her mind, the place was nothing but an industrial town, situated between the base of the Rocky Mountains, and the edge of the Great Plains. The only reason she thought it was popular was because it happened to be near the famous, fourteen thousand foot, Pike's Peak.

Astounded by the congested traffic, six and eight lane highways were filled. It was only a matter of time before she was asking Deke all about the area and attractions.

"Gosh Amy, it's one of the busiest, defense-related, industrial areas in the Western United States. It's not only home to Fort Carson, but Peterson Air Force Base, United States Space Command, Air Force Space Command, Falcon Air Force Base, along with Cheyenne Mountain Strategic Air Command. And that doesn't include the United States Air Force Military Academy, The University of Colorado at Colorado Springs, or Colorado College." Amy was reminded of the tour bus guides she'd heard about in Hollywood, listening to Deke ramble on about the city's attractions.

"Wow!" she exclaimed, and then quickly added, "So how long will it take for us to get the hell out of here?" Crowded cities with shady reputations always made her nervous. Surprised by her sudden change of attitude, Deke chanced a sideways glance at her.

"We should get to Green Mountain Falls in about fifteen or twenty minutes. My place is only forty-five minutes farther."

Deke had started to relax, feeling more that he was in his element as the mountains loomed to his left. But he convinced himself that he'd better keep a close eye on this little female hurricane sitting next to him. He had seen small tropical storms quickly develop into category 5 monster hurricanes, devastating many coastal towns caught unaware. This was one developing system that he'd decided he was going to watch very closely. Already this was proving to be a challenge. Just when he was sure to have her figured, Amy would dart off in the opposite direction leaving him dumfounded.

As the tension that was experienced at their initial meeting had starting to fade, he was sure he'd get her to open up about whatever secrets she kept so closely guarded. It was a good sign if she felt safe with him, and with just enough time to spare, especially since time was such a crucial component to ending this thing without anyone getting hurt.

Noticing her quickly developed freedom at speaking her mind, disgusted with the crowded cities that they drove through, he figured it might be something that could be useful. If her gander was raised enough by society's ills, she might tell him what he needed to know, sure to help them solve the dilemma. Then again, she might tell him to take a flying leap. But at least some form of communication would soon be established.

When Amy realized how much longer Deke said it would take she stared at him confused.

"Forty-five minutes farther, after we get to Green Mountain Falls?"

Deke jumped, surprised by her sudden impatience. Then he realized that it did sound like a long time. Deke explained, "Well, because after we get to Green Mountain Falls we have to take a narrow road just on the other side of town. That road winds its way up the mountain, eventually to the cabin. The forty-five minutes is a long estimate, just in case."

Amy seemed to calm down, pacified by his explanation. She remained silent for the next dozen miles; in fact, they exited the city limits of Colorado Springs, entering Green Mountain Falls nearly simultaneously before she spoke again.

The scenery had changed from one filled with super highways, smoke stacks, industrial complexes, and fast food restaurants, to one of breathtaking views; a paradise covered in thick forest, snow covered peaks, and rolling valleys. The transition left Amy almost stuttering as she labored at deciding which to next admire.

Deke had grown accustomed to seeing the sights, but was delighted with the way Amy fell in love with the place. It was always refreshing to be present for someone's first exposure to such beauty and grandeur. It always served as a reminder for him to never take such things for granted.

Similar to someone's first love, the mountains created emotions that ran deeper than any other thing Deke knew in existence. Even love, which in his experience only faded away with time. Instead, the mountains left an impression that furrowed a deep path through your heart, somehow managing to reshape the landscape existing in your soul.

Deke was contemplating God's unique methods for reaching into the hearts of men, daydreaming of the miraculous and magnificent opportunity given to mankind. When without warning, and totally unsolicited, he became aware that Amy was weeping. Her soft crying was an intimate moment that belonged only to her. Deke felt he wasn't supposed to witness such a private moment.

He could never have prevented or ever prepared himself for the overwhelming feeling of anguish that he saw in her. It was painful. Amy had walked through that pain all alone, daily. Reaching a point where despair and loneliness collide, the process finally shatters all the walls that are thought needed, then a greater work can begin within the heart.

As resistant and determined as a mountain range, Amy fought to overcome the everyday trials of life on her own, refusing to seek out any help, mistaking it as a weakness. She was unable to succeed against what had become her mountains. She, of course, had been mistaken, unaware that even the toughest of individuals need help with life's struggles.

Regardless of the tough display that was evident on the outside, God had somehow found a flaw in her armor, and while placing His hand over her heart, began to console her, whispering to her spirit. The desperate running from the guilt she felt over the death of her child had already been forgiven.

Amy had been paralyzed by fear and grief. She knew that the pain would have to be endured eventually. But Amy imagined fate had reserved a place in hell just for her. No longer capable of hiding, weeping with the travailing experience of a woman in childbirth, the pain flowed out from her like water. A birthing of sorts was taking place, to a freedom that she had never known to exist. Deke was witnessing a true deliverance in Amy, a spiritual deliverance, that until this moment, he'd only read about.

THE return trip to Amarillo seemed to take forever, but they made it in less than four hours, driving at average speeds of ninety miles per hour. Dan Baker argued constantly with Bill Frye. Nearly the entire trip was one solid argument. He didn't see why they had to follow Ranger Randal all the way back, but instead wanted Bill to pass up the black Bronco, just for the fun of it.

Bill insisted it would be disrespectful to pass up the lead vehicle in the investigation. Maybe Randal would get the wrong impression, thinking they didn't really have their priorities straight, weakening the strength of their bond. Dan thought Bill was full of bullshit, and said it without hesitation.

"You always come up with some psycho-babble bullshit to argue about any ideas I have." The statement was laced with humiliation, surprising Bill at first. A closer look was all that was needed; he saw how well his partner used manipulation.

"Why Dan, you cut me to my very marrow. I must apologize with deep regret if your hurt was inflicted by rationalizations I have used in the past. From this day forward I pledge to be more compassionate and caring." Bill thickened the comment to the point of his partner declaring nausea.

"See what I mean? I accuse you of being full of bullshit, and sure enough, an immediate eruption. You better get that condition checked out, I sure don't want to be infected with it," Dan replied. Both of them remained silent for the next hour, smiling pleasantly, each of them certain he had gotten the better of the argument.

Arriving at the location, Ranger Zach Randal immediately recognized the establishment; he was shocked to see that it was directly across the highway from where Amy and Deke spent the previous night.

"Well, I'll be damned!" he whispered to himself, then noticed Potter County Sheriff's Deputies had also arrived at the hotel, along with the Amarillo City Police Department. Right smack in the center of all the action, Zach saw Amy's Land Cruiser.

The realization that Amy had been so close to danger, combined with Vanessa's amazing ability to get so near to her with relative ease, sent shudders through Zach. Each time close encounters with such potential tragedies occurred, flashing images of young girls, hog-tied, and submerged in tubs of water with their eyes frozen in death haunted him.

Zach exited his vehicle with confidence, striding slowly onto the scene. Approaching the other officers, he felt their uneasy stares. Without a doubt, he knew their thoughts, not knowing whether they should admire him or fear him. He thought it was healthier to believe it was admiration. This was Texas, and he was the best damn Texas Ranger within a couple of thousand square miles. This was his back yard; rules were made as he saw fit. Everyone envied him, his confidence, his style, and were wise enough not to challenge his authority.

To Zach's surprise, the man in charge of the scene happened to be an old friend, one he'd worked together with for nearly ten years, back in the early days. It was a break that Zach needed. His old friend, Sal Domingue, was more than capable of handling this without him having to go behind looking for what they'd missed.

"Well, ain't you a sight for curing red mange from the ass of a Brahman Bull," Zach growled, lighting one of the small cigars.

The short stocky officer was a cross between a potbelly stove and a grizzly bear. His hand disappeared nearly to the elbow as Zach greeted him. The famous panic-producing handshake didn't rattle his friend. He chuckled as everyone around waited to see what damage he sustained.

"How the hell have you been Stump?" Zach was the man who tagged Stump with his nickname. It was the only reason Stump allowed anyone to continue using the unflattering title. His respect and admiration for the man who'd given it to him in the first place was paramount to anything else.

"This here vehicle look anything like the one you fellows lost down in Sweetwater Zach?" Stump inquired.

"Yes, I do think it is the very same one, Stump. How long has it been parked here?" Randal asked, sure that his old friend had found out everything there was to know about the vehicle.

"Hotel management says a young woman showed up in it late last night. Supposedly, she was a real looker, wanted to stay one night, which technically was two nights ago. She didn't ask for anything else, just a room. Come morning, she was gone. I think it's safe to say she didn't forget to take the vehicle with her. End of story."

This new development was nothing Zach could have ever imagined. The Ranger stood looking at the Land Cruiser, pulling on the cigar, flaming the end with long deep drags before speaking again.

"Name?" Zach asked. It was only for his friend's amusement that he continued with the questioning. The answers would not help him figure out a damn thing.

"Vanessa Jansen, MD, of the animal kingdom that is," Stump clarified.

"You need any help with this one, or is it true what I've heard about you?" Stump asked, almost as an afterthought glancing up at Zach. Randal looked down at his old friend, allowing him to continue with his questioning.

"I hear you've taken up with the canine species lately, specifically a Latin breed called Lupus-All-Alone-Us," Stump declared in response to Zach's inquisitive glance.

"Well, we all got our misfortunes. I guess mine is having to put up with name-calling," Randal confessed. He had heard it all once before, and knew from where the rumor came. But really, it was not a rumor. It was the gospel truth, but Zach would never admit to anything regarding that time in his career or in his life.

While playing with the loose ash at the end of the small cigar, he answered his friend out of respect only. "I guess it's true what they say about old law-dogs like us."

Stump looked thoughtfully at his old friend, sensing that something profound and unusual was about to occur. "What's that, Zach?"

"We spend a lifetime solving mysteries, still one mystery will forever evade our grasp. Why do we do it?" he commented.

Stump looked up at his friend, shared a sad smile, turned, and walked away.

Before he could get completely out of earshot, Zach heard Stump speak. "Take care law-dog. Ain't many of us left, and I'd hate to have to rescue an old-timer like you, especially at my delicate age."

Zach Randal could not help feeling sad in response to his old friend's comment. He was right about one thing; not many of them were left. Zach was quick at putting it out of his mind, and began searching through the Land Cruiser. He planned to question everyone that remembered seeing Vanessa, collecting all that had been left in the room where she'd slept. Why the hell had she left the Land Cruiser here anyway? It was a good thing the two of them had never became serious in their relationship Randal thought. She was much too smart for him to tolerate for very long, and probably would have had him robbing banks in his old age.

Undercover agents Bill Frye and Dan Baker had already entered the room where she had supposedly spent the night. What they soon discovered only deepened the mystery. Zach was tempted to close the whole case, and put an end to these new developments that were getting more bizarre as time progressed.

"Zach, I'm persuaded to think that our lady animal doctor never slept in this room, and may have left under the persuasion of someone, who we don't have the first clue about. In fact, we've just starting learning about her, and now she disappears without even taking her purse. It ain't something a lady does regularly, unless they got no choice," Dan Baker declared.

The way Dan wrinkled his brow when he made such assumptions was how Bill learned to gauge the accuracy of what he said. According to Bill, he had no doubt about what was discovered. The conclusions that Dan had made about this particular case were absolutely right.

The sudden discovery of Vanessa missing, without a trace of evidence to go on, had Zach wanting to sit with Amy, discussing everything covered from the very start of this investigation to the present. Then start over and do it again and again until he found whatever it was that she'd managed to hide from him.

Only if she convinced him of nothing, would he relent. He was so certain that she'd come up with much more than he had now, that he was tempted to try. Thinking better of it, he stuck with the same investigative techniques that worked for him all those years, to this point. They may be slower than the evolution of man, but they were tried and proven.

"Ranger Randal, you may want to take a look at this sir." Officer Bill Frye was peering into a black medical bag. A well-developed crease ran across his brow, furrowing deeply into his forehead.

As Zach walked over to Bill Frye, he wondered what chance of being correct did the creases in Bill's brow reflect. Zach's thought patterns were taking dives, and he had to force these crazy thoughts from his mind. He decided the only chance he had at remaining lucid, not posing a threat to his own safety, was to get the hell out of this town, and away from these two guys that reminded him more and more of Dragnet.

Not wasting a second more, Zach stopped dead in his tracks. Surveying the room, he formulated a quick impression. Seeing more than enough law officers present to handle whatever needed to be handled, he barked out a few orders and walked out.

Not missing a step Zach got into his vehicle, started the engine, and headed back toward the mountains. Deke Stone was placed on the team for a reason, and he didn't care if he had to chew the nuts off a grizzly to get to the man's house, he was at the point where being functional was only a step away from a pre-frontal lobotomy.

It was a frightful thing to be so starved for leads, only to discover that someone was determined to drown you with them. Grizzly nuts were looking better and better all the time. God he was close to the edge.

As the attending officers watched Randal walk out of the hotel, leaving in his vehicle, they assumed that he'd received another lead. It was only Zach Randal's good fortune that they didn't know the truth. Before exiting the room, Zach had instructed Bill to contact a Dr. Josh Sinclair at FBI headquarters in Wichita Falls. Randal wanted Sinclair to assemble a team from his lab personnel, and quarantine the entire room. With the room all to themselves, lab technicians could gather evidence, analyze it to their hearts content, and have the results whenever Zach called for them later.

He also instructed Bill and Dan to work with the boys from the Potter County Sheriff's Office, interviewing anyone who had heard, seen, or smelled anything peculiar. They could get with Detective Sal Domingue, who Zach affectionately referred to as Stump, have pictures of Vanessa and Amy faxed in from the Office of Motor Vehicles, show them around, finding out what information, if any, was out there. It sounded reasonable to the pair of officers, much more comfortable in a situation where clear orders were given. They proceeded to follow Zach's orders to the letter.

DEKE'S rough-riding Jeep, with its loud exhaust from a busted muffler, was nearly out of gas as they slowly made their way up the narrow mountain road. Several times, the Jeep had been only a few feet from the edge of the road; Amy realized they were on the edge of thousand foot cliffs. Panic was building as she held the dashboard, scooting off her seat, nearly landing on Deke's lap. He only chuckled at her response to what he'd become used to long ago. After climbing the twisting, turning, mountain road for eight miles, they were at an elevation of eight thousand feet. The air was thinner and much colder.

They pulled up to the small A-frame, log cabin, buried deep in a grove of aspen just below the surrounding snow covered peaks. Amy's stomach was now filling with butterflies from sheer excitement. This was the kind of place, and the kind of lifestyle she thought existed only in fantasies. The reality that someone had actually taken enough chances in life to gain such a gift filled her with a schoolgirl crush.

Deke of course was completely unaware of the transformation that was taking place in her. He was busier with the task of making sure they had enough dog food than he was with making sure Amy was settled in.

CHAPTER

14

GREETED BY THE incessant pain accompanying the humiliating stain of sexual violation, Vanessa batted her eyes until they adjusted to the light inside the cabin.

Emerging from the drug-induced state, she could think of nothing that may help her to recall the large amount of time that somehow was lost.

Vanessa was careful to wake without movement, quietly, but with constant thoughts about her escape. Still dark outside the cabin, Vanessa wondered what the area consisted of. The silence, which she had observed earlier, no traffic, only a couple of passing airliners, suggested complete wilderness. She sat listening for any familiar sounds of the night, wondering if it was the same night when she'd passed out, or the next.

She quickly came to one conclusion; the pervert was not in the cabin. For whatever reason, she couldn't say, but she worried about his return. Maybe he was only out on the porch, or inside the truck. One thing she was sure of, he was nowhere inside the cabin.

The easily detected aroma of after-shave had been memorized; it was what enabled her to estimate his distance. He had a teenager-like habit of nearly bathing in the sweet smelling aroma, over time, losing the ability to smell it himself, but managing to bring tears to other people's eyes. It was overpowering.

The night was cool, and she saw that the coal oil lantern was back on the mantle, the wick trimmed short. The golden, soft glow of light was soothing to her. Taking advantage of anything soothing, she closed her eyes for a moment's pleasure.

This man was proving to be one of her most difficult challenges in life. He called her Doc several times, hinting about having a relationship with someone named Amy, and the importance of some secret they shared together. He also rambled on with some kind of suicidal talk; a person named Jedediah was included in the conversation. She repeated the details to herself, trying to memorize everything, hoping for a spark of memory to return.

It was a mystery to her, but the fact that some type of darting pistol was hidden on the inside of her sweat pants made her feel that hope was still alive.

Vanessa decided almost immediately not to try escaping too soon; it would be an escape from one lost location to imprisonment in a lost world. Her chances were actually better with the over-sexed pervert for the time being. He was her provider and protector, as much as she hated to admit it, and she would never admit that to him, ever.

The low-pitched noise was barely perceptible when she first heard it, but with time, it increased in volume. Without a doubt, it was getting closer. Still, she had not picked up his scent, nor had she heard the usual noises that he made when elsewhere in the cabin.

In only a few minutes, the steady humming of the engine arrived, stopping just outside the cabin. Silence, creaking sounds, a slamming door, and heavy footsteps on the wooden porch. "Hello my love. Are you awake yet?" his voice nearly rattled the windows as she stretched out toward the fireplace, vomiting.

"I can't hear you. Are you hiding? Do you wish to play the game of seek and destroy, or is it hide and seek? I sometimes get them confused, once regrettably ending up having to kill two of my dearest friends. No, now don't get confused, believing that Jedediah could ever have been a friend. He was an enemy, and one of the worst sorts. As I had previously mentioned, he was not a very worthy opponent if seriously challenged. A waste of such waste is what I consider true waste." The deep rumbling laughter started.

The rambling confabulations of word salad monologue continued, being repeated every five or six hours. She struggled to piece things together, but before any sense could be made of the confusing talk, he'd stop.

She was quickly learning about his habits. Waiting for the loud entrance that, without a doubt, he'd make at any moment hoping to startle her and give him a little tickle of entertainment. Bursting through the door, he stomped loudly onto the wooden floor ending it with a jump. Vanessa didn't allow even a hair on her head to move. If her only victory was going to come in such a way, she planned to take them, savoring the win, while gloating as much as possible in his face.

He tried masking his disappointment at the failed attempt, but she made it clear with only a look, he was not fooling her. He began struggling with how well she seemed to be taking the devastating bits of information that he'd been leaking. He'd planned the tid-bits of horror, hoping they might shatter her composure. Instead, she had not even flinched at the news. Her own brother had been murdered, but she was rock solid. It was not a normal response. After thinking that he'd committed suicide only to discover he'd been murdered had to do some damage. He decided that the cracks were occurring, but only on the inside. Soon, he was going to witness a mental implosion. His plan was brilliant, but his blindness to her affliction prevented him from ever inflicting the kind of damage he'd planned.

THE name recorded on his birth certificate was Jack Vermette, it had also been the name recorded on his death certificate after the tragic accident. Contrary to belief, Jack was not dead, but a man without a family, even before the accident when he was legally alive.

No one questioned him when he listed his name as the same person killed offshore when crossing the border. He was a legal immigrant from Mexico. Jack moved back to the states from Monterrey where he'd spent three months recovering from his near death journey.

Nearly three years ago, when he was involved in that horrible boating accident while working for an offshore salvage company, he'd been badly injured, but not killed. Caught in crosscurrents and tides within the Gulf of Mexico, Jack's body was never located; the search team finally gave up, listing him as missing, certain that he'd been killed.

Helplessly adrift, Jack finally hit the sandy beaches of South Padre Island, off the shores of South Texas, just north of the Mexico border. The bitter life and death struggle had taken four days, drifting with the Gulf's tides.

A doctor working in a hospital where Jack was taken offered him shelter until he was well enough for travel. The Doctor's large family and the people living in a small village just outside of Monterrey assisted Jack. His recovery was quick, and the doctor consented to his plea that the authorities not be advised of his survival.

Jack had made up a story about being an escaped criminal from Louisiana; he'd been falsely accused of robbery. The elderly physician was a compassionate man, and effectively aided in giving Jack what he could never have attained through any other way: a brand new life.

Jack's recovery was attributed to his healthy status before the long Gulf crossing. The fact that he'd also escaped injury in the offshore tragedy, in which an entire dive crew reportedly had perished, was never revealed to the old doctor.

While sitting on the flat deck of a salvage barge, Jack was thinking about Amy. The cook emerged saying the mail had been delivered by helicopter. A letter had arrived for Jack.

Taking the envelope Jack saw that it was from Amy and nearly tore it in half, anxious to hear from her. His shaking hands opened the letter, and he briefly read the contents. A powerful shock passed straight through his soul. Crushed like a child receiving a slap across the face from a parent, a deep despair enveloped him. This was the kind of trip that would have no return. Returning physically still left his soul lost as the initial blow occurred. He would never accept what was in that letter.

Despite his wishes to die, Jack became the only survivor from the accident. Just as he placed the envelope into his pocket he heard the speedboat approaching. Within seconds, a horrific collision occurred. Six of the seven men on the salvage crew were killed. Jack lived. Against all odds, he had survived. Opportunity for revenge was being offered on a silver platter. The advantages of being someone dead were poor indeed, but if you were someone who'd managed to remain alive in death, the advantages were unique and immensely powerful.

With nothing but a few bucks and a tattered letter inside a torn envelope, he thanked the doctor and his family for all their kindness. Jack turned, leaving them behind. By way of a long journey, across the Gulf of Mexico, Jack Vermette had entered Mexico as a dead man. When Jack left Mexico, simply taking a short walk and crossing the border back into Texas, he'd decided to remain a dead man.

Months had passed since Jack re-entered Texas. Changing his hair style and color, he found it amazing how simple it was to roam freely about, undetected, without much more than a glance from strangers in the city of Sweetwater. His previous paranoia was unfounded as he realized most people were uninterested in anyone, except themselves in life. With the feeling of being invisible, Jack was soon stalking Amy without fear of discovery or detection.

The developments that had occurred within the last few months when Jack was away, he easily discovered. But having discovered such events, he now found they were slowly driving his emotional and mental states to extremes. Decisions made concerning actions that were to be taken became extremely unbalanced.

Jack learned all about the ranch from Amy, but had no idea that it was in such a secluded location. What he planned to do became all the easier. Hours upon hours were spent watching her. Many times, after the Beatles were taken inside at night, he would sit outside her window, watching her nightly routine.

The letter writing had been started almost immediately after returning to the states. Initially it was only because of her rejection of him that he harassed her. It was awesome as he watched her responses to the gruesomely written, harassing letters. Quite a pleasant feeling had been associated with watching Amy slowly unravel. Then, that Yankee Duncan boy became involved. He appeared harmless, and it was not until after the abortion that he saw the evil, but it was too late. His child had been sacrificed. Jack's anger was kindled to a level that he'd not thought possible.

After following Jedediah to his sister's home in Maine, Jack easily descended to a new level of violence, joyfully torturing, then murdering Jedediah Duncan. He thought of killing the sister, Vanessa Jansen, just for fun, but found Amy busy back in Sweetwater, befriending and confessing her secrets to that Texas Ranger Zach Randal. Randal scared Jack, but in a different way. He did not fear the man's physical ability, but something else did that he could not explain.

The night Amy and the son of her mother's friend, Deke Stone, left in his Jeep, Jack was not at the ranch. By the time he arrived, they had long been gone. What Jack did see, mistakenly thinking it was Amy making an escape, had been the nocturnal and secret activity of Vanessa Jansen. Her friend, Bob Davidson, the desk sergeant for the sheriff department where Randal's office was located, secretly dropped her off. Vanessa had taken Amy's Land Cruiser from the barn, driving north in pursuit of Amy and Deke. She'd hoped to spot the man she suspected to have murdered her brother, and also suspected as the one responsible for Amy's difficulties. His appearance on the scene had not been in the way she'd expected.

Vanessa had been trying to enlist the help of Sergeant Bob Davidson. The elderly desk sergeant was an old friend of the Humane Society, and their efforts to stop inhumane treatment of rodeo animals. Vanessa met Sergeant Bob Davidson at an annual convention held in Amarillo, eighteen months previous to her move to Sweetwater. When her world fell apart with Jedediah's death, she heard rumors that he'd associated with a woman from Sweetwater. Vanessa quickly remembered her friend Sergeant Davidson, calling for his assistance. He was a surprising wealth of information, explaining the ease and amount of information he was privy to with his position at the sheriff department.

Jack Vermette's error in thinking the woman veterinarian had been Amy only resulted in the ability to easily kidnap Vanessa Jansen. Thinking that the error may be put to some use, Jack assumed he would be able to garner information needed concerning Amy's location. That wasn't how things ended up, and Jack found himself stuck with a more than resilient opponent. Her difficulty in cooperating with him had already resulted in his decision to kill her. Delaying with his plan to kill Vanessa was due to his enjoyment of her recently. As he expected, he'd now grown tired of her, and feared Amy might escape to where he could never find her.

DEKE had been away for over a month from his A-frame cabin. He affectionately referred to it as the wife worthy of keeping. A serious statement when it was declared, but only to prove how much he missed her at times. Amy was surprised at his rudeness, confessing to still love his ex-wife. They never should have allowed him to become involved; his disability could cripple the investigation.

Busy checking the pantry, making a quick inventory of their supplies, he suddenly noticed the air within the cabin getting thick and heavy. Because of her sudden silence, Deke turned to Amy, realizing immediately that she took what he'd said wrong.

"Amy, when I refer to my wife, it does not have anything to do with a woman. The cabin is my wife, the very best wife a man could ask for. I love her. I love her for many reasons, but mostly because regardless of how far I may travel; however long I'm away, she never keeps me from going, and she's always here to greet me when I return. Never will be any second class plumbers, electricians, or builders of any kind remodeling, fixing, altering, or adapting anything that belongs to her."

Small talk was all they could manage at first. Arriving at Deke's place and beginning with the settling down routine was becoming…well, routine.

"With winter storms already beginning to drop significant snows, the mountain range itself will soon take over the weather for the next six or seven months," he said. The comment was meant to be more of a thought, but ended up coming out verbally. "What do you mean, the mountain takes over?" Amy was the one that he'd needed all this time.

Her innocent questions were a joy to hear, and a pleasure to answer. Life had become routine for Deke, until just a few days ago. Routine was something that he found very hard to live with, especially if you accidentally fell into those habits. "Whenever someone talks about the Rocky Mountains taking over, listen closely, and you'll find out why they call it that. But more amazing is how the mountains actually create weather for an entire continent. An entirely independent climate exist in the mountains, with peaks above fourteen thousand feet, countless lakes and streams, frozen tundra stretching for miles, and green forests with hundreds of plant species." Deke paused, watching the fascination on her face while picturing the scenery.

"But even more unique is how weather systems are actually created by the dynamics of constant change along the entire length and width of what we casually refer to as the Rocky Mountains. This unique and mysterious part of Earth is where God practices the most awesome of His miracles. It's one place where I can assure you, miracles still happen, and they happen every day." Deke spoke with such love for the mountains, and the One who had created the beauty he so admired. It made Amy begin to weep, again.

Deke was in one hell of a position; wanting to comfort her was only succeeding in reminding her about whatever was breaking her heart. She may think it was none of his affair. In that case, the secret might stay a secret, and he didn't want that to happen. It was the very thing Zach Randal warned him about, and had made clear a price would have to be paid if he messed up.

As Deke pretended to stay busy, preparing the cabin for the cold weather rolling down from out of the mountains, Amy sat before the fireplace. Occasionally she'd start to cry, then regain her composure, dry up, and fall back into despair, shedding more tears. He could tell she was being tortured by a very powerful memory, one that was pure emotion, and he wanted desperately to try helping her.

Deke coaxed Amy to come with him out on the front porch. Few sights were more effective in motivating and inspiring someone than watching the snow as it appears from out of the black, night sky, settling softly in the forest, in complete silence. The snow flurries that slowly drifted to the ground during the night would become a full force blizzard by sometime in the early morning hours.

The cabin had one bedroom, located in a loft that hung out over the cabin's den area. The bedroom was against the same wall the stone fireplace stood. The front porch was a small one. Only three months ago, he'd found two original cowhide wooden rockers at a flea market in the town of Delores, Colorado. Delores was in the southwestern part of the state, at the foot of the San Juan National Forest. He deliberated for a couple of minutes, and then bought them both.

The rockers fit perfectly on the small front porch. Soon, while the snow worked its magic, Amy sat, slowly rocking. Deke watched her as she lay her head back, closing her eyes, humming a tune softly to herself. From time to time, she'd open her eyes, just long enough to see that the snow was still falling, and that Deke was still with her. Once she was satisfied that nothing had changed, she'd close her eyes again, smiling happily, and resume her humming.

Deke was no genius, but he did admit he enjoyed learning, and learning about all sorts of things. He was driven, and that contributed to his self-teaching style. The world around him sometimes drove him to bizarre behavior because of his deep yearning to experience all that life offered. While he did confess that his knowledge of the earth had grown significantly, he admitted to experiencing complex and mysterious wonders that deeply puzzled and flabbergasted him; they left him speechless and dazed for weeks. This was one of those wonders. What he'd witnessed happening to Amy within the last two days, the abuse to her body and mind, were direct results of what she insisted to reflect upon, inflicting more trauma and stress upon her mind and emotions, venturing from the adaptive end of the behavioral spectrum to the maladaptive. His evaluation suddenly provided him with more than enough proof needed. Deke was unfortunate not to witness one of her first emotional spurts of growth.

Fear! Anger! Confusion! Regret! Love! Hate! Sadness! Joy! Comfort! Compassion! Security! Bitterness! Forgiveness!

What a collection of emotions, Amy had endured. Quickly he realized there were too many variations. Deke decided that to study Amy as she struggled through these obstacles would be identical to watching a patient die without helping, just to see the effects of death.

What an accomplishment, scrutinizing and analyzing, and all for the sake of psychology. He was disgusted with himself for even approaching the possibility.

Amy did not see the things Deke saw. She was unable to dissect and biopsy such things. However, his accomplishment was hardly worth mentioning compared to what Amy was experiencing. Deke found this to be a unique challenge, but while he was observing, Amy was scaling peaks.

Deke wanted it to be a simple revelation to Amy, not one with which she would have to struggle. It was because of his own personal struggle in life, and what he'd come to learn, he now felt he had to reveal those lessons to her. It had been the key, unlocking freedom's door for him. Deke silently prayed for Amy, and for himself, becoming aware that his task had now taken a turn. His entire life may have been for this single purpose. The importance of it did not escape him.

After losing his drive to attain the American Dream, Deke had immersed himself in the study of the human mind, searching for answers. The answers were long and hard in coming, and until the day came when he quit his searching, heading for the wilderness attempting an escape, had the answers been revealed.

While alone, deep within the heart of the Rocky Mountains, Deke relaxed, reducing his speed to a level below his previous, maddening pace. His energy level had been burned to a dangerously low level. In addition, while unaware and completely defenseless, Deke submitted, allowing a purging to start. Purged of the artificial barriers, stripped of his pride and arrogance, he was humbled to a place where his vision was cleared, returning to him what he'd lost long ago, and the ability to see.

Quite unprepared, but thankful, Deke received a gift, and discovered the answer. Filled with zeal and passion, driven by what he could not explain, Deke had often tried. His description was sorely inadequate, but quite unique.

Deke Stone was isolated in the wilderness, taken off guard, and became afraid. His fear was driven by what he considered was his insignificance, how small he felt when compared to the immense grandeur around him. With an increasing severity, the fear caused him to cower and shrink, beating him down to a level of despair where finally a transformation occurred. Before the fear could overtake him, Deke overcame, and his spirit was lifted. In a revelation, he was shown that the root of his fear was the very reason he should be considered special and significant. As insignificant as he was when compared to the universe around him was exactly the degree to which he was exceptional, and treasured from above.

Deke never looked at life the same way again. His prison, oddly, had been one of his own making. Freedom was found through a complete surrender. A surrender that was very different from what we think is involved with giving up. In truth, it is in giving up that we attain victory.

VANESSA Jansen and Jack Vermette struggled violently. Jack was actually enjoying the fight, impressed with her determination and effort. Vanessa managed to get partially free, but not before Jack had struck her several times with damaging blows to her head.

Miraculously, after several minutes, recovering from the blows, she regained her senses, and…her memory. As reality surfaced within her, she found herself facing the man who had murdered her baby brother, firing a.357 magnum through the roof of his mouth, and out the top of his head.

With the blistering speed at which Vanessa's memories were returning she also recalled how Jack Vermette prodded and poked at her, making horribly cruel statements referring to her brother, Jedediah, and his lack of courage. Insinuating Jedediah had died begging like a coward was more than Vanessa could tolerate.

Rage erupted from the injured, lady veterinarian, and with such intensity that the larger, much stronger Jack Vermette experienced a breathtaking moment of fear for the first time since taking the resilient woman captive. What he saw were changes within her, along with an incredible determination displayed. A surging energy had flown from her body, and effectively startled Jack.

The quickly evolving changes within Vanessa were physical manifestations of the vengeance that she'd been waiting to set loose for a long time. Finally freed from deep within her, vengeance had been brewing and getting stronger every day. Hate had taken up residence within her on that cold and damp morning after Jedediah's body was discovered. Brutally murdered and found in a bedroom closet, his body was left on display in a humiliating position.

For a moment, the murderer, Jack Vermette, became distracted by her sudden change, marveling at the courage before him. Vanessa had somehow managed to secretly remove the darting devise loaded with Ketamine, from the hidden pocket of her sweatpants. The small, toy-looking weapon gave her a confidence that she had only pretended to have before. Jack Vermette pulled back his head as he spotted the strange pistol, actually beginning to laugh. He was amused at what he thought had to be a harmless device, and the strange confidence that Vanessa seemed to have acquired with this toy.

Peaking levels of anger flooded from Vanessa at his laughter. With a sneer forming on her face, she squeezed the small trigger. The small dart entered and the Ketamine was injected. The small dart gun had suddenly changed from a toy into a potential weapon and finally into a successful form of self-defense.

Personnel within the medical profession use different variations in communicating with each other. Special code words and phrases are used in conveying information about the administration of medication. The usual routes of delivery are either intramuscularly, intravenously, or subcutaneous, when injected through the use of hypodermic needles.

For example: *On Board*, is a type of signal called out by either a nurse or physician whenever a particular cardiac drug is administered during a code situation. Nevertheless, the obvious message that the medication has been administered is not the only signal being sent. The more critical message being announced, which also happens to be the most important, is that the medication has been administered and it is not possible for it to be un-administered.

A bolus of a specific type of medication injected inside the body's tissue or bloodstream has been placed where any attempt to remove it is futile. Like a bullet being fired through the barrel of a gun, there is no way to have the bullet return down that barrel after the trigger has been pulled.

With a cry of accomplishment and victory in her voice, Vanessa yelled, *"on board!"* as a dumbstruck Jack Vermette pulled his injured and drug-filled arm away from the planned attempt to crush Vanessa's trachea.

Having grown weary of her, and the mute responses that he had been receiving to questions, Jack's rage erupted.

"JOHN! Get me Bob Davidson's home phone number will you," Ranger Zach Randal barked into his cell phone.

"Sure thing Zach. But if you want to talk to old Bob, he's still on duty, sitting up at the front desk right now. His shift doesn't end for another couple of hours." Before Zach could respond to his friend,

Sergeant Hadley's curiosity got the better of him. "What exactly is going on in Amarillo, anyway?" Hadley inquired.

"You wouldn't believe it John. That damn Land Cruiser of Amy's is stuck in the parking lot of some rundown motel with nobody in it. Hell, ain't even anybody around. Your boys made it to the scene, and I have them checking over the place, but they're pretty sure Vanessa Jansen was the driver." Zach was giving John Hadley the abbreviated version of what was found, but his mind had begun to run on all eight cylinders when he exited the hotel room. As clear as a missing plug on a finely tuned engine he had realized the key to what Vanessa was up to had been sitting at headquarters half of the night.

"So what is it you've come up with?" Hadley inquired. He knew that tone of voice he was hearing in Zach, and it meant excitement.

VANESSA Jansen had judged the moment as one to be taken advantage of, but she had judged incorrectly. In addition, when it came to judging the amount of punishment she could handle physically, again she had made a poor decision. Aware that this man was going to retaliate whenever she made her move, Vanessa felt the beating would be survivable.

After the attack, in a supine position on the mildewed mattress, her eyes gazing unfocused on Jack Vermette standing over her, Vanessa became aware as the life force flowed out of her. Blood was gushing out in spurts from the vicious laceration carved into her neck.

With a lightning fast response, Jack slashed Vanessa's carotid artery on the right side of her throat, just as the dart entered him. She went down immediately from the blow, and within three minutes, not a drop of blood remained for her heart to pump. With no blood to transport the crucial supply of oxygen necessary for her heart, the cardiac muscle began to fibrillate. However, her dangerous heart arrhythmia was of no concern; Vanessa had been dead long before her heart gave up the battle for survival.

When Vanessa's fibrillating heart finally ceased from the squirming death throes, Jack Vermette was already miles away from the cabin, driving toward Amarillo. Even though he had no way of knowing what drug Vanessa had used, injecting it into him with the small dart gun, he wanted to get closer to a main highway just in case he needed emergency assistance. He drove like a wild man down the dirt lanes, desperate to put as much distance between himself and the cabin as he could, which was a good fifteen miles from civilization.

Jack, being who he was, had lived a pretty adventurous life, and had experimented with many chemicals. As the Ketamine began to take effect, a smile of recognition came across his face. The unmistakable floating high produced by the drug was easily recognizable, and when he realized how easy the access to Ketamine was for Vanessa, Jack slowed the vehicle, pulling into the surrounding forest to enjoy the buzz.

CHAPTER

15

"WELL, YOU STILL want Bob's home number?" Hadley asked, after getting an update on what they'd found in Amarillo. Sergeant John Hadley wanted to be one of the officers in Amarillo, not stuck where he was. But when Zach Randal requested he stay at headquarters, explaining that nobody else could be trusted, Hadley had no choice.

"Hell! I wished I could have planned this some other way, but I guess this is the hand that the dealer has given us to play. Transfer me to the front desk. And John, I want you to monitor this conversation, okay?" he requested, then desperately started thinking about what was the best way to do this, and still do it as diplomatically as possible.

"Desk sergeant." Bob Davidson's voice droned out his title with about the same amount of enthusiasm as someone waiting for an enema.

"Hello Bob, this is Zach Randal." Zach's voice was just a tad louder than normal; he could blame it on the connection of his cell phone. It could also be one way Zach would use psychology to establish dominance over whoever he was speaking.

"Uh, yes sir Ranger Randal! What department do you need sir?" Bob Davidson's voice quivered just a bit, as he faltered over this unexpected call from the Texas Ranger.

"Don't need to be transferred Bob. I need your help." Zach had decided to play the Texas Ranger desperately looking for assistance on a stalled case. This would bring down any of Bob's defenses, and might even make him want to reveal everything. It was a way of getting the information from Bob that had become miserable keeping a secret.

Sometimes loyalties to friends kept cops from ratting out, but when Zach used this approach it had been effective in giving the one being questioned an easy out. Without feeling as they were being disloyal to anyone, they instead were helping to solve a high profile investigation. It had enough of a twist in it to work.

"Yes sir. What can I do for you Ranger?" The shaking in Bob's voice diminished, and he sounded just a bit more composed. Zach could only hope that the connection was clear enough on his cell so whatever he thought he was hearing in the man was accurate.

"We can do away with the formalities. Is that okay Bob? I don't have the time or the stomach for it right now. Besides, you and I have been in this together for about the same amount of time, ain't no seniority that I can see. With that out the way, I need information on Miss Vanessa Jansen. I'm just north of Amarillo, and up to my bottom lip working on this triple murder from out at Dodson's Cafe."

It was critical to even the odds just a bit, and rightly so, since Bob Davidson was at least ten years his elder. He wanted Davidson to think he was busy trying to wrap it up, and time was critical, which in reality it was. Without saying very much if anything about Vanessa or her possible involvement, he dropped her name on the desk sergeant. Bob wasn't buying, remaining silent.

"What I need from you concerning our friend Vanessa is to find out if she's mentioned anything lately concerning Amy Dodson. I'm worried that the good doctor is in a world of trouble, and has even gotten herself mixed up with this case." Still, Bill had no response.

"Without having to go into detail over this cell line let me assure you that certain facts about you and her, of which I am aware, will be put behind us and never brought up again, if you can give me the goods that I need to save a few lives. I know she's a friend of yours, Bob. So what will it be?"

Zach laid it out to Bob Davidson, giving him the impression that he knew about everything including their relationship. In fact, Zach did know some things, but the critical components were missing. Zach also gave Bob the impression that Vanessa was a friend who was in trouble. Challenging Bob, Zach made it clear that it was unwise to deny giving up the information.

Still no reply. Zach paused, anticipating and hoping Bob would just rattle off whatever he knew, but the desk sergeant remained silent.

"So cutting through this chase scene, I want to know, and Bob I really want to know now, why did you transport Vanessa Jansen to Amy Dodson's ranch in the middle of the night, with extra efforts employed for secrecy?"

Zach was getting weary of the entire situation, frustrated with the slow progress. He forgot about diplomacy, and lost the little bit of patience he had remaining. In terms that were comparable to letting cattle droppings fall with their distinctive plop onto the hot prairie, Zach outright asked Bob about that night, making it clear that dire consequences might be associated with refusing this request. Zach needed to get the cooperation of the desk sergeant now, making it crystal clear that he would not ask again.

After a short delay, with tension skyrocketing between the two men, Bob Davidson broke. Zach had called his bluff. Few men alive could boast about beating him at that. Davidson ended up to be completely innocent when it came to law enforcement and ethics; however, he was guilty of being a good cop and a good husband, doing whatever he could in ensuring he, and his wife's future. He had explained when and where he'd met Vanessa, how she'd contacted him before moving to Sweetwater and requesting his help in solving the death of her brother, labeled a suicide.

Zach was spellbound. Because of the bizarre web being spun, desperate to hear every detail, Zach had pulled off to the side of the highway.

"Why in the name of Zeus would her brother's suicide be linked to Sweetwater?" Zach asked, puzzled about the harmless events that brought Vanessa to Texas.

"Well, it was Vanessa's brother's close friendship with Miss Amy that she said resulted in him getting murdered back in Maine," Bob Davidson stated. He told Zach how Vanessa revealed her suspicions that someone in Sweetwater was responsible for her brother's death, someone that was some way linked to Miss Amy.

Bob poked around for her, never thinking much about her story. But when he checked with a couple of snitches he knew, Bob discovered Amy was seen with some man several months back. The same young fellow was also seen entering an abortion clinic a few weeks later, with Miss Amy.

Zach Randal's boat was rocked so hard with that statement that he had to shut the truck ignition off completely. He realized how severely handicapped he now was on the details, and that he would be on the line with Davidson for some time.

WHEN Jack managed to regain his senses, waking from the drug induced sleep, he was stunned to find the battered vehicle he'd been driving was now far from the edge of the forest, sitting with its front bumper hanging precariously over the edge of a cliff a couple of hundred feet from the valley below. Even with the day's light still an hour away, Jack could hear rushing water in the darkness from the stream below. Apparently, in his Ketamine induced high, Jack had been lucid enough to stop the vehicle just in time.

While the fog continued to clear from his mind, he chuckled silently to himself, tickled by the near tragic accident he'd avoided. It only re-enforced his conviction about his mission. He considered it justice that he endeavors to deliver, not a vengeance in retribution for his personal pain or suffering, but a righteous judgment to those who were involved with the murder of his child.

Daylight was just over the horizon getting ready to make its debut, evidence by the shadows slowly developing into deeper shadows within the darkness. When Jack finally cranked the truck's engine, heading in the direction of Amarillo, his mind was clear.

Vanessa's body would probably never be found, but if by some chance it were discovered, Jack would never be linked to it. The cabin where he'd been holding Vanessa was not his. The owner, regretfully, was where he could not be reached for questioning. His body had been buried in a shallow grave far from the location of the cabin.

The man Jack found living in the cabin had been severely mutilated; his face was missing both eyes and both ears. They were savagely cut away from him. In addition to the horrible disfigurement, the man's tongue was sliced out, using a razor blade. Jack felt proud of himself and his handiwork accomplished, all the more because of how he'd managed to keep the man alive throughout the entire ritual.

That veterinarian bitch, Vanessa Jansen, had not given him anything that he could use for locating Amy. Jack really was amazed at the lady animal doctor's toughness, even when taunted about how he had tortured, and killed her own brother. *"Hmm,"* Jack thought. *"What a woman that Vanessa was."* He relived the experience in his head. *"Truly was a shame that she had to die, Vanessa was good sex."*

Returning to the present, Jack decided to check out the Land Cruiser Vanessa had left parked at the hotel. He remembered having a set of Amy's keys, stolen from her vehicle one night after she returned home from shopping. They had come in handy. Even though he'd never used the keys to the Land Cruiser, her house keys gave him access to get inside and snoop.

It was a possibility that an address, or even a name, was left by Amy in the glove box. He would have to take care of that right away, while avoiding any law enforcement personnel. He could not allow them to get too close. He supposed that it was too late to find out why Vanessa had been driving Amy's Land Cruiser in the first place. It was the main reason he'd screwed up with his surveillance of the ranch. Following Vanessa in the Land Cruiser, he allowed Amy time to get away, without ever realizing it.

Jack was wise about Deke Stone. He knew how Amy had given him a room for the night, but only because Deke was the son of one of her mother's friends. Jack had heard all about the juicy affair they supposedly were having. The information came easy while he knocked around police headquarters, pretending to be paying a speeding ticket.

Just by coincidence, Jack walked by the break room inside the department, overhearing Deke Stone's name mentioned by two rookie officers dressed in plain clothes. In a brilliant move, he took two steps back sticking his head inside the break room. With a wide grin he whispered in a mockingly loud tone, "Hey, you guys. Don't talk about Miss Amy Dodson's cousin too loudly."

It was a blind attempt at getting any kind of information. His desperate behavior almost backfired on him as the two officers clammed up tight, looking at him suspiciously.

"Hey guys, I was just kidding," Jack said sheepishly, fearing the possibility of being questioned. His cover-up worked. The two officers looked at each other disgustingly before glancing back up at Jack, carelessly blurting out, "Yeah. Miss Amy's cousin my ass." Then, looking at his young partner sitting across the table from him, Jack heard the rookie say in a slightly lower voice, "I hear that guy knows more about the criminal mind than Quincy and Perry Mason combined."

Jack ducked back down the hall, avoiding any more conversation, but was puzzled by the rookie officer's comment. If Amy had managed to get away from her ranch, he could think of only one person who she would sneak off with, and that person had to be Deke Stone. That was an easy enough problem for Jack to solve, if indeed Amy had run.

Jack Vermette knew that Deke Stone lived in Colorado, on the side of a mountain somewhere. Jack also had no trouble discovering that Deke had been living like a hermit in the small A-frame cabin. What bothered Jack most about the information was how easy it had been to acquire. The ease caused Jack to become paranoid, thinking it could be a trap. His caution about being trapped had been short lived. Jack knew that he had a backup, and justice would prevail. He'd eventually find Deke's address on that mountain, and pay him a little visit. He soon forgot about the rookie cop's comment. The information might surface again, and Jack just might start putting two and two together.

"WHAT kind of fool lives on a mountain in the middle of the damn wilderness with nobody and nothing around him for miles, but he doesn't have a phone?" Zach blurted out, exasperated with the information being relayed to him by Sergeant Hadley.

"The kind of fool that doesn't want to be bothered, and the kind who ain't worried, certain about his ability to take care of himself. Maybe the fool brilliant enough to unlock the mind of the criminally insane," Hadley replied to Zach's sarcastic question unsure an answer was wanted. Hadley had come up with the answer after asking himself the same question Zach asked.

"What was that John?" Zach Randal asked, cursing up a small storm, missing John's response. Hadley doubted the wisdom of repeating his answer. Zach dismissed whatever it was John had said, and began to come up with an alternate plan to find Amy and Deke. More than anything, he needed to warn Deke that a new player was in the game, and one who was spotted-ass-ape crazy.

The information Bob Davidson had just imparted to Zach was effective in lighting a new and hotter fire under the stew they were boiling. As incredible as the account sounded to Zach, even if he had no other explanation, each developing aspect in this case had clearly placed his only suspect, Vanessa Jansen, in the clear.

Zach Randal's mood was transforming into one of extreme urgency. Whenever Zach Randal's mood changed too quickly for John Hadley to handle, the reason was directly related to a development that frightened Zach, actually becoming afraid. Fear that gripped Zach's heart, gripped it while he was listening to Bob Davidson. Thankfully, the fear lasted only long enough for him make a transition, using the energy and motivation caused by fear for another priority, one he classified as an extreme urgency.

Sergeant John Hadley was not looking forward to the hell that surely would break loose over some maniac chasing after Amy Dodson. He had seen Zach Randal become obsessed with a case before, and it nearly killed him. Unfortunately, in a roundabout way, the case had killed his wife, Katherine.

With an intensity that was immeasurable, the determined Texas Ranger had become so focused on the investigation that he'd quit eating and sleeping. His weight dropped so quickly that the County Coroner considered Zach's health dangerously fragile, losing so much in such a short time. Not only had a transformation occurred in Zach's mood, but also another transformation had taken place.

Hadley knew it sounded crazy, and it probably was, but other good, decent officers had also refused to talk about what they'd witnessed in Texas Ranger Zachary Randal. He had become a hunter. Not just any hunter, but one finely tuned to laser accuracy. Others saw the same thing in him. Zach had sharpened and honed his skills into a science.

Zach hated it whenever he was cornered, feeling like a hungry wolf in the dead of winter, starving for the kill. He had again become a desperate, dangerous, unpredictable killer. He was hunting.

"All right! Here's what we're gonna do." Zach broke John Hadley away from the old memories and started giving orders; "Call that sheriff that runs things up in El Paso County. What the hell is his name?...Wright, Sheriff Bill Wright, he's in the same county where Deke Stone has his cabin. Try to get him to go out to Deke's place, and take those two youngsters into protective custody. I'm on my way over, and I'm burning fuel." Zach was getting wound up like a coiled spring with this new information. Sergeant Hadley saw it coming, and he pitied the target Zach finally focused his sights on.

"After you've finished calling in bulletins, call me back, and give good directions on how to get to that mountain Deke and Amy are holding up." Flicking his cell phone off, Zach stepped heavily onto the Bronco's accelerator, heading toward Green Mountain Falls, Colorado. In a blur of metal, Zach raced, desperately hoping that he was not too late.

OFFICERS Dan Baker and Bill Frye had finished with their investigation at the hotel, and were heading toward the office of the Potter County Sheriff Department. Neither of the two men had any confidence in being able to get pictures from the Office of Motor Vehicles. They had serious doubts about their ability to fax anything, much less pictures. Even if driving permits had photo IDs on them, and were in the computer files at Motor Vehicles, it would be the first time in recorded history they pulled off such a task in less than twelve hours.

It was just like waiting to take the driving test; by the time you're tested, it's past time for your renewal.

As the two officers approached their destination they got a little turned around, finding themselves on a rarely used back street, right behind Potter County's headquarters. On the abandoned back street behind the sheriff department, the two officers spotted the tow truck that was supposed to be towing Amy Dodson's Land Cruiser to the impoundment.

Towing vehicles for impoundment was a normal procedure for any car or truck officers wanted to lock up, at least until a thorough going over had been completed by the folks working in lab. The scene that the two officers happened upon was anything but normal. The tow truck was pulled off to the side, away from the street, completely onto the curb. The driver was standing at the big Toyota's passenger door; half of him was inside the cab of the vehicle. He seemed to be rummaging around. It was disgusting, but it appeared that the tow truck driver was trying to rip off something from inside the Land Cruiser, which he evidently thought must be valuable.

Bill Frye and Dan Baker were in an unmarked vehicle, and saw no alarm in the man as they drove slowly around, intending to park in front of the tow truck. The fact that he was inside the vehicle when it was supposed to be locked did not surprise them. It was no big trick to open a locked car door when you had the tools to do it.

"This guy is not even worried about someone seeing him," Bill commented with amazement.

"Okay. The minute I throw the car into park, we'll approach him silently from each a side, and if we're good and quiet he might not spot us until we have him down." Dan coordinated their move, with excitement filling his voice.

Bill slowly shook his head. "It will never cease to amaze me, how much you like catching bad guys." The short comment was made just before the doors were gently opened. Walking at a quick, but silent pace, Dan and Bill approached the rear of the tow truck. Just as each of the two men arrived at the vehicle's rear bumper where the tow bar was hooked, they stopped. The driver that was digging around inside Amy's Land Cruiser was gone. They saw no sign of him anywhere. Looking silently at each other somewhat confused, Bill saw Dan's head explode as he took the hit.

An eruption of reddish-white spray materialized around Dan's head like a halo. A pink-tinged mist seemed to materialize from out of nowhere. Bill was shocked, unable to comprehend what was happening, and in slow motion. It was without warning that time resumed normal speed.

Bill Frye instantly entered a state of horror, realizing what had happened. He watched panic-stricken as Dan's body crumpled with a sickening crunch hitting the pavement. Dan was dead even before his body had stopped moving.

A loud ringing filled Bill's head, adding to the panic and confusion. Reflexes took over as he immediately crouched down. Feverishly, he began scanning the area. Bill was shaking as he drew his revolver. Then, following his training, he started backing up rapidly, seeking cover as he continued scanning about.

Tragically, Jack Vermette had been standing only a few feet behind Bill when he squeezed the trigger sending a bullet rupturing through Dan's skull. The concussion from the 44 magnum, and the incredible explosive force, had sheared away most of his head, creating a halo of blood and brain.

Bill found himself temporarily deaf from the blast; the constant ringing was effective in blocking out all other sounds.

A black evil, which later would result in some officers hesitating before they entered any scene, had been set loose through Jack Vermette. He waited calmly for Bill Frye to back up, toward him, the barrel of his weapon leveled at the back of Bill's head.

Just as the cold steel of the barrel on the 44 Magnum touched Bill's hairline, Vermette squeezed the trigger. Not the slightest effect was noticed in Jack Vermette; he turned, leaving the scene, while Bill's body fell over, head first onto the street. Nothing was left to his face as his empty skull hit the pavement. The sound produced was similar to that made when an empty coconut falls onto concrete.

Driving at a cautious speed, Jack had only a few minutes before he approached the hotel where Vanessa parked the Land Cruiser. He was startled as he saw a tow truck pulling the Land Cruiser, crossing him as it left the scene. Jack considered it his good fortune he followed the tow truck. On the darkest street behind the sheriff department, Jack made his move, easily coaxing the driver into stopping.

After a swift slice from the knife he carried, he pulled the driver's dead body out of the tow truck and away from the scene. Jack started to go through every inch of Amy's Land Cruiser, hoping she had left an address or sheet of paper with directions written on it.

The officers who were assisting Texas Ranger Randal with the investigation, Frye and Baker, never dreamed they'd encounter the man that everyone was searching for, the triple murderer, and now with Vanessa's disappearance, the kidnapper.

Jack's beat up old truck had been parked among the shadows on the dark street, out of sight from anyone arriving.

When Dan and Bill arrived, it seemed the only thing to be suspicious of was what the two officers witnessed happening. Naturally, they suspected the driver was a thief.

Unfortunately, instead of the tow truck driver looking to steal something, it was Jack Vermette. However, he was watching as the two officers pulled up in front of the tow truck, parking their unmarked cruiser.

Jack was a man who took advantage of any situation, and the moment he realized he was out of their line of sight while parking, he circled around, coming up from behind them.

Officers Bill Frye and Dan Baker were easy kills for Jack. Few men were capable of offering a decent challenge, and it was beginning to bore him. They were quick and clean hits. Without wasting a moment of time after the brutal, execution-style murders Jack drove away in their unmarked vehicle, checking out the bag of fast food that the two men left sitting on the seat. Munching on cold fries that Dan and Bill never had the chance to eat, Jack sang loudly along with the music on the radio. He was now Colorado bound.

CHAPTER

16

THE EPITOME of uniqueness can be witnessed every morning. Literally each morning is different from every other, past or future, different in every way since the dawn of time until the end of time. Creation is a dynamic event by design, and reveals itself to us in many forms. It has never, and will never cease with its progression. Set in motion by God, and by His word only will the advance be halted. The planet we occupy has been beneficiary of the most incomprehensible power in the universe. A power that provides us with each new day, unique, destined never again to occur. All the things that Deke saw as wondrous and miraculous, at one time, he rejected as philosophical babbling.

Deke was a likable person, but occasionally his philosophy of life spooked people who happened to be around him. Eventually, or inevitably, he would find himself alone, considered too deep a thinker by others. What people misunderstood about Deke were his passions, driving him to experience life at levels deeper than most ever knew existed. It was a certain passion for exploring life and its wonders in places where few men dared to wander. He took no offense by the distance people maintained from him. Deke understood their caution. Being so exposed, letting go of the emotional restraint as he did while journeying through life, could be very uncomfortable.

Maybe he was eccentric, a romantic, or maybe just a dreamer. Whatever the title, it had more healing power for the empty and searching souls of men than anything else others dared to believe. Deke's explanation for those having a hard time understanding his desire to drain every drop from life was simple: "Life is precious, but like many others, depression afflicts me too often. Because of the depth of this depression during times of attack, my only rational response is to counter depression by soaring to extraordinary heights at the first possible opportunity."

Above all other things in his life at this time, Deke knew one matter had taken priority: Amy needed healing from all the hurt she experienced. Just as importantly, she needed mending for her broken heart.

The freedom that life has to offer, regardless of any past error, had to be revealed to her. Regarding the deliverance, and her escape from the hurt, it was crucial that Deke monitor her closely. During such an emotional event, the tendency was to mistake the absence of hurting for an actual healing, leading to abandonment in the recovery effort. The result was the individual never reaching the root problem for their emotional turmoil.

Without a doubt, if she weren't careful, Amy would again fall into the same pain and depression. The tragedy would be the waste of time, money, and life. Life meant to be enjoyed, under normal circumstances.

The gift of life does not wait, but continues on its journey through time. A decision whether to climb aboard for the journey or accept being left behind has to be made. One must address the importance of this decision to either live life as a participant or to just observe life as a spectator. The choice is one that seems obvious, and is easy enough to make. However, what often is chosen is rarely carried out.

Deke Stone had reached a pinnacle of his life where decisions had to be made. Despite every obstacle, every pain, every failure, and each victory, he never, not for a single moment, regretted his choice in making that journey as a participant. It was the real thing for Deke, life in all its glory and splendor. Each experience was a unique, and sometimes bizarre event, but it was living, pure and undeniable, life at its best.

JACK Vermette was still singing to the songs playing on the radio. The car was only a year old, and he noticed how clean the interior was kept. Dust that accumulates along the edge of the air conditioning vents had even been wiped spotless. Over the visor were vehicle registration and insurance cards, all labeled, and easily accessible. Jack Vermette noticed all the signs that indicated an obsessive-compulsive disorder, which no doubt, brought misery to the officer who had owned the vehicle.

He shook his head slowly from side to side whispering, "Poor bastard, he really was sick. He should have thanked me for putting him out of his misery."

He had thought about going back to the cabin where he'd left Vanessa Jansen, dead on the mattress. Any information that may have been left in the Land Cruiser by Vanessa, or Amy, was now in the possession of Potter County Law Enforcement. On the other hand, maybe nothing was inside the vehicle for him to find in the first place. He dismissed the thought.

Vermette ate the two burgers left by Dan and Bill. The unmarked cruiser he stole from the two officers was well equipped. Complete sets of maps were discovered in an old, oversized map-case; Jack noticed it was made of pure leather. After glancing over the map, Jack was comfortable with his knowledge of the area, and well accustomed to the route he was taking from Amarillo. He emptied the leather map-case of its contents and stole it. He loved the smell and feel of leather.

The mind of someone who was capable of committing such brutality against another human being yet, also capable of functioning normally in society, considered socially charming, had the ability to develop control and restraint with years of practice. The extreme violence perpetrated by such an individual only came after elevating intensities in emotions from the many previous acts of violence committed.

Just as the normal individual becomes bored with the pleasures of life, seeking higher levels of activity for enjoyment, so does the mind of the criminally insane.

His first kill, was more than likely without extremes, producing feelings that were similar to an orgasm. But as time passed, killing lost its euphoric effect; increases in the degree of brutality were necessary to attain that first sensation he experienced.

He had entered a race, seeking that first high, which still had not been found, and the killings became more violent and extreme while his unbalanced mind panicked. A zealous and continuous search began, craving a euphoria that no longer exists. Living a life controlled by compulsive behaviors, he has no explanation for what he does, and he realizes that he has no control over this journey. It is a journey leading deeper and deeper into desolation and despair, leaving a wretched trail of dead bodies behind.

A distance of 213 miles separated Amarillo from Raton, New Mexico. The main highway, and of course, the quickest route to Raton, was Highway 87.

Anytime an investigation crossed a state line, with unknown individuals involved, the measure of difficulty increased significantly, while at the same time, the chances of solving the crime decreased significantly. The body of Vanessa Jansen would not be found for many months.

JACK Vermette was familiar with the man he referred to as that damned Old Texas Ranger. He'd crossed him in the hallway one day at the sheriff department while sniffing around for information about Deke Stone. It was common knowledge around Sweetwater that the damned Old Texas Ranger drove a modified black Ford Bronco. It was also rumored to be faster than the trooper cruisers.

Concentrating with a mixture of excitement and nervousness, Jack had set the Crown Victoria's cruise at sixty-five miles per hour. It was a safe speed to travel while avoiding attention from some state cop with radar. More than anything, Jack needed to come down from the adrenaline high he'd gotten from such a daring escape, executing the two detectives that were pursuing him. It was a close call that had energized him even more than he thought possible. Similar to the high sought after from cocaine, he was feeling the combined effect of euphoria and the rush of amphetamines. He knew from past experience that he was going to slowly crash, leaving him with an exhausting depression. It was no fun going through the crash, and contrary to some opinions, it was nothing like the feeling brought about after intense sex. However, the timing was going to be perfect, since two hundred miles of road lie ahead of him; he'd have enough time to recover. Laying his head back, adjusting the electric seats to a perfect fit, Jack made himself comfortable.

Roaring past the Crown Victoria, the black blur came from out of nowhere, zooming ahead of him. Caught in an unguarded state, Jack nervously stiffened up. Before the person driving the vehicle could get a look at him, they had zoomed far ahead of him. The hopped-up Bronco that was really flying down the highway impressed Jack. His smile of admiration quickly faded as he realized the vehicle was exactly like the one his nemesis drove.

The Bronco was easily recognized, but that's not what had suddenly scared Jack to sit up straight, gripping the wheel. In the east, the sun was coming up, casting light through the passenger side window of the Bronco at an angle just right for him to see that the big man driving wore a white Stetson. Recognition of the driver immediately conjured a feeling of fear in Jack. This encounter was too close; Jack's hands were shaking.

Wasting no time, he started looking for an exit, feeling certain that Zach Randal would turn around and come back for him, making an undetected approach from the rear. Jack knew he needed to get off Highway 87. Randal was not the same caliber of man as the men he'd just executed, and Jack was not ready for an encounter with him yet. He was planning to meet up with the Ranger, but only when the advantage was in his favor and a kill was certain.

ZACH Randal had many vices, most of which he'd kept hidden and were harmless. But one, which he had never been able to control, was driving at suicidal rates of speed. From the debacle that he and his fellow detectives responded to in Amarillo, he had turned around and taken Highway 87 north, toward Raton. After two hundred thirteen miles of wild driving, he'd enter Raton, jumping onto Interstate 25, hauling ass to Green Mountain Falls. That was the extent of his knowledge on the location of Deke's place, where Amy was hopefully safe.

Some people claim reality is stranger than fiction. It was unlikely that Zach Randal would respond to that question. Had the Ranger been aware of his immediate surroundings, and magically had some kind of seeing eye that showed him all the bizarre twists that were actually occurring around him, the possibility exists that Zach Randal would have appointed himself as judge, jury, and executioner.

Zach had no patience, and naturally his feelings were raw toward bad people, but he always kept that off the record, although, nothing else would give him as much pleasure as being judge, jury, and executioner.

Traffic on Highway 87 was light. Ranger Randal wasn't fooling around. He wanted to get to Green Mountain Falls, locate Deke and Amy, grab the Beatles, and give them the keys to his Bronco. Zach wanted to tell them, *'Head north and don't look back.'* He knew who was after them, and how dangerous this man was. Warning Deke and Amy would free him up just long enough to kill Vermette.

He had a real bad feeling about this case though, and that was what worried him the most. He wanted Deke and Amy to get out of town and into obscurity. Because he was a person with incredible influence, Zach knew he could convince them.

Passing car after car, driving at an average speed of ninety-five miles per hour, Zach was deep in thought, whipping by vehicles so quickly that in no time they were only small dots in his rearview mirror.

Out of the blue, Zach thought he recognized something. Maybe a place or a person that he couldn't place, it was a powerful *deja vu*. Struggling to figure it out, it was something he didn't need and hated when it happened.

Randal was afraid of the human mind. It frightened him every time he was assigned a case like this. He'd never admit to this fear, but the potential havoc and evil that the mind was capable of dreaming up was frightening, to say the least. Under normal circumstances, Zach knew people imagined doing horrible things to an enemy, but to actually commit a crime that has been dreamed is unlikely. In fact, only a handful of this type of behavior has been documented. People, Zach always thought, just weren't that black on the inside, crammed with evil. But apparently, someone was.

Swinging his head around to look behind him Zach suddenly realized that he had recognized that Crown Victoria!...That car looked just like Bill and Dan's unmarked vehicle!...They drove a black Crown Victoria...Who the hell was driving that one?...It damn sure wasn't Dan or Bill!

RINGO stood motionless. Deke was sleeping on the short couch, below the upper loft where his bed and Amy were. He almost screamed, petrified in fear, as he opened his eyes from the deep sleep, finding the big rust colored head of Ringo inches from his face. Thankful, he realized Ringo had just been watching him, returning to the old habit that Deke was first exposed to back in Sweetwater, while at Amy's ranch.

Closing his eyes, catching his breath, only resulted in a slurp across his face from Ringo's wet tongue.

"Hey! What are you up to boy?" Laughing at what happened, Deke ruffled the big Chessie's fur. It occurred to Deke that the Beatles had been inside the cabin since the night before. When he and Amy decided to go to bed, they were exhausted from the drive and the stress of the day's developments.

"Oh! I know what you want." Deke threw off the thick quilt that he'd covered with during the night. The weather was starting to change from a moderate snowfall into near blizzard conditions when he last checked.

Deke stood up, hearing a rumbling like drum beats coming down the stairway. John, Paul, and George had heard Deke moving about so they raced to investigate. All together, they began shaking and stretching to wake themselves. Deke watched as each yawned widely. The incredible size, on each, of the mouth, and with such large canine teeth, sent a shudder through him. Deke was thankful that the Beatles accepted him. He pitied the person that had to face them.

"Come on boys, let's see how much snow came down during the night." Deke opened the heavy door and discovered the snow was piled half way up the opening. Snow was piled to Deke's waist. He knew it was going to be tough getting anywhere in these conditions, they may be stuck for a few days.

The Beatles were standing at the door, tails wagging, looking at Deke with questioning eyes, anticipation building. When Deke realized that they were waiting for his command to go outside he quickly gave it.

"Okay, outside!"

The cabin seemed to shake from dog power as he watched the four brute Chesapeakes try to exit all at once. Banging against one another, and into the doorframe, the Beatles were leaping the three feet needed to clear the height of the snow before making it outside. The problem was they were jumping all at the same time, colliding while airborne. The scene was a comical display of rust-colored fur, struggling for the exit. It was a pleasant, but odd scene to watch.

In any other circumstance, with different dogs, fur would be flying when the fighting began. With the Beatles, even though they had that look of viciousness, they seemed to be making a game of it, laughing while trying to be the first. Deke started to laugh spontaneously. His laughter wasn't just a chuckle, but a guffaw.

It was as if someone had pulled the plug. The four dogs suddenly froze in their place, staring directly at Deke. Still laughing, but quickly lowering the volume, he looked at Ringo, then John, Paul, and George. Not an eye blinked between them.

"What?" Deke asked, bewildered. He remembered those wide jaws when they yawned and wondered what button he had punched to get this response. It was similar to buying a dangerous piece of hardware without instructions. Each controlling switch had different functions that you had to figure out, but by pressing one button at a time, hoping you didn't hit one that made it self-destruct.

"What?" Deke repeated, looking at the four refusing to move.

"They have been taught not to make any loud noises until after I'm wake in the morning. It's called consideration, and they have learned it well. But it looks like your training needs to be reinforced." Amy Dodson sat at the edge of the loft in a white cotton T-shirt. It left incredibly little for the imagination, but Deke stared anyway, deciding that his imagination needed a little boost occasionally.

"Okay, guys. I'm awake now. At ease!" she commanded.

The plug must have been replaced, because all four Beatles began to jump up toward Amy, barking with glee in their happiness. Deke wondered how she would respond if he joined in with them.

"Outside!" the command sounded like someone talking to a bird. Her voice was not a bellow across the mountainside, but it produced the desired response.

One at a time, with perfect timing, the Beatles leaped up onto the snow. Within a few seconds, they were out of sight, doing what dogs do.

Deke remained standing in the same spot, holding the handle on the door. With a bit of embarrassment he turned slowly from watching the Beatles run off, and back to Amy sitting at the edge of the loft. A part of him didn't want to look upon the enticing sight, and when he lifted his eyes to speak to her...she was gone.

In utter disappointment, he realized the shower was running. He smiled to himself thinking how life was some crazy ride. Even though he acted disappointed, in reality, Deke was relieved. It would only make an already confusing and highly charged situation more difficult.

While Amy showered, he changed into jeans and a sweatshirt. Since he was going to shovel snow from around the cabin's front entrance and check out how bad the drifts were on the narrow road leading down to the valley, he may as well dress for it. First, he'd start breakfast. Amy was pretty small, but a big eater.

The sausage and eggs were sizzling in the pan when he heard Amy dressing upstairs, she'd soon be coming down from the loft. It was silly, but he was suddenly uncomfortable.

"For crying out loud, it's not like you've had passionate sex all night!" Deke chastised the part of him that felt guilty for no reason.

Waiting for Amy, busily preparing their breakfast, Deke's mind shifted to what they had been unconsciously avoiding since Raton. They had not heard from Zach Randal, and he wondered about developments in the investigation.

Without a doubt, Amy was holding something back. Obvious to Deke through his analysis of what he had been told by Randal, plus the strange mood swings and depression that he witnessed in Amy, suggested a past regret, powerful enough to be very relevant. Whatever she was hiding, it must be very personal, and maybe an intimate part of her past.

Deke had tried to get Amy to talk, with no success. He began to regret his minor persuasions. He had no right to invade on her privacy. If Zach Randal had pushed her on the issue as hard as he knew Randal was capable, then it may have done more harm than good. Amy may have taken his pushing the wrong way, feeling the information was being demanded. Such heavy persuasion could have created a mechanism of defense to rise up from within her, the secret becoming a protected part of her, causing her to bury it even deeper, all because of a feeling that she was being violated.

If Amy feels like her mind has been invaded, and attempts are made to steal this secret part of her, the results could be serious. The possibility is very strong that she feels she cannot live without the secret, but at the same time, cannot live with it. It may help Deke in helping her. It also may take on new meaning, being transformed from what brought her pain to the thing that belongs to only her, and must be protected.

If that transformation occurs, then the chance of getting to it is nearly impossible. Deke may have to change tactics completely if they were going to have any success. He's not comfortable with this psychology bullshit. After all the years of college and graduate school, studying every damn form of twisted behavior, and every reason for it, he realized it was for the most part: a crock of shit.

Selecting a group of individuals, and conducting double blind studies was standard for most abnormal behaviors. Group response and behavior is evaluated, then documented. Stating this as behavioral proof, for whatever classification of abnormal behavior the research is studying, they begin to create what is called a symptom list.

It was all so much speculation that Deke couldn't see how they could accurately classify any research, claiming that it represents science.

Science is a definitive study, with solid evidence and proof that is undeniable.

Psychology is a study of various behavioral patterns, resulting from a particular stimulus, which cannot be positively identified. Stimulus of the type, which most often will not produce the same effect on any two individuals. Diagnostics are derived by taking certain segments of the population, anywhere from a couple, to hundreds of individuals, volunteering to participate in research. These individuals are subjected to certain conditions; their response is then documented.

Deke's objection to the testing centered around researchers taking the information gathered from the chosen test subjects, and assuming their responses were accurate in reflecting the rest of the population's behavioral habits. The tragedy was in accepting the conclusions, then documenting them as 'science.'

He realized that some areas of legitimate research were necessary in many fields of psychology, and he agreed with some of the conclusions, even witnessing as they had been put into practice, successfully.

The whole thing frustrated him at times, but he was knowledgeable in the studies performed, and in the documented cases of criminal insanity.

In addition, Deke had become involved with a research group that put together a large study with the assistance of grant money, to classify the bizarre behavioral patterns of psychopathic individuals, also sociopath deviant behavior. The study was incredibly interesting, and Deke really got into it. But he did not agree with the group's conclusion or with the study's results. Deke was adamant about the results being non-definitive for any solid conclusion. With so much bizarre behavior, to the normal mind it was indescribable, and he suggested that another study be conducted for comparison before classification, possibly even develop a behavioral base where other research studies would be able to utilize the result as a comparison model.

The research team disagreed. He had not been surprised, especially when he discovered that the grant also had been used up, without funding to complete the study or any additional research.

The result was simple. Since additional funding was not available, the test results were used for definite scientific documentation, in psychopathic and sociopath individuals.

Realizing this was not where he belonged, feeling too restricted, needing more space; Deke quit his graduate studies and began to travel. When he ran into the Rocky Mountains his heart told him it was the space he needed.

"Hey, that smells so good, I hope you cooked enough for me." Amy was as chipper as a bluebird. When Deke turned around and looked at her, he realized under the clothing she wore was not only a beautiful woman, but also a frightened little girl. He pictured a lost child in the middle of a mob of people. This child was crying in desperation, searching for help and safety.

Without a father all of her life, she'd lived with her mother who worked constantly for their survival. Amy was robbed of the nurturing from her mother who could not provide any because work was a thief, stealing the time right out from under them.

Amy finally bloomed into womanhood, compliments began to flow, and she suddenly starting receiving the attention for which she was so starved. But tragically, her mother became ill and died. The only permanent figure in her life was suddenly gone. The trauma must have been intense to her spirit, but from all accounts, she hid it well.

Deke knew that it was not hidden, but covered over, buried deep within her, afraid of the pain it would bring. Amy put a distance between herself, and the hurts in her life.

It was nothing so deep that Amy needed counseling, neither was it a psychological maze that had to be mastered before she could escape the past, enjoying the rest of her life. What Deke believed, and what had been proven through experiences that he himself encountered in life was that Amy was a woman who had not received the love and feelings of security, crucial in a child during the years of development.

Deke began suddenly feeling an urging from within, time was short, he was guilty, and selfishness had developed concerning Amy and his time with her. The fact that he was not being as honest as he should, in effect was a slap across the face.

Someone was somewhere close, maybe closer than imagined, and that person was a killer. Danger and the bleak fact that it was real and around them began to sober his mind.

"Hey, are you all right? You have such a serious look on your face." Amy immediately noticed a difference in him. Deke only looked at her, he did not answer.

"Come on Deke, stop it! You're scaring me." It was a turning point. Amy backed away from him. She was bewildered and he had scared her. Deke fought with the feeling for a moment, then obtaining the control he needed, relaxed, taking a deep breath.

"Amy, please forgive me. I've been thinking, and feel the time for us to speak has arrived. We must throw inhibition and caution aside, becoming honest beyond what will be comfortable, and find answers to stop who and what has set out to destroy you."

Had Deke not spoken so logically, humbling himself to a point where he was exposed and defenseless, Amy would have told him off. She had even prepared a response just in case the moment arrived when Deke would try picking at her brain. But, her intuition spoke loudly saying she could trust this man. He meant no harm, only to assist a fellow human being. The golden rule was applied, and every effort would be made not to hurt or embarrass her.

Looking at Deke, doubt written on her face, Amy responded, "All right Deke, what is it you want to talk about?"

Her words flowed like wine, and he wished she were toothless, barefoot, and fat. But being the way things were, he decided to endeavor, endure, and enjoy.

"Because of the seriousness of this situation, and questions that we have no answers concerning the future, I feel that it's time for a serious talk." He was trying to be gentle with her, but as he spoke, a change materialized in her eyes that he deciphered as skepticism and caution.

"Deke. May I speak first? I'm very concerned and worried about..." Deke held up his hand bringing her to a sudden stop.

"More than anything, that would make me feel much better, and I'm totally in favor of complete honesty." The comment was a sign for her to speak freely.

The breakfast was still on the stove, and the Beatles were capable of handling themselves, Deke and Amy each filled a large mug of coffee, making themselves comfortable in the small den.

"This horrible thing that's happened really has turned my world topsy-turvy. Deke, people have been murdered! I feel as if it's my fault. My heart has been shattered, and lately its been breaking into small little pieces that I am afraid will never heal." Her plea for help was obvious. Deke maintained control of his sympathy, even though the plea was very sad.

"I'm pretty sure that Zach Randal has filled you in on the details of the case, and he probably has told you my life story in addition. But Deke, I'm not sure that even I could relate my life story to anyone. Some parts of my life are very private, things that I will not reveal to anyone at any time regardless if a monster wants me dead for some reason or not. Men have things that are kept secret, but for the record, whenever a woman has a secret that she holds close to her heart it is a horse of a different color. No devils in hell will break that away from me. Before you ask any questions, let me explain one more thing. By a design that I suppose evolution is responsible for, since the very beginning of the human race, women have been oppressed. We have been cooks, cleaners, lovers, and mothers. Whenever the need would arise, we were expected to have gathered the eggs, butchered the hog, washed our hands, and cooked breakfast, among the many other chores that we perform.

"Secrets that women keep hidden, for whatever reason, are special, and the most intimate of their possessions. This is because they have been denied the privilege of possessing anything that was considered a threat by the man she's with at the time. All women feel the same, even though they might deny it. Too many men are with split-personalities keeping themselves well-hidden until all hell breaks loose, and when it does they begin to cry about how they are the victims." This was really a great story, and Deke thought it would make a great book.

He was relieved, and he felt that they were making progress. Amy was doing her best to be helpful and cooperative. Deke decided to spit out what he had to say, and let things happen.

"I appreciate what you've said, and I agree. I have no right to assault you in an attempt to get you to divulge personal and private matters of your life. It's wrong, and I will not have anything to do with that part of this entire affair. A killer is seeking to do you harm. For reasons that I cannot imagine Ranger Zach Randal has tangled me up with this investigation."

Amy was drop-mouth impressed with his declaration concerning her private affairs, but when he spoke of his entanglement, she looked hurt.

"Don't misunderstand Amy. It is still my choice to be helping. Maybe I know things that could be beneficial. For me to think I can solve this investigation would be arrogant to the extreme. Past experiences in my life have cured me of arrogance, and thankfully taught me that humility is where I belong most of the time." Admitting that he was only human, and not claiming to be anything special, was a breath of fresh air to Amy. The men that she had been associated with in her life would never admit to anything so tender in nature. Sitting on the love seat, where Deke had slept the night before, Amy tucked her legs under, and made herself comfortable. With a slight nod of her head, she urged Deke to continue.

What Deke felt he must say, was sort of rough. He was attracted to her; it was no use in trying to deny his feelings, especially to himself. The forces that come from emotions are usually in opposition to those of logic and reason, he was battling the two because of his feelings toward her.

With a deep breath he called on his courage and began, "Before I start, let me warn you, nothing said can be taken personal. Do not allow what is said to make you defensive. These are my beliefs, and they have been what has sustained me in a world that is cruel and unfair." With his clarification stated he felt a little better.

When Amy nodded again, eyes wide, she looked straight at him and whispered, "Okay."

Deke began, "Like many others throughout the towns and back roads of this country, you have suffered. You did miss out on important elements of life, and you were hurt and left lonely. To every one of the injustices I have one reply 'so what,' which applies to everyone who's endured similar obstacles in their life. The key to most problems that crop up in the course of a lifetime, comes with the realization that life is full of obstacles, expect them. Refuse the temptations of feeling sorry for yourself, learn to face negative events that come your way, determine to learn something, anything, from every confrontation encountered. Life is a journey that consists of good and bad events. Nothing exists that allows a person to pick and choose the parts they desire, casting aside those that are undesirable. The journey is a package deal with no guarantees of satisfaction. What determines satisfaction resides within you.

"The reality is that no everlasting party takes place for anyone to attend. The playing field is not even. Nothing in life is fair, and your rights are only the things that have been given to you by other flawed men.

"Reality is a brutal teacher, but receiving the brutality is a choice that the individual has to make. No perfect justice endures. Moments of heartache, moments of sorrow, and moments of pain that seems unbearable will happen. People will lie, steal, cheat, abuse, and purposely do all manner of things just to hurt you.

"Those are facts of life that need to be accepted. If not accepted the result will be an assault on the emotional level far exceeding the normal results in those who do accept these facts. Humanity is, and always has, been filled with those who are evil, those who seek out vengeance, for hurts that they've imagined as being the fault of other individuals. The facts can be compared to bitter pills, but whether bitter or sweet, they must be swallowed.

"In contrast to the facts of life that we struggle against, another list is at hand containing the facts of life which we seek. Time consisting of moments filled with joy, filled with laughter, freedom, happiness, contentment, satisfaction, peace, and even a deeper love than we thought imaginable await us.

"The decision to accept everything life offers is a wise move, leading to a fuller and more fulfilling journey. Time will always be our enemy, and that is why it is so critical that we not delay in making that choice. The choice is made easier when we realize the truth behind this existence, and that for every single evil and devastating collision we suffer through, an exact opposite is nearby bringing peace and joy in measures that are overflowing."

Deke was trying to express the awesome opportunities that folks have available in their life. He wanted Amy to realize that even in the midst of things happening to you that are so bad, life can still be so very good.

"Circumstances are irrelevant Amy, if you make this decision. Life is more important than anything of this world, and the time has come to stop and realize that fact."

When Deke finally stopped, he was afraid that he'd said too much. Amy sat before him crying the biggest tears he'd ever seen. He bowed his head, looking down, not wanting to embarrass her more than she already was.

The next few minutes seemed to drag by, lasting much longer than the five minutes they sat silent. Amy finally spoke.

"Deke, you're right. If only I were able to do those things you're talking about. I wish so badly for the happiness you talked about. But I don't know how to do it!" Amy tearfully confessed.

Because she was so meek, and with a poor self-image, Deke knew the process may be a difficult one for her, but he was sure she was capable, much more capable than she imagined. He wanted to help her. Lifting his head when she spoke he tried not to display any emotion. After her reply, his self-control was gone, and he responded, "I'll help you Amy. If you want the life that is waiting for you, a life filled with good feelings, excitement, fun, and happiness. I won't mislead you; obstacles will pop up, with trials to endure. But you'll find that when you encounter these hurdles the struggle will not be as difficult as before, and maybe, eventually disappear, leaving you with a new and stronger confidence." He had to force himself to stop. His desire to explain was so strong, but he knew of no other way to explain the experience; she would have to feel it for herself.

Those eyes were too much for Deke; he had a hard time with them before, now filled with tears the torture was close to unbearable.

Amy was broken. Her heart was completely exposed, and the wall she had constructed around her was beginning to crumble. He saw the desire in her, but a very important component must be utilized before attempting this process. While she was defenseless, and her ears were open to hear, Deke revealed the last step, "Before we can do anything Amy, I have one more thing I must say. This process of facing every fear and every pain goes hand in hand with a decision to forgive every person who ever caused you pain, that includes yourself.

"Forgiveness is paramount. Refusing forgiveness will result in bitterness, hate, fear, and depression; all leading you right back to the previous state of misery. After you have done that, it's such a simple and quick process to complete, and when complete, the decision can be made with no barriers." He noticed how the tone of voice he used for the last statement was much gentler and caring.

Amy's desire was so powerful that she began with the process while sitting on the love seat. Deke could actually see the pain and hurt begin to lift, and her countenance brightened magically before his eyes.

"You think with your help, we can do it?" The question was short, but loaded with information. Her choice of using the word we instead of I suggested togetherness, and he knew it was an unconscious choice, but now was not the time. They had enough on their hands for the moment. Deke looked directly into her eyes to answer. "Without a doubt. We can do what we feel needs to be done, and whatever we want in life will be possible." The definitive response seemed to satisfy her, and as her tears began to dry, she slowly unwrapped her legs from under her, and stood.

Deke figured she was getting herself another cup of coffee, but when she stood before him, she turned and slowly lowered herself until nose-to-nose with him. Those eyes were almost touching his, and the shock paralyzed him immediately. He became dangerously close to hyperventilating with this development. She had no smile on her face and her expression was one that Deke was unable to figure out.

Like satin blowing softly in the wind, she wrapped her arms around him and molded herself against his body. It was the worst, best feeling he could ever remember having. He recalled once riding on this super-duper roller coaster that was supposed to be the scariest and most exhilarating in the country. That was the only thing he could think of to compare this to, and then it got worse. As Amy hugged him, she began slowly squeezing tighter and tighter. He could feel her hot breath on his ear, and wished it would soon be over. Softly, she whispered, "I thank God for you. And I want you to help me, please!"

Deke finally found strength enough to raise his arms and return her embrace, but he was pretty sure that he was totally numb, and wouldn't feel a thing. Amy finally unwound her body slowly from him. With a smile, she sat back on the edge of the love seat.

The air was so thick that Deke felt he couldn't breathe. Just when he was about to panic, his body took over; a deep breath resolved the problem. He was not sure what his face looked like, but it was way too late to care with those eyes never leaving him. The time had come to end this distressing situation.

"Damn!" Deke commented under his breath. He knew better. Love was always more painful than it was pleasant, but this pain had a feeling that was different from the usual, and he sought it out with a hunger. For now, he knew they needed to get on with the business at hand.

"Amy, I think we need to clear up one issue. I've been entrusted to help with an investigation, and I will keep my commitment. What I need to know is do you have any idea who could be on this horrible rampage of killing?" Straightforward Deke placed it on her lap. It was a black and white question, yes, or no, but he needed an answer.

Without flinching, she looked deeply into his eyes. "Absolutely not!" The answer was solid, and he believed her. Of course, with her looking at him like that, he would have believed anything she said.

"Good. Now we can get on with solving this one way or another. But if anything comes to mind please don't hold it back." A change was taking place inside of him; he wanted to get this guy. The story was different now; he was in love with Amy, and someone was trying to kill her. Deke became the bodyguard that would take the bullet for her, and the best protection she could ever have.

Amy sat looking at this man, of whom for some reason, she'd discovered she could not get enough. She was hesitant, not knowing how he felt about her. A relief had washed over her body like a cleansing shower when he said that he would not invade on her privacy. The secret would not have to be revealed, and the incredible relief that followed still had her on a high. She still wondered if the secret had something to with all this, but could not imagine how. Deke had told her to put those worries that she couldn't do anything about aside; so, she did.

Just as Amy and Deke realized that the Beatles had been gone for a long time, from behind the cabin came the fierce and raging sounds of a furious battle.

CHAPTER

17

RANGER ZACH RANDAL grabbed his cell phone. This was going to be a first. He had never once called headquarters, hating the phone as he did. He allowed them to call him, but refused to call them. Too damn much technology was ruining the detective work, he'd said. In fact, it was a mistake on his part when he set up the plan with Deke where he would have to call them. After several frantic attempts, he managed to get Sergeant John Hadley.

"John, this here is Randal." The booming voice yelled into his ear as Sergeant Hadley answered the phone, hearing his friend on the other end. It would have been humorous to hear Zach's uncomfortable introduction at any other time, but Hadley had just received horrible news. The toughest part was telling Zach Randal. After putting it off as long as he dared, the phone rang with Zach on the line; no more putting it off now.

"Zach, I hear you fine, but before you say anything, I got some rough news." He hated this, and could not imagine what the statement he'd just made was doing to his friend. John Hadley waited patiently for Zach to prepare himself, and used the time to do the same thing.

"Okay, John, I'm ready for it, and don't hold back old buddy." About two minutes after Hadley warned him of bad news, he answered back. In the time between, he was mentally preparing himself. He was a tough old cob, but took it very hard anytime someone was lost.

"It's real bad Zach. But if you're ready...Dan Baker and Bill Frye have been killed." It hurt Hadley to have to do it, and tears flowed freely down his cheeks.

"Son-of-a-bitch! Damn to hell! All right John, get on with the details." His outward reaction was limited to two curse words. The man was an oak, incredible control. If John Hadley knew anything at all about Texas Ranger Zachary Wyatt Randal all of the pain, anger, and sadness of this incident will be concentrated, packaged, and re-directed, like the bullet in a rifle, with the cross hairs centered directly on the individual responsible for murdering these fine individuals.

Sergeant Hadley was trying to think of a way of telling him the details without pushing the old Ranger's emotions too far; he saw only one way to do this.

"Okay, Zach? Here's what Stump has put together, he called me about twenty minutes ago after evaluating the scene. He saw when Dan and Bill left the scene at the hotel. They were in route to the Potter County Sheriff Department, but for some unknown reason approached the courthouse from a small, dark, back street. Then things become even more confusing. The tow truck driver that picked up Miss Amy's Toyota was supposed to be bringing it to the impoundment. Unfortunately, the driver was discovered only a few yards away from Dan and Bill, also dead.

"The way Stump figures it, Dan and Bill just happened to come up on the truck with Miss Amy's vehicle in tow, and figures the tow truck driver was probably already dead. They stopped to check out the scene and were bushwhacked, I'm sure by whoever killed the driver. Stump wanted your opinion on this Zach, since the case started out with you. He believes it must be the same guy who took Vanessa Jansen." John took a deep breath, hoping the rundown was enough for Zach, but mostly relieved that he was finished.

As usual, Zach was not satisfied with what John relayed to him.

"What the hell does Stump mean when he says they were bushwhacked?" It was now obvious to Sergeant John Hadley that Zach had already turned the focus around, and was looking for a target.

"It looks like they were trying to approach the Land Cruiser from the front of the tow truck, on each side. Both were shot before they could reach the front of Miss Amy's vehicle." Hadley crossed his fingers, not wanting to go into any more detail.

"Go ahead and finish John, I want it all! I'm all growed up you know!" He was ruthless at times, and John knew that he was holding back his anger.

"Dan was shot in the left temple, probably a 44, shot from a distance of about fifteen feet. Bill was shot in the back of the head, execution style, and with the same gun. They were messed up pretty badly. The truck driver's body was found later in an empty lot not far away, his throat was cut from ear to ear. Whoever it was took off in the unmarked cruiser. Stump didn't find any other vehicle around that the killer could have arrived in, if he had a vehicle." Hadley hoped that was enough because that was all he knew.

"Okay. I guess that's all you know. John you're not going to believe this, but the reason I called is that I passed their cruiser about ten minutes ago, heading north on Highway 87. It was only about fifty miles out of Amarillo. I didn't get a good look at the driver, but I saw only one man in the car. I thought about turning back to look for him, but if he's as smart as I think he took the first exit he could find. By turning back I'll waste a couple of hours just looking for the bastard, and he'll get to Amy and Deke before I can find them. Now that I have the jump on him, I don't want to give up my lead. I'm traveling at a pretty good clip, and from what I saw; he's being smart and driving just below the posted speed limit. I've got to think on this John. Give me thirty minutes, then call me back, and have those directions to Deke's place, or don't bother calling back until you do."

Hadley heard the phone click as the line was disconnected. Zach had transformed into the Hunter, unpredictable, hungry, and desperate for a kill.

Sergeant John Hadley slowly lowered the phone as he hung up. Stress was causing his heart to race wildly. Two of his detectives, who had volunteered to help with this case, had just been murdered. He knew better than to blame himself, even though he had hand picked those men for this job. Thirty minutes ago he had nothing to do, suddenly Hadley had more than he could handle. The first thing he needed to do was get back in touch with that Sheriff Wright in Colorado. He had to find out if they were able to get Deke and Amy into protective custody.

LOCATING the next exit, Jack Vermette smoothly pulled the cruiser to the right and off Highway 87. That damned old Texas Ranger was messing up his progress.

The Dalhart exit, Highway 385, was a good exit to take, according to the maps in the cruiser; he was lucky to be just south of it. Now all he had to do was reroute his trip and get back on track. It was a small inconvenience.

When Jack realized how nervous he'd become just having that damned old Texas Ranger pass him on the highway, he shook for forty minutes, and completely lost the motivation he'd been feeding on. The adrenaline high that had faded away freaked out as his adrenal glands pumped another dose of adrenaline into his system as that damn Bronco roared by.

It pissed him off. He wasn't scared of anyone. That damned old Ranger was a used up and finished, old news, and Jack Vermette planned to be the one to kill him. It would be great to make the papers again. Like turning a light switch, Vermette's attention became focused on the map, and a quick route to Colorado. According to the map, he could take Highway 385 north until it intersected with Highway 412, just over the state line, into Oklahoma. When he got to Highway 412, he needed to haul ass south, back to Highway 87. The intersection was in the town of Clayton, New Mexico. His right foot pressed down in the cruiser's accelerator, and his speed increased a bit. He did not want law enforcement involved, but this new development was screwing up his timing.

Jack Vermette's nerves were rattled, and he was doing all he knew to unwind and get his act together. But nothing was working; so, he turned on the cruiser's radio, looking for a few songs to sing. Scanning the dial, he caught a weather broadcast. He knew a front had passed through because of the north wind that was ripping across the Texas plains. It was a north wind that was dry and brisk, the kind that made your teeth rattle, and would pass right through a person standing outside.

Listening to the weatherman drone on about the cold air masses and jet streams meant nothing to him. However, as he heard about the blizzard hitting the mountain ranges of Colorado, he took notice. Up to thirty inches of snow had fallen the night before in some parts of the Northwest. This was an interesting development and Jack felt certain it was going to be a part of his plan to butcher Amy, along with that damn old Texas Ranger. The old man would be his farewell gift to the state of Texas.

BOTH of them ran for the door at the same time. Getting out onto the three feet of snow that accumulated overnight was a different story. Amy was so frantic that Deke lifted her bottom up as she struggled; he pushed her up out onto the cold, white snow. Amy looked around at the wonderful beauty of the mountains that had magically been covered with the virgin substance. Deke was right behind her, and while trying to run to the back of the cabin slipped, falling twice, before getting a glimpse of what had happened.

The horrible sound of dogs when they're to the point of fighting is a sound that most people find difficult to withstand for very long.

As Deke rounded the corner at the rear of the cabin, he saw Ringo and John standing over the bloody, motionless body of a large German shepherd. Paul and George were laying a few feet away, unharmed, no longer interested, resting on the cool surface of lightly packed snow.

Amy was right behind Deke, and when she came on the scene, Paul and George got up quickly, afraid of what the boss was going to do. Ringo and John only looked at Deke and Amy, but did not leave from their post where the German shepherd lay, still motionless. Amy immediately slowed from her frantic approach to a calmer advance, slowly walking toward Ringo who was closest to her. When she was about five feet away, she stopped. Very calmly she called to him, "Ringo, come to me. Come." Amy knew how to talk to the Beatles. Deke was impressed with her, and the Beatles. Ringo's posture changed from the intimidating stance he displayed to a more relaxed attitude. Then, like magic, Amy held out her hand to him, and he walked straight to her. With Ringo by her side, she turned to John. The performance was repeated.

Paul and George had remained standing where they were as they arrived. When Amy turned to them, Deke saw something that impressed him so much he would have sworn the Beatles could outscore half the population if given an IQ test.

Paul and George had been watching everything from the minute Amy arrived. They stood alert, eyes sharp, ears perked up, listening intently. Still, they never moved from their location. As Amy turned to them, she called softly, "Now you two can come. Come Paul! Come George!" Right before Deke's eyes, he saw Paul turn his head and look at George, who was standing slightly behind him, then turn back and go to Amy's side. Not until Paul reached her side did George leave his spot and do the same. They had communicated. Paul and George wisely waited to hear what Amy would say, then spoke to each other some kind of message.

Once Deke overcame the Beatle's display of intelligence, he turned his attention to the dog that had apparently been killed by them. A large shepherd, wearing a collar with several tags, managed to create more confusion through its presence. Amy had walked back to the front of the cabin with the Beatles, she would let them inside, close the door and return. To see her or Deke fooling with their kill would be offensive and unwise.

As Deke checked out the poor victim, he saw that the throat had been ripped open. Several chunks of the dog were missing from different places. The fight had not lasted long, but the Shepherd was severely outnumbered. Amy returned and got down on her knees at Deke's side. Together they removed the dog's collar.

Inspecting the different tags on the dog collar, Amy and Deke spotted the miniature Potter County Deputy Sheriff Badge at the same time.

"What is this?" Deke said with surprise.

"Deke this is a police K-9 dog! What is he doing up here, halfway up the side of a mountain, in the middle of nowhere?" Both of them were blown away. It was crazy. With each new day, unexplainable events were occurring; from Deke's vantage point, it didn't seem to have any connection at all.

"Okay. We are sitting halfway up the side of a mountain, in a cabin with no form of communication; so, we can't contact the sheriff department. Plus, we've had a blizzard come down on us overnight, leaving three feet of snow on the mountain. Which means driving a vehicle down the narrow road for eight miles, getting back to civilization is out of the question, at least until the next big melt."

Deke wanted to run the situation through his head for the sake of organization. He said it aloud for Amy's benefit, since he was sure she would ask, unfamiliar with the mountain, and the ability that it had to trap you like a rat in a cage overnight.

Deke was getting more than just concerned about Zach Randal. Losing touch with them was not a quality that Deke could believe Zach Randal was capable. He was aware that the time and exposure he'd had with the Ranger was very limited, but Deke trusted his gut-feelings. This man checked out as a straight up person, in his opinion.

Back to the situation at hand, all he knew to do was put the K-9 where it would be safe from varmints, and the Beatles. As soon as they could get down the mountain, they'd go straight to the sheriff department. Sheriff Bill Wright was sort of a friend of his, and he wanted to do the right thing.

Amy agreed to his plan, and together they moved the big Shepherd to an outside woodbin, his body would keep. Taking the collar, Deke wanted to be sure it was turned over to the authorities.

While walking back to the cabin's entrance, Amy looked up at him. "You know, you have a pretty exciting life Mr. Stone. But I kind of like the excitement." Her smile was intoxicating. She looked up at him, anticipating an answer.

"Well, Miss Amy, what you kind of like, and the things that keep happening around here are not daily occurrences. It would be wise to hang around for a while, until you can get a clearer picture of what the Rocky Mountain lifestyle is all about." He wanted to drop a hint, but also maintain a distance. This dog's presence had him concerned, and he was very astute in predicting impending danger.

As they reached the front door Amy caught a chill, commenting on how much colder it had become in the hour that passed while they were outside. It amazed her. Before Deke could respond, telling her how quickly things happened at that altitude, the snow began to fall. It was falling at an impressive rate, a rate that surprised even Deke.

They laughed together for a moment about the coincidence. When Deke opened the cabin door, he bowed before her playfully, motioning with his hand for her to enter first. In response, Amy curtseyed playfully and they entered the cabin. They had no way of knowing how long they might be secluded in the wilderness of the Rocky Mountains.

CHAPTER

18

UNAWARE THAT THE man he casually discussed the weather with had in the last twelve hours brutally murdered four people, the gas station attendant finished filling the unmarked cruiser's fuel tank.

Jack Vermette followed him into the front of the run down old station. Turned into a mechanic shop from the filling station that it used to be, the station was located at the intersection of Highway 72 and Interstate 25, just north of Raton. Since traffic was light at the crossroads, Jack decided it was the perfect place to fill the dangerously low fuel tank.

All of Jack's money had been left behind, back at the cabin, as he made his desperate dash for civilization after Vanessa Jansen stuck him with that damn little dart gun full of Ketamine. Now, because of the disadvantage, he had to be real choosy about where he stopped.

The attendant was still carrying on about the weather as they entered the small room where the cash register sat. Jack suddenly wrapped his arm tightly around the man's face from behind. Pulling his head back and up, the last thing he'd see was the water stained ceiling tile of the little station that he owned. Jack slit his throat from ear to ear.

Not a sound was heard as a result of the repulsive act, not even the slightest bit of struggle from the attendant while he hemorrhaged to death. Within two minutes, he was dead. Jack dragged the man to the far corner of the station, dropping him in a dehumanizing heap. He returned to the small room where the cash register sat on a grease-stained counter, and quickly opened it.

Walking at a normal pace, so as not to appear suspicious or draw any attention, Jack climbed into the cruiser with the four hundred dollars he stole from the register. With a satisfied smile on his face from the good fortune, he resumed with his journey north.

He was making good time, but was concerned about the developing weather. If snow started to cover the highway, he may have to change vehicles. That damn, old, Texas Ranger had a big four-wheel drive vehicle, he wouldn't be inconvenienced. The more Vermette thought about Zach Randal, the angrier he became, determined even more to watch him die.

He was smart though, if his anger started to gain control of his actions a well-developed inner check and balance system usually stopped any irrational progression.

Through many hours of Middle Eastern Religious meditation techniques, he'd trained his body with self-discipline, a feeling of discontent would come over him like a wet blanket, and it made him aware whenever he started drifting.

Any out of control emotion was dangerous to Jack's plan, and it would effect his actions, hinder his progress, and change the outcome. Calmly he reached for the cruiser's radio, before long he'd found something to sing. In the unmarked cruiser, back on Interstate 25, and about to cross the state line into Colorado, Jack was singing one of Chicago's hits from the 70's, Feeling Stronger Every Day.

BREAKFAST was late, but they enjoyed it just the same. The Beatles were fed after calming down from their unfortunate encounter with the German shepherd.

"Okay, Amy, I give up. The suspense is killing me. What made Ringo and John kill that Shepherd, I mean I've seen dogs fight more times than I can remember, but they never went for the kill like that. Usually a strange dog is chased off with a good warning from the other. But I know what I saw, and it was a planned and carried out kill." Deke was stunned, but at the same time excited and fascinated by the development. To him, who had been with the Beatles all this time, witnessing such aggression was baffling.

"What was that approach all about, with Ringo and John?" he finally asked a single question that she could answer. Amy was back on the love seat, with her legs up underneath her, sipping on hot cocoa. She looked at Deke, who had been pacing around the cabin like a zoo animal. Using a calm voice, Amy stopped him in his tracks.

"Deke, why don't you come and sit down; so, I can talk to you, please?" He responded almost as quickly as one of the Chessies.

It was so comical that Amy let out a little giggle. The sound of that simple little sound from her was so bewitching that he wished he had never heard it, but he knew instead that he would never be able to forget it. Deke was sitting across from her at attention; sitting next to her was out of the question, even though she had patted the cushion when she asked him to sit down.

"Ringo and John have been trained to protect me. They are trained to protect by killing the intruder. They do not respond with such force unless heavily provoked, and usually will not kill unless given the command. Paul and George have been trained to respond in exactly the same way. Ringo and John are the first line of attack, while Paul and George act as scouts. If Ringo or John go down, then either Paul or George assumes their position." Very calmly, and in matter-of-fact terms, Amy explained in the most basic of ways what exactly the Beatles were capable of doing.

"Were they trained special, just for you?" he asked her, his eyes wide with amazement, wanting to know more.

"Yes!" was all the response she gave to the question, baffling him for a second before remembering to be respectful to her, and allow her to have those small secrets in her life, giving her an identity, making her feel special, and allowing trust and respect to grow unhindered.

"Oh! Okay, well what do we do about this miniature deputy sheriff badge?" The question was one he just picked out of the air, trying to change the subject, since it appeared she didn't really want to talk about the training the Beatles went through.

"I've been thinking about that poor Shepherd. Deke, have you ever heard of a K-9 being lose, on its own, away from the handler?" she asked. It was a good question that he'd not thought of. It was true, they were highly trained dogs, and a lot of money had been invested in each one that was recruited from canine obedience schools.

"What are you thinking, Amy?" Wanting to get her opinion on what he realized was something he was going to have to investigate.

"What if he was with someone, and they're watching us? Could the...the person...behind this be a policeman?" The question hit Deke like a brick. What in the hell had he been thinking? He was supposed to be constantly alert, yet instead he had let the little stars of love get into his eyes, blinding him to everything else around.

"Damn Amy! Where has my mind been?" he commented, standing quickly, realizing what he'd said. Amy only lowered her eyes, knowing exactly where his mind had been, and feeling that it was partly her fault. Deke looked at her quickly after making the statement, and saw her response.

"No, Amy!" he almost shouted, "It is not your fault! I just became complacent, being home made me drop my guard. Something is going on, and I'm going to get to the bottom of it."

"How? Deke! Please do not go!" He turned to her and saw the fear in her eyes. Those eyes, he felt like turning away. It was like looking at the Medusa, but with the opposite result.

"I have to. You'll be safe with the Beatles; they've proven that to me now. I promise not to be gone long." Deke was already searching for his snow gear before she could respond. He was not going to look at her again, not until he got back.

"Okay. I'll wait for you right here." From behind him, he heard her soft reply and winced, closing his eyes for just a second. 'No,' He said to himself, and continued gathering his supplies.

Within only a few minutes, he had what he needed. The Beatles watched curiously, but silently, from their spot on the cabin floor. Snow was still falling heavily outside, but the day was young, and Deke had to go.

"I'll be back soon, don't open this door for anyone." Deke smiled, looking at the Beatles as they watched him at the front door. He said, "You'll be safe."

Opening the door, Deke was surprised to find an extra six inches of snow had accumulated. Throwing his cross-country skis up on the snow, he followed after. When he looked behind to close the door he saw that Amy had walked up without him noticing. Standing with her hands on the door she said, "I'll lock it."

Deke was unable to avoid it, and their eyes locked. Yet, it was too late to back out, and he was already out the door, his mind made up. He just nodded his head to her, turned, and locked on his skis.

The snow was powder for the first six inches, but had a packed base as he slowly made his way. He decided to make a wide circle around the cabin, then work his way in by forming concentric circles until reaching the cabin. It was cold, colder than he'd realized. He and Amy had not been listening to the radio, and the weather broadcast that is frequently given. 'It is November,' he thought. They've had storms whip up earlier than that many times; so, he really shouldn't be surprised.

He did his best making adequate circles, but this was mountain terrain, and he had obstacles that normal front and back yards didn't have. Rock ledges with boulders bigger than buses were sticking up out of the snow. It was deceiving, how large some were until having to go around each one. Slowly making his way, looking out over the snow covered terrain, he was glad the sunlight occasionally was being blocked by storm clouds passing swiftly overhead due to the blinding glare off the new, white terrain.

After making two circles Deke was wearing down, he could find no tracks due to the new fresh snow, and was working his way up from below the cabin. A thick stand of short, fir trees sat at the edge of a sudden, thousand foot drop-off, about thirty feet ahead of him. It was a place where a deep scar had been carved into the side of the mountain.

Deke knew the spot well. He'd visited the spot several times just to sit and think. He found it one day while exploring, and accidentally almost fell over the deep edge. The stand of short fir was thick, concealing the sudden, sharp edge.

It turned into sort of like an inspiration point for him. He laughed to himself thinking that it was motivation he that needed now, more than inspiration. Climbing to the spot, he could not resist looking out at the beauty.

Snow had covered most of the fir where the edge was, creating an even more deceiving appearance.

It was inspiring. Resting for a few minutes while looking out Deke spotted something directly below the sharp cliff. It was a long way down, and he could not make it out clearly, but he thought what he saw looked like a man's legs.

A pair of hiking boots was sticking up out of the snow.

SHERIFF Bill Wright was on the phone with Sergeant John Hadley of the Texas State Police. Sergeant Hadley had just informed Sheriff Wright about the tragic murders that occurred in Amarillo. The sheriff was shocked by the bad news.

"Oh hell. I'm very sorry to hear that John. Shoot, I'm just nearly speechless. And you say this fellow may be headed up this way?" Sheriff Wright sounded like a good and decent man, with real compassion in his voice as he expressed his condolences.

"We do think that's the general vicinity this guy is headed for. He's a bad one Sheriff! I wouldn't take any chances with this fellow, he will not hesitate to kill, and is good at it." Sergeant Hadley didn't hold anything back; he didn't want a repeat of what had happened earlier that morning.

"Sheriff, before I let you get back to work, Ranger Zach Randal is very concerned about Mr. Deke Stone and the young lady that is with him. Have you gotten any news on those two?" Hadley was very polite and respectful, even though his request to the sheriff earlier to have them taken in for protection, apparently still had not been carried out.

"John I'm glad you asked about that, it nearly slipped my mind altogether. But I wouldn't worry about that couple, a deputy of mine took a hike up to Stone's place right after you called, he must have left sometime around four this morning. Probably, he'll be back at any time. He's sort of a mountain climbing fellow, and he's got a K-9 with him on the trip." The sheriff's answer caught Hadley unprepared. He was a little confused, and it took some time before he answered. "Did you say a deputy was taking a hike to Deke's place, Sheriff?" he asked.

"Why I guess you southern boys wouldn't know, would you? Sergeant we got three feet of snow up on Deke's mountain last night, and as we speak, the snow is again falling in pretty impressive amounts. Hell, they may get another three feet again tonight.

"The way I see it, ain't no way up the side except one old narrow road, and a person wouldn't even be able to find that road today. It gets blended into the mountain with no way to tell the difference between it and the mountain.

"Ain't nobody gonna be driving up the side of that mountain anytime soon Sergeant. You might want to pass that on to Ranger Randal. Maybe later we can get him up on horseback.

"Oh, and by the way, I was able to find an old set of directions that might help out. I'll fax them to you as soon as we hang up." The sheriff was a typical lawman turned politician, but he was all right. Sergeant Hadley thanked him, and they reminded one another that they would stay in touch.

John Hadley sat at his desk in Sweetwater, blistering, north winds whistling across the plains outside, and worried about his friend Zach Randal. It was bad news if the snowfall was that heavy in Colorado. It was even worse because he knew not a damn thing was going to stop Zach from getting up that mountain, especially when he was on the hunt. Just as he reached for the phone to call the Texas Ranger with an update it rang.

"John Hadley?" It was a voice that was familiar, but John could not place it at first. The information that followed shook away any cobwebs in his head, but at the same time sent his mind reeling. John hardly spoke a word while listening to Zach's old friend, Stump, detailing his latest discovery.

RANGER Zach Randal's cell phone rang just as he was crossing the state line from New Mexico into Colorado. The big Bronco was cruising, but the forty-gallon fuel tank was sitting on empty, he needed to find a gas station soon, and very soon.

"Hello John, give me an update." It was a given to Zach that it was Hadley calling.

"Zach. How are you?" As soon as he asked, John Hadley knew it was a stupid question, and wished he didn't have to wait for the answer.

"How am I? How the hell do you think I am John? I'm feeling about as good as a wolverine that can't find the damn rabbit that just ran between his legs. The truck is on empty, it's been cruising at about a hundred for the past 200 miles, and now I got sleet mixed with snow falling, getting heavier every mile. So how the hell are you John?" Hadley thought that Zach gave a pretty good description of his situation, but he had asked the question, and by God, Zach Randal, in his own way, answered him. Nothing was humorous about Zach's situation, but he had to chuckle a bit before answering him.

"I just got off the phone with Sheriff Bill Wright. He expressed his sympathy about Dan and Bill. I informed him that we think the perpetrator is headed up to..." Hadley was interrupted before he could finish.

"What about Deke and Miss Amy? I want to know if he went and picked them up like I asked." Zach's temper and patience were like quarter horses at the gate, chomping down hard on the bit, just waiting to be let loose.

"Uh, no Zach. Before you..." Again he was interrupted.

"Damn to hell John! What's wrong with those boys? Don't they know we got a situation here? This son-of-a-bitch we're after is rattlesnake smart." That was the first time Hadley heard Zach use that description in quite some time. The last time was when he'd caught that guy drowning those young girls in bathtubs. Zach Randal was not one to exaggerate. If Zach Randal made a statement about someone, or something, it was after he had deliberated on the subject for some time, and formed his own opinion. He must know more about this Vermette fellow than he wants to reveal. It sobered John Hadley, and wiped away the exhaustion that had been haunting him.

"Zach let me just tell you what Sheriff Wright said?" he pleaded with his friend, wanting to calm him down just a bit.

"Well, go ahead John, it's a free country." It was not a great response, but it was all that he needed; so, he'd try to explain.

"He said a deputy with a K-9 unit was climbing up the mountain to Deke's place, left this morning before daylight. Ain't no way for someone to drive up that mountain Zach. The only road going up to his place is covered solid with three feet of snow." Hadley didn't know if he got through Zach's hard head or not, but he tried. When he heard the response, he was relieved. Zach sounded a notch calmer.

"Three feet of snow huh?" he stated, questioningly. "That ain't any damn excuse John. I'm sorry old boy, it ain't you I'm unhappy with, but those boys don't realize the danger. It ain't for show when I ask for a favor from them knuckleheads. A psychopathic killer that will probably kill again within the next couple of hours is flying in that direction like a bat out of hell. But I'll get him John, if it's the last son-of-a-bitch I hunt down. Bill Wright can count on hell coming because I'm the one bringing it!"

He had never heard Zach so intensely driven before, and it had John worried. He knew that he needed to be there. He paused before continuing but could tell that Zach was not going to let go of his anger. It was something that he used for energy. He rode in on the back of anger, driving it; motivated by it, and the fear that it created. Until he'd finished what he set out to do, that anger would be his best ally.

Before allowing Zach to continue, or hang up on him, John blurted out, "And Zach, I just got a pretty disturbing call from Stump." A moment of silence followed as Randal adjusted to the statement.

John said it in a voice that was different from what he had been using just a moment before. Zach knew that voice, and also knew he was about to find out something that was a complete surprise. Resigning to the fact that he had no choice but to listen to another kink in the case, he grunted over the phone. It was his way of telling him that he'd gotten his attention.

Realizing that he'd stopped Zach dead in the middle of what was winding up to be a full blown fit of anger, Hadley reassured him, "Zach, I think this is the bit of information that we have been missing, the small piece that we've never considered. Well, hell! This is the break that we've been needing, but would have never been able to come up with, especially with what we think we already know." Hadley's rambling was becoming a maze. Zach felt as if he was being led around the block just to get next door.

"What in tarnation are you babbling on about John?" His patience could take no more, and Hadley was so stunned with the information that he wasn't sure how to tell Zach.

"Stump said that a set of keys were in the passenger side door of Miss Amy's Land Cruiser. A set of keys that were on a Dodson's Breakfast and Bar-B-Que Cafe key chain, along with a set of house keys, and a set to the café." Hadley stopped, leaving Zach hanging for just a second before wisely finishing with what Stump had reported.

"A big fat thumbprint was found on that key chain Zach. Stump ran it through the file, and he got a hit on the identification. But that's the confusing part, it belongs to Jack Vermette!"

Zach Randal was stunned. This was a development that he'd have never imagined in a million years. This was the thumbprint of a dead man! Only silence occupied the space over the phone line as Hadley waited for his friend to digest the blow. After what seemed like an eternity, John heard the recovered voice of his friend on the line.

"Well, if it were not Stump, I would never believe it. I'm sure he ran the print more than once. Right John?"

"Ran the same thumbprint three times, before he called me."

"Then we're sure that it's Vermette?" Zach questioned again.

"Stump said ain't no doubt about it." Hadley answered his friend's questions in short definitive sentences. He was aware that Zach would come up with everything he could, just to rule out the possibility of error. That was one thing that he didn't need at this point of the investigation: running off to chase phantoms.

"John, does Stump know who Jack Vermette is, or was?" the big man sounded awestruck.

"I told him myself Zach. I couldn't believe it either. Stump even ran Vermette's employment license. Since he had to be registered for offshore dives in international waters Stump thought a mistake had been made. Vermette is still listed as dead. Legally dead. His body, you remember, was never located. Coast Guard just assumed he had ended up as cut bait for the crabs and red snapper."

"No, I didn't know that! You mean that son-of-a-bitch was declared dead without anyone ever finding a body? I mean…I knew that he had been declared dead, but I thought the body was eventually discovered washed up on some beach, that is whatever hadn't been eaten by the sharks." Hadley heard Zach's voice coming back to life; he was recovering quickly, and was once again making the transition from being stunned to becoming the Hunter.

"It happens all the time offshore. They don't find every body that's involved in those accidents." Hadley didn't know who he was defending, but he knew what he said was true.

"Put out a bulletin on this character, Jack Vermette, apparently he did survive his death. Tell the boys that he's back from the dead, and alive somewhere."

CHAPTER

19

ZACH KNEW HE may be running into an investigator's nightmare, not to mention the legal nightmare. Every law enforcement agency in the country would get the same response whenever accessing anything on Jack Vermette; deceased, accidental death in offshore waters south of Texas. With his memory seriously jarred, he did remember Amy dating that fellow for several months. It was no secret between him and John Hadley. They'd both worried about her, after discovering from sheriff deputies patrolling West Texas, she was dating some big, time bachelor, living somewhere around El Paso.

When the report that an entire diving crew had been killed in a boat accident offshore stated that Vermette was one of the men killed, Zach began to breath a little easier. He worried about the little brunette, who seemed all alone in the world, even if Amy pretended capable of taking care of herself.

The absence of any grief response in Amy, about the man's death, was taken by him to mean one of two things. Either she wanted to maintain the secrecy of their relationship, even after his death, hiding her grief, or it meant that their relationship was not such a big deal, and had been dissolved long before the accident. He had never thought about the fact that maybe she feared him, and was relieved by the reported outcome of the accident.

SEVERAL hours later, Sergeant Hadley's phone began ringing at the Nolan County Sheriff Department in Sweetwater. No one answered. Getting no response after the second ring did not surprise Zach. He was afraid this might happen, in fact, he saw it coming. He knew John Hadley, and he also knew that the amount of stress and emotional turmoil behind losing two good officers would be too much for him to handle. Zach had misjudged the timing, probably by only a few minutes.

He regretted missing John, but knew that if it had been him sitting at that desk, he would have done the exact same thing, probably would have done it long before John. He apparently decided that he'd had enough, and finally just got up and walked away from the desk.

Zach Randal would have bet his next paycheck, with anyone, John Hadley was driving north, toward Colorado like a bat out of hell, in an attempt to get in on the action. Zach smiled, he couldn't remember how many days it had been since he did that. With the Bronco's heater set on high, the driver side window all the way down, and cruising at ninety-five miles an hour, Zach continued north into Colorado. Fumbling with the small, cell phone, made even more difficult with his catcher's-mitt hands, he finally managed to get a mobile operator, connecting him to the El Paso County Sheriff Department.

"Hello? Yeah I can hear you. Who is this?" Zach Randal was not in the mood to play phone tag with anyone.

"Get me Sheriff Bill Wright!" he commanded.

"Sir, Sheriff Wright is not available at this time, but I can have him return your call as soon as possible." The first person that answered the phone had transferred him to this individual, who knew how to screen calls.

"Well, I don't care if the sheriff is not available, I want to talk to the man, not marry him. Now you've made a good attempt at screening this call, but I'm sorry to inform you that it didn't work. Some you win, and some you lose, that's a lesson son." On occasion, when Zach Randal was involved in an investigation, the amount of adrenaline surging through his veins would wind him up tight, and without fail he'd find some unlucky person, and nearly twist their ear off.

"Now, the next thing I want to teach you is my name, it's Texas Ranger Zachary Wyatt Randal, and I'm hunting down a man who's killed seven people, that I know of, and four of those folks were killed just this morning. Bill Wright would be doing himself a favor speaking to me before I arrive at your location. Currently I'm just north of the town of Walsenburg, which is north of Trinidad. So, you can clearly see that I'm headed straight to you, sitting with that phone in your hand. My vehicle has a forty gallon fuel tank, and it's just been topped off, Interstate 25 is smooth and flat, and my speed is somewhere around ninety miles per hour. The reason I'm telling you this...Oh, I'm sorry, what is your name?" Randal was weaving a trap, and the young man he was speaking to was getting ready to fall right in.

"My name is Officer Daniel, Ted Daniel," the young man answered hesitantly.

"Good! Officer Dandelion, the reason I'm explaining this is because what I need the sheriff to do for me will take a little time to accomplish, maybe a couple of hours, I can't be sure. Anyway, until the sheriff is finished with my request I'll be sitting right next to you, we can share old war stories together. Now, the longer you have me waiting, the more time I'll have to sit and visit with you." Randal finally got to the point of his story. The time it took telling it was shorter than he would have had to wait, dealing with folks screening Sheriff Wright's calls.

"The sheriff will be with you in just a moment Ranger Randal." Officer Ted Daniel sure was efficient. He was true to his word too, in no time at all Zach got results. "Sheriff Wright." The next voice Zach heard on the phone was of Bill Wright.

"Bill, this is Zach Randal." Before Zach was able to say anything else, he was interrupted.

"The Texas Ranger, Zach Randal? Hunter Zach Randal?" Sheriff Wright asked in a disbelieving tone of voice. His reputation not only followed him, but this time had beaten him to where he was going. For a second Zach hesitated, deliberating whether or not to answer the son-of-a-bitch.

"Damn right this is Hunter Zach Randal, and I ain't got time for all this bullshit! I don't know about you and your boys Sheriff, but right now, my officers and me are working to find a killer, and he's coming your way bound and determined to murder someone in your county. Now if you want the bad publicity of having been warned ahead of time, but you were unable to prevent these killings, fine. But if not, let's cut through the fat, and get to the meat of things." Zach hated talking to the sheriff that way, but Bill Wright had pushed the start button, and once Zach got started, he decided to get his money's worth; besides, everything he said was the damn truth.

Once the two men got their wires straight, the conversation didn't last long. Zach's request would take less than two hours, if things progressed without problems. Sheriff Bill Wright was in agreement with what Zach wanted to do, and his entire department would be at Zach's disposal upon request. Before the two men hung up Bill Wright delicately gave an apology for his disrespect to the Ranger. In return, Zach apologized for his demanding behavior.

"Zach, I'll do everything I can to help you catch that piece of scum, and I'll have what you requested ready, hopefully by the time you arrive." Sheriff Wright sounded like a different man.

SERGEANT John Hadley was cruising with his blue lights flashing and siren blaring, up Interstate 27. He was making good time, already halfway between Lubbock and Amarillo, but still he was far away. Frustrated by how long it would take him to get to Colorado, but he was still determined. He'd been a good soldier sitting at that damn desk like Zach Randal had asked him, but he saw no reason to continue. Two good detectives, friends of his, had been executed by some son-of-a-bitch, and he wanted in on the chance to get him, the hell with what Zach Randal thought about it.

John Hadley was the only friend that Zach Randal allowed in his life, especially since the death of Kate. In reality, Zach was always a loner. Having such an unusually brilliant ability to anticipate criminals, and with his notoriety, it was difficult to be a regular person with people. They would end up wanting to know this or that about his work, and Zach did not talk about his work with anyone. It was a dirty and disgusting world that he lived in when working, and not worth discussing in public.

John was the only man who came to Zach after Kate's death at the funeral, shaking his hand with a humble and compassionate voice, telling him, *"I don't know what to say Zach, I'm sorry. If you need, let me know."* Then he walked away to let the man grieve alone. Zach had appreciated the honesty, and even more, he appreciated him not coming up with bullshit like, *She's in a better place or God works in mysterious ways.*

Zach had wanted to smash the preacher in the face when he'd said that Kate, the woman he'd loved more than life was *"In a place where she could now find peace."*

"Why the hell couldn't she find peace with me?" he had asked John one day with tears running down his cheeks. It was tough for John Hadley watching the big man cry, but he did, and he did it without offering a single word of consolation. He did it without giving a single opinion about why, and that was what Zach wanted most. John couldn't give his opinion about why Kate was dead because he didn't understand any more that Zach did. Their friendship began because of no pretense between them.

The speedometer read one hundred ten miles per hour as the state police cruiser sailed north. He was going to get to where the action was before it went down if he had to fly. For some reason that he could not figure out, John had a bad feeling about this one. Zach had always come out clean from the toughest of manhunts, except for the time he was shot by that State Police Investigator. Even that had not slowed him down, it only pissed him off, and he became even better at his job. This killer was different for some reason, but John could not figure out what made him feel that way.

Poor, old Bob Davidson had taken it hard after he'd realized how deep Doctor Vanessa Jansen had managed to become involved in the nightmare, and now she was missing, presumed kidnapped by the same man who executed Dan Baker and Bill Frye. The old desk sergeant had to be relieved from his post. He was so upset that John Hadley insisted he go home, taking a few days off and spending them with his wife. Thankfully, Zach dismissed Bob Davidson's involvement as innocent; it was not a violation of the law to assist a friend in need. The incident where he was seen dropping Vanessa at Amy's ranch under the cover of darkness, amounted to nothing more than him doing a favor for a friend. Issues and developments were flying through John Hadley's head at the same speed that his cruiser was making its way up Interstate 27.

ZACH was convinced that Jack Vermette, an old flame of Amy's who he thought had been killed in a diving accident, was the person who killed the three women at the cafe, who had been sending Amy the anonymous letters, who kidnapped Vanessa Jansen from the hotel in Amarillo, and who finally ended up murdering Dan and Bill.

What convinced Zach was the single most disturbing fact in the case from the very start. It was a fact that he hated to admit, but it was as true as it was disturbing.

Zach Randal had had no idea who was behind all this mess, and that was when he realized he'd been trying to conjure up enough speculation to actually suspect someone who was totally innocent.

HADLEY began to focus his thoughts on every aspect of the case. It was a long way to Colorado, and he decided to gear himself for whatever the circumstances may be when he arrived. The El Paso County Sheriff Department was not expecting his arrival, but he was certain that after Texas Ranger Zach Randal invaded their domain it would never be the same again. John Hadley's arrival, on the other hand, more than likely would never be noticed.

ATTEMPTING any kind of descent from this height with no equipment, and in the middle of another approaching snowstorm, would be suicidal. Deke stood on the edge of the precipice straining his eyes to make certain that what he thought he saw was indeed a pair of hiking boots attached to a man's lower legs. As far as he could tell the boots were motionless, and from what Deke could remember, a row of large, jagged stones sat lined up at the bottom of the crevice just below the fresh layer of snow, exactly where the man's body had landed head downward.

Guilt and an obligation to respond tore at him for a while, until he finally convinced himself that the man was dead. He could do nothing for him, and to chance a descent in such conditions without the proper equipment would indirectly jeopardize Amy as well as him.

With one last look, Deke turned away and started back for the cabin. The snow was beginning to come down harder; it was without a doubt that the narrow road leading down had blended completely into the mountainside. Deke was not concerned about anyone attempting the ascent, and he was certain that he and Amy were not going down. Snowbound in the small cabin at any other time would have been a dream come true, but this was no dream, and he knew a Texas Ranger who was certain to try and reach them.

Sheriff Bill Wright had to have been contacted by Zach Randal by this time. The last thing Deke and Amy heard from Zach were his strict instructions to continue north to the cabin, staying until he was able to rendezvous with them. Zach was in the process of finding out more information about Vanessa Jansen's involvement in all of this. For some unknown reason, Vanessa had been tailing them. Heightening the mystery behind her reason for following Deke and Amy to Amarillo was the fact that she'd rented a room in the hotel directly across the highway from where they had stayed. Deke was also puzzled about the way she'd managed to gain access to Amy's Land Cruiser, locked up in the barn, and why.

It was difficult to imagine Doctor Vanessa Jansen tailing them up Interstate 27, somehow undetected by Zach, and she was obviously a close friend of Amy's. According to Amy, she was somewhat of an introvert, and this was behavior opposite of her character.

It was Amy who came to her defense when Zach suggested she was involved in the crime, stating they'd previously made an arrangement that Amy's Land Cruiser was at her disposal at any time she needed it. Still, Amy found it difficult to explain Vanessa's actions, shrugging it off when asked to give any rational explanation.

Deke was quick in detecting a peculiar response in Amy, suggesting no reason to suspect Vanessa Jansen of having anything to do with the horrible events she'd experienced. The lack of concern that he saw from her, even with the involvement of her Land Cruiser, set him on edge. He did not like her devoid of an emotional response when it came to such a large development in the case. Zach Randal had just about been chewed in two by Amy whenever he'd made the strong assertion, stating that Vanessa was a key player in the letter mailing campaign, and maybe even responsible for the collection of human body parts in small packages that found their way to Amy.

Deke realized how out of shape he'd become in the last few weeks, panting and heaving as he reached the rear of the cabin. The spot where Ringo and John had ruthlessly killed the shepherd was already neatly covered with fresh snow. Not a trace of blood remained where somehow this beautiful German shepherd, and a K-9 unit Shepherd at that, wandered into the path of the Beatles.

"I'm home!" Deke stated in an uplifting tone, trying to minimize the seriousness of the situation they were in. He was surprised not to find anyone waiting at the door, either to greet him with a worried look, or greet him with wet slurps on his face. The interior of the cabin was empty and deadly silent. That silence had him seriously spooked, and on the edge of panic, when suddenly he heard a barely audible sound that seemed to melt the snow accumulated on him from the exhausting hike.

"Deke! We're up here." Looking up from his awkward position outside the front door and at the top of the three feet of snow, he was unable to see from where the small voice had come. Quickly he placed his cross-country skis up against the logs of the outside wall, and jumped down into the cabin. Amy was peering out from the edge of the loft with what seemed to be a wall of rust-colored fur around her. John, Paul, George, and Ringo stood so close to her that it seemed impossible that any man would be able to come within ten yards without being attacked by one of them.

"It's only me men," Deke stated playfully, he was their friend, and avoided everything that might cause an attack.

"They would never hurt you, Deke. They know that you are a friend, and they would protect you with the same ferocity that they've been trained to protect me," Amy cooed from the loft, ruffling their fur and smiling at them.

"How are you doing? I'm wondering what the hell you're doing in the loft?" he asked humorously.

"It's a safer place than downstairs. Anyway, you've been gone such a long time. I hope you never leave me like that again?" she confessed, looking at him with her eyes narrowing, displaying an emphasis to her statement. She knew exactly what she had said, and was not backing off from what it implied. Deke was busy knocking the snow from his boots, and fought the urge that swept over him to look up. He knew those eyes were waiting to lock onto his, sending him into another whirlwind of emotions. Continuing with his chore, cleaning the boots, Deke reminded himself of what he had just found and suddenly how important it was to find out where the hell Randal was. Having no phone had been great at his small mountain hideaway until now, but the more he thought about it the more concerned he was about how they were going to contact the Texas Ranger.

He had spent the better part of the morning searching around the cabin for anything unusual. Now that he had found something, he was at a disadvantage to investigate.

Snow had been falling heavily, and Deke noticed how the daylight was beginning to fade. Earlier, the sunlight could be seen occasionally reflecting brightly between storm clouds off the snow-covered terrain, but the weather was quickly deteriorating with the mountainside appearing suddenly shaded from the thick, pewter-colored, storm clouds.

"It did take longer than I anticipated. Because of the snow being so wet at the surface, my balance was seriously challenged. But all went well as soon as I finally managed to get moving and…that was about the time that I discovered the German shepherd did have someone with him." He dropped the discovery on Amy like a ton of bricks. Divulging the surprising news, Deke allowed himself to look up at her. He was sure to be safe from her enticing looks with that bit of disturbing information now shared.

"Who was it? Where are they? Did you talk to them?" Amy was full of questions, firing them off at him faster than he had time to respond.

Looking away from her, Deke began to unbuckle his cumbersome boots.

"I suppose it was a he. All I really saw was a pair of hiking boots he was wearing. And I didn't get a chance to speak with him, he was dead," Deke replied in a calm matter-of-fact way.

"Dead!" Amy repeated the word so loudly that even as Deke looked up at her in surprise he saw the ears perk up on Paul, George, John, and Ringo. They turned their heads also looking at her, puzzled by her sudden outburst.

"Was it the killer?" Her follow-up question was much lower in volume. She was still having a hard time regaining her composure.

ENTERING Pueblo, Jack Vermette had long ago reduced his speed significantly. It wasn't fear or caution from law enforcement that made him reduce the cruiser down to an aggravating forty miles per hour. More begrudgingly, it was the weather. Conditions had become perilous, with some stretches of highway having been shut down altogether by the highway department. With the increasing rates of snowfall, some areas were receiving up to six inches an hour. Only major highways remained open, but were being closed to traffic by sundown.

Jack's frame of mind had deteriorated, becoming more and more unpredictable with each mile that he was not allowed to resume at a more tolerable and acceptable pace. Already his mind was imagining that damned Old Texas Ranger arriving at Deke Stone's cabin, like some kind of hero on the back of a white stallion, rescuing Amy Dodson from peril, carrying her away in a cloud of dust as they rode off into the sunset.

Within the severely twisted mind of Jack Vermette a plan had long ago been thought out, a plan to his liking, in which he would become the hero. Instead of riding in on a white stallion, he would be riding upon a pale horse. The same color as the last horse of the Apocalypse, which hell and death rode. His dead child would become beneficiary and Jack would become the hero, avenging his murder, which had been committed by a mother void of morality. The heathen who had assisted her in the despicable act had already been tried, sentenced, and executed. It was a pity that the sister of the heathen had to pay with her life also; however, Justice was blind, and for all of the innocent victims caught beneath Justice's scales of balance, she wept not.

With every mile, another form of inflicted torture was imagined by Jack, upon who he had begun referring to as the whore. Once Jack had made the transformation from reality to one of a created fantasy, mimicking the Divine Vision witnessed by John the Apostle while exiled on the Island of Patmos in the first century, it stuck.

Jack Vermette's insanity had plunged to a new depth, responding to the extreme panic and stress brought upon him from thoughts of losing his chance to exact retribution against Amy. The new development changed his previous self-image from one that was still vulnerable to danger, one of human status, to a self-image of divine origin. In order to ensure the punishment that he had in store for Amy, he was forced to equate himself to someone god-like, without fear of suffering failure, injury, or even death.

In short, the madness raging within him moved to a deeper dimension, associated with his perceived status as a victim. The transformation necessary to continue his mission with confidence, while ignoring certain factors completely outside of a realm where he could control the outcome, such as the developing weather, was simple. Without the slightest amount of effort, and without ever becoming aware, Jack developed what would eventually be labeled as the Messiah Complex.

CHAPTER

20

RANGER ZACHARY WYATT Randal entered El Paso County, and had been driving north through the famous area for the last twenty minutes. Zach was mindful to examine the area closely, looking for particular signs obvious only to lawmen that would give him a pretty good idea as to what kind of leader Sheriff Bill Wright really was.

The dreary and cold conditions, which had descended upon the area within the last seventy-two hours, severely hampered normal activity in the county and Zach's ability to judge the effectiveness of the sheriff. However, the small, quiet communities and neat, well-kept, business districts along this route left him with the impression that Bill Wright held a tight rein on the population.

However, Zach's initial impression was shattered as he entered the outskirts of Colorado Springs. The large city was impressive, but run-down warehouse areas with the slum-like conditions of some of the neighborhoods located away from the tourist and Interstate routes disheartened him. In all fairness, Zach soon became aware of how much larger this city was than Sweetwater, along with many of the other Texas cities that he held near and dear to his heart. Realizing the immense scope and size, and with what he knew was a diverse populace, the Texas Ranger cut Sheriff Bill Wright a bit more slack before making a final evaluation on his job performance.

Weather conditions had evolved from the light snow that had been falling, into blizzard like conditions. His Bronco was equipped with the ability to switch into a four-wheel-drive status, and Zach had stopped several miles back, locking the front hubs, engaging the vehicle into a four-wheel-drive high gear. The gear allowed him to travel at highway speed, but with the advantage of all-wheel drive. The slick and frozen road conditions had slowed him only slightly as Zach continued on his way. His frustration however, came when he was held up in traffic behind the many accidents that had occurred along the route. Zach had to force himself to employ what little patience he was gifted with while making his way into the city.

AMY'S question had taken Deke by surprise. It wasn't so much the question that had him concerned, as much as it was the answer. The answer would be significant in more than what was just obvious, providing them with an identity to the one they had feared for so long, but even more importantly, it may provide them with his location.

If the man that Deke had seen was the killer it meant they no longer had anyone to fear. However, if the man Deke had spotted over the precipice, head down in the snow, was not the killer, then who was he? And what was he doing up here? Why had an El Paso County Sheriff Department K-9 dog accompanied him? It didn't take long for Deke to realize how important the answer to Amy's question might be, and he also realized that he would have to go back and somehow find a safe route to the bottom of the precipice, and identify that person.

Deke looked at Amy with regret in his eyes. She descended slowly, down from the loft with John, Paul, George, and Ringo beating her to the bottom of the stairway. Without a word, Amy walked to the sofa love seat, grabbing one of the throw pillows. She sat back holding it tightly against her chest. She watched in silence as Deke began re-lacing and buckling the cumbersome ski boots.

Deke was shaking his head in disgust; frustrated with himself for not realizing what had to be done when he'd first spotted the body. For some odd reason, that he was unable to think of at the time, he'd only been concerned with getting to the cabin, and out from the cold, back to Amy.

Without looking back up at her, afraid of seeing her response, he confessed, "I'll have to go back."

"Why?" Amy questioned him, astonished at his quick turnabout from appearing to settle down into one of going out again in the frozen weather.

"The person I saw was at the bottom of a steep gorge. Whoever the man was, his head was buried in the snow. Apparently falling, he was killed." Glancing at Amy for just a second to find out how she was responding to the information, Deke saw raised eyebrows, and a world of puzzlement.

"It's a place that I know well. The ledge is easily misjudged, with a short stand of trees hiding where the edge of the gorge drops off. But the edge has an eight hundred foot drop for anyone who takes the wrong step." Deke's voice was void of emotion, as if he were giving a commentary on some television documentary about *Wild Alaska*. He was trying desperately to make his case for the argument that he knew would soon start. He had finished lacing his boots, and with the final snap of buckles while kneeling on one knee, he turned and faced her.

Immediately she knew what the look meant, and began to protest before he could explain the importance of going back alone to identify the mystery stranger at the bottom of the scarred mountainside.

"I'm going with you. I can't stay here alone for another minute Deke. Even with the Beatles, it's just more than I can handle." Amy was relentless with her appeal. Still, as she continued with one reason after another, the strength of the argument began to subside. She knew he had no skis for her to use, and even if he did, she had no idea how to use them. And it surely was not the time for first lessons. Amy's face reflected the defeat that she was so determined to avoid, fearing another long period of time being alone, while Deke was out in the blizzard conditions raging on the mountainside.

Deke had not moved from his position, but only lowered his head to avoid looking into the eyes that he knew were pleading. Pleading for a decision that would be against his better judgment and one that he had barely enough strength to avoid making. He stood slowly as Amy became silent. It was a silence that spoke to him clearly, accepting the situation, and allowing him to do what had to be done, and without having to explain why.

Deke turned from her and opened the cabin door; the snow had piled up a few inches higher in the short time that he'd been in the cabin. In a reassuring tone, he turned back to Amy.

"I'll be back as soon as possible, you'll be fine."

With a quick jump, he was out and back onto the snow. This time; however, Deke noticed that Amy did not come up behind him to shut the door. He reached down pulling it closed, and faced the blinding snow that was coming down at disturbing angles, driven by the howling wind. Deke began to construct a plan how of he would descend the jagged eight hundred feet to where the body had ended up sticking out of the snow like a Popsicle stick.

JACK Vermette had a plan, but it was a tricky one. Already he was entering the city limits of Colorado Springs, but his progress was pathetically slow. He was still ignorant as to where Deke Stone's little cabin was located in the wilderness. He had no idea what town, what highway, or what mountainside it was he'd heard Deke lived on. What little information Jack had discovered he'd heard only in passing, and the accuracy of that information was subject to question. However, he did remember a couple of rookie cops saying something about Deke Stone's knowledge concerning the criminal mind.

It was a vague memory, but Jack was desperate. His mission had taken on a new urgency, especially with that damn old Texas Ranger somewhere in the area. It angered him, not only because his plans were in danger of being foiled, but also because Zachary Randal scared him.

His plan was simple, but a real long shot. Jack liked the fact that it was a long shot, his luck had been incredible so far, and when the cards are falling in your favor the temptation to continue gambling gets all the more powerful. If the cards fell in his favor with this, he was sure that nothing could possibly stop him.

In the northeastern section of the city, just off the Interstate 25 business route, sat The University of Colorado at Colorado Springs. It was the only University that Jack had ever visited in the state, but that had been years ago. He was sure that they must have some type of science or psychology department. If his hunch were right, then they would have some type of mailing list for the individuals who either received journals from the department or corresponded with the Division of Psychology. If those two rookie cops, he had accidentally overheard in the break room of the Sweetwater Sheriff's Department several days ago, knew what they were talking about, then Mr. Deke Stone just might be on that mailing list.

Jack Vermette continued north through the city in the direction of The University of Colorado, feeling more and more confident as he neared the campus.

SNOW was thick as spit, and instead of the normal blizzard conditions that most people are aware of when the white stuff floats down vertically; this snow was layered horizontally in sheets across the mountainside. The wind howled unceasingly, sounding like the pipe organ that haunted Don Knots in the old movie *The Ghost and Mr. Chicken*. Deke remembered seeing the movie that was supposed to be a comedy, but the way the old pipe organ had sounded really spooked him. Its evil wailing was something far more sinister than just a humorous tune. Phantoms danced with glee on moonless nights to the tunes played on that pipe organ, and Deke's wild imagination had him as jumpy as a groundhog in a snake's hole, hiding from a grizzly bear.

After about ninety minutes of struggling, watching the path closely to make sure he didn't make the same fatal mistake the individual he was going after had made, Deke reached the edge of the deep scar that formed the craggy, mountain gorge.

Nearly invisible, the fatal step was even more concealed by the drifting snow. As Deke stretched his neck out over the side, peering through the whiteout that had covered the mountain like a wet blanket, he was sure that he would be covered by a foot of snow. Still, he had to get some type of bearing on where the person had fallen. Deke was wise enough to know that when he reached, and if he reached the bottom of the gorge, everything would look as alien as the surface of the moon, having no similarity to the way it looked from eight hundred feet up.

The line of jagged stone that sat at the edge of the gorge bottom made a semicircle. It was easy to see before the last two feet of snow had fallen, and this guy looked like he had fallen right onto that rock edge. The only thing that was barely visible were the tips of the jagged rocks sticking out hideously in the deepest part of the gorge. He remembered when he first spotted the person sticking out of the snow; it looked like the teeth of a shark had surrounded the man, and he was being swallowed. With his bearing about as good as he was going to get it, Deke cut back across the mountainside at ninety degrees, heading down for a hundred yards. It was not going to alleviate him from having to descend the dangerously steep cliff, but it would take some of the angle of descent out of the initial portion.

Cutting back across the mountainside, again moving toward the gorge at a more reasonable angle, Deke approached the lip of the drop. Damn, he hated to have to do this. At least he was not as winded as he had become earlier that day. Removing his cross-country skis, leaving them standing in the snow, he would be able to locate them later. They would also give him a target to climb for, provided he made the climb down and was able to climb back up. He turned and began descending into the gorge, facing the side of the cliff. It took only three minutes, having descended only six feet; to bust his mouth against the hard granite-like stone as he stopped his fall after losing his footing on the ice covered face of the cliff. The only consolation was that his face was numb, and he didn't feel it much. The copper-tasting, warm blood in his mouth was the only way he even knew he'd busted his lip.

"*Oh well,*" he thought. It wasn't the first time, and for some reason Deke knew that if it was the only injury he sustained he would be damn lucky.

Straining to hold on to the sharp, rock edges with his ungloved fingers, he was amazed at his casual attitude while attempting the suicidal descent. With a grunt of recognition, it occurred to him that this must be the kind of behavior love produces. He damn sure couldn't think of any other reason for his current predicament. He was freezing, flat against the side of a cliff, his mouth was busted, it would be dark before long, and he was pretty sure that he was hopelessly stuck.

Feeling like a rain-soaked kitten at the top of a screen door trying to get away from the wet, Deke realized that, just like the kitten, he was hanging on for his very life by the tips of his fingernails.

ZACH became tired of looking at the depressing sights within the warehouse districts of Colorado Springs and the inner city. Originally, he took to the city streets thinking that he would make up for lost time since the Interstate was so clogged with backed up traffic and ice. Tiring of the many stop signs and drivers managing to get their cars stuck sideways across narrow streets, blocking most of the traffic, he shot back up onto the Interstate 25 business route. Ignoring the slow and sliding vehicles that honked and swerved to miss him as he merged into traffic, he made his way toward the El Paso County Sheriff's Office.

Estimating that he was only twenty to thirty minutes from their location, Zach realized that darkness would arrive before any worthy attempt could be made in getting to Deke's place. It was difficult, but he began to slow himself down, conserving the energy that he knew he'd need first thing in the morning. The pace he'd set, burning the amount of energy he was burning, would not be healthy for him to maintain throughout the night, even though he wanted like hell not to slow down.

JOHN Hadley had been driving like Sadam Hussein's Royal Guard racing across the desert to escape the carpet bombing delivered by the Air Force's B-52's during Desert Storm. Not all of them made it to safety, but by God, the ones who did considered it the biggest victory of their life.

Entering Colorado, he felt better. He was fairly sure that the real action would be put off until the next morning, and that gave him plenty of time to find Zach Randal. The directions that he'd received from Sheriff Bill Wright were pretty detailed, and John Hadley understood Deke's place was at least fifteen miles north of Colorado Springs, somewhere up the side of a mountain where no addresses to speak of existed. Deke lived about eight thousand feet up a mountain that was called Pop's Soapbox. A little cabin that he'd built was accessible only by way of a narrow dirt and gravel road that hugged so tightly against the mountainside it was called Mamaw's Staircase.

Yes, John felt sure no attempt would be made to get to Deke's cabin until morning's first light. That was only if the amount of snowfall overnight did not make Mamaw's Staircase impassable.

DRIVING north, trying to remember how to get to that damn college campus, Jack Vermette nearly swallowed his tongue when a powerful, black Bronco suddenly swerved up onto the ramp. The driver never even looked back as Jack swerved to prevent a collision. He sat on the cruiser's horn in protest, but quickly backed off when, to his disbelief, he realized that he'd nearly slammed into the damn Texas Ranger Zach Randal. Jack was so stunned that the unmarked cruiser he drove slowly slid to a stop, banging into a side rail, while he watched the madman behind the Bronco's wheel zoom out onto the ice covered highway without even skidding.

Quickly, Jack made a critical decision, and it meant an immediate change of plans. To hell with a possibility of any mailing list. It took only a second for Jack to realize that the damn Texas Ranger he'd come to hate so much knew exactly where he was going. Zach Randal had just been designated as Jack's personal guide to wherever Amy was hiding. If he stayed just far enough back, behind the mad Ranger's black tank of a truck, he was sure to be taken straight to the place that he wanted so desperately to locate. As far as Vermette knew, Zach Randal had never been introduced to him personally, and could not be certain what he looked like. He was sure the man did not recognize him through this damn blizzard. He had enough heavy clothing on to disguise him; besides, it was the unmarked cruiser that would give him away, if anything. He would have to remedy that as soon as possible, but this tour service had just started, and he set his sights on the black Bronco's taillights. This was getting more exciting with every hour that passed. How could his mission not succeed when he had such divine intervention?

SHERIFF Bill Wright had managed to get everything they needed before the last light of day faded away over the western mountain range. He did not make a habit of getting personally involved with a hands-on commitment for just every law enforcement official that passed through his county, but he was making this a special occasion. He wanted to be on the heels of Texas Ranger Randal if any type of action occurred. This was a high profile case; he had already checked it out with officials back in Texas and New Mexico. Whoever Randal was, he was no small potato. Texas Ranger's didn't usually take off across the country after some petty thief, especially if that Ranger was all alone. From what he was able to piece together from different sheriff departments, Ranger Zach Randal was one peculiar law dog. He didn't like company, and tolerated advice even less. Bill Wright had already made up his mind, he would do anything he could for Randal, but the cooperation was going to have to work both ways. Either Randal would bend enough to give him half the credit for any arrest made, or walk up that mountain alone without the use of his horses or directions.

Two miles just northeast of the famous Pike's Peak, at the edge of the roughest terrain·encountered by settlers crossing the country in the mid-1800's headed west toward California, Bill Wright waited. He had instructed one of his deputies to escort Texas Ranger Randal to his location as soon as he'd arrived at the sheriff's office.

Bill Wright was sitting on the front porch of one of the many cabins utilized by his office whenever organizing trail rides and volunteer posse details. The cabin sat in a small valley near the Continental Divide, at the eastern edge of the Rocky Mountains. Sheriff Wright often used the corral for different events, and even more importantly, it was only four miles due south of Pop's Soapbox where Deke had built his cabin. From where Bill Wright sat, he saw only one route up that mountain. However, Mamaw's Staircase was covered with several feet of snow, making it inaccessible except by horseback.

Sheriff Wright had been careful enough to select two of his best deputies to accompany him and Ranger Randal up the mountain. His best deputy had never returned from the early morning hike to Deke's place that he was supposed to have taken. It wasn't like the boy to get lost or fail to carry out an order by Sheriff Wright, but the young deputy had been known to override orders whenever weather conditions warranted. He was probably snuggled up with some snow bunny in front of a fireplace, laughing at what Sheriff Wright and Zach Randal were preparing to attempt.

THIS had to be without a doubt the most unexplainable situation Deke had ever gotten himself into; other than the time when he married that girl with a stinger. He was unable to move up or down, despite his many attempts during the last forty-five minutes. And things were getting worse. The longer he remained clinging on the cliff face the more the ice built up and the darker it got and the colder he became. He wanted to laugh at himself, but when he thought about what Amy must be going through back at the cabin, knowing that it was getting dark and he was still not back, made him nearly panic. He was still a good seven hundred and eighty feet above the gorge's bottom, where the person, whoever it was, had managed to fall, killing them. It was a fate he was entertaining thought about himself. What in the heck was he going to do? He saw no way that he could make it back to the ledge where he'd started his descent. It was taking everything he had just to hold on to the sheer cliff at his current location. Likewise, he saw no way that he could descend any more without losing his grip altogether. It looked bleak. Deke began looking around for what he had put off as long as he could: the best place to fall.

AMY started rummaging through the two closets and beneath the stairs in the cabin at least thirty minutes before it became dark, looking for any kind of clothing that would help keep her warm while she went looking for Deke. She was frantic. With six pairs of oversized socks on her feet, and four pairs on her hands, she'd managed to get an old pair of hiking boots, that Deke had stuck in the back of one of the closets, onto her feet. She had also found several pairs of Army fatigues. He must have worn them back in college. Amy managed to tie them tight enough around her waist by using an old, striped, silk tie, she'd found hanging in the same closet. She was hoping the pants would stay up long enough to keep her butt warm.

Only one thing had convinced Amy that she must go out searching for Deke, but it was the one thing in which she had the most faith. For the last hour, Ringo had not moved from where he sat facing the cabin's front door. It was as if he were transfixed on a single spot of the wooden door, staring at it, waiting for Deke to return. Then, for the last twenty minutes, he started whining in a low mournful wail. It was the sound of grief. Ringo knew something that the other Beatles seemed oblivious to, and Amy was convinced that he could lead her to wherever Deke was stranded, or hurt. Amy was still searching for one last piece of equipment that she felt she could not do without, a flashlight.

It was during her search Ringo started a different behavior. His wailing became more intense, insistent. Then, standing at the cabin's door, he began scratching at the wood feverishly. As his intensity escalated, Ringo began biting at the wood. He was going to find a way out of that cabin if it were by removing the door one splinter at a time.

Amy finally located a large 9-volt battery, and after summoning all her courage, she turned to the Beatles. With the exception of Ringo, still busy at the door, John, Paul, and George, sat in a half circle watching her every action, puzzled, but made anxious by her bizarre activity and the fear that they could smell.

"Let's go!" She'd relented to the fact that it was a bad idea, but she was determined to die if that's what it took to bring this chapter of her life to an end.

When Amy pulled the door open, she was greeted by the dark, the bitter cold, and the unforgiving wilderness of the Colorado Rocky Mountains. Like an enemy, patient and powerful beyond belief, the cold and dark mountain seemed alive, waiting for her. Ringo, unable to contain his state of troubled frenzy, bolted away from her and into the jaws of the waiting darkness, disappearing almost immediately across the eerie and frozen, white covering of snow.

The storm was still raging with snow falling heavily, but in the half darkness of the mountainside, it seemed to have lessened a bit and the fresh snow that covered the ground had a luminescent glow. As Ringo bounded across the virgin flakes in search of his lost friend, Amy could not help but think about Sir Arthur Conan Doyle's fictional tale about a wild hound that haunted the Moors of England. Linked to a family cursed by the ghostly beast, the novel was titled *Hound of the Baskervilles.*

Ringo's departure stunned Amy. She had never once been deserted by any of the Beatles, for any reason. This development aroused sadness in her as she watched him flee into the white night. Ringo's passion moved her, almost romantically.

Flicking on the big flashlight and training the beam in the direction that Ringo headed, Amy followed his paw prints. John, Paul, and George tagged along beside her, sniffing curiously at the snow without complaint.

CHAPTER

21

ZACH WAS SURPRISED, as he arrived at the El Paso County Sheriff Department. A young but able looking fellow was waiting for him. He wore a white Stetson, and immediately, Zach approved of the deputy who introduced himself as Ted Daniel. Officer Daniel updated Randal on the situation, as far as the weather was concerned. Then, he informed Zach that he was instructed by Sheriff Wright to bring the Ranger straight out to the small cabin where the sheriff was waiting.

"No sir!" Zach said to the offer from the deputy to drive him out to the mountain hide-away. "I insist that you ride with me. It would be an honor for me to personally carry your scrawny little hide in my department vehicle," Zach stated, smiling as he pointed to the oversized Bronco sitting atop the thirty-five inch mud tires.

The young deputy smiled approvingly, answering, "I thought you'd never ask." Then, ran over to the truck and climbed into the driver's seat. Zach Randal sauntered over to the big, four-wheel drive, and with a hop jumped up onto the passenger-side running board, handing Ted Daniel the keys.

"Fire this mother up, Ted my boy. Consider it payment for the troubles that you and the good sheriff have gone through on my behalf." With the command given, the two officers, who could not have looked more opposite from one another if they had been ordered from the Sears and Roebuck catalog, roared away in the big, black Bronco.

Sitting in the unmarked cruiser, hidden behind a delivery truck a block away from the sheriff department, Jack Vermette watched the brief encounter between the two men. More than anything, he was shocked to see the young deputy get behind the wheel of the Bronco before they drove away. The meeting seemed to amuse Zach Randal. Jack saw a rare smile on his face as he climbed into the passenger seat.

Sliding down low to avoid detection, but without arousing suspicion from the act of trying to hide, Jack waited until they were a couple of blocks away before cranking the cruiser up, following them at a safe distance. He had not been able to switch into another vehicle like the one he would have preferred. Since the car he was now driving was well known by the damn Texas Ranger, it made him more nervous than usual. This was a precursor to possible screw-ups, and Jack hated screw-ups. Even if unavoidable, situations that were less than desirable were in themselves loaded with danger, the kind of danger that was sitting on coiled springs just waiting for the trigger mechanism to shoot them out in all directions.

It created mass pandemonium in his psyche, which, ironically and inevitably, led to an increased possibility of potential screw-ups. Jack didn't like thinking about all the factors involved. It hurt his head to concentrate on anything of that nature anyway. After all of this mess was cleared up and all the loose ends were tightened, or neatly clipped, Jack wanted to turn over a new leaf.

He'd decided, while recovering in Mexico that he had too much raw talent and energy hidden somewhere inside to allow another day to waste away. Jack had always wanted a family, and thought he was very close to having that very thing when Amy decided to end her pregnancy. He knew that it was all because of that Satan-worshipping boy, Jedediah Duncan, Vanessa's young brother. What resulted from that event was what made him who he was today.

EXITING the city, headed in a northwesterly direction, Zach and Ted made their way through the snow filled evening and into the majestic scenery of the Rocky Mountains. The young officer, Ted Daniel, handled the slippery conditions on the dark and narrow winding roads with skill. He and Zach made small talk while covering the twelve or thirteen miles to the small hide-away, where Sheriff Bill Wright was waiting. Zach thought very little about discussing the case with one officer while on their way, when he'd have to go over the whole thing with another as soon as they arrived. Although the distance was only a dozen miles or so, the big Bronco did not arrive at the cabin until an hour later.

Exiting the two-lane, state road, they drove the final mile on not much more than two strips of slick, frozen mud, where the tires of four-wheel drive vehicles had worn paths through the wild grass and brush of the mountain valley.

The yellow glow of a lantern could be seen through the cabin's windows as Ted and Zach exited the Bronco, plodding through two feet of snow to the front porch. Zach was glad when he saw a faint line of smoke coming from the chimney on the cabin's rooftop. He had just been entertaining the thought of sitting before a warm fire while nursing a glass of blended whiskey. As they were knocking snow from their boots at the front door, Sheriff Wright burst through from the inside. With a smile on his face, he stuck out his right hand to Zach, in his left he was holding a half-empty glass of what Zach figured was well-aged bourbon.

"Well, I'm pleased and honored to finally meet you, Ranger Randal," Bill Wright stated, wide-eyed as he watched his big hand swallowed up by the ham-sized paw of Randal.

"The pleasure is all mine Sheriff, but we can get through the pleasantries after I've gotten seated, warmed over, and wetted my whistle if you don't mind?" Zach motioned to the glow and warmth revealed through the open door of the cabin.

"Absolutely!" Sheriff Wright responded, leading the way through the inviting door while Zach followed, and the quiet deputy who he'd nearly forgotten all about followed him.

"Oh." Bill Wright stopped short in the doorway, appearing to have suddenly remembered something. He turned looking past Zach, at the young officer, Ted Daniel.

"Ted, would you mind going out behind the cabin to the woodbin? We'll need a few good-sized logs for tonight, I didn't get a chance to bring them in earlier." Sheriff Wright didn't even wait for an answer as he turned back entering the warm domain that was before them.

Zach noted the exchange, wondering how the young buck would handle the belittling event. He was pleasantly surprised and impressed when he heard Ted Daniel respond, "Sure thing Sheriff. Is that all you need doing for now?" The words were spoken respectfully.

Bill Wright didn't even bother to answer, and after a moment, Ted Daniel turned energetically on his way to the woodbin.

"What's your pleasure Ranger?" Bill asked Zach, walking over to the small wet bar in one corner of the small structure.

"Whatever you suggest Sheriff, as long as it gets here in a hurry." Zach's response was made as he casually surveyed the rustic interior of the place. He was pleased with the decor, and realized immediately that this kind of lifestyle was the answer to the question he put to Sergeant John Hadley earlier, wanting to know what kind of person lives like this, but without a phone. He knew exactly why a phone would be ignored living this way, and knew exactly what he was going to do after this whole affair was over and done with.

He found an old rocker made from rough-cut aspen sitting by the fireplace. As he settled into the rocker, he realized the seat was warm. Apparently it was where Bill had been sitting when they arrived, but Zach made no effort finding another chair, he was comfortable.

"Here you go Ranger." A mason jar converted into a drinking glass was handed to Zach filled with an amber liquid and two cubes of ice. He thanked the sheriff, slowly rocking while testing the beverage. A nod of his head told the sheriff that he approved. Only then, did Bill Wright turn and take a seat across from Zach on the fireplace hearth.

After a couple of moments and after Zach had mentally unwound, he realized his age was showing and he deliberately made an effort to appear less exhausted.

"Bill, why don't we get the first obstacle out of our way? You can call me either Randal, Zach, Zachary, or son-of-a-bitch, but you don't have to call me Ranger or Sir. Okay?"

"Okay. Likewise for me Zach," Bill answered him.

By this time the wit was seeping back into Zach, and just to tip the scales a bit he responded, "Bullshit! I'll call you what I damn please and you'll like it or else." The response sounded so real from Zach that it took a minute for Bill Wright to get the joke, but when he did, they both laughed loudly. Zach's sudden and bizarre quip was effective, and the walls that were building between them crumbled. Both men were relieved by the break in the ice, but were interrupted by Ted Daniel, who walked into the cabin noisily lugging a couple of huge logs.

Noticing the loud laughter between the two men ceased as he walked in, Ted looked around suspiciously, "What?"

Laughter erupted again. This time realizing the humor, Ted Daniel also joined in with the stress reducing behavior. As the men relaxed in the warm cabin, their laughter echoed through the valley. Zach silently wondered how long he would have to play this game before getting down to business.

fOLLOWING along behind the young deputy and that damn Texas Ranger on the slick and winding mountain road, Jack Vermette started having difficulty with the cruiser, specifically, in holding it on the road. The Bronco made a ninety degree turn to the left, and afraid to lose his blind guide, Jack accelerated just a bit too quickly. Before he knew it, the cruiser had turned sideways. Unable to correct the severe angle, he held on. The guardrail in the curve was sturdy, but the thought of striking the low barrier while out of control had a negative effect on Jack; after all, it was a cold and dark night, and he had no idea where the hell he was or how much farther he had to go.

The heavy cruiser was moving faster than Jack thought, but he managed to straighten the angle, sliding headfirst into the rail. When the collision occurred the guardrail easily plowed through the front grill and into the car's engine. He was unhurt, but the cruiser was finished. With the engine dead and disabled, the cruiser sat harpooned like a whale by the guardrail. It was stuck and so was he for the time being.

Jack sat in the silence of the snowy night wondering what, if any, options were left.

AFTER discussing the trivial crap that lawmen discuss after first meeting, Zach broke away from the usual by asking how long it would take to get to Deke's place.

Looking somewhat uncomfortable, taken by surprise, Sheriff Wright first looked at Ted Daniel, then back toward Zach before responding.

"Well Zach, that's a difficult thing to answer without knowing how much more snow we might get tonight. Hell, we really don't know how much snow is on Mamaw's Staircase to begin with. That will be the determining factor of us having any chance at all." The sheriff gave his response in a shaky voice, revealing to Zach that he was no way near sure of himself, or their chances of getting up that mountainside in the morning.

Zach said nothing at first, pausing for a while. The slow and disgusting way he shook his head from side to side; however, left no question as to what he was thinking.

"Bill, I've driven a hell of a long way, overcoming many obstacles. Yet, I arrived in about the shortest amount of time possible. I never doubted the fact that I would get here, only the amount of time that it might take for me to arrive. Now that I have arrived, the last thing I feel like doing is playing patty-cake with you or anyone else on this planet. One more time I'll ask you about how long do you think it will take for us in the morning?" This time as Zach asked the question, his voice had a notable change. He was not only asking for an answer, but demanding an answer, and the assurance that they would indeed be getting to Deke Stone's cabin in the morning.

INDIVIDUALS, who are in danger of its debilitating effects, are rarely prepared for exhaustion until it suddenly is upon them. Even more, the bizarre development is often a result of inactivity. Deke had been perfectly ready to accept the possibility of becoming tired, but only after strenuous activity. For the last couple of hours he'd been relatively inactive, unable to move more than a few inches. Yet, to his dismay and confusion he unexpectedly discovered that he had become completely exhausted.

He also discovered, to his utter disappointment, that regardless how many times he scanned the ground below him, or how intense a study of the terrain he made, it remained the same distance from him as when he first came to be in the current situation.

The word delirium came to Deke's mind, as he carefully examined the rock formations below the spot he was stranded.

Suddenly, he remembered that while in graduate school he and his colleagues occasionally chose a relatively mysterious word from the English language with which they played a sort of mind game together. After choosing the particular word that met everyone's approval, each would individually take turns coming up with a different synonym. The first person that failed to think of a synonym within two seconds would be out of the competition. The object of the game was to avoid pausing before coming up with a correct synonym. The person quick enough to outlast the others was declared winner.

Prizes varied depending on the month, or the week, or the day of the week, or how much money they were able come up with between them. Deke was an excellent competitor, easily winning most of the word games they played.

Stranded, his face buried closer to the rock wall than he thought possible, Deke felt time standing still. The word *delirium* was haunting him, and automatically Deke began rattling off synonyms emerging from within his brain.

Madness! Delusion! Insanity! Fever! Lunacy! Confusion! Chaos! Baffled! Puzzled! Bewildered! Stupefied! Deranged! Havoc! Mayhem! Loss of One's Faculties!

He paused…It was the first time that he had to pause to think of a synonym. Deke knew then he had lost the game…It was his sign…He jumped.

The snow had been falling for so long that all he could see for the last hour was the blinding white. As he fell backward off the cliff, he looked up. Through the white haze, for just a second, he saw something he recognized. But he was too far away to be sure. Disappearing into the soup of white, into the deep gorge below, Deke faded quickly. Yet, at the top of the gorge, from the edge of the cliff he'd descended…Ringo let out a loud wail in response.

THROUGH the blinding blizzard and three feet of fresh snow, Ringo had located Deke. Just as the big Chesapeake arrived where the well-concealed edge above the gorge was located, he watched Deke loose his grip, falling away into the blinding white without a sound.

Miraculously, as Ringo saw Deke disappear into the white fog of snow, the darkness increased. Realizing what had happened; Ringo began running along the gorge down the mountainside. After several hundred yards, Ringo spotted an area where the descent was more reasonable. Leaping without hesitation, he began climbing down into the deep scar of the mountain. With amazing agility and speed, he descended into the darkness.

Ringo had left Amy and the other Beatles far behind as he took off from the cabin. Amy was still struggling with the flashlight, following Ringo's paw prints through the snow. The amount of fresh snow still falling had nearly covered over Ringo's path and the farther Amy followed, the slower her progress became. Paul, John, and George had no idea what she was up to. If able to understand her plight, they could have easily helped by sniffing out Ringo's destination. The cold was numbing, and Amy was not dressed for her trek. In addition, she was not prepared for the brutality of the terrain and its unforgiving nature.

For two hours Amy and her companions managed to wander repeatedly in one giant circle. By the time they reached a spot only three hundred yards behind the cabin for the second time, Amy realized how tragic her decision to search for Deke had become. She had lost the trail of paw prints left by Ringo long ago. Frozen, nearly blinded by the snow and wind, Amy walked into the side of a large boulder jutting out of the mountainside. As she fell to her knees George, Paul, and John surrounded her. The cleft where the boulder met the ground was barely large enough for her body as she squeezed down in an attempt to escape the bitter wind. Snuggling in against her, the Beatles attempted to provide warmth. It might be the only thing giving her a chance of survival. As her swollen and burning eyes closed, Amy whispered to John, Paul, and George, "Thank you for being with me guys, and being so faithful over the years."

CHAPTER

22

SITTING BEHIND THE wheel of the wrecked cruiser, Jack wondered how long he might have to wait before a vehicle came along this winding, desolate, cold highway. From watching the cruiser's digital clock on the dashboard, Jack saw that nearly an hour had gone by, and not a single vehicle had passed. With the storm still making an impressive show of strength, he didn't think many people would be braving the narrow road, and didn't have much, if any, expectations of being rescued. As he pondered how he'd get out of this situation, Jack reminded himself that this was a mission, a mission to establish an equal balance between the righteous and the irreverent. Justice was at the heart of this mission. If for any reason the outcome was not successful, he was not to blame. His involvement, he believed, was irrelevant. Yet, because the forces controlling directions had chosen him, he believed his destiny was one of greatness. This event and the many missions he would be entrusted with in the future had now defined the purpose of his existence.

Lost in mesmerizing, bizarre, and wandering delusions of grandeur, Jack is unexpectedly blinded by the reflection of headlights appearing in the rearview mirror. Shaking his head to clear his mind, he watched as a vehicle drove up behind him, stopped, and the driver side door open. Hurriedly Jack exited the cruiser, not wanting to be caught at a disadvantage, having no idea who the man was.

"Howdy. Are you all right?" The man's voice sounded friendly and genuinely concerned.

Shielding his eyes from the blinding headlights, Jack could only see the black outline of a man wearing a cowboy hat approaching him from the front of the vehicle.

"Uh, yeah. I'm fine, but afraid I can't say the same about my car," Jack answered. His voice was a little shaky as he tried to determine if any threat could be detected in the voice. That was okay, since it only made him sound like he was shaken from the accident. The effect made him appear all the more innocent.

"Well, I have a cell phone here and we can call for an ambulance, but if you think you're all right...are you sure sir?" The man approached slowly, studying the stranded situation of the cruiser. Still, Jack was unable to see the man clearly, although such a concerned and helpful individual with such respectful manners left Jack with no other option but to feel completely safe and non-threatened.

"I don't think I've suffered any injury, except maybe to my pride. No ambulance can help that, but I'm thankful for your concern." With just a slight chuckle mixed into his response, Jack knew his acting would soon reward him. He walked toward the individual behind the cruiser, extending his hand to introduce himself.

"My name's…" Jack stopped abruptly.

The tall man approached him, moving to the side of the bright headlights where Jack could finally see him. Wearing a white Stetson, and about twenty-five years old, the deputy sheriff extended his hand grabbing hold of Jack's, shaking it firmly.

"Deputy J.B. Walker," he said introducing himself. He looked at Jack, anticipating an exchange of introductions. Deputy Walker tilted his head slightly, a little puzzled.

Jack nearly panicked, making a mistake and responding by striking out at the young deputy, but held himself together, respecting the man's bigger and heavier frame. If his opponent were any good at hand to hand confrontations, Jack may find himself shackled and headed for jail before knowing whether or not the man had any idea of who's hand he was shaking.

"Oh! I'm sorry deputy. My name's Ja…Jasper…Frank Jasper." The lie was not his best performance of the night, but the young deputy bought it easily enough.

"I'm afraid that I need a little more practice at driving in this snow and ice. Before I knew what had happened the car was sliding, and not much I did helped me to get it to stop. I was trying to get back to the Interstate, toward Denver." Jack began an act of being the innocent tourist, who had tragically become lost in the storm.

"Denver! Well, Mr. Jasper I'm afraid you've taken a wrong turn somewhere along the way." Deputy J.B. Walker chuckled as he rubbed his chin with his hand, looking over the scene.

"Yeah, I will admit that I'm as lost as a Louisiana fur trapper in an Egyptian pyramid."

Immediately, Jack adopted a Cajun accent, hoping to receive a little sympathy.

The deputy looked directly into Jack's eyes, holding the stare for just a second too long. Then he looked away, walking to the front of the cruiser to inspect the damage.

That stare probably wouldn't have amounted to anything that aroused the deputy's suspicion, but it was a second too long and too intense for Jack to trust. The moment the young officer's back was turned, Jack moved swiftly.

In a flash the knife was out, and just as he had opened the service station attendant's throat earlier that morning, Jack carved a deep gash from one ear clear across to the other. Letting his victim down slowly, he held him from behind. Jack marveled at how ineffective the struggle was whenever arterial blood spurted three feet from his victim's neck.

By the time Jack had gently allowed the deputy to fall to the cold, snow-covered roadway beside the cruiser, he was dead. Only then did Jack notice the large revolver strapped to his side, and he quickly unsnapped the holster, stealing the pistol. He also dug around in the man's pockets for anything useful, but found nothing. Backing up from the scene, Jack approached the bright headlights. After he'd scanned the area, finding nothing that would incriminate him, Jack turned to climb into the deputy's vehicle. He was shocked when he realized that he had to reach up to grab the door handle.

Deputy J.B. Walker drove a big four-wheel drive pickup, equipped with a Skyjacker lift kit and a brand of gigantic tires that Jack had never seen before. Reaching up, he climbed in. After familiarizing himself with the interior and controls, Jack threw the big truck into reverse.

The deputy had pulled so close to the rear of the cruiser that Jack had to back out, driving around his impaled car. He suddenly felt an odd jerking behind him, and a sound like moving metal, it reminded Jack of the sounds associated with a big tractor-trailer. Slamming onto the brake petal, he looked behind. That was when he discovered that this truck had a damn horse trailer hooked to the heavy-duty hitch.

It was too great a development for Jack to attribute to anything else but the divine forces that had been guiding him on this mission. The horse trailer contained a beautiful chestnut gelding, saddled and ready to ride.

"Look here Zach, I've taken my entire department and put it at your disposal trying to accommodate you and get that couple out of any trouble they may be in." Sheriff Wright was a little insulted by Zach's demands, and was yet to hear the first word from him signifying any gratitude.

"Now I don't mean to be disrespectful, but I too am a man of authority. Let's work together on this thing and we'll be successful, otherwise you can rent a team of mules in the morning from an old Mexican who lives on the mountain forty miles from here, and go at it all alone. I don't want you to have to do that, neither does Ted, nor does Joe Bob. We're here to help you with this."

Zach didn't respond for some time, sitting and sipping on his drink. When he had sufficiently, but secretly, chastised himself for such rude behavior he decided to call a truce, realizing the stress was a result of his personal involvement, and not anyone's uncooperative behavior.

"Wait a second!" Zach suddenly responded. "Who doesn't want me to go to that Mexican for his mules?" he asked.

"Hell, none of us does Zach." The sheriff had not caught onto what Zach was really asking.

"That's not what I mean. You referred to yourself and Ted, and then who else?" Zach asked, looking intently at the pair sitting bewildered before him. All at once, Bill realized what Zach was after.

"Oh! I see what you're asking. Before making the arrangements to help you get to Deke's place, I thought long and hard about who we should have with us on that ride. Ted here is one of my best deputies, and I have another fellow who is just as effective, and just as good in the saddle. His name is J.B. Walker, but we just call him Joe Bob. He should be on his way over here about now. I had him pulling a late shift this afternoon, and after his shift he's supposed to pick up his mount before driving here to meet us tonight," Bill Wright explained briefly to Zach who he meant when he referred to Joe Bob.

"I see," Zach stated. Taking a deep breath, he then decided that he would begin with his apology. After properly taking care of that, he started with the particulars behind the case.

Zach began with the women at the cafe, then who Amy Dodson was, and why Deke Stone had become involved. He explained who Jack Vermette had been, who he was now, and what they suspected Vermette had done to Dan and Bill. Finally, he told them why his personal feelings were so damn raw about the entire thing.

"Damn!" the young Deputy Ted exclaimed.

"Double damn!" It was the only form of expression that Ted Daniel could come up with to emphasize his astonishment after Zach had finished with the details.

"And you think this same guy is responsible for all of this?" Sheriff Wright was just as awestruck as his deputy, but managing to hold his amazement at bay. After all, he was a seasoned officer and not supposed to be as impressed as some young deputy, but in reality, he was.

"Bill let me make a confession before I give the reason for believing Jack Vermette is our man. In fact, this confession may be all I need to say for you to understand." It was the second astonishing event of the night. To have the famous Texas Ranger, Zachary Wyatt Randal, make a confession. It left them spellbound. Sitting before Zach, looking like two pioneer kids sitting before a roaring fire and listening to stories from Davy Crockett, Sheriff Bill Wright and Deputy Ted Daniel were cross-legged and entranced.

"When all this started with Miss Amy, I'm afraid I was still suffering from the effects of a previous case." Before Zach could continue, he was interrupted.

"You mean the case of the bathtub drowner!" Deputy Ted Daniel blurted out with excitement. Bill looked at his young deputy disapprovingly before apologizing to Zach, and asking that he continue.

"That's okay, Bill, and you're correct Ted. He was without a doubt the most ruthless, immoral, and pure evil human being I had ever run across in my entire career. What I'm going to tell you boys is something that I have never spoken of before. I'm not sure of all the reasons behind telling you this much, but when this is all over with you might have figured out some of those reasons yourself.

"What that animal did to those poor young ladies...well, I never did allow the press or anyone else get hold of the details. I could not tolerate having the things that were done repeated for everyone to know. The horror and the humiliation that each of those families had to go through was beyond anything acceptable as it was. I never even revealed that information to the families. What good could have come from such foolish arrogance on my part?

"Anyway, I said all that to bring me to another point. That's right, even now I will not reveal what happened to those girls; so, don't ask. What I will say is that the effects of what I witnessed were...how should I put it...life changing. That's about the only way to describe it; because I have never been the same man that I was before I started that investigation. In my mind, even though in reality I know that I am not to blame, I failed those young girls. I was not good enough to save them. A damn lunatic had bested my skill as an investigator.

"When I returned home after several days of interrogations and paper work from the arrest, I found my wife dead. She had killed herself in our bedroom by putting a bullet in her brain. I, of course, was devastated. Had I been home for her when she needed me most she would be alive today. Kate had been sad for some time, and I had failed her also." The Texas Ranger who was a legend, sat before those two men with a trembling chin. Bill and Ted were also fighting off tears.

"I continued to Ranger after Kate's death. It was all I had left, but things were different. My patience was not as good as before, and some men suffered because of it. My techniques changed, and as I'm sure the both of you are aware, I acquired a nickname. They started calling me Hunter. I must say it's a pretty accurate description of what's happened to me, especially on a few of the latest investigations I've handled. However, this case has taken on an even deeper significance. You see, Miss Amy is a dear friend of mine, and I will not, I repeat, I will not fail her! So help me Lord, if it's my last act on Earth, I'll save her. I'll save her for every one of those poor girls that I couldn't save before, and I'll save her for Kate too.

"Something else about this case that I think you should be told, Mr. Deke Stone is probably one of the most brilliant psychological profilers in the country. Many institutions have blackballed him because of his radical and rebellious theories on the criminal mind, but that fact is exactly what makes him so unique and effective. He's the kind of thinker I'd want on my team everyday. Unfortunately, in this case, I had to hijack his services, and he has never had all of the facts to work with; therefore, he's been severely handicapped. His ability to solve this mystery has never been possible due to my inability to provide him with enough information. The man is top notch though, and has put his life in serious peril just to help Amy and I. Admittedly it's probably more for Amy's sake than mine. That don't hurt my feelings none.

"Back to what bothers me most. As evil and as twisted as that damn bathtub-drowning animal was, and even though I thought I'd never see worse, the man that we're after right now wrote the book on bad.

"It's not just the small packages that he's sent to her, packages containing the eyes, ears, and even the tongue of some poor fellow which had been cut right out of his mouth. But he did all of that without leaving a single trace of evidence.

"Neither is it the fact that three women at the cafe were skinned alive, brutally attacked, and horrifyingly mutilated but *how* had he managed to spell out the name of AMY by using skin peeled from the women, pinning it on the wall, and do all of this in less than twenty-four minutes.

"It's not about how he executed two good detectives, friends of mine, blowing the contents of their skulls into the middle of the street behind the Potter County Sheriff Department. They were detectives that had been assigned to this case, and who were good at what they did.

"But it *is* about how this guy thinks, what he thinks, how brilliantly and how quickly he thinks. It's about how consistently perfect his crimes are left, quickly and cleanly, and *all* about the fact that this man *was*, and still *is* listed as deceased. Even more than that, it's about finding a single thumbprint, one print left on a simple key chain. One print that if it had not been found, Jack Vermette would still be thought of as dead, never suspected of having anything to do with any of these horrible crimes, when in reality he is responsible for all of them. And please believe me when I say that he's responsible for many, many more. Months from now, and I know this because I'm damn smart, we'll still be finding out about acts of violence that were committed by Jack Vermette.

"Why is he doing this? That's the two hundred and sixty-four thousand dollar question. Yet, not a single person that I know of has the answer. That is the biggest reason to fear him and to never underestimate him. To this day, I have nothing that can be considered as motive. Since I have been out of contact with Miss Amy, and unable to inform her of who the suspect is, she still thinks Vermette's dead. Whatever her opinion is about why this man would commit such depraved exploits has yet to be obtained. Unbelievable acts of torture and murder committed without any reasonable or unreasonable excuse. That is why I fear him. Nothing that I can imagine is beyond his capability."

Bill Wright had whole-heartedly listened the entire time while Zach gave his apology, confession, and convictions, but he was troubled about how much time had passed. He was troubled because of the lateness of the hour, and about Joe Bob's failure to arrive. According to Bill's calculations, the young deputy should have arrived long ago. It was not like Deputy Walker, and created urgency within Bill to act, rather than to sit and do nothing.

Both Zach and Ted excused themselves to the cold and dark exterior of the cabin to relieve themselves while Bill nervously put a pot of coffee to brewing. Walking back into the cabin Zach approached the kitchen area, and without any encouragement from Bill, Zach asked where he thought they should start searching for the missing deputy.

"Wha...how! Hell Zach, if you weren't on my side you'd scare the beejeebies out of me," Bill confessed in surprise.

"If I were not on your side my friend, you'd be dead." The ruthless reality of Zach's statement sent a bone-chilling shiver through Bill. He was not afraid of Zach, but the Texas Ranger had brought to mind the fact that someone was going to be one hell of a force to reckon with.

"I am worried Zach, but you're responsible for that." Zach was surprised by the accusation. "Bill, I'd much rather you worry than have blood on my hands for letting you be killed," he responded. Zach calmly grabbed a cup, filling it with hot coffee. He was right, and Bill regretted the statement.

Bill Wright had the most intense look on his face that Ted had ever seen. He was placing a couple of more logs on the fire that he'd retrieved from the woodbin. Turning to Zach, Ted saw that he was sitting in the comfortable rocking chair he'd located, quietly sipping on his coffee.

"What's up with Sheriff Wright?" Ted asked in a low voice after placing himself on the hearth, warming up from the outside chore.

"Your partner, Joe Bob, may have run into some problems. Bill says he should have been here long ago, and he's pretty torn up about it." Calmly, without any degree of panic, but to the contrary filled with concern, Zach briefly filled Ted in. Just as their exchange ended, Bill came out from the kitchen. He too was sipping a hot cup of coffee; the anticipated job ahead of the three men was effectively creating a chill in their bones even before leaving the warmth of the cabin.

"First thing we'll have to do is saddle up the horses. Ted give each a small portion of oats, put an extra five pounds in your saddlebag, I'll be out to help with the saddling in a few minutes. But get a mug of hot coffee before you head out again." The orders from Bill Wright meant one of two possibilities, and maybe both possibilities.

Bill was leaning against the mantle above the fireplace. They had been up most of the night, daylight was only an hour or so away. Staring into the fire, Bill asked Zach for his opinion, "Do you think we'll find any trace of Joe Bob if we try at first light?"

Bill was a smart cop; he had to have been at one time or another. Zach saw the logic of his question, admiring him now more than ever for humbling himself enough to ask for advise. Zach was aware of how much Bill wanted to get out and search until he found his deputy. It had to do with protection, and how a sheriff feels that it's his duty to make sure none of the officers who work for him are harmed.

It was damned difficult for Bill to sacrifice searching for his young deputy to ride up the mountain. Especially when way deep inside each of them, they shared the belief that Deke and Amy were as safe as they could possibly be. The couple was snowed in, but that also meant that everyone else was snowed out.

Zach was still sipping on his coffee. He gave the question some thought before answering.

"Nope. If Jack Vermette has somehow been able to get to him, God forbid, won't be much of anything left for us to find, except maybe a body. As much as I regret what may have happened, some good may come from it." Hesitation accompanied the last statement from Zach. The nature of what he was suggesting was repulsive.

As Bill shot a pair of rage-filled eyes at Zach, he explained, "Don't misunderstand hoss, just wait until I explain. If you're still nail chewing mad after hearing me out, then you can have a chunk of me. Okay?"

"Well, get on with the explaining, we don't have much time." Bill Wright was a hurting man right at that moment and Zach felt for him, understanding more than he had ever wanted to about what was going in Bill's mind.

"Give me a rundown on your young deputy, what he's driving, weapons he might have, and what time you think he might have met with any misfortune?" Right away, Bill's anger evaporated, realizing for what Zach was fishing.

He was right; it could be that good fortune was associated with what might have happened. Bill filled Zach in on the information. He could not be certain of all the particulars so guesswork was all they had for the time being. It was enough to at least to get them motivated, and out into the freezing wind and snow flurries.

SERGEANT John Hadley was running on pure adrenaline for the last several days, and he felt it as his energy level started to bottom out. As close as he was, he would not allow anything to stop him. Back in the old days when working seventy and eighty hours straight, John and Zach rarely had enough time to eat. But they drank coffee by the gallon, and always seemed to get through.

Time has a way of changing things, and had really screwed up the way coffee was made. At every chance, John bought a Styrofoam cup filled with the brown brew, but what was passing for coffee these days used to be called locust piss when he was a kid. It tasted as bitter as green pecans and was thinner than the tissue paper in the bathroom where he'd bought the lukewarm stuff.

Throwing his latest sample of coffee out the cruiser's open window, John did his best to follow the directions to that horse ranch in the mountains where Zach and Bill Wright were holding out. The young deputy he'd contacted at El Paso headquarters wasn't able to give him an escort as he hit Colorado Springs forty minutes ago, but he did his best with giving directions, which Hadley followed pretty easily.

He estimated another half to three quarters of an hour before getting to where the men were. As he drove through the dark and cold, snowy night, John became aware that the directions were easy to follow since no other roads were available to take, except the one he was following.

If he messed this up, getting lost in the process, Zach would never let him live it down. Smiling to himself, Sergeant Hadley thought about the possibilities, escaping the humiliation from Zach meant he might even have to retire. At times, he thought that was not such a bad idea.

The narrow road was a winding and twisting affair that kept a man on the edge of his seat, and Hadley had nearly slammed into the back of a vehicle. Suddenly it had appeared from out of the gloom with the rear end sticking out on the road in a narrow curve.

As he slammed onto the brake pedal John began to slide, but immediately releasing the locked brakes he allowed the ABS system to slow him to a stop without ending up in the back seat of the phantom vehicle.

John could not believe what he saw sitting right in front of his eyes. The wrecked Crown Victoria that was twisted up into the guardrail had to belong to Dan and Bill. Snow had almost completely covered the gruesome form of a body stretched out across the highway, lying on the cold pavement beside the Crown Victoria. John knew the body probably wasn't someone he knew; certainly, it wasn't any of his fellow officers. But who was he?

CHAPTER

23

DAYLIGHT WAS PEEKING out from over the mountain range in the east as Deke amazed himself by opening his left eye. Considerable effort was required; fighting against the side of himself that had been his worst enemy as long as he could remember. Insisting to the contrary of what he could plainly see, telling him that he was dead. Apparently, he had not been killed from the fall that he'd taken, jumping off the steep rock face of the cliff the night before.

Deke emerged victorious, overcoming the loud and arrogant voice that lived inside his head. Desperately struggling to obtain a clear head, he began recalling details of the previous day. Remembering the most recent events might give him a glimpse of his life as it was before, Deke thought, and he opened his right eye.

His scream was so unanticipated and shocking that he could only respond with another even more shocking scream. He quickly convinced himself the reason was to clear his lungs from the snow that he'd swallowed.

Hideously large when only a few inches away, Ringo's face was literally against his when he first spotted the rust-colored shaggy hair. Deke never dreamed that one of the few grizzlies still roaming through Colorado would end up being the thing that took his life.

Ringo didn't even lift his chin from the snow, rolling his brown eyes at Deke, obviously unimpressed with the screaming released directly into the big dog's floppy left ear.

"Ringo my boy! Gooood morning to you!" His elation soared beyond the depth of the gorge. He remembered a last resort jump, blindly into the darkness.

Like a kamikaze pilot flying his Zero gracefully above the enemy, tragically discovering that he's out of fuel. Deke had said a prayer and aimed for what he thought was the softest spot, blinded to the treacherous terrain below.

Slowly, with the smallest of movements Deke began to check himself out. He had ended up falling through the top of several snow laden fir trees. The treetops were forty to fifty feet high, and luckily, had broken his fall. Deke discovered that he had landed on his back, but in a semi-sitting position, facing the cliff wall. Thankfully, the snow had accumulated enough to cushion his fall even more, and after inspection, Deke was pretty sure no bones were broken.

Ringo must have found him sometime during the night, curling up around his body to keep him from freezing. The big Chessie stood from the position next to him, stretching his long body and yawning widely.

As Deke stood testing his legs, he felt the many bruises that he'd taken while passing down through the fir branches. Several of the evergreen's limbs were scattered around him, sheared off by his body as he plummeted to the ground.

Even with the soreness he felt in his extremities, Deke was thankful to be alive, considering it nothing short of a miracle. It was still early morning, but Deke could see that the storm was not about to relinquish its grip on the mountain. Snow began to fall moderately again as he looked around. He had to orient himself to his approximate location; a task was waiting to be taken care of since he'd made it to the bottom of the gorge.

With his bearings pretty much taken, Deke and Ringo headed off in a northerly direction, up the face of the mountain and deeper into the throat of the gorge. The chance of him finding the mystery upside-down-person was slim since the body had probably already been completely covered with new snow by this time. But as long as he was here, Deke had to make the effort. Looking down at his new friend walking beside him, Deke marveled at the courage and the love of a dog.

AMY had always heard that uncontrollable shivering was a sign that the body was desperately attempting to produce heat, and that hypothermia had set its deadly grip into a person's core. The uncontrollable shaking and shivering is part of a vicious cycle. Burning up what remained of a person's energy, shivering was a desperate attempt by the body to heat itself up; sadly, it rarely can produce enough heat to combat the decline that has already been set into motion. Whenever the point is reached where shivering has ceased, coma and death are usually not far behind.

Knowing she must get up and get moving did not stir Amy into action. An irrepressible urge to close her eyes and go to sleep had taken over.

Without the strength to fight, Amy surrendered to the powerful seduction. Daylight was just breaking, and with George, John, and Paul, surrounding her small, balled-up shape at the base of the huge boulder, Amy slipped into a deep sleep.

WITHDRAWN into the emotional feeling of despair after losing such a young and talented man as Joe Bob Walker, Bill Wright hadn't spoken two words while helping Deputy Ted Daniel saddle the horses. They were in the small barn that was attached to the coral. The animals they were using were beautiful, massive specimens that could take the punishment of climbing through deep snow at steep angles. Bill had a feeling when all of this started that it was going to be an amazing adventure. He was right, but he hadn't anticipated such dire consequences, and the extreme danger to which he'd be exposing his young deputies.

Ranger Zach Randal was as cool as a cucumber. Bill watched him closely, and was impressed by the big man's confidence; it seemed to surround him like an aura. No wonder Zach's persona was so alluring to everyone who knew him.

At one time Sheriff Bill Wright scoffed at the admiration given to such men, assuming that the average Texas Ranger was a desk jockey who rarely, if ever, went into the field to track down and apprehend a criminal. Bill Wright's response to the heroic efforts that were attributed to Zach Randal, after capturing the serial killer responsible for the deaths of so many young girls, was cynical to say the least.

"Hell, all that Ranger did was get lucky. That so-called manhunt was only one arrest. We chase down a dozen or so of that kind of criminal every other day. He just got good press coverage on what was probably a simple take down. We don't brag so much about what's an everyday occurrence for us." Bill's comment had been quoted and printed in that weeks major addition of the *Denver Post*.

Bill Wright was thinking back about the foolish response that he had given to some zealous newspaper reporter. He'd been jealous about the notoriety given to Texas Ranger Randal, and had exposed his feelings by commenting negatively. He secretly hoped that Zach had not read his comment in the paper back then. His foolish judgment of Zach Randal was something that law enforcement officials should resist above all, especially with the experience of seeing guilty men later proven innocent. Bill was intent on apologizing.

The amount of danger that these Texas Rangers placed themselves in daily, tracking down the worst of society's evils, stunned him into complete repentance. Bill Wright was arrogant, and at times totally obnoxious, but he was also man enough to know and admit when he was wrong about somebody. When it came to Zachary Wyatt Randal, Bill had been dead wrong from the get go.

Light from the morning sun struggled to pierce the thick veil of snowfall covering the mountain range. Ice crystals in the atmosphere thousands of feet high resulted in cloud formations that could weigh thousand of tons. As the day progressed and heat from the rising sun warmed the heavy-laden ice clouds, they began to melt and descend in the form of rain. Because of the extreme altitude from which the rain fell, and the temperatures at that altitude, the rain again freezes into a solid form before reaching the ground. This solid formation reaches the Earth in the form of snow or ice.

Possessing a crystalline composition of ice so elaborate and complex, each individual snowflake is completely unique in its configuration. With such complex and beautiful ice structures floating down from out of the sky, sunlight pierces each at a different angle and the intensely brilliant glare can be enough to brighten an entire mountain range, even on gloomy and cloudy days. Reflections can be so bright that anti-glare sunglasses are needed to assist individuals traveling across mountainsides, preventing what is referred to as snow blindness.

With the reigns of each bridled horse held tightly in his hand, Deputy Ted walked toward the cabin. Bill was busy digging through his truck, apparently looking for something before joining Ted and Zach at the cabin. When Bill finally arrived, he had the searched for items in his hand, and passed Zach and Ted each a pair of dark Polaroid sunglasses for them to use.

"Use these, even if you think you don't need them. The bright sky and its reflection off the snow on the mountainside will have you snow blind before we get half of the way up. Then I'll have to leave you tied to a tree to keep you from walking off a cliff, while I finish with this little piece of business." Sheriff Bill was beginning to get his old personality and good humor back.

"But if the wind gets too strong put those goggles on instead, the ones that are in your saddlebags. I just thought the sunglasses would be a lot more comfortable for us to begin with." His concern for them touched Zach, but in a different way. Maybe the man wasn't such an asshole after all.

The three men mounted up. Zach was an old horseman from way back, and was as comfortable on the back of a horse as he was in that rocking chair in front of the fireplace.

"If everyone's ready, I think we ought to head straight for Mamaw's Staircase. If we find the snow too thick and piled up in drifts, then I know of another pass we can try farther up the valley." Taking charge of the small rescue posse, Bill spurred his horse, and the others followed suit.

It had been decided that they would ride single file, the lead horse breaking a path and making it easier for the one behind. After Bill's horse tired, they planned to change positions giving his mount a rest. Deputy Ted took up the rear position behind Zach, who had not spoken since leaving the cabin. He was perfectly comfortable with Bill taking charge, unthreatened by another man's abilities. It was the mark of a man who was sure of himself, and his own competence.

As they made their way through the snow toward the mountain called Pop's Soapbox, Bill kept a monologue going. Talking about the various sights along their way, he sounded like a tour leader. It didn't bother Zach at all; in fact, Zach was pretty amazed by the knowledge that Sheriff Bill seemed to have regarding the mountains and forests surrounding them.

In the course of his commentary, Bill said he estimated it would take three to four hours just getting to the base of the mountain that they were heading. If Mamaw's Staircase were accessible, the ride up the mountain to the level where Deke had built his cabin would take at least another five or six hours. His estimate, he declared, could be relied upon only if they were lucky and suffered no delays.

The saddle that Sheriff Wright used for his horse had a rifle scabbard with the butt of the rifle accessible near the saddle horn. The rifle was pointing down near the front flank of his horse. Zach had no idea what sized caliber the rifle was, but he also saw that Bill was wearing a leather holster with a large caliber revolver stuck deep inside.

As Zach studied the two men, he noticed that whenever they switched positions and Deputy Ted took the lead, the young deputy also had a rifle scabbard on his saddle. Much less fancy, it consisted of a simple leather sock, tied with a leather strap at the butt end. He kept a lever action Marlin 30/30 in the scabbard, loaded.

Zach Randal was once again wearing the Colt Python.357 Magnum. It had been such a controversial topic when he'd refused to wear the pistol while on duty. He claimed too much of an intimidation factor was associated with it, making it nonproductive whenever he was on an investigation, especially when dealing with an untrusting public while seeking information regarding criminal behavior. Yet, the pistol was in its holster, and on his side.

Zach didn't need any other weapon. He predicted any confrontation that he would have with Jack Vermette was going to be up close and personal. A rifle wasn't necessary when dealing with that guy. If he were far enough away to be out of Zach's reach, then he would be where Zach couldn't see him anyway. No rifle was capable of killing a man that was out of sight.

NARROW, winding, mountain roads that were covered with fresh snow, and in some places had drifts several feet high, snaked up into the mountains for miles. Jack had been wandering up and down around the area where he last saw Zach Randal and that young deputy. Becoming frustrated by his vain attempt to locate them, Jack saw that he was now running low on gas in the big truck he'd stolen from Deputy J.B. Walker. Jack even started to second-guess himself, thinking Randal and the deputy had pulled a fast one on him. He was afraid they weren't anywhere around, having fooled him, leading him to a secluded mountain range to get him lost. Then, they'd let him freeze while he was desperately looking for a way out.

He returned to his senses after asking himself what the young deputy that he'd killed was doing out here in this wilderness? And why was he pulling a horse-occupied trailer? Jack was delirious from lack of sleep, but the fatigue did not worry him, it only made him less predictable and quicker at making decisions to kill. He considered it an advantage. Fatigue worked in his favor.

It was insane. He thought it would be easy to pick up the tracks of the big Bronco. Since he had encountered no traffic, clear tire tracks should be easy to follow in the snow. He continued to drive along looking for Zach's tire tracks. He did not worry that he'd be left on foot if the truck ran out of gas. The horse trailer behind him had all the transportation he needed, but unfortunately, he'd still be lost.

Not until he saw the first signs of daybreak did Jack realize his folly. It had been snowing all night, quickly covering any tracks that were left along the road. He had probably driven right over the same spot that the damn Texas Ranger had used to get to Deke's place. Jack felt that he had blown it; Amy and Deke Stone were probably rescued soon after he lost sight of the Bronco. They were now in the care of the El Paso County Sheriff Department and that damn, old Texas Ranger.

According to the information Jack was able to obtain about Deke Stone, he lived on the side of a mountain somewhere outside of Colorado Springs. Jack was definitely somewhere outside of Colorado Springs, and he was definitely on the side...of a mountain?

He was not on the side of a mountain, but traveling around the many mountainsides through a valley that stretched for miles leading nowhere. He admitted to himself that he'd gotten lost, but he also knew what the hell a mountainside looked like. If that damn old Texas Ranger, Zach Randal, had picked up Amy and her friend, Dick, it definitely did not happened here.

Even though Jack found new questions to ask, he was unable to find any of the answers. He was renewed by the possibility that maybe he had not missed the encounter between Zach and Amy, but remained discouraged since he'd only managed to complicate things more than they already were.

A long straight incline to what seemed like the edge to a smooth point of higher elevation stretched out before him. He had stopped the big truck to preserve gas, thinking over his predicament. It could easily be another valley over that rise. Cranking the big engine Jack shook his head in disgust, thinking, *"One more mile, I'll check out that rise. If nothing is on the other side, I'll initiate Plan B."*

Jack knew that no such thing as a Plan B existed, but talking to himself often reduced his anxiety. He only wished that he didn't have to lie to himself so often. He'd forgotten all about the divine intervention that he'd decided was going to be responsible for his success, or blamed for his failure. But divine intervention was only forgotten until Jack topped the small hill, looking down into the valley below.

About half a mile from where he was, Jack could clearly see a small cabin. A leaning barn barely managing to remain upright stood just behind the cabin, along with a small coral that looked like it might be attached to the leaning barn.

This odd but interesting development had suddenly turned what had been a total failure into what he could say would be an assured victory. It was not due to his remarkable find of the small cabin, shaky barn, and small coral. The feeling of victory had everything to do with the unmistakable black Bronco Jack also spotted in front of the cabin. Apparently, and recently, it had crossed the snow filled muddy pasture between the gentle rise where Jack sat, and the flat, open valley below where the small cabin and barn were located. It appeared before him just as Jack had begun to question his mission. Feeling like a man cleansed of shame, and vindicated from false charges, he'd been rescued from potential persecution.

The sardonic smile that had sickeningly been smeared across Jack's face began to slowly vanish as he sat monitoring the location. Very little, if anything at all, was happening inside the cabin. He couldn't see if any lights were on since daylight was breaking and Jack was facing east, the sun's filtering rays fuzzed up his vision.

Jerking himself up from the lounging position he'd taken as he watched the place; Jack reached for the ignition and fired the engine up. If he were too far away to see anything, he would just have to get closer.

The big truck lumbered down the narrow path into the wet, muddy, snow-covered pasture. The trailer followed like a lost puppy, easily pulled through the pasture by the truck. As Jack approached the cabin, he could see behind the small building and the space between it and the barn. Suddenly he could see other vehicles that were parked between the cabin and the leaning barn. Paranoia and fear rose within him without warning. Still, it wasn't the two vehicles parked which initiated the sudden frenzy.

Jack floored the accelerator on the truck, sending mud, snow, grass, and everything else in the pasture flying twenty feet into the air. He'd nearly lost the horse trailer spinning around and making a U turn. Pulling the trailer in such a tight maneuver behind him had nearly tilted it over. It balanced on two wheels of one side, before slamming back down and stabilizing. The exiting truck's engine screamed like a terrorized woman. Reaching the top of the rise again, he bounced the rig back onto the narrow road and resumed his departure with the same frantic pace.

HEARING the sound of a vehicle, Sergeant John Hadley came out of the barn to investigate. He had just cleared the space between the two buildings when he spotted the big truck creeping through the pasture approaching the cabin, like a predator looking for the kill.

In a blur of speed and without warning, the big truck began spinning and turned around. It was such a bizarre and odd display that the maneuver could only be what John recognized as an escape attempt.

Running in the direction of the fleeing truck, John was unable to get a look at the driver. He saw the horse trailer being dragged behind it, but that was all he saw since the pasture looked like it had been thrown into the air behind the truck.

He would have to let it go. John had other priorities that had to be taken care of, and getting that mare in the barn saddled was one of them. Briskly, Sergeant John Hadley spun back around, heading into the barn. He had missed his friend's departure but only by about an hour or so. He would be able to catch up with them as soon as he'd figured out the direction in which they'd gone.

CHAPTER

24

APPROACHING THE LOCATION where he'd estimated the fallen individual had landed; Deke and Ringo both sensed an uncomfortable, creepy feeling. Everything looked different from down here with so much snow covering the landmarks he used to mark the area, and Deke soon became frustrated. While looking about, kicking at the higher drifts of snow to reveal anything that might be buried, Deke began to realize that his determination to identify the stranger had diminished significantly. He was now, more than ever, concerned with getting back to the cabin and Amy. All at once, his attention shifted to Ringo. Why was he alone, and where were the rest of the Beatles?

Meanwhile, Ringo had wandered to the edge of the cliff wall at a location that resembled the corner of a room. Easily definable, Deke saw that the corner made an excellent landmark for future use in the canyon. From that location, Ringo set out in a straight line to where Deke was standing. Approximately twenty yards before reaching Deke, Ringo stopped abruptly. Feverishly, he started digging in the snow; within seconds, he'd uncovered the soles of two boots. All of his previous thinking had disappeared as Deke raced to join in with the digging. As the pair uncovered the bottom half of a man, head down in the snow, the digging became nearly impossible to continue. Whomever this person was, from his waist up or rather waist down in the snow, he was frozen solid.

Using his bare hands, and Ringo with his paws already bloodied from the frantic search, Deke saw they would not be able to pluck the body from the frozen ice pack. Exhausted, they stopped briefly to rest. How would they ever discover the identity of this individual? It was clear that their struggle was useless yet; Deke was too determined to give up after getting so near to finding out the identity of this individual.

Lying on the side of the small mound of snow they'd removed from the bottom half of the body, Deke began to study the person's clothing. That was when he saw the small corner of a leather wallet sticking out of the back pocket. Reaching out, Deke slowly pulled the wallet from the frozen pants. He found himself trembling at the prospect of what he'd discovered. His anxiety had reached such a critical state that to finally make a positive identification was more stressful than he had anticipated. Opening the frozen wallet, Deke was not overly surprised to see the El Paso County Deputy Sheriff's badge. What he did feel was an overwhelming disappointment, and a tremendous amount of confusion. What would a deputy sheriff be doing up this high on the mountain, and apparently with a K-9 dog? Reaching inside the wallet, he discovered the man's name was Paul Scott, twenty-seven years old, and a resident of Colorado Springs. He remembered a fellow named Scott. On one of the cross-country trail rides that Deke had taken with the sheriff's posse a Deputy Scott also rode. If he remembered correctly, this was one of the individuals who were supposed to be specially trained at high altitude, mountain terrain survival. It meant one thing that superseded all other facts; this was not the individual that was after Amy.

A new priority instantly had established itself with the man's identification discovered. Meanwhile, Ringo had resumed with his effort to uncover the man. With a firm and unquestioning command from Deke, Ringo ceased with digging.

"Come on boy. We've got to get back to the cabin. Amy's in trouble." With the wallet stuffed into the pocket of Deke's thermal suit, he began scanning the vertical face of the gorge in an effort to find the easiest and quickest way up. With the new layer of snow that covered the sharp decline, Deke saw no quick way, regardless of the difficulty, for the two to climb out of the deep ravine. Turning to Ringo, Deke saw it as his only chance, hoping the big Chesapeake would understand.

"Ringo! Go home! Find Amy!" Deke tried his best to give the command in a voice that sounded authoritative. Attentively, Ringo's ears stood up. With only a moment of hesitation that nearly made Deke panic, Ringo looked up at him with an expression of complete understanding. Then, he took off in the direction from which they had come. If not for such an overwhelming confidence in the Chessie, Deke would have called him back, for it appeared to be the opposite direction that they needed to go. But instead, he found himself trudging through the snow attempting to keep up with Ringo.

Occasionally, while forging ahead, the Chesapeake would stop to allow Deke to catch up. Before long, they reached a side of the deep canyon gorge where the ascent was reasonable, and within the hour, they were at the top of the cliff face, headed in the direction of the cabin. With luck, they would be back within a couple of hours.

SHERIFF Bill Wright, Zach Randal, and Ted Daniel were making good time. It was about twelve o'clock when they reached the foot of Pop's Soapbox Mountain, stopping at the base where Mamaw's Staircase ascended in a spiral and winding path up the mountainside. As Bill Wright had expected, Mamaw's Staircase was blanketed with an additional three feet of fresh snow, on top of the two feet of snow that had already become packed.

"Well, we can try hugging the side along the way, and hope that we don't wander too close to any of the hidden edges covered by the snow," Bill stated as he examined the treacherous ascent. His statement had been made more to himself than to anyone else in particular, realizing how difficult and time consuming the climb was going to be.

"How long do you estimate the climb to take?" Zach Randal was also studying the side of the mountain, silently thinking how hard the climb might be on the horses, but before he could state his concerns, they were answered.

Bill Wright looked at his watch, and glancing at the sky above tried to predict what the unstable weather would do in the next few hours.

"Zach, from what I can determine we may be able to beat darkness if we start now, but only if we don't encounter any problems. The horses will do fine. Their ability to withstand the climb is not what concerns me." Bill's reply was only half-assuring.

"All right Bill, now that we've established the confidence that our horses can make the climb, and that it doesn't concern us, you have my undivided attention. What is it that you're not telling me but does concern us?" The Texas Ranger was quick to pick up on the worry that Bill Wright would rather have kept to himself. Turning away from his intense study of the mountainside to face Zach, the sheriff calmly stated, "Avalanche."

With a slight kick to his horse's flank, Bill Wright turned away leading his horse to the edge of the narrow path, starting the climb.

Zach was flabbergasted by the reality of what he'd never even considered as a threat. Of all the things he had weighed as possible deterrents in attempting to get to Amy and Deke within a reasonable amount of time, while they were still safe, this was one that he'd never imagined. A rare moment occurred in which he found himself speechless, and without any quick-witted response to what Bill Wright had so calmly declared.

Zach Randal spurred his mount following the sheriff for the slow and difficult ascent that faced them. Ted Daniel, who had been quiet for most of the trip, remained silent as he followed behind Zach.

SERGEANT John Hadley managed to saddle the only remaining horse left behind in the small barn attached to the coral. An old gray that he'd judged to be wise to mountain traveling, and one that hopefully was up to the challenge. While he was saddling the big gray, John noticed how calm and passive the animal remained. His expectations had slowly dwindled to almost nothing by the time he took the big stud out of the barn and mounted him. Much to his astonishment, he was barely in the saddle when the big gray bolted, following the trail left behind by the three horses that carried his friends.

John Hadley was determined to catch up to the trio even at the expense of his mount, but was relieved to see that this horse was just as interested in following the trail as he was. It could have been the wisdom of the big gray to follow, fearful of whatever alternatives awaited not pursuing after his companions. Regardless of the reason, John hung tightly to the reins as his mount double-timed it to their destination, wherever that was.

FREEZING from the bitter cold that seemed to pass through his bones, Jack Vermette sat at the edge of the rise looking down at the small cabin in the valley. As soon as he saw the uniformed officer make his exit on the big gray, Jack returned to the truck he'd stolen, and again began driving down through the pasture below. He didn't know who the law enforcement officer was, but he could not take the chance of having a confrontation with anyone at this stage of the game.

His main concern at this time was to locate warm clothing for what he had guessed was going to be the next step to this bizarre adventure. The fact that he had managed to acquire possession of a mounted horse, that obviously was going to be used by that deputy he'd so easily bled to death, made him ready to follow wherever that damn Texas Ranger had made off for. He was steadily leading Jack to Amy's location. Randal was proving true to his reputation, refusing to let anything stop him from his duty.

Once inside the cabin Jack rummaged around, wasting precious time before locating a small closet with enough thermal underwear in it to keep him from freezing to death. All bundled up, he opened the trailer and mounted the stallion that was inside. He hadn't expected the horse to be any trouble, and to his delight, the animal was as steady as a rock.

Before setting out to follow the deep tracks left by the others, he considered whether he should try flanking the group. Jack wasn't even sure that the officer who just left was going to meet up with Zach Randal or not, but it was the only good lead he had on Amy's possible location. He would have to go for it and follow behind cautiously. Because of the snowfall, and being unsure of how far or even where they were heading, Jack stuck to following the tracks as doggedly as a bloodhound, relishing the opportunity that awaited him ahead.

BRUISED and battered from his desperate leap off the side of the deep gorge that he'd taken the night before, Deke found himself rapidly running out of steam. He had not anticipated the deep snow in his eagerness to get back to the cabin. Trying to follow Ringo, as he made his way back, had left Deke with no other option but to leave his cross-country skis back at the spot where he'd tried descending the cliff in the first place. With the snow still coming down he lost sight of Ringo altogether a couple of times, and had to struggle with everything left in him just to make the next few desperate yards before again catching a glimpse of the rusty coat of fur ahead.

Then, what Deke had feared most finally befell him; he lost sight of Ringo, and after fifteen minutes of looking was unable to spot him anywhere. Despairing at his situation, Deke sat in the deep snow catching his breath. Where could Ringo have gone? The snowfall made his location so deceptive that Deke had no idea where he was on the mountainside.

In utter hopelessness, Deke looked skyward and yelled out in frustration, "Ringo!" Much to his relief he heard a distinct answer to his outcry. Only fifteen yards to his right, a single *'woof'* was heard. Crawling to the spot where he judged the sound had come from, Deke was stunned to discover the balled up figure of a body lying at the base of a large boulder, now surrounded by all four of the Beatles.

Initially, Deke was shocked by the discovery. The person was dressed in layers of old army fatigues tied around the waste, and with what appeared to be a necktie. Several pairs of socks were covering the person's hands. It only took Deke a minute to recognize the loose fitted clothing as his own. To his horror, the balled up figure inside his old clothes was Amy! His fatigue once again seemed to vanish as he reached out for her, cuddling her body close to his, he could feel warmth emanating from within the odd-looking collection of apparel.

As protective as the Beatles were about Amy, Deke was relieved to see that his quick, reflex action of grabbing her up into his arms had been accepted without protest. The fact that she was in a deep sleep was obvious, almost immediately. Yet, Deke still made several attempts to arouse her, but to no avail. Although her body still felt somewhat warm, wrapped in the assorted clothing, he was aware that if the temperature within the core of her body was only a couple of degrees below 98.6 it would still feel warm to him in the sub-freezing temperatures on the mountain, but at the same time, she could be hypothermic and in serious danger.

Lifting Amy's eyelids, Deke was relieved to see a good pupillary response to light; they didn't remain fixed and dilated. It told him that she hadn't suffered any brain damage yet. He'd reached her in time, but it was still crucial that he get her back to the cabin and out of this weather.

Still holding her unresponsive body close, he realized the depth of his love for her. This strange little woman, whose life he had stumbled into, had somehow captured his deepest feelings of affection, and he was terrified at the possibility of losing her. Looking about, desperately racking his brain for a plan of action, Deke was afraid that he was far too weak to carry her. The result may be both of them freezing in this horrible storm that had descended from out of nowhere, imprisoning the mountain in a suffocating blanket of white death.

The Beatles soon picked up on the seriousness of the situation and became restless, starting to pace around. That was when Deke came up with an idea. Wild as it seemed, he realized it was through desperation that the most desperate of actions succeeded. Removing Amy's arms from the sleeves of the army jacket she had on, Deke tied the two sleeves together in a knot above her head. After he had re-bundled her inside the jacket, he removed the tie from around her waste and tied one end to the knotted sleeves. With what remained of the length, Deke managed to slip through the collars of both Paul and John before tying a final knot. As they stood side by side, John and Paul looked as though they understood his intention, and Deke prayed that it would work.

Still unsure of the direction to take getting back to the cabin he looked at Ringo and gave the command, "Back home boy! Back to the cabin!"

With a look of intelligence that would probably haunt Deke for the rest of his life, Ringo took off. The next command was even more important for their survival. Looking down at John and Paul, he made the request with pleading in his voice, "Okay! Go!"

Magically, resulting in more delight than he could ever remember experiencing, Deke watched as the two big Chesapeake Bay Retrievers effortlessly and smoothly began dragging Amy behind them in the direction Ringo had disappeared. Patiently, George waited until Deke began his struggle to follow the caravan before keeping pace beside him. Together they started making their way in the direction of his cabin.

MANAGING to get nearly half of the way to Deke's homestead, following Mamaw's Staircase up the side of Pop's Soapbox, the three men stopped to evaluate a sharp turn ahead of them. They had done well with little trouble, and were becoming more and more positive, feeling that they might make it before dark.

Looking back down the trail through the falling snow, Zach spotted an object some distance from the base of the mountainside. Nearly too far away for the naked eye, a dark spot was moving in the direction of the mountain. Slowly but steadily, in a straight line, its movement was detectable after several minutes of observing. Bill and Ted concurred that it was definitely someone on horseback heading in their direction.

"Hell, maybe it's Joe Bob. He might have gotten delayed by something." Bill was being more hopeful than he was realistic. After all, Joe Bob was at least eight hours late by the time they'd left that morning, and very few things would keep a man from obeying direct orders from the sheriff for that long.

"Look!" Ted cried out suddenly, pointing nearly straight down the side of the mountain at the spot where Mamaw's Staircase began its winding, swirling ascent. Only slightly more discernible they saw someone else on horseback. Except, this figure was moving a bit more quickly than the first, in blind pursuit straight for them. The man was huddled tightly against the face of the mountain, determined to follow along the narrow path.

"My Lord!" Zach exclaimed in astonishment. Looking back at the Texas Ranger, Bill's eyebrows creased with concern.

"What is it Zach?" Still peering down below them at the base of the mountain Zach Randal didn't want to believe what he thought his eyes were revealing, but the resemblance was too much for him to cast aside as impossible.

"I'm fairly certain that the man on the horse directly below us is Sergeant John Hadley. He's the man who first called you from the Texas State Police. He's on our side, and a damn good asset if the need should arise." His recognition of who was on their trail sounded harmless, but Zach's voice carried a far more sinister ring to it than the contents of his statement had revealed.

"So, I guess that's okay, but what's that sound of dread in your voice all about?" Sheriff Bill asked, not for a second fooled by Zach's quick reversal of his initial impression.

"Well, it ain't old John that we got to worry about. In fact, it's old John that ought to be worried. If my guess is right, that fellow following behind him is Jack Vermette."

CHAPTER

25

ВАCK INSIDE THE cabin, Deke quickly kindled the few embers that were left in the fireplace into a roaring blaze. Amy had still not awakened from her deep state of unconsciousness, and Deke wasted no time stripping the wet and baggy, ridiculous looking clothing from her. Still shaking from near frostbite, in addition to the extended amount of time that he'd been exposed to the frigid weather, he struggled with the last few items that she wore. Fighting his way to the upstairs bedroom, he left Amy on the rug before the fireplace. Deke stripped the thick blanket away from his bed and ran downstairs to wrap it around her.

As Deke took the last step in descending the stairs, he turned for the fireplace. Without warning, he faltered, nearly falling flat on his face. He'd been so consumed in his rush to warm Amy's body that the beauty of her nakedness had been completely overlooked. Standing rooted to the spot where he'd come to a dead halt, holding the thick blanket in his hands, he became flustered. The confusion of the moment finally caused him to turn away, embarrassed at his momentary loss of control, staring at her nakedness. He was embarrassed by his behavior. Then, as if slapped on the back of his head by reason, he returned to the seriousness of the situation, racing to swaddle her within the dry warmth.

Sitting before the raging fire, supporting her body against his, Deke began slowly coaxing Amy back to the land of the living. Eventually, she aroused enough to take small sips of the hot soup that he'd prepared. With only a couple of hours of daylight remaining, he patiently nursed her back to the point where he no longer feared for her life.

Warm and safe, Deke carried Amy up to the bedroom where he placed her gingerly on the mattress, still swaddled like a papoose in the blanket. She would need to rest for a while still, especially after the exhaustive struggle her body had endured.

After broiling a huge rib-eye steak to show how deep his gratitude was for each of the Beatles, Deke collapsed before the warm fire. Thoughts of the developments, which had occurred within the last twenty-four hour period, consumed him. Why was a deputy sheriff walking through a blizzard on the mountain near his cabin? Did someone send him? Who could possibly have known that he and Amy were here?

It was well after dark by the time they had arrived two nights ago. Could anyone have seen them as they arrived, driving up the mountain? And most of all, where was Zach Randal?

The questions assaulted his brain like a pinball machine with all the stainless steel balls set loose at once. Pinging at the corners of his skull in wild and erratic directions, each thought prevented him from focusing on any other thought. Then, another would zoom across his mind, derailing any concentration that he'd managed to establish. Leaning against the back of the love seat before the fire, Ringo stretched out snoring loudly by his side as Deke drifted off into a restless sleep.

WATCHING as the scene below them unfolded at a crawl, Zach and his two companions deliberated about what to do next.

"At the speed John's moving I don't think whoever's behind him will ever catch up." Bill Wright's observation was accurate. Still, a certain amount of deadly discomfort remained with Zach. His friend was probably in the most dangerous situation that he'd ever faced in thirty years, and Zach had no way of knowing if he was aware. The obligation that Zach felt to warn his friend was being sheared in half by his equally important obligation to reach Deke and Amy, and likewise warn them of the impending danger. The least of his duties would be telling them who was discovered as the one after Amy from the very beginning. He knew he must prepare Amy for whatever it was she may have to face, and maybe even obtain some piece of information that would assist him in stopping the son-of-a-bitch, killing him if need be.

"Ain't no question in my mind who that fellow is behind John. In fact, it's the first thing I'm certain of since this whole damn tornado got to spinning. It's exactly what I should have expected from the start, and what I had hoped would happen whenever I convinced Amy and Deke to take this wild goose chase in the first place. The only flaw in my plan was having the guilty party already decided on in my head. In the meantime, the real murdering bastard probably kidnapped my prime suspect from right before my eyes."

Zach was baring his soul to the two men, who somehow understood the immense amount of emotional energy driving him. An energy that had been driving him for what was probably the past few years.

"I must confess fellows, this has been an investigation that started in the gutter and has done nothing but move downstream ever since. The only redeeming event in this whole affair came as a result of execution style murders carried out on two good men. Their death was far from a good thing, but the thumbprint that was obtained from the scene was how we discovered that a dead man was responsible for all of this. I pray to the One who listens to old law dogs like me, that the death of those two fine men be not in vain, and that I have the distinct and eventual pleasure of watching the bastard responsible die slowly and painfully."

That was not supposed to be verbally stated by any Texas Ranger, but it was often felt deep within the hearts of the officers, who had to sift through bloody and disgusting crime scenes in order to obtain the shreds of evidence needed to bring perpetrators like Jack Vermette to trial. Usually, in their trademark quiet style, Texas Rangers remained tight-lipped as they slowly and methodically gathered information and evidence. While deep inside, they were silently screaming out in protest at the thought of suspects responsible for the savage and unbelievable crimes were still walking around alive.

"Bill, I'm at a crossroads. No matter how I twist it, I'm being pulled in two directions that are impossible for me to go in simultaneously. You make the call on what we're going to do. I fear that too much emotion and personal feelings will blur any clarity and rationalization that I might have if I have to come up with the answer and decide." It was a powerful statement that most people would have mistaken as a weakness, but Sheriff Bill Wright and Deputy Ted Daniel sat and witnessed the turmoil Zach Randal had just put himself through in order to come to the decision. It was jaw dropping admiration that they experienced as Zach uttered the bravest words either of them had ever heard. It was what they nearly had forgotten existed in a better world, once upon a time. It was honesty. It was bravery. It was character. It was rock-solid integrity.

Stalling for time, trying to absorb what the Texas Ranger just admitted, Sheriff Bill Wright looked at his watch, then up at the snowy sky.

"Damn Zach, don't drop this responsibility on me unless you're willing to walk with me through the possible consequences." It was a declaration no less powerful than the one just previously made. With a nod of his head, agreeing to the conditions, Zach made the commitment that was requested of him.

"All right then." Bill Wright seemed to shift into a different mode, one of deep conflict in which he already regretted the decision he was going to have to make. Standing up in the stirrups of his saddle glancing down over the mountainside at the slow progression of events unfolding below, he made his choice.

"Ted, I have no other way to call this one partner. I'm going to have to ask you to double back, intercept Sergeant Hadley, and inform him of his pursuer. Let Hadley decide what the two of you will do next. Let him know I want him to assume all authority when you've reached him, and that's on my orders. As long as the two of you know that you're being followed, you'll have the advantage. Ranger Randal and I are going to continue up the mountain with the desire to get to that cabin before dark. You got that?" The decision was especially difficult after experiencing the gut wrenching feeling that he had already lost one young deputy to that madman.

Deputy Ted Daniel didn't even flinch at the orders. Listening to the sheriff with an attentiveness and dedication that any man wished he possessed, the young deputy responded, "Yes sir!" Then, without another word spoken, turned his mount carefully on the narrow path and started down. Sheriff Wright watched him as he began to make his way back down Mamaw's Staircase; calling after the deputy, he made one final statement, "You be damned careful. You hear me son?" The final sentiment was filled with the emotion of a father instructing his child, and did not escape the notice of Zach Randal. Deputy Ted only waved a hand over his head in recognition of the command, busy concentrating on his descent.

Bill Wright turned, looking back at Zach. "If any shots are fired we'll find out soon enough. I just hope the avalanche that's started by the shooting doesn't catch us out in the open." As before, Bill calmly stated his concerns before spurring his horse and resuming with their winding ascent.

RISING before him like some prehistoric volcano, Jack gazed upon the mountain as it came into view. The man ahead of him approached the massive monument at such a quick pace that before Jack knew what had happened he had disappeared. A shelf or crevice of some kind appeared to have been carved into the side of the mountain, and to Jack's delight when the man before him finally re-appeared, it was clear that he was ascending the side of the mountain along what Jack decided was an old roadway.

Jack was hesitant to follow this man, undecided whether or not to approach the narrow access onto the mountain. It was obviously the same route taken by his nemeses, that damn Texas Ranger, Zachary Randal. He surmised it had to be only because it was the only route visible.

Settling in behind a patch of scrub brush tall enough to still stick out of the deep snow, Jack decided to wait and watch. He was no longer afraid of being unable to find his prize. If Amy were anywhere in the state of Colorado, he knew it had to be somewhere on that mountain. Forces he had come to recognize as his divine guides had instilled the certainty of her location within him. They assured him of success with his mission, having brought him this far Jack saw no possibility of failure or defeat. The righteousness that was at the very core of what he had been compelled to participate in, by nature could not suffer defeat after having reached this crucial stage. Such an impossible result was against the law of nature. Now more than ever, Jack felt secure with his endeavor.

Consistent snowfall on and around the mountain, combined with Jack's state of fatigue and the fact that he had no eye protection, plus the intense strain that he'd been putting his eyes through, eventually resulted in Jack seeing things that were not real. It was not hallucinations that he began to suffer from but more correctly a state of magical thinking.

While behind the stand of brush, confident that he was completely camouflaged and hidden from sight, Jack failed to recognize how easily it was for anyone looking in his direction to see him. It was nearly humorous. Jack was like the child who, when covering his eyes to play peek-a-boo, thinks that his inability to see others is equal to the other person's ability to see him. In effect, his reasoning was if he could not see Zach Randal ascending the side of the mountain, then through some law of nature, Zach could not possibly see him.

As suddenly as the bizarre patterns of this delusional state would appear, they vanished. Left in a state of momentary confusion, Jack's mind would feel as if he were awakening from a deep, dream-filled sleep.

Clearly, Jack was beginning to unravel. Suffering from such extreme delusions of grandeur, his decision-making went from one extreme to the other. Denying the reality of the deep emotional trauma he'd suffered, combined with the incredible feelings of rejection he'd experienced, without a doubt, resulted in a complete loss of touch with reality.

Feeling he'd been chosen and had somehow been elevated to a higher level of existence, created an inconceivable amount of evil to manifest itself in a new form. Dangerous beyond description, and capable of acts that defied understanding, Jack Vermette graduated from the primitive and crude behavior often labeled as animalistic, to a more intense evil. Intelligent and unpredictable, this behavioral category of dangerous species was called human.

Without warning, Jack was reminded of the rush and exhilarating adrenaline high he'd experienced with each sacrificial kill he made, and was immediately struck by a craving for the euphoric bliss again. With a confidence that rarely exposes itself when seeking to do that which is inhuman, Jack emerged from behind the patch of tall brush. Boldly he approached the mountainside, following in the tracks left by the horses that had passed before him. Previously without a hint of the plan that he knew must be devised, Jack suddenly knew exactly what he must do. As he persevered to climb the mountain where Amy was hidden, he'd execute each and every individual encountered along the way. It was the only way to ensure a safe outcome. Riding high in the saddle with his chin out in defiance, Jack relished the assignment that was now before him as he narrowed the distance between himself and the officer ahead.

DARKNESS was steadily approaching, and the time was unmerciful for those desperately struggling to escape the desolation that seemed to accompany the cold, bleak and lonely terrain. A feeling of dread sometimes accompanies an individual on horseback, crawling through deep snow while ascending a mountain where one false step brings nothing but a thousand feet of air. To a greater degree, is how the misery can be multiplied ten fold as the sun starts to descend below the snow-covered peaks. Gradually, the sun's light fades away and shades of gray become darker and darker until finally producing total darkness. Until it climbs from the opposite direction at dawn, the sun is sorely missed.

Sheriff Bill Wright and his companion, Zach Randal, experience the feelings with such intensity that a taste of desolation is thick within their mouths for hours after darkness has established its presence.

Reaching the end of the narrow road called Mamaw's Staircase, the two men detect the smell of burning wood somewhere up ahead. Within minutes, it is Zach Randal who first spots a dim glow of yellow light floating deep within the thick stand of aspen stretching before them. It is the light from the fireplace, shining through a window of the cabin. Cold, hungry, and exhausted, the men make their way toward what is considered to be the equivalent of a palm filled oasis in the middle of the desert.

AWAKENED from his brief slumber by the sound of deep, throaty growling, Deke was initially confused and frightened. Shaking his head and stretching out of the muscle cramped position that he'd fallen asleep in; his attention was drawn to the cabin's front door. John and Ringo were standing before the door, and looked like they were peering straight through the wood at something on the other side. The throaty growl, rattling from the pair, resonated with a threatening message. Glancing about the cabin, Deke located the other two Beatles, George and Paul, lying at the top of the loft where Amy was still asleep. Their growls were just as menacing, but not as pronounced as the pair standing at attention before the door.

All of a sudden, the significance of what he was witnessing stunned Deke. Like a bolt of lightning from a cloudless sky, the shock paralyzed him into a near catatonic state. What was he supposed to do? He had no weapons inside the cabin. But wait, of course, he had four of the most effective weapons he could think of, the Beatles. As their growling became a steady rolling sound throughout the cabin, hackles rose up on their back, and the fur around their tail puffed out. The effect was definitely intimidating; giving them an appearance that reminded Deke of the horrible werewolf he'd seen in the movie, *American Werewolf in London*.

It was creating a situation that he was not sure how to handle; it was embarrassing, finding that he was wishing Amy were awake. On the other hand, what would she do if she were awake? Deke pondered the question that he'd posed to himself, rationalizing its appropriateness by reminding himself that after all they were her dogs. It was not long before he realized he would have to act. Any kind of offensive action was better than having to respond defensively.

The storm was still depositing a fair amount of fresh snow on the mountain outside, and the sun had dropped below the western horizon. It was not pitch-black dark yet, but well on the way.

Deke could hear nothing outside as he placed his ear against the thick front door. The few windows in the cabin were long and narrow, placed only on the second floor when the cabin was built. Ground floor windows served no purpose if the snow outside had piled up eight feet high against the walls. In a wilderness cabin, windows served only two purposes. Their first usage was the obvious one of allowing sunlight to enter. But the second, and more important purpose of windows on a mountainside cabin, were to allow a means of escape should several feet of snow render the door useless, frozen, and unable to be opened against packed ice. Unfortunately, the windows that Deke installed were long and narrow, solid pieces of half inch thick glass with no way of being opened. From his loft, they were convenient to survey the cabin's surroundings without having to get out of bed.

Still, Deke could hear nothing, but the reaction from the Beatles told him that his ears were not what he should be relying on. Hesitantly, and with disgustingly slow movements, Deke opened the front door. Inch by inch, as the opening widened he watched John and Ringo, frozen rock-like with anticipation. Deke feared they might hurt themselves. At precisely the moment when Deke was least prepared, Ringo and John exploded forth from their suspended state of animation, crashing against the portion of door that blocked their exit. Their departure jerked the heavy wooden structure from Deke's hold with such force that it stung him to his elbow. Flashbacks of his childhood and being stung by cracked baseball bats whirled through his mind.

Up, out, and through the thick veil preventing detection, they rushed after whatever had captured their interest. Deke could not help but shutter, imagining the fate of whatever the target of the two powerful canines happened to be.

As soon as he began closing the door, shutting out the darkness, the cold, and the danger, Deke heard a sound. Cocking his head slightly in response to the strange familiarity, imitating the behavior he'd witnessed so many times in the Beatles, Deke was certain he'd heard that sound before. Again, the familiar noise pierced the darkness. In stunned relief Deke exhaled, and wondered if he should believe what his ears were

301

telling him. It seemed too far-fetched to accept without first applying a healthy dose of doubt. What he thought had been too much to ask, had indeed come true.

The Texas Ranger's loud and playful yelling could be heard echoing from out of the thick stand of aspen that surrounded the lonely little cabin.

"So ya'll missed me did you? Well, I bet not half as much as I missed you fellows." He could be heard playfully talking to John and Ringo, Deke pictured the scene he'd witnessed at Amy's ranch, Zach Randal rolling on the ground like a school boy wrestling with the big dogs, loving every minute of it. Their deep growls were nothing more than the style of play employed when battling the big man, enjoying themselves more than Deke could ever recall seeing. As the big man materialized from out of the darkness, he approached Deke. His huge right hand was extended in greeting. Deke's emotions were running the gamut of extremes, his initial desire to leap into the Texas Ranger's arms barely held in check. Gambling once again with the future use of his right hand, Deke reached out and watched as his limb was swallowed to the elbow by Zach's friendly handshake.

"How the hell you been Deke?" his question was so casual yet, Deke stumbled and stuttered so badly that he couldn't answer.

"That bad is it." Zach's evaluation was quick and accurate.

"Well, we're going to remedy that condition once and for all, that is if you still need the help badly enough to pay up front for the services. Total charge so far comes to about one pot of hot coffee for my friend here and myself." The confusion and fear that was plastered all over Deke's face must have appeared worse than it actually was because Zach Randal's face suddenly hardened into a look of concern as he reached out for Deke at the open door.

Before Deke hit the floor behind him, exhaustion finally taking its toll on his body, Zach caught his leaning body heading backward in defeat from the last two days of abuse.

The last thing Deke remembered before he lost consciousness was the voice of Zachary Randal yelling.

"Damn that son-of-a-bitch and every ounce of heartache and suffering he's brought upon so many good and descent people. Bill! Get your high society ass over here and help me with this brave young man."

CHAPTER

26

FOR SEVERAL HOURS, Sergeant John Hadley experienced one of the most difficult struggles he'd ever faced during his many years of public service. Fighting his way over the rough and frozen terrain, leading the way while walking before his horse, he held tightly to the reins. He knew this fight was being waged for a slightly different reason.

POWERFUL emotions are involved whenever two people develop the deep trust needed for what is sometimes referred to as a friendship. True friendship requires a unique and rarely experienced emotion, which, in addition to being very powerful, has an even more important strength, mysterious in nature. The mystery does not originate from some kind of magic, but from something totally different, and so unique that on occasion can create a spiritual bonding between the two individuals. A bonding of the human spirit so powerful that it even surpasses the ties formed between members of the same family.

This was the situation that Sergeant John Hadley found himself in one day after reaching out to console his friend Zach Randal. Zach had fallen into a deep pit of despair, unaware of anyone he thought capable of understanding. However, the one man that proved his willingness to extend his compassion was Sergeant John Hadley.

Katherine Alicia Randal had been buried only the week before, and such a heavy weight of sadness had been crushing Zach that he had not the strength to cry out for help.

Some men believe their grief must be endured alone, while others that have been down that road of hardship establish within themselves an integrity so great it remains indestructible and untarnished by the trials they bear through life.

John Hadley's wife had been killed when she was only 29 years old. A drunk driver smashed into the car that she was sitting in, waiting for a traffic light to change. The drunk was reported to have been traveling at over eighty miles per hour, and his big truck smashed her compact car into an unrecognizable heap of metal.

Twenty-five years later, John is still deeply in love with her. He was never to marry again. John was never negative about life nor was he bitter over the things that life had dealt him. This special outlook he possessed became the reason that Zach Randal asked him for help, sort of like a personal guide to ensure his survival for at least the next few years, or until the pain associated with Kate's death would become tolerable.

A rare and very special bond forged itself between the spirits of the two men that day. A bond that was powerful enough to send John Hadley feeling his way up a mountain in total darkness, terrified of hidden dangers buried below the deep snow drifts on the mountain, and all the while his bones aching from the indescribable and bitter cold. Even with such an extreme sacrifice surrendered on his part, John never uttered a word of complaint. He does it for his friend, because he knows his friend would not hesitate to do the same for him.

The gray horse that John had found in the barn behind the cabin soon tired from the fast pace that he had set. Reaching the halfway point in their ascent John sensed the moment when the horse began to falter. It was sometime after sunset and darkness began to spook him. As midnight arrived on the mountain, John was still leading the horse by hand, taking extreme care with every step that he made in the black night. He was determined to reach his destination, where he hoped his friend Zach Randal had made it to safety.

Snow continued falling, but it was not nearly the deterrent that darkness was capable of being. Earlier in the day, sometime that afternoon, John thought he saw a man across one of the ravines encircled by the same narrow road he was following. Hoping to meet up with the individual, he followed the road that doubled back before twistingly heading in that general direction. John estimated that not more than thirty minutes of time separated them from each other. He anticipated that it would take at least that much time to reach the location where the ravine had cut through the terrain.

Yet, nobody descended the mountain to where John was, nor would he ever locate the man, even after being certain that what he saw was real. Like some ghostly apparition, the man and his horse had somehow vanished.

Could the snow have created an illusion, which he mistook for a man riding a horse? Without slowing from his pace, John began to increase his periodic scanning of the mountainside. A newfound anxiety had suddenly formed within him, as he doubted the possibility of what he had seen as being some kind of snow ghost. It had been a man. If any snow ghost were on the mountain to worry about, they had been responsible for making the man he saw vanish.

Preoccupied, deliberating in the darkness, John missed his next step, stumbling forward headlong. While faltering, vainly attempting to grab onto something to prevent falling, Hadley dropped the reins he'd been holding tightly in his right hand. Terror gripped him, as he perceived the extent of his fall. Thinking he would hit ground at any second, John was puzzled when, to the contrary, his plummeting only increased in momentum.

Sergeant John Hadley's world was flying by as he wildly reached out with his arms, hoping for some miracle. Out of nowhere, abruptly, he seemed to accept what was occurring, marveling at the relative comfort that he began to feel, knowing all along that one day he was going to have to face death. He uttered no cry as the long descent seemed to last forever.

DESPERATELY looking about with eyes that felt as if they had been scorched with a red-hot poker, Jack found himself instantly afraid. The darkness was not what he feared as long as he was able to hear the slow continuous movements of the man he followed, making his way over the treacherous terrain.

Jack was flanking him up the mountain when out of nowhere fear struck. If not for the blind luck he'd been having since the very start of the suicidal climb, the mission would have abruptly ended.

With his attention diverted momentarily, he came face to face with another young deputy climbing down off the mountain. Thinking fast, he tried to play dumb with the deputy, confusing the man before having to kill him, but that was when his luck ran out.

Jack would never figure out how the deputy recognized him, but it was obvious when the young deputy's mouth fell open, surprised to see Vermette on a horse right before him. Reaching for the pistol at his side, he was just a bit too slow for the more experienced and self-confident madman three feet in front of him.

Moving faster than he was used to, Jack looked around for anything available to keep from being captured or shot. Surrounding the two men were thick, heavy branches of fir trees swooping down in an umbrella shape.

The deputy's hand had just barely touched the butt of his revolver when Jack grabbed hold to one of the long branches loaded with green foliage. Quickly he pulled it back toward him, releasing it before the deputy could act. The heavy branch whipped forward like a slingshot. The deputy's horse responded violently as it slapped hard against his big nose. Jack seized upon the moment by spurring his mount straight into the young deputy's horse. The powerful collision happened just as the deputy's horse reared back onto its hind legs.

Both horse and rider fell backward with a loud and sickening thud. Unfortunately, the deputy was under the weight of his mount as they fell, crushing him. Not another sound was heard as the young deputy died. Eyes wide and filled with fear, his mouth frozen open in a silent scream.

Jack studied the scene feeling very shaky, he had never witnessed sudden death from so innocent an accident. The morbid display on the cold ground before him brought tears to Jack's painful eyes. It was such a beautiful death.

Jack marveled at the unexpected change of events. In less than two minutes the success of his mission grew more possible and only two minutes ago, the young deputy had been alive and well, searching the mountain for Jack Vermette.

Jack focused his attention back on the descending darkness ahead of him, listening for any kind of movement from the other officer that he had been following. What if all the commotion that just occurred had spooked him? He could be setting a trap to catch Jack, preventing him from his destiny, allowing Amy to live. Jack sat motionless as he began imagining scenarios. No sound was heard, but no soul would locate Jack before he was given his opportunity to set right, that which was wrong.

Once, while working far out in the Gulf of Mexico, Jack had read a book filled with quotes. The author had not been one that he recognized, but he was impressed by some of the things written. One quote he'd found particularly interesting was memorized by Jack.

"Pray not for judgment upon those who stand in opposition to you, but rather pray that they embrace in you what they oppose, effecting greater ease for your rule."

The waiting seemed to last forever. One minute, followed by ten minutes, then adding twenty more minutes to the time that passed, yet Jack made not a sound. It was unnerving and required patience, a commodity that unfortunately Jack had never managed to store within him. He could no longer play this game, and loudly made his way to the spot where he thought the other man had been.

The big gray stood alone under a thick fir, pawing at the snow trying to find a morsel of anything to chew on as Jack arrived. He could find no sign of the officer, and for several tense minutes, Jack Vermette studied the situation. Eventually, he deciphered what had occurred.

AWAKENED by the unique aroma of coffee, Deke found himself on the love seat before the fireplace. The usual peace and quiet that he was accustomed to at the cabin had been shattered by loud voices. Passionately the voices were discussing a topic in which they had very different opinions.

As the fog cleared from Deke's head and his level of awareness stabilized it became obvious that the two voices he heard belonged to Zach Randal and Bill Wright.

The so-called disagreement that he'd picked up in the two voices, innocently enough, had been about how many ice crystal formations were possible in a snowflake.

Zach Randal immediately noticed the fact that Deke had awakened. Although Deke had no idea how long he had been unconscious, judging by the way he felt as he sat up on the small couch it could not have been much longer than thirty minutes.

"Damn Deke! You okay, son? You've been out for nearly thirty minutes." With a deep concern, Zach approached him.

"You certainly passed out like a man needing a nap. Hell boy, if I wouldn't have caught you a knot as big as a bowling ball would be on the back of your head." Zach Randal had taken a seat on the hearth of the fireplace. Displaying a sense of urgency, Zach began to question Deke, clearly disturbed by the physical condition in which he'd found him.

With an equal desire, Deke wanted badly to question Zach on important issues of the last two days. The question that came next from Zach twisted such a perplexing look on Deke's face that it stopped Zach cold, and patiently he waited for an answer.

"Come on Deke, you shouldn't have to consult any map to answer me. All I want to know is where is Miss Amy, and is she safe?" The picture that automatically popped into Deke's head upset him, creating even more of a delay in answering Zach's question.

The picture he was having trouble wiping away from his mind would never have become a memory before today. He had stripped the wet clothing from her, and recalled how he'd nearly swallowed his tongue coming down the stairs with a blanket. All he had wanted to do was wrap her in something dry and warm.

"One more time just to see if we can break a record here. Where is Miss Amy son?" The amount of patience he heard within that plea from Zach revealed more information about the size of the big man's heart than anything else Deke had heard since meeting him on that fateful morning.

Initially the difficulty that he was experiencing had him pretty frightened. Only after Zach had worked with him for a while, calming him, and just exhibiting that incredible patience was Deke able to begin explaining their wild experience.

The amount of punishment that Deke's body had been exposed to sort of disabled his ability to form the words that his brain was struggling to express. It was a scary time, and at first Deke thought he had experienced some kind of stroke or brain damage. Zach Randal began laughing at Deke's fear.

Although insulted by the laughing, Deke couldn't do much. He was so dependent on Zach helping him with the problem, and even began pleading with him. Deke knew only that he wanted to return to normal, and quickly.

"Deke my boy, you have not suffered a stroke. However, I have no idea of knowing, one way or the other, about any previous brain damage you may have had." As soon as the words were out of Zach's mouth, they produced a facial expression like nothing he had ever seen before. That was when the laughter began.

Amazingly, it was the laughter Zach managed to coax from Deke that magically repaired the short circuit in his brain. Laughter that came out in what sounded like hiccups at first, but as Zach prodded and poked him, the laughter began coming out smoother. In no time, he was carrying on as if he had never had a short in his head.

Of course, the first thing out of Deke's mouth was Amy's location.

Then, he told the two men about her close call, judging that she would make a full recovery in no time. Adding to his account was the amount of gratitude that he felt for the Beatles. Without the Beatles, both he and Amy without a doubt would be dead, if not by freezing to death, surely as a result of something else.

"Because we have so much that has to be covered in such a short time I'm going to go upstairs to check on Miss Amy." Nothing about Zach's statement could be mistaken for asking permission, he was making a declaration of intent.

But before Deke would allow him to walk up those stairs and see Amy, he needed to advise Zach of one small fact…Texas Ranger Zachary Randal's face flushed beet-red.

"Bust my damn buttons! I trusted you to protect Miss Amy, Mr. Stone. You were trusted with taking care of something very valuable and precious. Wasn't nothing in the deal that guaranteed any privileges, and you were not to sample the fruit at the earliest possible opportunity, especially while deputized and in an official capacity."

Deke was making apologies while at the same time trying to explain his innocence. The situation playing out in front of Sheriff Bill Wright must have appeared hilarious, because the big man suddenly began chuckling.

After five more minutes of time had passed, with Zach and Deke frantically continuing the exchange of comments, they gradually realized that Sheriff Wright was no longer chuckling, but had begun roaring with laughter.

The two who were butting heads became silent as they watched Bill Wright point an accusing finger in their direction. Tempers began to climb from the finger pointing, and Bill Wright had not realized the danger behind his behavior.

Zach, realizing no harm had been intended, soon excused Sheriff Wright. What came to be realized by all three of the men was how special this woman, Amy Dodson, was to them.

Settling down, and getting on with the business at hand, the highly charged and important questions were handled first, allowing stress produced by each of the issues to slowly lessen until eventually, it evaporated from them.

Emotional responses became less volatile, which reduced the amount of stress, which resulted in emotional responses becoming less volatile.

Zach apologized to Deke after discovering the heroic measures that were taken when rescuing Amy, which also explained why she happened to be in Deke's bedroom, completely naked. Relief was felt all around, and Zach returned to his pre-explosive state.

Decisions were also arrived at concerning how much information should be withheld from Amy. More importantly, they deliberated about what information Amy needed to have revealed to her.

They knew it was not a popular strategy to keep secrets from her. A previous reaction about that very thing nearly resulted in Amy totally rejecting both Deke and Zach from her life. Only by using their best manipulative skills had they avoided a tragedy. With that event still fresh, they made up their minds using the same plan as before, hoping that Amy wouldn't discover it this time.

"We may not have another opportunity such as this to go over everything; so, with Amy still sleeping we'd better take advantage of it." All of them were in complete agreement.

They covered much of what happened since Rotan and Vanessa Jansen's disappearance, but an incredible amount of evidence had been discovered since then, and more importantly, for the first time in the investigation, the evidence had produced a prime suspect.

"Deke we've made some mighty important discoveries since the last time I spoke to you. Some time back, Miss Amy was involved with a fellow who went by the name of Jack Vermette. At the time, nobody knew much about this fellow, and it was obvious that she didn't want the relationship advertised around Sweetwater, kind of secretive about it.

"Well, after several months of seeing the fellow, who at the time lived somewhere around El Paso, he was reportedly killed offshore, a boat accident of some kind."

Zach was watching Deke closely to make sure he was getting all of the information. At the same time, Deke was glued to Zach, hanging on every word he said, somehow sensing how incredulous the information was going to be.

"Amy never said anything about the man, and I never asked. I figured she just decided to keep it a secret. Or maybe the affair didn't work out to her liking. Anyway, and this is the part that grieves me the most, since I didn't put two and two together when I should have, it was several months after his death that she started receiving those disturbing letters. And not too long after the letters, the small packages with body parts started showing up."

Ranger Zach Randal was taking his time, making certain that the previous short circuit in Deke's brain was not hindering him from understanding the significance of what he was revealing.

However, Zach Randal should have known that even before he was able to complete his story Deke Stone would have it figured out.

"Jack Vermette didn't die in that accident, did he?" Deke asked.

With a sudden look of astonishment, Zach quickly replied, "No!"

Before Deke could interrupt him any further, Zach plunged ahead, "So far I've calculated at least six people that I'm pretty sure he's murdered. That includes the three women at the cafe, one tow truck operator, and the two officers that I had helping me out in Amarillo with the disappearance of Dr. Vanessa Jansen. They were executed that same night on a dark street behind the Potter County Sheriff's Department, by someone digging around in Miss Amy's Land Cruiser."

A grim-faced Zachary Randal gave the last bit of information. He had the kind of look that resulted from the mixture of rage and sorrow, a combination that Deke saw as incredibly frightening.

"What makes you think that this Vermette fellow was the one responsible?" It was a question from Deke that Zach was poised to answer.

"His thumbprint was on a Dodson's Breakfast and Bar-B-Que Cafe key chain they found hanging from the passenger door he unlocked to get inside the vehicle. It was Miss Amy's key chain Deke." Zach didn't relish having what was considered irrefutable proof; it had been obtained through a price that was way too high to pay for getting it, specifically, the lives of Bill Frye and Dan Baker.

"My Lord! Those two men were killed that very night? We had no idea. Then, Vermette must have been hot on our trail from the very beginning." Deke was stunned.

By this time, Sheriff Bill Wright had made himself useful by heating up a pot of soup. He served Deke a large mug full of the rejuvenating liquid, and he sat up hungrily drinking it down.

Zach continued to fill him in on the rest of the details that he'd managed to put together, including the fact that Sergeant John Hadley may be on his way up the mountain, but with who Zach was afraid might be Jack Vermette right behind him. Zach even voiced his opinion that Vermette was probably responsible for killing one of Sheriff Wright's deputies the night before.

Without any intentional effort from Zach, he put the fear of the Lord into the two men sitting before him. This character Jack Vermette sounded like an invincible and invisible killer, almost like *Bram Stoker's Dracula.*

Deke was not ashamed to admit that a healthy amount of fear was lurking deep within his heart for the woman he had become so attached to, especially since he had no idea what Vermette even looked like, his physical size, his demeanor, or even his personality traits.

With this bit of information, Deke snapped alert, remembering what it was that had nearly killed he and Amy to begin with.

Looking directly at Sheriff Wright, who had up until that time remained silent allowing Deke to be filled in by Zach on all that had developed, Deke's brow creased. He didn't want to tell him what he'd discovered.

"Sheriff, I hate to tell you this, but I found one of your deputies at the bottom of a steep ravine. I'm afraid that he'd fallen in the storm. Here's the wallet that was in his pocket." Deke handed the shocked, white-faced sheriff the deputy's billfold. Realizing the impact that the information had on Sheriff Wright, he added in consolation, "I'm pretty sure the impact from the fall killed him instantly."

Bill Wright stood silently before them and opened the deputy's wallet slowly before losing his composure and turning away. They both sensed his grief and also turned, looking away.

"He was sent up here to warn you and your lady friend. Sergeant Hadley made the request. I sent him up here before realizing how serious a situation this was. I guess his death is my fault." The big man's department was taking a heavy toll from all of the mess, and it was obvious that not only was he grieved by it, but he was also pissed.

"That ain't true Bill. None of this is your fault, and I won't let any of us get started on taking turns to see who's to blame for this part or how much. Just one man's responsible for all of this crap, and by God, I aim to see him pay one way or another. Not that it will reverse any of what has happened or bring anyone back, but it will ensure that no more folks end up dead as a result of his sick mind."

Zach stopped short, suddenly realizing that after everything, he still had no idea what Jack Vermette's motive was for starting this rampage of death and destruction.

"That reminds me Deke my boy, now that you have most of the variables in this game of death scrabble, why don't you fire up that high-priced brain of yours, and figure out what possible motive this varmint Vermette could have for terrorizing that poor little lady?"

Before Deke could protest the uselessness of having any such information and that it would avail nothing to their situation, in addition to any attempt at grilling Amy on what she may know about it, they heard the faintest whisper of a voice come from the upstairs loft.

"I'll tell you what his motive is." Amy stood at the top of the stairs, surrounded by the solid and vigilant Beatles.

CHAPTER

27

ALL THREE MEN stood at once, bumping against one another in their haste to show proper manners, while fearful not knowing how much of their conversation Amy managed to hear.

She remained at the top of the staircase, completely calm and appearing fully rested. It was obvious to the three men however, that she had not taken notice of her current state of dress. Amy was still wrapped inside the large blanket that Deke had stripped from the bed to bundled her up.

With a nonchalant flip of the blanket, Amy intended to shed the extra weight before descending the stairs. That was when the three men realized her intentions, and all at once, raised their hands in warning. But it was too late.

With a cry of surprise, the blanket fell away exposing her to the three men who, by this time even as difficult as it was, managed to turn their faces away sparing her the extreme embarrassment. They heard as Amy made a speedy recovery of the apparel, announcing somewhat uncomfortably that she was once again decent. Now, swaddled like an Egyptian mummy inside the blanket.

The shock of finding herself stark naked, unable to recall if she had been the one to disrobe her body, derailed her previous train of thought. She was rather speechless in fact, and that was when Deke saw his opportunity to rescue her from the intrusive feelings of guilt that were about to force her into revealing the deepest and most sacred part of her soul.

"No! I refuse to submit Amy to any more probing and prying into her privacy. That madman responsible for all of this is the only one who can positively identify what kind of motives madmen have. To begin anew, with speculations or theories would be more of a punishment to her self-worth and integrity than I will permit. Gentlemen, I for one do not believe that we have the right to delve into a woman's privacy, dissecting each and every misguided thought or step taken throughout her life, just to be able to say we made a gallant effort in solving the mystery behind some tangled and twisted person's mind. While in the end, we will still have no idea as to what the true motivating factors might have been. In any case, any possible motive we discover has at this point become irrelevant."

Deke's declaration of intent and his rationalization for that intent took the other two men by complete surprise. Zach Randal and Bill Wright both switched their gaze from a bewildered, but relieved Amy, to the smaller man standing between them, who without warning, had taken over as her guardian.

"Shucks Deke, if you'll give me and old Bill here a couple of minutes to figure out exactly what it is you just said I might want to challenge you." It was a well-placed response to Deke's defense of Amy; Zach Randal knew all too well what Deke declared so boldly was in itself the best thing that could have happened. It spared him making an enemy of himself through attacking Amy, and at the same time, allowed him a way out before getting too deep, only having to crawfish backward from a severe tongue lashing when Amy finally did lose her patience with any additional probing.

"Okay, I thought it over, and by golly whatever you said makes damn good sense to me. What do you think about it Bill?" As smooth as his reputation, Zach Randal slid right back into Amy's good graces, throwing the ball in Sheriff Bill Wright's corner to bobble for a while.

"I never heard a better example of common sense in all of the courtrooms in Colorado." Sheriff Wright was true to form, sounding like the politician that he was.

TEMPERATURES plummeted that night as the four refugees sat inside Deke's small cabin. The amount of snowfall was not as heavy as it had been for the past twenty-four hours, still a good three to four feet piled up against the outside of the structure. Between the three men, they had managed to dig away most of the snow at the cabin's front door. At a distance that was about fifteen feet, a ramp of shoveled snow gradually climbed up from the cabin entrance separating it from the top layer of snow that blanketed the mountain. Amy had recovered fully from her embarrassing incident at the top of the stairs, and after having a bowl of Sheriff Wright's soup; she again retired to the loft. Even though she felt rested her body had been severely taxed, and she soon realized that she needed more time to rebound from her nearly irreversible hypothermic episode.

315

The three men sat around the fire discussing what their next move should be. Zach and Bill wondered if anyone else had managed to make the ascent. Bill Wright worried about Deputy Ted Daniel, hoping he'd met up with Sergeant John Hadley. He figured they decided to turn back toward the camp; it was his only consolation to why they'd not heard from them yet. Or had they run into Jack Vermette somewhere on the mountainside, been ambushed and killed and were buried somewhere in the deep snow?

Nothing else was said between Deke and Zach Randal in reference to the possible motive that must be driving Jack Vermette. He had apparently been normal enough at one time for Amy to become involved. What could have happened since then was anybody's guess. Maybe it was something from the accident that he'd survived, causing such psychotic behavior. Possibly an injury of some kind or even severe emotional trauma leading to post-traumatic stress disorder, a diagnosis that in the past was often misdiagnosed and abused by those seeking to push some political agenda.

Who could tell, or really know what was going on inside the mind of such a disturbed individual. Deke secretly held to the belief that only one person possessed the key to solving that mystery. He also believed that Amy was positively certain she knew exactly why this mad butcher was after her, but Deke vowed to himself never to try to discover what that key was.

Zach wanted to know the motivation more than he needed to know it. Like most lawmen, he imagined a courtroom drama unfolding in his mind with the prosecuting attorney unable to give the court a definite motive for such bloody and bizarre actions. Motive was often the most important piece of evidence to many who sat on a jury. Nonetheless, as Deke had so eloquently detailed earlier, motive was nothing but verbosity when all other evidence pointed to guilt beyond a shadow of a doubt.

Defense lawyers were famous for creating mountainous masterpieces of horseshit in courtrooms across America. With all the passion and pomp of Shakespeare, they railed on and on regarding motives, unless of course, a motive was established against their client. Then they would avoid any reference to motive with everything that was in them, declaring it ridiculous to assume it could be of any significance.

Anyway, Ranger Zach Randal had been thinking like a lawman, wanting to avoid the possibility of anything muddying up the water. It only came to him later that whether Jack Vermette had any motive or not, in the end it would mean very little, especially since dead men never saw the inside of a courtroom anyhow.

Sheriff Bill Wright sat before the fire consumed within his thoughts. It took no degree in psychology to quickly figure out that the man was embroiled in warfare, struggling with himself, against himself, in spite of himself. The torture that he was inflicting upon his mind was about as useful as teats on a boar hog. Yet man is the most complex of all creations, aware of measures that lead to naught, but powerless to prevent the sequence of events that will play over and over in his head, as if the past might some way be altered to change the outcome of the events that now create such despair in his soul.

Zach Randal and Deke Stone sat quietly watching him until the degree of misery became obvious. Staring blindly into the red coals of the fireplace, Bill Wright would occasionally mumble something to himself under his breath, then in response to the words that only he was aware of, the big man would jerk forward with rage, shaking his head and pounding his fist against his knee.

The self-abuse finally became too much to witness, and Zach was compelled to interfere. Standing, Zach walked up directly behind Sheriff Bill stopping when he was about a foot away. Zach looked down at the pitiful sight.

"Bill, how tall are you my friend?" The question was way off key, and took both Deke and the sheriff by surprise. Still, Deke Stone had more faith in the old Ranger than anyone he could think of, and instantly knew that Zach was up to something. He obviously had come up with some kind of a plan to help rid the sheriff of this unwarranted grief.

"What's that Zach?" Bill Wright looked up at Zach standing behind him, confused.

"Now I know I don't stutter you dime-store, dip-shit, wanna-be cowboy. I asked *how tall are you?* And while you're chewing on the answer to that question let's see if you can handle an even tougher assignment by telling me how much weight you pack on that rack of rattly bones of yours?"

This was no joke, Zach wanted answers to the odd questions, rudely challenging Bill Wright to come up with them.

The sudden intrusion upon Bill's private and personal attempt to self inflict harm upon himself by Zach, kind of aroused the sheriff from his despondency. A look came upon him that suggested he might be returning to reality.

"I'm not sure I appreciate your tone of voice, and neither do I appreciate those condescending remarks. Now what the hell do you want to know my height and weight for Zach?" Even in the foulest of moods, Sheriff Wright was trying to be as patient as possible with the burly old Texas Ranger. It was not going to work.

"Well, I figure you're about one or two inches taller than me, giving you the advantage; so, I don't feel bad about that. And with a little imagination, I guess I could estimate your weight to be somewhere around two-sixty. Am I close Bill?" Zach was sizing up the sheriff, who by this time was standing, facing Zach Randal. The challenging move from Bill Wright didn't even cause a stir in Randal's composure. Still talking to the sheriff, Zach began to shed the tight and confining leather jacket that he was wearing. He unbuckled his holster from around his waist, and removed the trademark white Stetson. Placing the items neatly and gently to the side, Zach crossed his arms, and again demanded an answer.

"Well, am I close country bumpkin, or what?" Shaking his head in mock disgust Zach decided not to cut him any slack.

"Where do redneck, shit-kicker fellows like you come from anyway?"

"Look here Randal. I'm not in the mood to play head games with you, now just back off okay?" Sheriff Wright was heating up, but was allowing Zach a way out of whatever it was he was brewing.

"Head games! Boy, now you know you don't qualify for such advanced training. If I wanted to play head games with someone I'd get old Deke here, or even one of the Beatles to give me enough of a challenge to make it interesting. The only head game you probably know how to play is when those cheap hookers are offering an alternative to posting bond." Before Bill Wright could respond to the off-color remark, that truthfully threw Deke into another orbit, he continued, "If you must know melon-head, I'm sick and tired of watching you throwing your own little pity party, whining like the head cheerleader upset because it's homecoming, and she's on her period. It makes me want to deputize the damn horse that carried me up here just so you'll have someone else to add to that skeleton crew working for you. At least the damn horse will have enough sense to do what he's told, won't fall off of any cliff, and won't go around catching bullets." Deke finally caught on.

Zach was making reference to the young deputies that had been killed or gone missing from Bill Wright's department. The point that he seemed to be driving home was that each of the officers had made their own decisions that had unfortunately ended with disaster, not one of them had been following direct orders from Bill Wright the moment disaster struck. The only possible conclusion to all of this, and what Zach wanted Bill to realize, was the error he'd made by assuming blame.

It was a case of legitimate grief quickly transforming itself into unwarranted guilt. Adopting the bastardized emotion, Sheriff Bill Wright had mistakenly assumed responsibility for actions, which had been created from the depraved and immoral behavior of one man, a man who could not be controlled and who was ultimately to blame for every harmful event from the start.

"So let's me and you get busy, either wipe your butt or blow your nose, but get serious, because if it's an ass whipping you're intent on delivering to yourself I'm pretty sure that I'm more qualified to give it than you are!" Zach Randal was prepared to bring it to a bloody end if necessary, but both he and Deke saw when the message hit home. Sheriff Bill Wright deflated quicker that the soccer ball Deke and Amy saw George sink his teeth into several days ago. No more fight remained in him. He became aware of the foolishness of his behavior, and with a miserable look on his face reached out grabbing hold to Zach Randal. Tears rolling down his chin, all he could do was look at Zach stating, "I know, I know, but Zach I loved those boys like they were my very own."

Zach Randal supported the big man against his chest; it was a chore that he'd had to perform a couple of times in the past with other officers. As perplexing as it was, some people considered Zach's ability to recognize and reverse the destructive cycle as nothing short of a miracle. He considered it about as useful as red piss, and wished that he'd never stumbled across the strange ability.

ZACH Randal's wisdom told him that Jack Vermette was an extreme exception to all the rules. Rules that normally kept human beings from rising to the point of a deity: the god-level prevented them from experiencing what were considered divine appointments. So far, and to

319

Zach's dismay, it appeared as though nothing in this world could prevent, or deter Jack Vermette from the task that he had set before him.

Everything was falling in his favor, whether by chance or divine intervention; the man had not once been thwarted. This was most unfortunate since it only confirmed any previous delusions he may have had. As far as Jack was concerned, Zach's experience told him that they were going to be out on the dance floor with this fellow until the very end of the song. He could not envision any opportunity that would present itself allowing him the option of cutting this guys legs out from under him, letting them all go home a little early.

It was well after midnight with only a few hours of darkness left. Soon they would find out just how much of the storm clouds remained to deny the sun's light from shedding its bright and piercing warmth onto the surreal looking, white terrain of the mountainside. With any luck, the weather might allow them to double up and head down the mountain toward safety.

Bitterly, cold temperatures existed outside with a toasty warm fireplace on the inside, Miss Amy was fast asleep, safe in the loft, and Bill, Zach, and Deke busily pondered their situation. Almost too many developments had taken place over the last several days, and after several attempts to pass on each small detail surrounding each of them, the three men finally abandoned their effort, realizing that the amount of drama associated with each occurrence had lost its appeal.

Without warning, a loud rumbling noise suddenly came from the loft. The men turned heads so quick in response to the commotion that each of them held a hand to the side of his neck from the near whiplash. As it turned out, they nearly were injuring themselves from the amount of anxiety existing between them. The drum rolling sound had come from the heavy footfalls of all four Beatles, as they ran down the stairway together, stopping at the front door staring at it as if it would open of its own accord.

"Okay, this is at least something that I've seen once before," Deke stated while getting up from before the fireplace and walking toward the door, allowing the Beatles to exit quickly and do their business. Maybe they'd even roam around the cabin for a while getting some exercise. It would do them good to get out for a couple of hours, immune to the cold as they were. Besides, the fact that Miss Amy was safe for the time being went without saying. If three grown men could not protect her, what could a Chesapeake Bay retriever add when it came to guarding her?

As soon as Deke cracked the heavy door open, a brisk stab of cold weather entered, and the Beatles rushed out resembling a dust devil made of fur. Within seconds, they were out of sight, and Deke wasted no time closing the door. The darkness and cold night behind the door reminded him of the smell of death he'd been exposed to in mausoleums that he and his friends used to break into at a Catholic cemetery where he'd attended high school in South Louisiana.

INCREDIBLY cold and dark within the small wooden shack, Jack still considered it a blessing to get away from the elements. It had been a long climb, and only through slow and methodical searching for tracks in the snow was he able to pick up the tracks left by the horses carrying Zach Randal and Sheriff Bill Wright. Winding his way around the mountainside, Jack followed the horse tracks until coming to this place. Without a doubt, it was the storage shed just outside of Deke Stone's cabin. Jack had been inside the small, cramped building for at least three hours, and whenever a lull in the wind occurred he could actually hear the other men talking inside the cabin. Even though it was darker than the inside of a pig, Jack didn't risk snooping around the cabin. The damn windows were two stories high anyway, and he doubted that he would be able to find out more than he already knew.

First and foremost, little Miss Amy Dodson was inside that cabin, along with those four-legged devils that she called the Beatles. Secondly, that damned old Texas Ranger was with her and his new crime fighting buddy, the one, and only Sheriff Bill Wright. Third, Deke Stone, the all American Albert Einstein in the world of abhorrent, psychosocial, sociopathic, and mental disorders, was also inside. Fourth, Vermette knew that no additional deputies were on their way. Finally, the only variable he saw to being a possible deterrent was that fool old man that had taken a fall. All the kings' horses and all the kings' men would not be able to put that sorry bastard back together again.

Jack Vermette laughed aloud at his quick wit and good fortune.

"Hell yes, we got it made now don't we Lassie?" The bizarre statement accompanied the poking and prodding of the frozen, mangled, dead body of the German shepherd discovered inside the shed. Even though he had no idea why the dog was inside the shed, he enjoyed the company, and was without complaint even if their space was limited.

For the three hours that Jack stayed cooped up in the tiny space, he reflected on all that had taken place in the last few days. It was true, he had been lead by some powerful forces to get to the place he now found himself, but that was the troubling part to his meditation. Once he'd made it to the area on the mountain where Deke's cabin was, sneaking into this small, but lifesaving shelter, the guiding forces that had been by his side encouraging him with the needed help for so long, seemed to have simply vanished. A strange and frightening dread suddenly filled the place where he sat, like a room that had suddenly had all of the oxygen sucked out, and had been filled with a thick dust. Jack felt a panic rising from deep within him. An awareness, that was rapidly becoming crystal clear, consumed him with a fury. Finally, Jack was left to face the fact. He was alone.

Efforts to simply breath had taken on a new meaning. All of his previous plans, which had become such a high priority, were seriously jeopardized.

Minutes passed slowly. With great difficulty, he fought the urge to run from the small shed screaming at the top of his lungs. If Jack succumbed to the almost irresistible reflex, the resulting failure, after the many months of work and planning, could steal from him a great destiny he was convinced now awaited him.

A period of time that seemed to last much longer than what he knew had actually passed, finally reduced his anxiety level to a point where his breathing became less labored. He'd stopped perspiring and when he glanced at his open hands, he saw that they were no longer trembling.

Every child senses the presence of a guardian angel at one time or another while growing up. Jack smiled when he realized he was no longer alone. His divine assistant was once again by his side. Relief and a large measure of confidence welled up in him as he realized it had only been a test. Checking on his loyalty and determination, the powers that be had once again judged him as beyond reproof. Greatness was definitely going to be a part of his destiny. One final step was separating him from his magnificent future, and he was anxious to be done with it.

CHAPTER

28

REALIZING WEATHER CONDITIONS were not going to improve enough to gamble an attempt descending the narrow trail called Mamaw's Staircase, especially if they were doubled up with two riders per horse, the men made a decision an hour before daylight to remain in Deke's cabin.

Whenever brief moments of time that were not saturated with fear flickered by, they were actually able to think rationally. Rational thoughts shared by the men throughout the night seemed to suggest that their present location offered the best protection against any possible attack, along with shelter from the prevailing weather for an indefinite amount of time. Still, only minutes after coming to such conclusions they would begin getting nervous and jumpy. Like caged animals they suffered the bombarding and relentless moments where a desire to get home overruled all other feelings.

It was during the coldest and darkest hour of day, and the last hour before sunrise, that Deke realized nearly four hours earlier that he had let the Beatles out. They had not come scratching at the door wanting to get in, and for just a brief moment, a stabbing pang of worry pierced his being. At that very moment, Zach Randal declared the fire needed more wood, and he'd bring in a couple of loads if Deke gave him directions to the woodpile.

The momentary distraction by Zach's question sidetracked Deke's previous concern about the Beatles. He switched thought patterns, turning to Zach with directions to the woodpile, and which of the stacks might be best to burn first after having dried over the summer. Offering to accompany Zach and help with the task, Bill was turned down, but asked by Zach if he knew how to cook. The sheriff proved quite capable of wearing the chef's hat, and proceeded to get breakfast started. It would be after daylight before the pestering of Deke's sub-conscious mind managed to again break through to him, but by that time it was going to be too late.

DELIBERATING on a plan of action, Jack Vermette was nearly at his wits end with frustration before he was shocked into action. For the longest time it seemed Jack had entered a void. The cold, dark, cramped shed offered nothing but the sound of a steady, shrill wind passing through the cracks of the wall. He had almost become lulled into a state of sleep by the steady whistling, abandoning all thoughts on how he would be able to finish his mission. It was right at that point of impaired awareness, in that thin sliver of time when he was not sure if he'd fallen asleep, he was shaken alert by frantic scratching at the bottom of the shed's door. Sitting bolt upright, his mind raced to identify the development, while at the same time assessing the possible danger. Terrified of discovery, Jack experienced the primal reflex known as the fight or flight response. His choice was made in an instant.

Fate again had smiled down on Jack, providing a way where previously none existed. His only concern now was to find a way into the cabin without alarming those inside, and doing so within a reasonably short time. He was again exposed to the bitter elements of the mountain's weather, succeeding in eliminating his biggest concern, and the most lethal of his opponents. Quite unexpectedly, a solution to what was the most difficult of his problems had been provided.

All along, he knew the greatest challenge would be facing the viciousness of the Beatles, and their protectiveness of Amy. Since their unexpected discovery of him in the shed, and his agile ability to cling to the top rafters while letting them in, he'd successfully locked them out of his way. Hanging above their heads, Jack managed to exit the shed through a hole that he'd broken in the dry wood of the roof. The training that the Chessies had gone through before Amy adopted them would, on this occasion, work against them. All four of them remained silent as they watched Jack escape, refraining from the loud barking they were capable of.

Hunkered down against the back wall of the small shed in the pre-dawn darkness of the morning, Jack escaped detection by Zach Randal, who crunched through the snow only fifteen feet away from him while hauling firewood to the cabin. For a second Jack deliberated making a quick kill, eliminating another one of his threats with a swift slice of his knife, but decided against it, aware that it would only alert the others to his presence, and prevent him from ever gaining access to the cabin. He had to think of a way to get inside before the others became aware of his presence, and before they'd realize, and respond to the immediate danger he represented. Besides, Jack didn't want to waste a good kill without his victim aware of what was happening.

Fear manifested in a person who for the first time was confronted with the finality of their death, was rare and beyond description. While each of his victims responded in very similar ways, each also had a response that was very unique to the individual. Jack coveted the ability to create such an emotion, anxiously anticipating each response. He was anxious for Amy's response; it would be as none yet witnessed.

No! He would not squander a kill. It would be sinful for him to waste such an opportunity when he knew each of them had been planned as special tools for his growth.

While reflecting on the many circumstances that brought him to where he was, Jack wondered if that damned old Texas Ranger had been able to read the clues sent to Amy. The packages containing what he'd considered clear directions were an explanation and the reason behind his need to punish her. He thought it was all so very clever.

The abortion was an act against the very fiber of mankind, and the reason he wanted to remove her from this life. Amy had violated a superior authority: the male species. By her rebellious action, selfishly seeking a release from the bonds that had been created between them, and servitude to him, she had stirred what was already troubled waters, creating ripple effects that had so far been successful in keeping her from where she belonged in the first place: with him.

Packages containing eyes, ears, and a tongue, from the unidentified male were meant to speak to Amy, clearly revealing what was to come. From the very beginning of their relationship she'd stubbornly refused to advertise the fact that they were seeing each other, and on a regular basis. Hiding the truth, she exhibited behavior that went to the extreme. She'd insisted meeting only at previously decided locations, far from either of the communities where they lived, before even taking a weekend outing with him.

She'd puzzled Jack with this secretive mindset, teaching him about the old wife's tale: Hear no evil. See no evil. Speak no evil.

Amy claimed it was very practical when applied in daily life. Even though her sin and rebellion had been carried out in secret with the help of Jedediah Duncan, the act was closely monitored. Jack wanted to teach her that she had no way of escaping the truth.

See no evil. Hear no evil. Speak no evil. They would prove to be terms of folly.

ENTERING the front door of the cabin, Zach Randal dropped an armload of firewood onto the floor getting the immediate attention of Deke and Bill Wright. Upon hearing the loud crash of wood, Bill spun around drawing his weapon in surprise. Since Deke was watching Zach as he walked in, his response was much calmer.

"Zach, are you all right?" he asked, fearful that the Ranger may have suffered a heart attack from the exertion.

"Hell no I ain't all right! And I guess the only reason I'm still alive is because the son-of-a-bitch plans to look me in the eye when he kills me!" Quickly bolting the door behind him, Zach had obviously encountered something to create such a drastic change in his speed, and his excitement level.

"What? What's going on? Who's gonna kill you?" stammering like a virgin in a whorehouse, Deke felt the tension level within the cabin rise quicker than the rabbit population in Australia after guns were outlawed.

Sheriff Bill Wright holstered his revolver, and calmly turned back to the stove to shut off each burner.

"The bastards here, ain't he?" Bill Wright was making a statement more than asking the question.

"You got it Bill. Right off, I noticed tracks from the Beatles leading inside that old shed in the back. I just continued without even taking a breath, but didn't spot him until I was on my way back. He was balled up behind that shed, against the wall and out of the wind. How he didn't see me when I spotted him is beyond understanding. I spotted him just as big as a preacher behind a blackjack table. Without so much as a flinch, I figured he'd try and get me from behind, but when I didn't feel the blade I knew he felt sure that his presence was undiscovered."

All of a sudden, the interior of the cabin went from a wait-and-see mode to frantic attempts at preparing a state of readiness. Energy levels surged within the three men as a frenzy of activity was started. Except, it was apparent that they had no idea when, how, or where to apply this new knowledge about Jack Vermette's location.

What was Vermette's next move going to be? When would he decide to make that move? How should they prepare for what may happen, at any time or any place?

"Boys, I'm sorry if the way I just responded burned away a couple of years from your lives, but it seems obvious from the tail chasing that we're doing, ain't a catfish's whisker of difference from what we were doing before, to what we're doing now." It was true. Zach just happened to be the first to realize that despite all of the excitement created from seeing Vermette outside the cabin, it benefited them very little, if anything at all.

Deke Stone and Bill Wright stopped dead in their tracks. "Well, what do we do?" both of them asked in unison, looking directly at Zach Randal.

"Damn good question," he answered them, looking around at the inside of the cabin as if an answer to their question was written on the walls. He didn't want to admit to the feeling of helplessness that was coursing through him, but if he didn't come up with an adequate and workable plan soon, the two men would clearly see the befuddlement plastered across his face.

He stood in the small cabin that was surrounded by several feet of snow from the blizzard conditions realizing for the first time that not only Amy was being hunted by that psychotic terror, but he too had become prey. An overwhelming and familiar feeling swept through him that he knew as being from an ambush. The swelling rage that boiled from within him was kept in check, Zach felt sure the opportunity to render his sentence upon Vermette was near.

The fact that one man had become so mentally and emotionally warped by something that he perceived was done to him, inflicted by a person who Zach knew to be incapable of intentionally hurting anyone, had him bewildered. The more he pondered about Vermette's reasons in hunting Amy down like a dog, along with the people who were trying to protect her, the more he saw a stain that had to be rubbed out.

Zach eyes were looking in the direction of Bill and Deke, but it was plain to them that those eyes were focused on something else.

"I don't know about the two of you fellows, but I feel like I'm playing in a deadly game where the other side won't give up the ball. Playing just defense has limited my scoring ability, and I'm the kind of guy who likes to inflict damage, scoring as often as possible."

Bill had heard about the predator skills the Texas Ranger exhibited, but until that moment he had never imagined how intense or to what degree Zach Randal actually became a hunter. Right before his eyes, a transformation took place.

Zach looked like a peaceful mountain man only minutes ago, hauling wood inside the cabin for the fireplace. Now, his appearance was more like that of a starving wolf, hot on the trail of a crippled caribou. A twinkle of anticipation was shining from his eyes, but even more disturbing was how a smile worked its way onto his face. It was a hideous smile hiding behind a serious face, a gleeful smile like the smile of a wolf watching his prey slowly lose the advantage.

"What do you plan to do Zach?" Deke had noticed the change in him, and more than anything else, worried about what he had on his mind.

"Deke my boy, it should be obvious to you what needs to be done, something that I should have done long before allowing that human disaster to get this far. Being at a disadvantage for so long has created a serious handicap in my game plan, preventing me from doing the very thing I do best." Zach walked over to the side of the mantel above the fireplace, grabbing his jacket hanging from a wooden peg. Slowly, while slipping his huge arms inside the thick, leather jacket he looked at his two friends standing stunned before him.

"I'm going to hunt him down and kill him!" he declared.

Bill and Deke looked at each other in surprise, not knowing what to say or do. Zach noticed their worried looks, offering a deep chuckle in response.

"Don't worry boys, I'm not asking that you come with me. In fact, my better judgment says leaving the two of you here, just in case I'm not successful, will be the best backup I can think of. A scared and innocent little lady needs protecting." Zach looked up in the direction of the bedroom loft, a strange and sad appearance of regret on his face.

"If the two of you don't mind, I'd like to have the first crack at making sure she stays safe and innocent, before all this damn mess has the same effect on her that it's had on me." His appearance changed from the sweet and sorrowful look to one filled with anger and bitterness.

Neither of the two men, standing captivated before him, was able to offer a single word in opposition to his plan. The words spoken by Zach Randal were filled with a mysterious intimacy. It was his moment, and they had no right in trying to prevent him from doing what he knew he had to do.

He bundled himself up, checked his weapon quickly, and after briefly nodding to Deke and Bill, walked through the cabin door closing it tightly behind him.

HUNKERED down behind a thick stand of trees some fifty yards from the front of the cabin, Jack Vermette waited. He had to find a way inside that cabin without exposing himself, and he had to do it before he froze to death.

With that damned Texas Ranger so close to him while hidden against the old wooden shed, escaping notice, Jack experienced a sudden thrill. It only proved what he'd suspected all along about the man; he was getting too old for the job.

Jack's confidence level was elevated a couple of notches as he watched that damned old Texas Ranger walk right past him. He might as well have been blind, missing Jack as he sat, nearly fully exposed. After watching the big man enter the cabin and close the door, Jack made his way to the clump of trees where he now sat.

Unexpectedly, the door opened again. Jack sat stunned as Zach Randal exited. The Ranger closed the door behind him and stood in the middle of the deep alley of waist high snow the men had cleared a path through earlier. All Jack could see of the Texas Ranger was where his slender waist started, clear to the top of his head. But he saw enough of the Ranger to recognize the Colt revolver now awkwardly holstered at his side.

Zach stood silently in front of the cabin looking at his surroundings with a cold, hard stare. Jack Vermette suddenly went from his previous state of cold shivering to a cold sweat. Whatever had gone on inside that cabin for the last few minutes somehow had a drastic effect on the Ranger's behavior. He'd changed from Jack's recent impression of the old, blind man carrying a few pieces of wood, into a determined man with enough ferocity to have Jack second-guessing everything. Survival dictated conclusions obvious only to Jack; the Texas Ranger was off his rocker, or trying to impress others standing guard.

Ranger Randal continued scanning the terrain, standing as big as a lighthouse for Vermette to see. He was aware that he was being watched, but had no idea where the watcher, Vermette, was.

If conclusions that were reached by him and Deke about Vermette's mental and emotional state were correct, it wouldn't take too much more of this behavior to draw Vermette out from where he was hiding.

Zach had exited the front door without the faintest idea of what he was going to do, not even the smallest hint of a plan existed in his mind, but something had to be done. As long as Vermette was under the assumption that he had an upper hand over the three men, with Amy hopelessly trapped like rats in a cage, his cockiness might just be enough to swing developments in a hell bent direction. That was where Zach wanted to prevent things from going.

By being exposed, outside of what Vermette imagined their cage, the doubting process might begin and any previous beliefs of victory might vanish from Vermette's mind.

It was a tedious and very dangerous affair to stand fearlessly exposed to such rebelliousness. Zach planted himself at the entrance, as immovable as a hickory tree. He didn't want to give away the fact that he'd seen Jack, preferring for him to think only the skills he possessed as a lawman had revealed to him Jack's presence.

If Vermette was half as deranged as Zach suspected this arrogant behavior might be enough to boggle Jack's thinking, screw him up just enough to get him to talking, then Zach could take advantage of the opportunity by putting a bullet in his head. If his bold behavior failed to draw out Vermette, Ranger Randal may have to employ a more shocking approach.

Vermette was quickly becoming spooked by the Texas Ranger's strange behavior. The Ranger could not possibly know where he was, although twice already Jack thought he'd caught moments where he'd looked right at him, making brief eye contact. He stood displaying an arrogance that was rapidly creating doubts, and a measure of fear. Vermette instinctively knew that he had to do something to end any overconfidence before it was allowed to drain the self-assurance that he'd managed to instill in himself.

Just as Jack was about to reach a breaking point, he decided to circle around the side of the cabin, below the Ranger's line of sight approaching from the right. He used the side of the cabin to keep his advance on Zach's position stealth, completely hidden away from his target.

Upon reaching his destination, standing just behind and to the right of the Ranger, Jack looked down at the top of his white Stetson that he wore.

Vermette had intentionally allowed himself to be deceived concerning the Ranger's competence, fabricating a lie to degrade and topple Zach from his elevated status, and Jack kept repeating that lie to himself. Instead of allowing the potential of future problems to remain from this old man, he decided that he'd kill him, and be done with it. He would breathe a lot easier with him out of the way. Slicing him from ear to ear, he'd leave him at the cabin door for the other victims to find.

With the skill of a serpent, sliding silently around the corner of the cabin, Vermette crept up behind Zach. Skillfully pulling his knife from the sheath in his boot, he never got the chance to lift it any higher than his knee.

Without warning, Zach Randal let out a yell with a voice that was so thunderous snow seemed to fall from the tree limbs.

"You'd better think long and hard about what you're getting ready to do boy! I'm coming after you! Make no mistake about it! You won't live another day. You want to why?" With slow and deliberate manipulative assuredness, Zach allowed a smile to cross his face. "Because I know where you're hiding."

Upon hearing the booming voice rumble from the Texas Ranger, and for reasons that he would never be able to explain, Jack remembered a story that had given him nightmares when he was a child: It was from the Old Testament.

Thousands of years ago somewhere in the Middle East, the Wrath of God destroyed the ancient cities of Sodom and Gomorra. It was as fire rained down from heaven that Lot's family made their escape. Instructed by angels, that were dispatched by God, not to look upon the cities while the brimstone consumed them, Lot's wife was unable to resist. Ancient texts tell us that she momentarily looked back at the place that was her home. She turned back, taking only a brief glimpse, but immediately turned into a pillar of salt, forever remaining at the spot where she stood.

Whether or not he'd mistaken the voice of the Ranger as an announcement from Almighty God himself or not, badly shaken and fearful of the Wrath to come or destined for the same fate as Lot's wife, Jack could not say. It gladly would turn out not be his main concern anyway. In fact, more than any event in his life, the echoing voice of Randal's perfectly timed bluff had produced a response in Jack that he'd never experienced as a grown man, one that he had no idea how to handle.

While holding the razor sharpened knife in his hand, only two feet behind his target, just seconds away from slicing through his neck cutting clear through the throat and scraping the front of his cervical vertebrae, that booming voice filled the air. Fear gripped his heart so strongly that his chin began quivering, and his vision became blurred from the tears.

Finding he was in a situation changing so rapidly actually stupefied Jack. From a moment filled with anticipation preceding the kill, he'd unexpectedly switched to an uncomfortable, unavoidable, and incapacitating fear, rendering him helpless.

If Ranger Randal would have turned his head only slightly, or at that second glanced sideways from the corner of his eye, he would have caught Jack standing only feet behind him, immobilized, frozen in fear, and vulnerable.

Again, as if by magic, Jack would have divine interventions materialize rescuing him from certain disaster. No one would see or hear as Jack painfully retreated to the corner of the cabin, creeping along the wall to the rear of the small structure.

The shock and fear that damned, old Texas Ranger created by yelling had effectively destroyed Jack's concentration, he was unable to go through with the kill. A golden opportunity had presented itself to Vermette, and just as quickly, it suddenly vanished. The struggle to regain his composure and retreat was as difficult as anything he'd ever done before. The strength he used to overcome each of the horrible feelings that were being experienced had been developed over many years.

It was just as well, for after the old man bellowed out his statement, Jack was afraid the other two men in the cabin may have come running out, alerted to the danger. Regardless of Jack's advantage, if the odds were stacked that heavily against him, he was smart enough to know that he would have never stood a chance.

In the meantime, incredibly offended, Jack made use of the wet snow that was piled high against the back of the cabin. Wiping his face and chest to shock himself from the stupor that had developed, his arrogance, and bravado had unexpectedly begun to crumble. The momentary setback seemed to strip away all of the false pretense that he had perfected within himself.

Had Zach Randal really been aware of him sneaking up? If so, why had he allowed him to escape? He realized that his nerves must be frayed beyond his ability to comprehend. A welcome response were elevated levels of anger growing within him, and he vowed to bleed each of them like hogs butchered for Mardi Gras celebrations at some Cajun village in Louisiana.

Confused, stunned, and exhausted, he could not think of how to gain the advantage over the three men, getting beyond their protective barrier, and most of all to Amy. As he pulled his shirt, jacket, and gloves back on, he saw a strange metal plate near his feet, just below the snow. The odd plate of steel was fitted right into the side wall of the cabin. Because of the whole he'd dug in the snow refreshing himself, it had been exposed.

Intrigued by the roughly finished steel plate, Jack estimated its size two feet by two feet. A hinge on one side resembled a handle; it could only be to open the metal plate like a door. Opening into where or what he did not yet know. Closer inspection revealed what he'd seen before on the backside of fireplaces. A metal plate could be opened on the outside of the chimney to evacuate ash and debris that had accumulated inside. The ash was swept into a small bin beyond a similar one installed inside the back of the fireplace. Later, opening the outside metal plate one could dump the collected ash.

However, the plate that he'd found covering this passageway was larger. It could only be used for one thing. Quickly, Jack decided to peek around the corner of the cabin, checking to see if Zach Randal was still standing like a geriatric billboard, allowing him time to investigate this new discovery.

If it was anything similar to how his luck had been running, it was going to provide him with the break that he needed most, and assist him in carrying out punishments that were long overdue.

Jack had been exposed to many different lifestyles during his career along the Gulf Coast. From the Mexican immigrants living in tin and cardboard shelters to the Cajun trappers who built marsh cabins made of saw grass and Spanish moss, each had distinctive styles and relatively ingenious tricks of various kinds that were utilized in making the raw living conditions easier.

South Louisiana has always been known for extreme heat and humidity. Yet, another side exists to the state's bizarre and extreme weather. Winters across the flat marshlands can be the most brutal in the country. Soaked from the damp climate and frequent storms brewed with the help of the Gulf of Mexico, in addition to blistering and bitter north winds that whistled in with cold fronts unimpeded by the flat terrain, the Cajuns survived by keeping warm, but more importantly, by keeping dry. Loads of wood was burned throughout the winter, and to burn properly the wood had to be kept dry.

Built into the back of the cabin walls were trap doors that usually led to small storage areas within. This room resembled a large box or square cabinet area inside the cabin that was usually against a rear wall. Often the inside frame was used as a bed, placing a blanket or cot on top of the boxed area. Inside the box, which either was accessible from a small side door, or a chute built into the outside wall, was enough dry wood stored for the entire winter. As the wood was used up for the fire, more wet or damp wood replaced it, allowing time for it to dry and be used whenever needed. The clever design also allowed an average-sized man a way to gain entrance into the cabin without much of a problem.

RUSHING to the closed door that Zach was on the other side of, Deke and Bill quickly exited the cabin curious as to why he was yelling. They discovered a calm Zach Randal standing several feet from the entrance, lighting one of the small cigars he forever carried in his shirt pocket. Nothing seemed the matter as the two men bolted outside toward Zach.

Spinning around at the sound of their exit, Zach suddenly realized the reason for their concern, quickly explaining that his outburst was only an attempt to lure Vermette from hiding. Unfortunately, his attempt had failed miserably.

Without realizing how critical one brief and innocent moment could be, Deke and Bill had not hesitated to exit. Worry about the safety of Zach Randal was their first error, creating the opportunity for tragedy.

Totally unaware of how potentially deadly the change in their location might prove, the three men stood together outside of the cabin. Relief overwhelmed them when they found Zach was safe and unharmed. And soon the small talk began, as they attempted to pry into the Ranger's head to find out what he was planning.

Deke and Bill had run from the cabin in such a hurry that neither of them bothered to grab weapons, or even a coat to protect them against the cold. It was no matter, they thought, since they would soon be returning inside. That was, if they ever returned.

Zach was facing Deke and Bill, standing between him and the open cabin door. He hesitated in revealing any possible plan of action, when in fact he had no such plan. It had resulted in producing an elusive tone in his voice.

Frustrated by their lack of direction, in addition to Zach's strange aloofness, Deke and Bill were alarmed to see Zach's eyes open wide with fear. A mortified appearance suddenly came over him in the middle of his attempt to reassure them. Such a bizarre reaction from Zach produced a horrible dread that ran through their bones.

Turning quickly, with a panicked response, facing whatever it was that Zach had spotted, Deke and Bill stood helpless and watched as Jack Vermette, who was standing just inside the cabin, slowly closed the heavy, wooden door. They listened dumbstruck as he latched and bolted it secure from the inside.

CHAPTER

29

FRIGHTENED BEYOND MEASURE, the three men jumped for the closing door all at once. Failing in their desperate attempt to stop the madman certain to murder Amy Dodson who, while sleeping soundly in the upstairs loft, was completely unaware of what had just transpired.

Deke found himself rapidly slipping away from reality as the scene played over and over in his mind. The hideous smile on Jack Vermette's face had sent a clear message while he slowly closed the heavy door. As solid as it was, Jack knew of no way for them to possibly break through before he was able to commit whatever sick deeds he'd fantasized about for so long.

Hauntingly, each replaying of the scene was driving Deke closer to the edge. He began pounding wildly upon the door; at the same time, all of the knowledge that he'd acquired in the field of psychology, running through his mind. Tactics would have to be employed to remain functional.

Denying what he feared might happen to Amy was his only defense. Establishing a root belief that Amy would not be harmed, regardless of how accurate this basis of deception was, allowed him to continue mentally and emotionally, giving him time to devise a strategy to set her free, destroying the threat that had suddenly arisen.

He felt the power behind a pair of enormous hands slowly and gently wrap around his wrists, effectively stopping his outburst of madness. Madness rose from an attempt to do something, anything to prevent Vermette from continuing with this wild spree of senseless carnage. Just what he was trying to accomplish with his frantic behavior, Deke couldn't say, he had no clue.

"This ain't the way Deke. Relax little buddy. We got to think. And we've got to think fast. I need your brain kicking on all cylinders; so, get a hold of yourself, this isn't over yet." Calmly, and with a strange tone of assurance, Zach spoke almost in a whisper. He was right, and Deke quickly restrained his outburst of emotion, grabbing hold to reason while he was still able.

Sheriff Bill Wright had already run around to the other side of the cabin in an attempt to find out where and how Vermette had gained such easy access into the cabin. Within seconds, he was back, carrying his revolver in his hand.

"The son-of-a-bitch found the door to the dry wood cellar, climbed in through it. He must have been sitting in the woodbin just waiting for the opportunity when we wouldn't be ready. I tried to get in, but he must have latched it closed from the inside." He was winded from all the excitement and his quick sprint.

By that time, Zach had also started an inspection of the area. Looking closely at the snow cover around the cabin, bending down on one knee, he was only a few feet to the right of the doorway.

"No! I don't think he's been in that wood cellar very long at all. I think luck just has a way of finding him with every step he takes. And that's one fact that has me more worried than anything right now."

Deke had been staring at the door, quietly like an encyclopedia salesman waiting for someone to answer the doorbell. How could he have forgotten about that damn door to the wood cellar? It had obviously been left unlocked. Who would think of someone entering a four-foot square door? As soon as Zach made the comment, his head snapped up resembling a sleeping dog smelling food.

"Oh my Lord! That's exactly right!" Deke returned to reality with a sudden understanding to many of the questions he'd been asking himself.

"From what you've told me about this Vermette fellow, and the few deductions I've been able to make concerning his state of mind, or more correctly his degree of insanity, it seems a regression in his cognitive status is occurring. It's as if he goes from one stage of development to another, depending on the circumstances surrounding him. The stages are called developmental periods, common only in adolescents and even younger individuals. In addition, there seems to be a lot of magical thinking combined with a savior-like identification on his part. Anything he experiences, which happens to be the result of coincidence or pure luck, will be considered a sign. He may even attribute his good fortune to divine intervention, something that is ordered by God to assist him. It's very possible that Jack Vermette thinks of this as a mission. A mission, through divine appointment, that he has been chosen for." Deke stood staring off into space. His brain was clicking at warp speed trying to profile Vermette.

Sheriff Wright and Zach hadn't moved from where they stood, listening to the bizarre description of this madman. From what they were able to understand, this was more than just a madman, he was a curse sent from hell under the false assumption that what he had been doing, and was about to do, was the will of God Almighty.

"So what exactly does that mean, from a standpoint that's helpful to us?" Sheriff Bill was taking it all in, and had quickly cut through the analysis to what was most important. He was afraid that it was not what they wanted to hear from Deke.

Refocusing his gaze from wherever it had been, Deke looked into the inquisitive eyes of Sheriff Wright.

"What it means to us Bill is that this is the worst of all scenarios, that is, if my conclusions are correct. Vermette is so persuaded by some kind of self deception that regardless of any facts revealed to the contrary there is no way he will think otherwise, his mind has been made up. He is also under the impression that he cannot fail, and that is where the real danger lies because it means he cannot be reasoned with. It's likely that he also believes that he's invincible, cannot be killed, or harmed in any way. He's being provided with divine protection from God. The reasons behind the horrible killings probably have something to do with what he perceives were sins committed. His motivation, for those who think it's crucial to establish the fact that Vermette is motivated by something, is punishing Amy for sins, or the sin she's guilty of."

Having such an incredible revelation come to him at this particular time was disturbing. Deke felt that if he would have had such knowledge beforehand he would have had a chance at derailing much of what happened. Even if he couldn't have prevented the deaths of Bill Frye and Dan Baker, he could have at least prevented what he was facing now.

Zach had been listening quietly, pondering on what Deke had just said. His mind was hard at work. This was it, do or die, sink or swim, kill or be killed. He could remember other times in his life when all he did was live for such an opportunity. It was in fact, what he had been living for since losing Kate. When the odds were against him, and the danger to his life was greatest was when he felt most alive. This time it was different. Zach had been fighting since this investigation had begun to prevent this very thing from occurring. Reflecting on all that had happened within the past few days he could not help but ask himself,

"Had he really been fighting to prevent this, or subconsciously had he fought to create it?"

Whatever the answer, he had to make sure that Deke didn't start blaming himself for what had happened. He needed that boy to provide him with every possible twist and turn of deranged thoughts within the head of that man inside the cabin. Amy's life would be totally dependent on how brilliant an idea they could come up with, and on how quickly they were able to come up with it.

"I hear what you're saying Deke, but I also know what you're thinking and haven't said." Sheriff Bill holstered his pistol, and walked over to Deke. Zach joined them at the doorway to the cabin.

His responsibility was to get everyone on the same track. He knew that if any one of them started ripping himself apart, thinking they should have done this or that, it would only result in dragging them down. A combined effort of knowledge, wisdom, and gut instinct from each of them was going to be the key to getting Amy away from Vermette. He knew that a chance still existed to save her, their last chance.

"Okay, I'm only going to say this once; so, you two listen closely. What we got here is a very damn big problem, but make no mistake we also have one last opportunity to solve it, and get Amy out. Deke, I know that brain of yours is heating up; so, don't jam up your sprockets by letting guilt throw a wrench in the works." An immediate look of guilt materialized on Deke's face, and Zach knew he had hit the nail on the head, and just in time.

Bill looked at Zach, amazed. He too saw the look on Deke's face, and wondered how this Texas Ranger had managed to get so damn smart over the years.

"Don't ask me why, but I don't think Jack Vermette is going to harm Amy just yet. He hasn't come all this way, and gone through all the trouble he's encountered just to have it end so quickly. I believe he wants to savor this for as long as he can, and that means keeping her alive for as long as possible. He may even want to kill us first, making her watch, to spice up the works. So we still have time, but we're going to have to utilize every little piece of experience and expertise we have between us to figure a way out of this mess." As Zach spoke, a calm settled over them. Whether or not he believed what he was saying it made sense to Deke and Bill.

At the point when they had to helplessly watch Vermette slowly close that door, smiling with evil intent, everything had seemed lost. Bill and Deke thought the worse. It was over. They had screwed up, with no way to fix it. Yet, the thought processes within Zach Randal's head had not allowed him to dare think failure. Negativism was the catalyst for defeat, and Zach had learned many years ago that he had to stay as far away from those thoughts as possible. Instead, his mind had been focused on the simple fact that he now knew exactly where Vermette was, and all he had to do was devise an ingenious plan to get him within striking distance. It was plain and simple, the enemy's location had been identified, the life he had committed to save was in jeopardy, and he had one final chance to remedy the situation.

"Deke, here's what I think we ought to do first." Zach didn't have the slightest idea of what to do yet, but knew they had to start somewhere, or go crazy not doing anything.

"You and Bill run over to the shed and let the Beatles loose. I still don't know how he managed to lock them up without killing them, or being killed, and I truly hope they're okay. I'll stay here and try to taunt Mr. Vermette into a challenge. If for some reason I'm not here when the two of you get back, set those dogs loose with the command to find Miss Amy. Maybe the fact that they're out here sniffing around will intimidate him enough to make a mistake." The plan wasn't anything close to brilliance, but at least it was something.

REMARKABLY reminiscent of the time he'd spent with Vanessa Jansen, Jack Vermette stood by the huge bed in the loft watching Amy as she slept. Looking at her this way had a strange effect on him. Memories of the happy times they'd spent together came flooding back. As deeply as she had hurt him, with all the hate he was harboring, a spark of adoration for her still remained. She was beautiful, and had been everything he'd looked for in a woman, but she had turned out to be evil. Choosing to dishonor him through deception, destroying his seed, which grew within her? The child was an heir for his family, and from his very own blood, the only one to carry his genetic makeup into the future. For all time, as long as that child produced offspring, and that offspring produced in turn, and so on, his genetic fingerprint would have survived. Yet, because of the rebellious actions of the woman he'd chosen to begin this lineage, everything was lost.

Jack was going to make her suffer for committing so grievous a sin. A sin that was not committed against God alone, but against his child, and above all, against him. However, before sentencing would be carried out he had a few questions that he wanted answers to.

Very slowly and with great effort Amy began to stir. She was still very weak, having not yet made a complete recovery from her close encounter with death. As she turned her head and slowly opened her eyes, she looked to the foot of the bed and saw Jack, gazing down at her.

Initially her response was one of fear and unbelief. She quickly reasoned that the vision must be a nightmare, and that she was still asleep. Unfortunately, her head continued to clear and as soon as the fog diminished, she realized that it was no nightmare. An evil and deviant smile was smeared across Jack's face as he wickedly took on a wolfish appearance.

Amy was groggy and weak, but she was alert enough to come to the conclusion that what she had secretly feared all along had now come to pass. As hard as it was to reject all thought of the possibility that Jack had killed everyone before waking her, she stuck to her intuitive belief that everyone was alive and well. He had somehow tricked his way into the cabin, and the others may not even be aware of what had happened. Confusion flooded her mind but one thing was clear to her; if she were to survive, she would have to act wisely.

MONTHS earlier, Ranger Zach Randal had made a valiant effort to discover what Amy was hiding from him. In his questioning of her, he was quick to recognize the fact that she was keeping something a secret.

He implored her to reveal whatever it was she was holding back, explaining that it could be the key to whoever was behind the terrorization. Amy denied having any such secret, ashamed to tell him of the abortion. The more Zach pressed her the greater her resistance became. Finally, Amy had reached a point where she became so resistant that she'd decided the secret would remain hidden within her until the day she died.

Through it all Amy continued to reason with herself, saying that it could not have anything to do with the abortion, since the father of the child was dead. The report that Jack Vermette had been killed in a diving accident offshore ended any possibility of his involvement. Since he was not involved in any way, nothing could be gained by revealing her deepest secret. Since nothing could be gained, she had no obligation to reveal it.

Finally, Zach relented and accepted the fact she could contribute nothing more. As the investigation continued, Deke Stone was brought aboard. It was at that time she began to wonder. Had Jack really died in that accident? Was he behind all of what was happening? After all, she had mailed him a letter telling him of her plans, ending their relationship. Determined, Amy had convinced herself that he had never received the letter. He was dead long before it could have reached him, or was he?

Deke had also been quick to recognize the fact that she was hiding something, but his approach had been more humane. However, realizing nothing she had to say would change what was happening, and since it was such a private part of her, he believed he had no right to extract the information like a tooth without the use of an anesthetic.

Amy was touched by his sensitivity. Little did he know, she had nearly decided to reveal everything to him. The pain and remorse associated with the decision she'd made to have an abortion, was driving her to seek comfort from someone.

Since first meeting Deke, that horrible day her employees were murdered, her feelings for him had intensified. He was the kind of man she'd been looking for when she first met Jack. Sadly, Jack turned out to be insecure and insanely jealous. However, Deke revealed a compassionate, caring, and mature side to himself that she had always suspected men to possess. His greatest asset was the fact that he did not care if he appeared kind and gentle, he was uninhibited by what ruled the actions of most men. It was just when she'd decided to confide in him that Deke announced his opinion about the interrogation tactics employed on her, and how cruel they were. Instead of being a disappointment, his declaration only made her love him more.

EMERGING from the deep sleep that she'd become captive to for the last ten hours, Amy quickly realized that in order to save her life she would have to devise an immediate plan.

Apparently, Jack had not been killed in that accident. Oddly, she was not shocked at this discovery. It became clear to her that Jack had been behind all of the carnage and death from the very beginning. Instead of showing him how dreadfully afraid she truly was, Amy decided to play on his sympathy.

She would begin a game of manipulation, certain that the chore was going to be difficult. Playing a game that she knew Jack had mastered long ago was going to be very dangerous to say the least. She knew of only two people in the world better at manipulation than she was. One of those people was Zach Randal. Of course, his manipulation was always used for obtaining whatever information he needed to solve a crime. The other person that she knew to be a master of manipulation was Jack, who always used his skill for selfish and evil reasons.

"Oh my God! Is it really you Jack? Thank God you're here!" she blurted out. Before he could respond, she pretended to look around the room suspiciously. "Are the others gone?" she questioned him. It was difficult to hide the shock of finding him standing at the foot of the bed. His response was what she'd hoped. Taken aback by her sincerity, appearing to be happy to see him, had effectively thrown him for a loop.

"Yeah, It's me." He tried to answer her in as mocking a tone as possible, but she clearly detected surprise and confusion in his voice. Amy was not going to allow him time to think, it would be a fatal mistake not to try and overwhelm him.

"But the others, are the others gone?" She looked around frantically with fear in her eyes, giving him the impression that she was very uneasy.

The response that her behavior produced in him encouraged her. This was puzzling him, his attitude was changing, and he appeared to act as if he were being protective.

"Yeah, they're gone. Don't worry about them right now," he said, somewhat confounded.

"Are you all right? Where have you been?" Amy put on a show of bewilderment. She saddened her eyes, and strained out a few tears. Jack became powerless whenever she put on the scared, little girl act. Amy was praying that it worked just one more time.

"I'm so scared Jack. They've had me prisoner in this cabin for days. I tried to escape yesterday and became lost and almost died. Now that you've come to help me, maybe I can get away. I don't understand what's been happening." She decided to pour it on as thick as she could. This was going to be her only chance; so, she may as well push it to the extreme.

Amy knew quite well that in every man lies a secret fantasy of rescuing the damsel in distress, becoming the shining knight on his white horse. It was just as strong a desire in Jack. If she could make him believe she had been captured, and that she had not been running in fear of him, she may be able to confuse him long enough to get free and away.

The look on Jack's face was revealing a break in his concentration, but a hint of suspicion was still obvious to Amy. Knowing that she had to hit him with everything, and hit him where he was most vulnerable, she decided modesty would have to be a thing of the past. This was her life she was in danger of losing.

Still wrapped in only the heavy blanket that was on the bed, her clothes in front of the fireplace where they continued to dry, Amy rose up kneeling before him. The blanket fell loosely around her hips, and completely exposed her nakedness.

"Please help me Jack. Tell me that you'll help me to get out of here." Pleading before him, naked and vulnerable, Amy reached out wrapping her arms around his neck.

ZACH walked slowly around the cabin, straining desperately to hear anything that might be going on inside. He heard no screaming, no loud arguments, no cries of despair, nothing that he could attribute to being from a struggle or an attack. It was puzzling. What was going on? He decided to remain quiet and make no attempt to taunt Vermette. From what it was that Zach was not hearing inside the cabin, it might work against him if he inflamed the man's anger at this time.

From the little bit of information he'd been told about Vermette, Zach felt certain the man was a walking time bomb. But then again, probably much more about the man was unknown than what he'd been able to find out. If anyone knew him, it was Amy. Because of that one fact he started thinking that maybe the reason he wasn't hearing anything from inside was because Amy had taken control of the situation, at least temporarily. A smile found its way onto the big, man's face as he became more and more convinced of what he suspected.

Deke and Bill Wright had made it to the small shed out back. Sure enough, they found the Beatles snuggled up against each other, inside and unharmed.

344

"That son-of-a-bitch is smart," Deke commented, observing the opening that had been busted out of the roof.

Bill looked up at the spot where Jack had apparently made his escape. "Yes he is a crafty fellow. How we're going to get him out from that cabin while Miss Amy is still alive, I just don't know. You built the place like a damn fortress. I'm sorry to say Deke that I don't think we have a chance in hell of getting inside."

Deke stopped dead in his tracks, looking thoughtfully at the man that he had quickly come to respect. Risking everything, Sheriff Bill Wright had accompanied Zach the entire way, and had even lost some of his best deputies in the process.

"What? What are you thinking?" Bill saw that familiar look of an idea as it flashed through Deke's head.

"You're exactly right Bill. Ain't no way for us to get inside that cabin. Any attempt would only exacerbate the situation, creating a heightening in Vermette's anger." Deke had started pacing around inside the small shed, partly from his intense concentration, and partly to help work off the chill that he felt enveloping him.

The effect of the cold would soon get the better of them, especially since they had not grabbed coats when running out of the cabin. He closed the flimsy wooden door while he and Bill were still inside, and before the Beatles had a chance to get out.

"All Vermette has to do is delay whatever his plans are for a couple of hours and we'll be nearly incapacitated from this weather. He's got to have figured that out by now. We can't break in, and I'm sure he knows that too. But hopefully, someone else also realizes ain't no way for us to get inside." Thinking aloud about the situation had Bill beside himself with curiosity.

"What? Tell me what's going on in that damn topknot of yours. Who else would know about our situation, but Randal?" Exasperation filled Sheriff Bill's voice.

Deke stopped pacing. "Amy! She's got to realize that she's on her own by now. She'll see right off that the Beatles are not inside, then it will hit her that we're missing also, and she'll come to the realization that the only person who can stall Vermette, or get him confused, is her."

Sheriff Bill Wright looked at him, cocking his head to the side as if undecided whether to believe this lame-brained conclusion or not.

"You're telling me this is our idea? This is the brilliant plan we're gonna come up with to save that poor girl, and get Vermette?" His questions were saturated with sarcasm and doubt, unwilling to accept what Deke was trying to convince him.

"Exactly!" Deke replied. He sounded like the Sherlock Holmes character created by Sir Arthur Conan Doyle, the infamous detective who worked for Scotland Yard, and had lived at 221 Baker St. With an air of confidence, he often responded to his sidekick Dr. Watson, "Elementary, my dear Watson. Elementary."

Hurriedly they exited the small shed, leaving the Beatles locked inside, heading back for the cabin where Zach was waiting.

CONFLICT was rapidly rising within Jack's mind. Amy was suddenly at his feet, naked and begging. What she was begging him for had nothing to do with how he would decide to respond. It was the fact that she had now chosen to put herself subservient to him that was tremendously pleasing. All he'd ever wanted was for this beautiful creature to be his most prized possession. But...she had deceived him!

"What is this shit? Do you think after what you did to me I should rescue you?" Jack suddenly snapped out of the dream state where Amy had so effectively lulled him.

She never took her arms from around him; instead, she slowly lowered herself, tightening her drip around his waist, placing the side of her head against his stomach.

"Jack darling, what are you talking about? I never stopped loving you. The day I was told of your accident the world stopped spinning. It was as if I had fallen into a deep and dark area of space. For months I couldn't eat or sleep, I actually thought that I would have to seek professional treatment." Her acting was superb. She raised her face looking up at him. With her actions portraying total submission, she continued, "How can you say those things to me? I'm so afraid they might come back and...and...they took my clothes from me Jack." Again, she had him, and she watched the effects of what she'd just said.

Jack's face became beet red, and veins distended out from his neck. From past experience she knew that his anger was kindled, and that his possessiveness and jealousy were taking control of his thoughts and emotions. As long as Amy could keep him filled with the crazy anger that accompanied the green-eyed demon of jealousy, she had a chance.

Jack looked around the cabin, thinking of what to do. Then he remembered the questions that he wanted answered.

"Why did you write me that letter?" His question rocked Amy so badly that she nearly lost control. She had been sure that he'd never received the letter, but he had. Quickly she realized he was going to question her about the abortion. She had mistakenly written about it in the letter. Now she was certain that this was all about her rejection of him and ridding herself of his child. While dating he often spoken about when they would have children. Finding out about her intentions to abort the pregnancy must have driven him over the edge.

"What letter are you talking about?" She continued to look up at him with pleading eyes.

"Don't mess with me Amy! You know very well what letter." His anger was intensifying. She saw that trying to deny things would only made them worse; an alternate approach would have to be used.

He already knew of the abortion, and that was most probably the thing that had caused him to snap. To try hiding it, or to deny the fact that she'd had an abortion would expose her as being guilty, trying to deceive him. Amy knew she would have to think of a way to admit to the abortion. All at once, she burst into tears.

"They made me write that letter to you Jack. They said they would take the cafe from me if I didn't do exactly as they said. I did what they said, but secretly had planned to contact you for help. That was when I received the news about the accident. I just knew they had to be the people responsible." With forced emotion and an extra burst of tears, she plunged ahead, "They...they...took away our child. I was forced to have an abortion!" By this time, she was wailing loudly, sobbing into his shirt.

Her performance was convincing. The revelation was so incredibly different from what he'd believed for so long. She felt as his body began shaking. Almost uncontrollably, the shaking surprised her, but she continued sobbing into the front of his shirt. Finally, as he regained control of himself, he looked into her eyes.

"Who did this to you Amy? I swear I'll kill the son-of-a-bitches! Just who are these people?" His voice had changed. No longer was the suspicion apparent, he bought the entire story. Like a catfish taking hook, line, and sinker, Jack swallowed it whole. For the first time since waking up she began to think she may live.

"Tell me who did this to us." When Amy heard him use the word us, she knew it was time to begin with the next phase of her plan. Her only problem was that she had no second phase to her plan, and for a moment began to wonder if her optimism had been premature. She might not live after all.

CHAPTER

30

ARRIVING BACK AT the cabin, Deke and Bill saw no sign of Zach. Just as Bill was about to yell out for him, Deke raised his hand in protest.

"We don't want Vermette to hear. It's best that he thinks we've left. Don't ask me why, but we have to make him think we're not as interested in saving Amy as it appears." Hearing what was said, Bill Wright wrinkled his brow in confusion. He was not certain that he agreed with this new strategy, but it wasn't his show. He'd have to trust in Deke's instincts for the time being, at least until he found Zach and filled him in on everything. For all he knew, the boy might be losing it, coming apart, and they'd have to tie him up in the shed just to get anything accomplished.

The two of them started walking around the right side of the cabin, running into Zach Randal. He was standing against a wall, directly under one of the high, narrow windows. As they walked up to his position, he held a finger in front of his pursed lips indicating for them to be quiet. Sneaking up to him slowly, Bill was the first at his side.

"What in hell's fire are you doing?" The behavior he was witnessing was odd to say the least, and for a moment, he thought this was a new type of surveillance with some wild technique to gauge negotiations.

"What's it look like I'm doing, playing tennis? I'm trying to listen to what's going on inside; so, keep it down for a minute." Zach was aggravated by the interruption, and in short order had placed them on notice not to say another word until he Okayed it.

Deke leaned back against the side of the cabin next to Zach, a satisfied smirk on his face. Bill Wright was beginning to feel like a rookie cop. Instead of becoming offended, Bill leaned up against the wall next to Deke, making an attempt to see if he could hear anything also.

After a few minutes of standing and observing Zach Randal, who seemed to be hearing something on the other side of that thick, log-constructed wall, both Deke and Bill heard what sounded like far away, muffled sounds.

Sure enough, when they'd stood long enough, quietly listening, locking out all other sounds, they were able to distinguish voices.

Apparently, Jack and Amy were having some type of discussion, and it sounded as though they were being very civil in doing so.

"What the hell is going on Amy?" Zach asked the question in a whisper, intrigued by what he was hearing. It was apparent that she was up to something, but exactly what was anybody's guess.

Shifting his gaze from the upper window to Deke, Zach whispered, "Well, you've been spending a lot of quality time with her lately, what do you think she's up to?" Zach wanted a confirmation to what he suspected, but didn't want to reveal what that was until he had strong corroboration from someone, preferably Deke. Too much was riding on this, and if they were supposed to bow out letting Amy assume control of the situation, he didn't want to be the single person responsible for making the decision for their inaction.

Deke didn't have to be asked twice. He was waiting for the opportunity to run his theory by Zach anyway.

"It might sound crazy Zach, but I think Amy figured it out real quick that she was on her own. No Beatles, and no us when she woke up. The one person alive who knows what Jack Vermette is made of is inside with him, and from the bits and pieces I'm hearing through the wall it sounds like she has the upper hand for the time being." Deke confirmed exactly what Zach had assumed. Even though he didn't want her having to compromise herself, and be put in the position of having to manipulate Vermette, Zach was damn proud of her.

"You really think she might be able to pull this off, and stay alive?" The big Texas Ranger was raking himself over the coals emotionally for allowing this to happen, and Deke recognized his fatherly tone immediately.

"Zach, if anyone has a God given gift to effectively manipulate a person…Yes, Amy can do this, and she will." His affirmation of what he believed and the confidence that he stressed in making the statement, was somewhat exaggerated.

Deke wasn't sure of what she had to deal with, but he had some idea about the degree of difficulty. As long as she didn't break and was able to keep her story rolling with some consistency, she had a chance. Still, Deke began to pray silently as the three of them stood in the snow below the window, concentrating to hear whatever snippets of information they could. They all knew a time would arrive when they would have to make a move. Each of them wanted to be dead certain about that exact moment, if it arrived at all, taking full advantage of whatever Amy was busy setting up.

STRUGGLING every foot of the way, Sergeant John Hadley finally reached the top of the steep cliff. His hands were blue, raw, and bleeding. It didn't bother him much since they were also completely numb. Face down in the snow at the top of the deep gorge where Sheriff Bill Wright's deputy had fallen, and where Deke was nearly killed trying to find out the deputy's identity, John Hadley thanked God for allowing him to survive.

After stumbling in the dark and tripping, headfirst into oblivion the night before, he found himself stranded on a small outcropping of rock and snow. Only a few shrubs and bushes surrounded him. He'd fallen nearly fifty feet, but was not injured, only knocked unconscious. As daylight arrived, he began looking out over the precipice from where he'd landed. That was when he got sick.

He was at least fifteen hundred feet above a rocky flat that stretched out forever below him. Laying his head back where he'd landed, John rested for a few more minutes, waiting for the light of day to completely arrive, then maybe he'd be able to see where he was going. It had been the darkness that tricked him into making that near fatal step, and he was not going to make that mistake again.

Five solid hours of climbing and traversing sideways across the mountain had led him to the gorge. Quite unexpectedly, he found that he'd walked right up on a pair of legs sticking out of the snow. Hideous looking, the boots on the feet were right at eye level. When John realized what they were, it sent shivers through him. Without even bothering to inspect the body, he continued walking until reaching the face of the cliff, then he began climbing.

Now, at the top of the deep gash that scarred the mountainside, he decided again to rest for a while. He could be of no good to anyone dead, and even if alive he'd be more of a hindrance and a burden, especially if he couldn't walk; so, he'd rest a few minutes before continuing. Zach might be in trouble and need his help. John Hadley would not be able to live with himself if he let those people down.

OBVIOUSLY distraught at hearing the words that were spoken by Amy, Jack appeared completely befuddled. Relaxing from the stiffness in his posture that he'd shown standing at the foot of the bed, he suddenly reached out, placing one of his huge hands on the back of Amy's head. His sudden change of behavior worried her, but she knew it was just the break she'd been hoping. When he slowly began stroking her hair in an effort to console her, she knew it would soon be time to make her move.

With tears still running down her cheeks, Amy continued her sobbing act. Since she'd been taken completely by surprise, unprepared for any kind of confrontation such as this, she decided to wait on Jack. Whatever his response was to her declarations of innocence, being forced into writing him the letter, and even forced into the abortion, determined the direction she'd have to take next. What happened next not only surprised her, but also created a sense of guilt within her.

With more gentleness in his touch than she'd ever experienced, he slowly pushed her away. Holding him tightly around the waist, she felt his huge hands reach down, removing her arms from him. If his demeanor had not been so courteous, Amy would have been terrified, expecting him to harm her. Instead, he pulled at the heavy blanket that had fallen around her hips, and covered her nakedness.

"Put this back around you Amy. You'll catch a chill in this cabin." As shocking as this show of concern for her seemed, she reminded herself that the same man had horribly butchered three of her employees. The terrible acts of violence that so many people had become victims to were all because of his demented and warped emotions. He may be treating her with compassion now, but if the wrong buttons happened to be punched by Amy, Jack could explode, changing in a matter of seconds, mercilessly mistreating her in ways that only she had experienced, but had never divulged to anyone.

Amy obeyed his suggestion, her head still bowed in submission. Tears ceased flowing, but she decided to keep the act going with a lot of sniffling. It wasn't difficult since her crying had created a runny nose that wouldn't stop.

Jack stood back from the bed and began pacing, occasionally looking in her direction. He was entirely sidetracked and deeply disturbed about this development. Finally, after a few minutes he stopped. Placing his arms across his chest, he tried to stiffen his posture and appear wary of what she'd just confessed. It was clear he'd come to a conclusion.

"Am I supposed to believe you? Is that your story? Is this the truth?" Jack questioned her.

Amy's mind was so overloaded by all that was happening that she was nearly a basket case from suppressing the fear. However, because he'd decided to question her once again, despite her convincing performance, she spontaneously threw what's referred to as, a bitching fit. With an outburst that stunned even her, Amy lashed out at Jack.

"Is it the truth?" Appalled by his doubt she repeated his question. It was obviously insulting, and from her tone of voice, Jack regretted ever having asked the question.

"After everything I've been through, and all that has happened to me in the last few months, even after having to experience the awful and shameful feelings that the abortion created, you stand here with that pompous and arrogant attitude having the audacity to ask me if what I said was the truth? Jack, do you actually think I enjoyed what happened? You think I planned such pain and discomfort for myself because I was bored? You have just hurt me more than you can know, I was a fool believing that you had come to help me, believing that you still loved me!"

Amy again began to cry, but this time her tears were from pain that she really had experienced following the abortion. Her declaration about the shameful feelings that accompanied the act was the truest thing ever uttered in her life.

Jack's arrogant posture crumbled as he felt the sting that her words inflicted. As he watched Amy break down, moaning sorrowfully from the pain, he realized she could not possibly be faking such a deep and painful grief.

All of a sudden, moving so quickly Amy instinctively raised her hands attempting to protect herself, Jack threw his arms around her, embracing her apologetically.

"All right! I believe you. Tell me who made you do those things. I must know who and why they tried to destroy us." Rocking her gently, holding her tightly with those huge and powerful arms, Jack made it clear that he wanted the names.

Amy fought to pull herself out of the black pit of depression the memory of the abortion brought back. Who indeed could she attach this blame to without endangering their lives also?

353

IMPATIENTLY, Deke, Zach, and Bill Wright, remained standing in the snow against the wall of the cabin. Intermittently, a conversation of some kind could be heard through the logs of the cabin. Jack's voice remained restrained for the most part. Whenever he spoke, they could only distinguish a few deep, muffled words. However, it was clear when Amy was speaking, the tone of her voice made hair stand up on the back of Deke's neck.

Upon hearing the heated voice of Amy, Bill Wright turned to look at Zach. His eyes were wide with amazement as he whispered, "She's a little hellcat ain't she?"

Ranger Zach Randal remained silent; his expression did not change while listening to the few fragments of the exchange going on inside. The intense concentration within him was obvious, as well as his determination to decipher Amy's intentions. His confidence slowly dwindled away as he realized how improbable their chances were of anticipating the exact time when she would lure Jack Vermette into a vulnerable state.

MEMORIES came flooding back through his mind. What had been a nightmare for so long had slowly undergone a metamorphosis. Now it was only a bad habit. He no longer found himself being haunted about his chance to save a young woman's life, and how he'd misjudged it so badly. She had drowned only minutes before he and that state investigator barged into the room. The killer was apprehended, but his chance had been foolishly squandered. Minutes passed while he waited on that investigator, and all the while the girl was slowly drowning.

After Kate's death, Zach started reading the Bible. Finding solace in little else that existed on Earth, he'd decided to give it a try. He found that he especially enjoyed reading the books of the New Testament written by Paul the Apostle.

In Zach's opinion, Paul must have been a very courageous man, and he admired the style of such a man. Paul attained such a high status within the Christian movement that he actually feared "exalting himself beyond measure." What he meant was he feared thinking of himself as better than other men were.

In his second letter to the Corinthians, to prevent himself from being "exalted above measure" Paul revealed that he was given a "thorn in the flesh." A messenger of Satan was sent to buffet him lest he become exalted. What the thorn actually was no one knows for certain, but it kept him humble.

For the sake of his own survival, Zach was forced into accepting the awful blunder as his "thorn in the flesh." It would forever keep him humble, reminding him to follow his instincts regardless of anyone's opinion. No other women would die on any investigation he was in charge of, especially as a result of someone else's opinions. His "thorn in the flesh" had become his ally.

FEVERISHLY racking her brain to come up with someone that she could blame for the fabricated lies in her story, Amy kept drawing a blank. She knew of no such individual evil enough, whether in reality or in her imagination.

Jack continued to console her, but his efforts were not quite as intense as when he'd started. Without a moment's hesitation, he again asked the one question that would prove one way or the other if she were telling the truth, "Who are the people responsible?"

All Amy could think of was stall...stall...stall.

"Jack, please don't make me talk about it now. Let's just get out of here." Pretending the memory was too painful, Amy tried to sidestep identifying anyone. She was not sure where Deke and the others, or even the Beatles were, but she knew they weren't inside; so, they must be somewhere outside. She would focus on nothing but getting through that door where someone could help her to escape.

Jack had not yet responded to her plea. He was reading her, wanting to see if what she'd claimed was truly preventing her from revealing names of individuals. She had already chewed him out for questioning her honesty, and he didn't want to go there again, but for reasons that he was unable to figure out something was wrong with the entire story. Jack was thinking. If Amy had managed to fabricate such a stunning account in such a short time, she was either much smarter than he'd ever imagined, or he'd been successful in driving her out of her pretty little head.

"As soon as I find out the people responsible we're getting out of here. But, I need that information first Amy. Now, you get your clothes and get dressed. And while you're getting dressed, you need to begin to think about giving me some names. Unless of course, you don't know who they are, but I don't think that's the case." Jack was patient, giving her time to come up with a guilty party. But Amy could not think of anyone. Rising from the bed, she stumbled, nearly falling down the stairs. She'd not realized how weak she still was from her ordeal, lost in the blizzard.

"Whoa! Careful darling, I would hate to lose you now," he stated, catching her before she fell.

All of a sudden, Jack's expression changed. With a look of puzzlement he asked, "It's not because you're trying to protect someone, is it?" It was a damn good question, and she nearly jumped at the opportunity, before realizing it would spell disaster faster than anything would.

"No, Jack! I would never consider protecting any animal capable of inflicting this much pain and fear on anyone." Her response was stated with sadness. She was speaking the truth, although he'd never know that the animal she referred to was him. Amy was determined; if it were possible to get him within Zachary Randal's reach, she would do it. She knew one fact very well, if Zachary Wyatt Randal got within his reach Jack would be stone dead before he had the time to blink.

Stalling was her only alternative. Maybe stalling long enough would provide her with an answer to his persistent questioning. Just as the thought passed through her head, Jack delivered.

"It's not the same people who tried to take the cafe away after you're mother died?" It was perfect. How Jack had remembered that incident was beyond her. Back before they'd begun dating she'd told him about what happened. It was during one of those weekend workshops in El Paso for small business owners.

Amy hadn't even thought about the Chamber of Commerce members who attempted to railroad right through her. Powerful people were forever trying to intimidate those who were at a disadvantage.

She had not yet finished high school when her mother died suddenly. The County Chamber of Commerce tried to deny issuing Amy a license to operate. Reasons given were highly questionable.

They said that she was underage, and since the previous owner, her mother, was deceased, the cafe had to be sold at public auctioned. The sheriff department would be in charge of the auction. It must have been someone in the sheriff department, aware of such an injustice occurring, who contacted an attorney that chose to remain anonymous. The attorney petitioned the Chamber of Commerce, and their decision. Before the matter could ever be brought to court, Amy had another birthday. Reaching the age of eighteen effectively rendered the entire issue moot. She'd reached the legal age. Soon afterward, Amy was issued the proper documents and Dodson's Breakfast and Bar-B-Que Cafe was off and running. "Jack you can't fight them all alone. I've gone over it in my head again and again. If we accuse them of anything, it will be our word against their word. I'm not even sure that I can prove anything. It will start the nightmare again, and I'll have to live through that horrible event all over." Her answer did not confirm that the Chamber of Commerce members were guilty, but then again, it was lacking anything that denied their involvement.

Jack's response was explosive. She had no idea he'd become so angry when she started her monologue about why she didn't want to pursue the issue, but he was wild, unbalanced with rage. She decided only one thing remained that she could do at this point, even if his reaction was violent.

"Jack please, why don't we just leave it alone. We can start again, without having to go through any of that fight. Let's get out of here while we still can." She was not far off with her prediction. The intensity of his anger could not have increased, but his resolve for revenge did.

"Leave it alone! You want me to allow the people who ruined my life to go free, unpunished!" His anger had elevated to a level making him totally unpredictable. Amy was afraid, but saw it as an opportunity to keep him preoccupied, without the chance of him become leery to anything she said.

All of her clothes were dry, and she'd finished dressing. They had descended the stairs together, but as she went over to the fireplace to dress, Jack stayed at the foot of the stairway. The rage that surged through him was so powerful that he'd stayed rooted at that very spot the entire time she dressed. She had to walk over to him and physically try to pull him away from the spot.

"Come on Jack, let's go while we can." Amy began to get worried; she was so close to escaping, or at least close to getting outside of the cabin. If she was relying on Zach to help her, she had to get Jack outside, where she knew Zach was waiting.

"Come on Jack! If the others come back we may never get a chance to leave here." The moment she mentioned the others, Jack snapped out of his narcosis. Blinking rapidly, he allowed Amy to pull him to the door of the cabin. Once she had him moving in that direction she refused to be slowed. Sliding the huge metal bolt, unlocking the door, she pulled with all her might. Jack was nearly catatonic, refusing to help Amy with the door, standing directly behind watching as she struggled.

It refused to budge, stuck tight, probably frozen by the snow and ice that accumulated in the outside frame.

MONITORING every sound detected coming from inside the cabin, Deke, Zach, and Sheriff Wright were aware of something very heavy happening. They'd moved from their previous position, Zach approaching the door from the right with Deke and Bill approaching from the left. They would ambush Jack if he came out, refusing to allow Amy to be held hostage.

SOMEHOW, Sergeant John Hadley had forced himself to lug through the deep snow, reaching what looked like a tool shed, it resembled an old-fashioned, double-seater outhouse. His eyesight had gotten worse with time from freezing temperatures and severe winds, and he thought it strange that this building would be out in the middle of nowhere. Squinting to refocus, he looked just beyond the tree line ahead for any sign of life. He would have to continue farther, and began his approach toward the old wooden shed.

He hadn't walked very far when, curiously from somewhere ahead, he heard whimpering sounds. Puzzled by this development he stopped, but as he did the sounds did also. "Funny!" he thought. If he hadn't known better, he'd have thought the whimpering noises sounded like dogs.

"Dogs!" he yelled.

With renewed vigor, John Hadley trudged through the snow, heading for the small shed. Little did he know, because his eyesight had been too affected to see very well, Deke's cabin was less than one hundred yards from his position.

SCRAPING against the ice that had built up around the door's frame, Amy was overjoyed to feel the heavy door slowly opening.

"Come on Jack, we have to get moving." She would not relent in her determination to get him outside and in the open.

As Amy cleared the threshold, pulling on Jack's hand behind her, something caused him to snap alert. Jerking his hand away from her, he stood inside the doorway looking around with uncertainty.

"Come back here damn you," he growled. Amy had begun to climb the wall of snow that lined the sides of the walkway at the front entrance. She'd nearly made it, but had not gotten far enough away when Jack reached out, grabbing her by the seat of her pants. Violently, he pulled her back toward him.

Zach watched alarmed, holding his breath at Amy's near escape. They had not been ready for such a rapid exit from her, and before anyone could assist her in getting away, Jack had a tight hold on her. With one arm around her neck she was helpless and not going anywhere.

From where he was hiding, just to the left of the doorway, Deke saw her failed attempt. He yelled unintentionally, jumping onto the pathway between the deep piles of snow, protesting as Jack jerked her off the snow bank and roughly into the crook of his arm.

The sudden shock of hearing the voice of a man yelling sent Jack backing up, trying to get inside the cabin. But Deke had beaten him to the entrance, stopping his retreat. Within a split second, Jack had pulled a large knife from the sheath in his boot, pressing the blade against Amy's throat before anyone could get a clear shot off.

"Let her go Jack!" The voice of Ranger Zach Randal pierced the frozen air as he walked out from the right side. He was holding his .357 Magnum in both hands, pointing it straight at Jack's forehead.

"Let her go! Ha! Are you getting senile in your old age, you damned Ranger?" Everything that Amy had worked to accomplish was gone in that one second. She had gotten so close, but at the last possible moment, Jack regained his purpose, overflowing with madness.

"I ain't letting her go until I've watched the last drop of your blood soak into the snow." His features had changed; he was an animal, challenging everyone that got in his way.

"So is this the little going away party that you planned for us Amy? Well, thank goodness we didn't miss anything, I would hate for you to have missed what's going to happen. You know, I brought a little surprise for you too." The insanity had taken control of any previous touch with reality.

With Deke behind him, Zach to his right, and Sheriff Bill on his left, Jack was left with few options. Slowly, while dragging Amy along like a rag doll, the knife constantly at her throat, he began walking through the alley that they'd managed to dig through the snow at the entranceway.

Unwilling to gamble on a headshot, Zach and Bill lowered their pistols.

The human element would not allow them to take any chances with Amy's life. Jack was in control of the situation until through some miracle things changed.

It was a development that Zach Randal and Sheriff Wright had both been in before. The tables had turned; it had now become a hostage situation. All good law enforcement officials know not to gamble with crazed killers, especially when hostages are involved. It effectively forced them to switch strategies. They made up their minds to shoot quickly, and at the first opportunity.

Deke was going to grab Amy, and pull her to safety. That was supposed to give them at least one, maybe two, seconds of time while Vermette tried to sort out the confusion. In that two seconds, Zach was confident he'd be able to place a couple of .357 slugs through Vermette's head.

When Amy had come out from the cabin, she had not put enough distance between Jack and her position before trying to climb onto the high snow bank surrounding the entrance. Deke had been on the same side where she tried to make her escape, but he did not have a chance to get into position, and Zach watched helpless from the opposite side of the entrance, also unable to get to her in time.

Only a few feet from Vermette, Amy had struggled to climb the steep snowdrift. Vermette had quickly become suspicious at her frantic attempt, easily reaching out and pulling her back to him. The masquerade was over.

Now, a knife was at her throat, and Amy's life was in peril. All the training he'd gone through told Zach he needed to try reasoning with the man, stalling for time, negotiating for the sake of the hostage's life, but deep down inside he knew this man could not be reasoned with. Zach Randal wanted nothing more than to raise his pistol and put one between his eyes, and he was a good enough marksman to do it, but the thing he could not overcome was that human element.

The human element placed a question of doubt within him. What if he took the shot and missed? What if Amy moved at just the wrong second and he shot her? What if after shooting Vermette, the blade of the knife had sliced her throat open? They were questions that he could not ignore, for he was not certain of the answers. Despite his desire to kill this man, he could not bring himself to gamble on his ability when Amy's life was in the balance.

Glancing over at Sheriff Bill Wright standing on the opposite side of the entrance, Zach saw that everything he was feeling had also gone through his companion's mind. The lowered pistol in Bill's hand said everything he needed to know. Neither could the sheriff bring himself to take that chance. Facing the crazed Vermette who thought nothing of the chances he'd taken getting here, Zach felt it a curse that he too could not be insane.

"You'll never get away with it Jack! Drop the knife, and just maybe I'll think about letting you live today!" Zach said. His words were forceful, and spoken with such confidence that even Deke feared what Randal would do next.

"You damned old Texas Ranger. I've been looking forward to dealing with you for a long time. I thought it would have been perfect to have Amy watch as I made you beg for your life, but things have changed. And I must say that they have changed for the better, because now you can watch while her blood stains the snow. Now throw those pistols over here to me." His last sentence was said with a measure of coolness. So sure he was controlling the situation, Jack planned to disarm them, and take them on one at a time.

"I can't do that Jack, it's against everything I know as an officer. Plus, how do I know you won't just kill her anyway?" Zach did his best to stall.

With added pressure to the knife blade against Amy's throat, a clear, thin line of blood materialized on her neck.

"If you don't do as I say she'll die right now! Is that a good enough reason for you?" The pressure stopped just short of slicing her neck open. Amy wasn't aware she was bleeding until she saw the terrified look on Deke's face. Simultaneously the three men who had sworn to protect her, stopped breathing. She said not a word, but the fear in her eyes revealed her plea that they cooperate. The pistols that Bill and Zach carried hit the ground at Vermette's feet with a thud.

"Now that's more like it. You're smarter than you look old man. It's going to be a pleasure watching you die." They saw no signs suggesting he was in any hurry. He was at the peak of his madness, and planned on taking all the time in the world dragging on with his plans, and savoring every moment.

"Jack. Listen to me." It was Deke. He was still standing at the door of the cabin behind Vermette. He knew this man was hell-bent on going through with his mission and that he had no way to stop him; he still had to try to stall him for as long as he could. Deke had no idea if he'd be able to even get his attention since he seemed oblivious to anyone else's appearance, but Zach and Amy. He knew that he had to try.

Surprisingly, Vermette swung around to face Deke. He appeared stunned for a moment, forgetting that Deke had jumped between the high snowdrifts at the entrance to the cabin.

"Young Mr. Stone. It really is a pity that you became involved in this. Just because your mother happened to be a friend of Amy's poor, dead mother, has ended up being a stroke of bad luck for you, hasn't it? But since you're not really involved here, I might let you live. I admire the fact that you felt it your duty to try to help. What you didn't know about this bitch was just how evil a person she really is. Do you know how serious a sin she is guilty of?" It had worked. Deke didn't know how long he could keep the man's attention, but as he realized where the discussion was going he knew he had to sidetrack him. Amy's attempt to protest what Jack was about to reveal was thwarted by the huge hand across her mouth, but Deke saw her panic.

"I really don't care what sin you think she's committed, I love her," Deke declared.

The effect was instantaneous. Jack creased his brow, and doubt was visible in his eyes.

"What's the matter Jack? You didn't think any men better than you existed? Or did you know deep down inside that, you're not half the man you've pretended to be? I think you're a coward, a piece of scum, unable to handle rejection from a woman. Why don't you let her go and try taking on a man for a change?" Deke's challenge was met with laughter. He had succeeded in getting his attention, but as he'd feared, more intellect hid behind the madness than what was obvious. It was just as Randal had stated from the start. Make no mistake about it, the perpetrator may be sick and perverted, but crazy he's not.

Humored by the feeble undertaking, Jack Vermette turned where he could keep an eye on all three of them, enjoying his ability to thwart their attempts at stalling him.

"This is better that I'd hoped. But to be honest with you guys I'm getting tired of these games." He looked into the fear-filled eyes of Amy, and placed a wet kiss on her lips. "Well babe, times up. I'm sorry you crossed the line, but rules are rules. Say good-bye to your friends. I'm sure they'll be meeting you in Hell," he said smiling.

SCRATCHING feverishly at the flimsy wooden door, the Beatles smelled John Hadley long before he arrived. Not knowing what else to do, John opened the door.

In a rust colored blur that seemed to explode at his feet, John realized he had just released the four, big, Chesapeake Bay Retrievers, and they were headed fast in a direction that didn't take John very long to decide he must follow.

Struggling through the deep snow, John set off as quickly as conditions allowed. He was tired, freezing, and bruised badly from his fall, but he knew the Beatles had taken off in a direction that would lead him to the others. John only hoped that by setting the dogs loose he had not made a stupid blunder. Maybe they had been locked up on purpose and unthinkingly he had foiled whatever reason was behind it. They had taken off at such a quick sprint that he had no chance of keeping up, but at least he could follow the prints they left behind in the snow. He cursed his fatigue, fighting with everything in him to ignore the pain.

MATERIALIZING from out of nowhere, John, Paul, George, and Ringo struck with a ferocity that stunned everyone. From a world surrounding them that seemed to have been bleached white, Zach, Deke, and Bill, saw a blur of Beatles only a second before they hit Jack Vermette.

Deke was quickest to realize what was happening. Amidst the pandemonium that ensued on the frozen ground before him, he was able to grab Amy and pull her to safety. She was completely limp, and he feared that Jack had made good with one last slice from the knife.

Jack Vermette was on the ground; his screaming was hideous as the Beatles attacked. A rage had consumed them. Showing no mercy, Jack was being ripped piece by piece from four sides with no way to protect himself. The attack was inhuman, causing chill bumps to run through the three men who stood watching, unable to do anything to stop it. The sounds that came from the Beatles were enough to frighten any man from getting too close. Fear gripped them as they wondered to what extent the four, big Chesapeakes would go.

Jack's pleas for help fell on deaf ears; they could do nothing even if they wanted to, nauseated by such a savage onslaught.

It didn't take long before Jack's body resembled a rag doll, shredded by the Beatles who were taking turns shaking any remaining limbs with their powerful jaws, making sure of the kill.

Hideously disfigured by multiple chunks of flesh ripped mostly away from his head and throat, Jack Vermette was dead.

CHAPTER

31

QUICKLY INSPECTING THE wound on Amy's neck, Deke was overwhelmed with relief to discover it was nothing more than a superficial cut.

"Amy! Are you all right? Amy! Please wake up!" Deke was busy trying to arouse her fatigued body. At least he knew she would live, and that thought brought tears to his eyes. He was surprised to discover that he couldn't stop them from flowing.

Sheriff Bill Wright joined Zach Randal; they stood looking at the shredded remains of Jack Vermette. Not much of a man was left on the ground before them. The Beatles had quieted down, their task completed. They rested on top of the snowdrift, licking what blood had been spattered upon their thick coats.

"My Lord!" Zach whispered. "Well, I guess it's only right." He seemed to be speaking to himself as he looked upon the mutilated body of the man he'd wanted to destroy.

"What's that Zachary?" Bill Wright questioned him.

"Huh? Oh, I guess what I mean is, it's only right that he wasn't killed by me, or you Bill, or even Deke. We all had our reasons for wanting to eliminate the planet of him. Mine was because of, well, because of personal reasons. Yours was having strong suspicions that he'd murdered a couple of your best deputies, and Deke, wanted him dead because he was threatening the life of the woman he loves. We were weak, hesitating when we shouldn't have because we're human. That little hesitation and weakness is something that the Beatles don't suffer from. The fact that Amy was being held hostage by some crazed murderer, who had a knife at her throat, carried only one meaning for them. Their master was clearly in extreme danger, and they acted accordingly. They only knew to watch over her. The one person that they'd been trained to protect. Hesitation was something never bred into them, and because of that lack of hesitation, Miss Amy Dodson is alive today. They did their job, and they did it well." Bill and Zach looked over at the four, big Chessies, calmly lying on the snow near Amy and Deke.

"And the best part of what's just occurred is the pure modesty they possess. The need to be recognized for doing what they're trained to do, and what's expected from them, does not exist. Without arrogance, or pride, but instead, an incredible courage. All they know is they protected their master, and now she is safe. If only we could emulate that kind of modesty as humans. I think we'd be a different kind of people, a better people." Turning from the morbid sight before him, Zach walked away.

Amy was awake and alert. She'd apparently fainted, resulting from a combination of things. Deke held her tightly in his arms, filled with thankfulness that she was okay. He kept her from looking back at the spot behind them, where the white snow looked something like the canvass of a mad painter, with only the color red to sling from his brush.

Sheriff Wright joined Zach where he had stopped a few yards away to light one of his little cigars. Striking the match Zach looked at him.

"You know only one thing puzzles me about all this," he confessed.

"Yeah. What's that?" Bill asked.

"When you two came back from the shed, it seems that I remember you telling me that the Beatles were left locked up."

"That's right, we did leave them locked in the shed. We were afraid they'd get Vermette stirred up, and screw up our plan," Sheriff Wright confirmed.

"See, that's what I don't understand. How the hell did they get out?" Zach's curiosity was about to get the best of him. At that moment, a voice yelled out from the rear corner of the cabin.

"Hell bells Zachary! I let those damn dogs loose! Don't you know you can ruin a dog that's house broke if you keep him locked up too long?"

Both men spun around instantly. Sergeant John Hadley was on hands and knees, but he had made it.

"Damn good thing I came along when I did. I just knew you'd gotten yourself into a heap of trouble, and needed a little help." John smiled at his old friend Zach Randal, who was now running through the snow toward him.

Hearing the voice of John Hadley, and watching Zachary Wyatt Randal run clumsily through the deep snow, Deke and Amy went from crying tears of joy to joyful tears of laughter.

Above them for the first time in days, the snow stopped falling. They watched as brilliant rays from the setting sun pierced through thinning clouds lighting up the sky in amber. It was going to be a beautiful day.

ABOUT THE AUTHOR

One might say that Joe Richard has been around the block of experience a time or two. An avid outdoorsman, he was raised in the richly Cajun cultured area of South Louisiana known as Acadiana.

He is quick to point out that while his experiences in life may have prepared him with writing material, the actual writing would have been easier accomplished if he'd only passed high school English his senior year.

At the age of fourteen, he began his work history in the town where he grew up as a disc jockey for a local radio station. After working in radio for five years, he chose a new profession as advertising manager for a newspaper.

From that experience, he moved on into the medical field. After working for nearly a decade as a Nationally Registered Paramedic, Joe Richard went back to college where he quickly acquired his degree as a Registered Nurse. From the excitement of an emergency room to the quiet atmosphere of a retirement village, he tried it all.

Surprisingly, his attempt at writing was set in motion by a simple dare from his wife. It has become the most challenging, most stimulating, and most rewarding endeavor in his life. *Blind Pursuit* is one result of his newfound vocation.

Joe Richard has two grown sons. He and his wife enjoy the outdoors together, traveling extensively across the country.

Printed in the United States
4615

9 781403 305510